MONTE COOK'S ARCANA EVOLVED

THE DRAGONS' RETURN

MW00512889

TALES FROM THE LAND
OF THE DIAMOND THRONE
BY
MONTE COOK
ED GREENWOOD
KRISTINE KATHRYN RUSCH
JEFF GRUBB
AND OTHERS

EDITED BY SUE WEINLEIN COOK

MALHAVOC PRESS

MONTE COOK'S ARCANA EVOLVED:
THE DRAGONS' RETURN

VI
INTRODUCTION
SUE WEINLEIN COOK

I
ESSENCE OF THE DRAGON
WILL MCDERMOTT

26
NOT ALL THAT TEMPTS
BRUCE R. CORDELL

45
THE MAD MOJH OF ONTETH
ED GREENWOOD

62
ENVOY
JEFF GRUBB

86
OATHSWORN
MARY HERBERT

112
PRIDE
WOLFGANG BAUR

136
VOWS
RICHARD LEE BYERS

159
THE SAND VEILS
LUCIEN SOULBAN

181
THIS LAND IS IN OUR BLOOD
STAN!

207
MANIPULATORS
KRISTINE KATHRYN RUSCH

234
LORESIGHT LEGATION
KATE NOVAK

255
MEMORIES AND GHOSTS
MONTE COOK

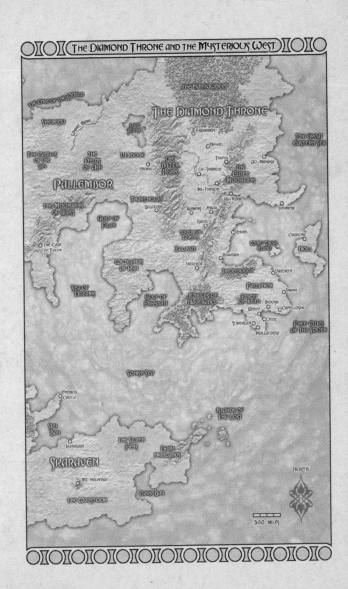

The Harrooi Deep

The Diamond Throne

The Edge of the World

Sheryth

Comet River

Lake Asoon

Ghadanov

Howel

The Great Eastern Sea

The Castles of the Sea

The Fields of Ash

Verdon

Eborn

The Bitter Realm

The Elder Mountains

Thog

Ek-Manar

De-Pairos

Ru-Pairos

Pallembor

Thurthoran

Bullton

Varel

Gammo

Jerbo

Younber

The Nightmark of Glass

Gulf of Nihil

Kavel

Gorwyn Land

Cabisha

Nogal

The Cave of Teeth

Northern Valleys

Esnora

Zalanna

Veterot

The Redroot

Matorth

Sea of Dreams

Cold Lands of Ulag

Forest of Silence

Igana

Border of Silverheim

Pallarion

Forest of Xholm

Inosh

Cibil Loph

Gulf of Firelight

Renvi

Cuios

Free Cities of the South

Schewlen

Mir Loroth

York Sea

Erebos Castle

Islands of the Lost

Stra Bay

Hornlion

The Silken Peng

Emer Highlands

Skaraven

North

Mt. Nelversil

The Coalstorm

Dark Bay

300 Miles

SUE WEINLEIN COOK
INTRODUCTION

Six thousand years ago, the dragons dwelled in peace. But in the absence of their mighty liege, Erixalimar, they dabbled in dark experiments that led to the birth of the dramojh: foul demon-dragons whose unchecked battle-lust and powerful magic threatened to wipe out their creators. Returning from an exploration of the western lands, Erixalimar found his realm awash in blood, his people near death. He did the only thing he could do: sought the help of the gods to rid the world of the dramojh. And once the bloodthirsty creatures were gone, he took his people away to the west, leaving their homeland to heal in the hands of mortals.

But the power of the dramojh surpassed all expectations. After more than four thousand years, the demon-dragons returned to plague the land once more. This time, the intercession of the Hu-Charad—noble giants from across the eastern sea— exterminated them once and for all and saved the mortal races from further centuries of enslavement. A long-forgotten treaty forbade the giants from entering the dragons' home, but the wyrms were no longer there to uphold the ancient pact.

And now, seventeen hundred years later, the dragons finally return to find that the Hu-Charad have made the realm their own, rebuilding the draconic homeland into a place they called Dor-Erthenos, the Lands of the Diamond Throne.

Ferocious or friendly, grand or grisly, dragons always make intriguing and complex characters. And a short story anthology is the perfect venue to explore the complexity of the draconic character, as well as the complexity of the circumstances surrounding their return.

The twelve talented authors in this book all see the arrival of the wyrms in a slightly different light: Some of the dragons seek power, some thirst for blood, some want to reconnect with ancestors, and some just want a place to call home. Whatever their inclinations, these dragons bring with them unique ancient magic tied to the land, arcane skills to help creatures evolve into more powerful versions of themselves, and a new client race of dragon-men: the dracha.

The response of the Diamond Throne residents to the dragons' return is just as interesting and complex as the dragons themselves. The giants see the creatures as a new threat to the land. The reptilian mojh view the return as a much-prophesied answer to their prayers. And the descendents of the dramojh, such as the slassans and squamous lir, have reason to tremble, for the dragons want no reminders of the evil demon-dragons. Other mortal races see the dragons' presence here as a cause for fear, an opportunity for profit, or a call for great courage.

Much of this story is yet unwritten. Why did the dragons choose to return now after so long? Will they drive the Hu-Charad back across the sea or work with them to reshape the realm once more? These are questions that only your own imaginations can answer. For now, enjoy the story as it evolves.

WILL MCDERMOTT

ESSENCE OF THE DRAGON

S carathar's knees ached. Not from walking—though there had been plenty of that this past week. The apprentice's thighs and calves had tingled as if pricked by a thousand needles the entire second day, and then throbbed for two more as the needles worked their way down to the bone. But that pain had become no more than a permeating twinge at the threshold of awareness.

This new pain came from standing. Different joints and muscles were being tested by an interminable vigil at the edge of a boulder-strewn field. Scarathar shifted his weight from one foot to the other in an attempt to ease the load on his knees.

His weight. *His* knees. Scarathar still found it hard to think of himself as anything but male. But it wasn't. Neither was it female. Scarathar was mojh. The apprentice gazed down at his . . . its . . . body, recently transformed during an agonizing, monthlong ritual. Scarathar's gangly body had elongated by more than a foot—most of that in the legs—and was now covered in green scales.

I

To Scarathar's left, Arganoth seemed to have no problem standing for hours. Claw tips touching, the master was obviously deep in thought. Arganoth was shorter and stockier than Scarathar, especially around the protruding hip bones. Many of the master's scales had yellowed over the years, giving the old mojh a mottled coloring like leaves in Tenthmonth.

Scarathar wondered, not for the first time, why the venerable mojh had chosen him . . . it . . . for this journey. There were more experienced, more deserving, more solemn members of the sect. Many had even volunteered for this honor. But Arganoth had asked for Scarathar. And all mojh knew the dragons spoke to the master in dreams, so none questioned the decision—none but Scarathar.

So they stood at the edge of the field. Scarathar shifted again and stared at the vast meadow dotted with boulders the size and general shape of small houses. Other than rocks, there was nothing of interest. The beige grass was cropped so close that Scarathar decided it must be grazing land. But the apprentice could see no animals—only large, cubical boulders.

Scarathar could wait no longer. "Why do we stand here at the edge of this bare plain, master?"

The elder mojh didn't look up, and the apprentice knew what was coming before the words were spoken. "All that needs to be known is already written."

Scarathar suppressed a sigh. Mojh stoicism had been nearly as hard to bear as the lack of proper pronouns. Scarathar stared at the master and thought about sitting down to open the leather-bound Annals he had carried all the way from Kish. The respite would have been welcome, but the correct passage came unbidden to Scarathar's enhanced mojh mind:

> *When the heavens align, pointing the way from West back to East, the time will have come to prepare for the return of our lord. Master and apprentice shall venture forth to*

find that which is necessary for the restoration ritual: the blood, breath, heart, essence, and legacy of the dragon.

The thick tome held the prophecies, visions, and revelations of generations of masters in the Nithogar sect. It was said that Arganoth had been the conduit from their dragon lord for nearly a quarter of the text in the Annals.

Another passage loomed in the apprentice's mind's eye.

On the eve of the tenth morn following the heavens' portents, the blood of the dragon shall be found amongst the ruins of the gods. The swift stones shall point the way.

It was indeed the tenth day since the Dragon's Claw constellation had appeared, pointing east from the setting sun. Long shadows loomed now as the sun set behind the two mojh. Still, the rocks looked anything but swift to Scarathar, who began to wonder if the master could possibly be wrong.

Then, as Arganoth's shadow touched a boulder, it moved. The boulders, once as stoic as the master, began to slide across the plain like sailboats in the Gulf of Firesight.

Unlike boats, though, the rocks moved erratically: starting and stopping with no warning, changing directions or spinning to retrace paths in an instant. If there was a pattern to the movements, the apprentice could not see it. It was total chaos.

Scarathar heard a loud crack and turned in time to see slivers of rock cascading over two colliding boulders. A deafening screech split the air as the grey slabs slid against one another.

The apprentice took a step back—ready to run if necessary—just as Arganoth darted into the maelstrom. Scarathar hesitated a moment, prepared to wait for the master's return, but a flash of movement out of the corner of its eye told the mojh it was time to go. Scarathar sprinted after the master just as a ten-foot-tall boulder careened past, nearly clipping the apprentice's scaly foot.

Scarathar's clawed feet pounded a staccato beat on the hard ground as the young mojh followed the mentor through the Field of Running Stones—which, until this moment, the apprentice had thought to be a myth. A boulder whipped past as Arganoth side-stepped and turned left. Two more house-sized rocks slammed into one another behind Scarathar, showering sharp pebbles onto the apprentice's scaly back.

Scarathar had but one thought, one hope: that the venerable mojh could see the path to their goal, could discern a pattern in the chaos. But the master moved almost as erratically as the boulders, turning to avoid some swift-moving stones, then racing right at others. Pain sliced through Scarathar's thighs and calves with every pounding step. But the young apprentice knew that to slow or stop would mean death.

Scarathar began to wheeze as new pains shot through its lungs. The apprentice couldn't last much longer at this pace. Ahead, Arganoth avoided an oncoming boulder, forcing Scarathar to dive out of the way. The boulder caught the apprentice on the tail, whipping the young mojh around.

Scarathar landed hard. Out of breath, sore, and slightly dazed, the apprentice looked blearily at the bloody tail, which was a foot shorter than it had been a moment ago. Past the bloody tail stump, Scarathar saw a wall coming up fast.

The apprentice's clouded mind realized the danger too late. Scarathar tried to roll out of the path of the boulder, but there was no time and nowhere to go. The mojh raised scaly arms over its face and felt its body being sharply jerked back. . . .

Several moments passed. Scarathar's double eyelids slid open slowly to see the master's mottled body standing above. The apprentice stared blankly at the elder mojh. As if in response to the unasked question, Arganoth pointed up. Above them was a small hole through which the young mojh could hear the scraping sounds of sliding boulders. The master had gotten them to safety.

Without a word, Arganoth walked off into the darkness. Scarathar took a moment to wrap the oozing tail stump with a piece of leather from the pack, checked for other injuries, and got up to follow. They were in an immense subterranean chamber. Scarathar couldn't even see the walls and hurried to catch up, rather than risk getting lost in the dark.

As Scarathar came up behind Arganoth, one side of the cavern came into view. The curved walls towered fifty feet from floor to ceiling, forming a mammoth circular chamber. But more than that, the walls were honeycombed with thousands upon thousands of alcoves. The "ruins of the gods" mentioned in the Annals were a great dragon burial chamber!

As Scarathar stared in awe, Arganoth began examining the wall. Realizing what the master was doing, the apprentice moved closer to help scan the alcoves for the aura of magic. Scarathar edged away from Arganoth around the chamber, searching each section of wall for anything magical.

About halfway around, the young mojh was nearly blinded by a flash of aura from an alcove near the top of the chamber. Scarathar turned to call out, then decided to climb the wall and retrieve the item alone. This must be why Arganoth chose me, thought the apprentice, looking up at the alcove-filled wall. An excellent climber as a human, the mojh apprentice scaled the wall easily with long limbs and strong claws.

Halfway up, Scarathar's wounded tail slapped hard against the edge of an alcove, shooting pain up the length of the young mojh's spine. Unwilling to show weakness in the pursuit of the master's task, the apprentice grimaced and continued climbing, eventually pulling its sore body into the glowing alcove.

After checking the blood-soaked tail bandage, Scarathar scanned the chamber. It was strewn with bones and debris, making it difficult to pinpoint the source of the aura. Scarathar knelt to sift through the remains. The bones seemed to be mostly teeth, claws, and a few scales. But these were dragon scales—five to ten times larger than mojh scales. They would be worth a fortune to armorsmiths in one of the giants' cities.

The apprentice considered pocketing a few, but dismissed that thought as an artifact of its previous life. At the bottom of the pile, near the back of the alcove, Scarathar found the source of the magical aura: a ten-inch-long, bone-white claw, sharpened to a razor's edge along its entire length.

"The master will be pleased," thought Scarathar, scrambling back down the wall and all but forgetting its wounded tail in the excitement. But if Arganoth was pleased with the apprentice, the master's stoic face never showed it. The old mojh simply stuck the enchanted claw in a pack and left the chamber.

Later that evening, after leaving the Field of Running Stones, Arganoth mounted the enchanted claw onto a dull grey hilt, instructed Scarathar to build a fire and prepare the evening meal, then sat down with the weapon held in both claws to meditate.

After checking the bandage on its wounded tail again, the young mojh built the fire and roasted a hawk for dinner. Still the master sat grasping the blade. The apprentice pulled a wing off the hawk and ate while watching Arganoth. "How could a bone-claw dagger be the blood of the dragon?" wondered the apprentice out loud.

"All that needs to be known is already written."

Scarathar looked up at the master's face. Arganoth spun the bone dagger around and sheathed it in one fluid motion, then reached out and tore a chunk of meat from the roasting bird and began to eat.

Scarathar had studied several sections of the prophecy before dinner and knew there was precious little about the blood of the dragon. The only relevant passage stated:

The blood will open the heart. The blood courses through the heart and unveils the legacy.

As far as Scarathar could tell, it was gibberish. But the young mojh knew that to ask the question again would bring no new information. So, like a good mojh, the apprentice said nothing. Amazingly, the master broke the silence.

"I must eat and rest," said Arganoth between bites. "Study the Nithogar histories and prepare for our departure. Tomorrow we begin our journey to the Bitter Pit to capture the breath of the dragon. All must be ready by the first day of Twelfthmonth."

Scarathar stared. It was probably the longest speech the master had ever made. The importance of so much verbal communication was not lost on the apprentice. The young mojh tossed the remains of the wing into the fire, pulled the Annals from the pack, and began reading about the great Lord Nithogar and the Dragon War.

> The Conclave of the Dragons was in disarray. After signing a treaty with the giants, a people called the Hu-Charad, Erixalimar had left the Land of the Dragons for the uncharted west. War between the dragons erupted in his absence, as metallic and chromatic vied for control of the Conclave. Unto this turmoil came the great Lord Nithogar.
>
> In his bid to lead the Conclave out of chaos, Lord Nithogar, who, it is written, "could swipe his claws into other realms as easily as men could dip their hands into pools of water," brought to his brethren items of nearly limitless magical power found in a forgotten dimension— the tenebrian seeds.
>
> But those controlling the Conclave forbade Nithogar from experimenting with the seeds, which they deemed "the spawn of the netherworld." Denied his attempt to openly explore the power of the seeds, Nithogar met in secret with a select group of allies. . . .

* * * * *

"Idiots," sighed Nithogar as he twirled a seed aimlessly on the floor. The spinning, amber-colored rock sparkled in the firelight. Nithogar slapped the seed away, sending it flying across the chamber.

"Patience, my darling," purred Jelissican. "We do not need the Conclave to reveal the secrets of the seeds."

Nithogar looked at his lair-mate, who had placed a reassuring claw on his shoulder, and sighed again. "Of course you are right, Jelissican." He smiled a large, toothy smile and then strode across the chamber to an enormous hearth. Several tree trunks crackled in the roaring fire. Nithogar plucked the seed from the white-hot embers.

Nithogar's red-tipped black scales gleamed in the firelight. From a distance, the two colors merged together, giving him a coppery hue. He stared into the depths of the glittering rock. "Can they not see the power we can gain from these seeds?"

"They are fearful old fools," said Cridonag, a young red dragon whose wings were still too small for proper flight. His main duty at the moment was to keep the hearth stocked with fresh trees. "Or perhaps they covet our new power."

Nithogar let the inclusive pronoun pass, but Sedonaral, an ancient green with gem-encrusted scales, clapped Cridonag across the horns as he carried an oak toward the hearth. "'Our power'?" she asked. "Your only power, pup, *is* our power, and don't you forget it!"

"Leave the boy alone," said Bandogras, a mature black lounging at the far end of the chamber. "We were all reckless and hungry for power in our youth."

"Yes," agreed Nithogar, "But in our youth, Erixalimar and the wretched Conclave held all the power." The great dragon looked around the cavern at his tiny cabal, which, in addition to Jelissican, Cridonag, Sedonaral, and Bandogras, included

Windigar, a ferocious white dragon with twin scars running the length of her body, and Gunthilor, whose blue scales and quick mind shone brighter than all but Nithogar himself.

Nithogar dropped the cooling seed onto an amber pile in the middle of the chamber. "Our group may be small, but Gunthilor believes that by infusing these seeds with our own essence, we shall gain immense power—enough to wrest control from those fearful fools and rule this land as it should be ruled."

"But the Conclave ruled the experiments too dangerous," said Cridonag. "They forbade you to proceed."

Sedonaral slapped the young red with her tail. "The Conclave has problems of its own," she said. "While our brethren battle for control of these lands, the Conclave has no time to enforce fool-ish edicts."

"We should not dismiss the fears of the Conclave so quickly," said Jelissican, pushing the two rivals apart.

Always the diplomat, thought Nithogar.

"We must proceed with caution," she continued. "There is great power in these seeds. But that power must be tempered with intellect and understanding if we are to win this war with-out destroying the land we seek to rule."

Nithogar stroked the scales along the length of his beloved's neck. "We shall take all due precautions, my love. But if Gunthilor is correct, our efforts can tip the balance of the war and put an end to all this needless strife."

Nithogar stared at the pile of seeds at his feet. "As Cridonag said, the power is ours."

* * * * *

A week of walking across the Southern Wastes had hardened the muscles in Scarathar's legs and created a pit in the young apprentice's stomach. Mojh could go days or even weeks without water, but the heat forced the duo to move from shadow to shadow to regulate their body temperature under the hot sun.

The southern foothills of the Bitter Peaks reached higher into the sky before them each day until they arrived at what Scarathar knew was their destination. The young mojh had read the appropriate passage several nights earlier.

"The breath of the dragon erupts from the dragon's mouth. Capture the breath and venture forth to the heart."

Their path wound up a dry river bed to the mouth of a cave cut into a rocky outcropping. A slab of rock swept over the top of the black maw before them. Part of that natural arch had fallen during some ancient cataclysm and now partially blocked the opening, jutting out like the jaw of an enormous beast.

The river bed led past the stone jaw and down into the blackness. An acrid cloud of black mist billowed out of the cave mouth. The dragon's breath, indeed!

Scarathar's nose and throat burned as the two mojh descended into the cave. Their eyes adjusted to the darkness, revealing a rather featureless cavern that meandered back and forth where the ancient river had etched its way through the softest pores in the rock.

The foul mist thinned once they passed the entrance, giving Scarathar's throat some welcome relief. The apprentice glanced up and saw a black cloud hugging the ceiling. It ebbed and flowed above them like an inverted river coming up from the depths of the cave. They walked in silence for a time beneath the vaporous river. The cloud seemed alive. It moved like a snake, surging forward in fits and starts and slithering across the ceiling. Mesmerized by the undulating dance, Scarathar almost bumped into the master as they came to a small chamber.

Smooth walls betrayed the unnatural origin of the circular room. Above, the black cloud still roiled, enveloping the ceiling and spilling into the rough tunnel behind them. In front of Scarathar was the source of the miasma: a bubbling pool of viscous liquid that dominated the small room.

The substance almost glistened in its utter blackness. Each bubble that popped released a small puff of acrid smoke. While they watched, hundreds of bubbles swelled, burst, released their poison, and sank into the black soup.

Kneeling at the edge of the dark pool, the master plucked a vial from a belt pouch and leaned out over the bubbling liquid. Arganoth's thin hand hovered over the pool, clutching the vial between three claw tips. Scarathar began to worry that the master had succumbed to the fumes, for Arganoth swayed back and forth, the vial moving in a slow, elliptical path over the pool.

The master's arm plunged toward the glistening liquid just as a large bubble burst. A puff of black smoke erupted into the mouth of the descending vial. After corking and securing the smoky tube back in the pouch, Arganoth rose and left the chamber without a word.

Scarathar followed a moment later, not bothering to hurry. With the breath of the dragon in claw, it was time to trudge to the next location in their unending pilgrimage. The apprentice wasn't eager to get started.

After pushing through the curtain of smoke at the mouth of the tunnel, Scarathar sensed that something was wrong. The master was nowhere to be seen. Relying on old instincts, the young mojh stopped to listen. Amid the whistle of the wind could be heard the scrape of claw against stone—which could be Arganoth—and a low growl.

The sounds came from beyond the fallen slab. Scarathar scampered up the side of the boulder and crawled to the far edge. The master stood perfectly still, arms splayed wide, in front of a ten-foot-long, golden-scaled beast.

The creature had a feral head ringed by a shock of fur, but its body was covered in scales that reflected the light of the sun. Ribbed wings, like those Scarathar had seen on sketches of dragons in the Annals, sprouted from the beast's back.

The tableau in front of Scarathar held for a moment, giving the apprentice time to slip a dagger out of its sheath. The vicious-looking beast must have heard the scrape of the blade. It tensed and jerked its head to the side to scan the rock.

Scarathar flung the dagger at the beast.

Arganoth screamed, "No!"

The creature leaped straight up toward Scarathar.

The dagger skipped across the beast's scaled chest as it flapped its wings once and rose into the air. The creature landed on all fours, nearly on top of Scarathar, and raised its head.

"Cover your ears!" yelled Arganoth.

It was too late. A deafening roar washed over Scarathar like a sheet of ice-cold water, leaving the apprentice disoriented and gasping for breath. Scarathar could do nothing but watch as the creature reared up for a lethal strike.

As it raised its claws, a jet of flame blasted over the rock, enveloping the beast's head and shoulders. The force of the flame knocked the creature onto its side.

Scarathar tried to move, but aching muscles wouldn't cooperate. All the mojh could do was lie there staring into the beast's gold, glaring eyes. Wisps of smoke rose from its burnt mane. It bared its teeth and growled as it rolled over to stand again.

Before the beast regained its footing, Arganoth appeared above them both, bone-claw dagger raised overhead. The beast swiped at the master from a half-supine position, but the weak blow couldn't penetrate mojh scales. Arganoth hesitated a second, then slashed down in a blindingly fast arc.

The beast dropped again, and this time it would not rise. Its eyes dulled, and a crimson streak blossomed across its chest as a stream of blood spilled onto the rock.

Arganoth pulled Scarathar away from the dying beast and sat next to the apprentice. Scarathar tried to sit up but found it impossible. Looking up at the master, the young mojh swore there was a tear trickling down one cheek.

"What was that?" asked Scarathar once feeling had returned to its muscles.

"A dragonne," said Arganoth. "Luckily just a pup, but we should not have killed it."

"Why?"

"All that needs to be known is already written."

> The war between the dragons raged on, and the chromatics were losing ground against their enemies. Our lord knew the time had come to rally his brothers and sisters under a new banner. The experiments had succeeded beyond the cabal's highest expectations. Infused with dragon essence, the tenebrian seeds had germinated and produced beings with the strength of dragons, but with the blood lust of demons.

> With an army of these dragon scions—these dramojh— at his disposal, Lord Nithogar's cabal came to the aid of their chromatic brethren and turned the tide of the war. And yet all might have been lost if not for the intervention of a most unlikely ally. . . .

* * * * *

Nithogar landed on the hilltop and surveyed the battle raging above the desert. Cridonag landed at his side, but the great dragon ignored the whelp. The small red was useful in his own way, but Nithogar knew that battle was not the best use of the young dragon's particular talents.

Nithogar, Jelissican, Sedonaral, and a company of dramojh had ambushed a small band of gold dragons. The scions had erupted from beneath the sand as the golds flew past and tore into them with sharp claws and teeth.

To Nithogar's eye, the dramojh were beautiful creatures, an elegant meld of dragon and demonic spider. Their serpentine bodies slithered through the air as easily as snakes through the grass, held aloft by great, ribbed wings. But on the ground, the dragon scions could scuttle far faster on their eight, multi-jointed legs than even the quickest dragons.

Nithogar had watched as three dramojh ripped scales from the neck of one gold dragon and sank their teeth into exposed muscles like wildcats feasting on a herd animal. Two other dramojh plunged their spearlike legs deep into the gold's back for purchase and began ripping out the spines from its wings, shredding the leathery membranes as if they were leaves. Unable to fly on the tattered remains of its wings, the gold fell to the sand, broken and bleeding.

Another platoon of dramojh scuttled back and forth like crabs on some nearby rocks, ready to assail escaping enemies with foul magic. Nithogar had followed one such gold dragon into the sky. Before he could even breathe his flame, a cloud of black particles enveloped the retreating gold. The dragon screamed and plummeted from the black cloud, a horned skull where the dragon's head had once been.

After that, Nithogar had retreated to the hill to direct the attack and watch his beloved. Green and golden, Jelissican circled above the battle, using her breath and claws to force stragglers back into the fray.

He had lost track of Sedonaral, however. Nithogar scanned the battle for the troublesome green to no avail. Fearing more that she had abandoned them than that she lay dying, he pulled a dragonstone from a pack. After passing a claw over the red-dish stone to activate its magic, Nithogar spoke. "Sedonaral, where in the West are you?"

The stone lay silent for nearly a minute. Nithogar was about to repeat the call when the rock vibrated and Sedonaral's sharp, clipped voice emanated from it. "Busy now. Chasing stragglers. Leave me to my work."

Nithogar quelled the urge to fling the stone at the nearest

enemy and simply dropped it back into his pack. After controlling his anger over the green's continuing insolence, the great dragon turned to the young red beside him and asked, "What news do you bring of the cabal?"

"You have nothing to fear from Gunthilor or Windigar, my lord," said Cridonag. "Gunthilor is completely loyal to you and the cabal, while Windigar's only appetite is for battle, not power."

"Yes?" said Nithogar as bolt of lightning arced across the desert and cut a retreating gold dragon in half. "What of the others?"

Cridonag quivered under his master's icy stare. "Bandogras is difficult to read and extremely careful, my lord," he said. "But my spies continue to gather information."

"Obviously I can trust Jelissican," said Nithogar, "but what of Sedonaral?" He scanned the raging battle, looking for the gem-encrusted green.

"She may be a problem—"

At the sudden silence, Nithogar glanced to his side to see Cridonag half-falling, half-running down the hill. The next moment a cloud of noxious gas enveloped the hilltop. Through the vapors, Nithogar saw a gold dragon diving toward him, claws bared. How had the gold gotten through the lines? Nithogar thought he saw Sedonaral flying high above, watching him.

Nithogar tried to turn toward the attack, but his muscles wouldn't respond. The gas had weakened him, and he nearly fell over. The gold was almost upon him. He could see death in its eyes. Nithogar opened his mouth to breathe. . .

Something flashed past Nithogar and slammed into the gold, driving it to the ground. The great dragon could see what looked like two gold dragons locked in combat—one not much bigger than a wyrmling.

When the smaller figure raised its head and roared, Lord Nithogar knew it for what it was. Unfortunately, its attack had little effect on the gold, which ripped the dragonne apart a moment later. Nithogar belched acid at the wounded dragon as it advanced up the hill, then opened his mouth again and seared his attacker's acid burns with a torrent of fire.

All that was left of the gold was a smoldering, blackened corpse. Later, after the battle, Nithogar and Jelissican gave the dragonne a proper burial. Then the great dragon flew off to find that craven toady, Cridonag.

* * * * *

During the days after the dragonne attack, the master seemed even quieter and more subdued than usual. In silence, they had clambered up and around the dragon breath cave, found where the dry river bed emerged, and followed it for two days into the mountains. Scarathar could feel a rift opening between them.

In the evenings, Scarathar read the account of how the great lord Nithogar was saved by a lowly dragonne and began to understand why Arganoth revered them. But it was just an animal, wasn't it? The young mojh knew better than to ask this question aloud and continued to study the Annals, eventually finding an appropriate passage.

> The world is an interconnected web of existence of which
> we are all a part. All creatures revere the great lord
> Nithogar, caretaker of the land. In our lord's absence,
> it falls to the mojh to tend the web.

After reading the passage, the young mojh considered apologizing for the rash behavior that had ended in the dragonne's death. But Scarathar still couldn't grieve for the death of an animal and knew the master would detect the insincerity.

So the rift between them grew as they climbed into the mountains in silence. Near dusk on the second day they struck out along a gorge that descended into a chasm. Eventually, the chasm narrowed enough to force them to walk single file.

Finally, Arganoth stopped. Not a single word had passed between them since the attack. Even though Scarathar had pored through the Annals for hours, the young mojh was unsure what they would find in this featureless and claustrophobic chasm.

Scarathar glanced at the sheer walls, which seemed to come together high above. Only a sliver of sky was visible, and the apprentice couldn't tell whether it was day or night. Nothing existed for them now but rock walls streaked grey and brown.

Arganoth slid ahead but held up a claw, indicating that Scarathar should remain. The apprentice saw an alcove in the wall where the master had stood. It was small, not much more than a shelf cut into the cliff. Scarathar's eyes—trained long ago to notice minute details—also saw a small crack running across and down the wall.

Arganoth motioned for the apprentice to take a closer look. Scarathar moved forward and peered into the alcove. The base of the shelf was etched with an intricate design that looked familiar, but it was difficult to tell exactly what it was. Something seemed odd about the etching. It had obviously been carved with great care. The whirls and lines were perfectly formed but cut quite deep into the stone—deeper along the edges of the design than at the center.

Scarathar heard Arganoth shuffle closer and glanced up to see the claw dagger raised and ready to strike. Scarathar's arm shot up to defend against the strike, but the master grabbed it and forced the apprentice's clawed hand into the alcove, over the center of the design.

"Master, I . . ." began Scarathar.

The claw dagger plunged into the back of Scarathar's hand, emerging through the palm. As the apprentice screamed, blood ran down the bone blade and trickled onto the shelf. The dark liquid flowed into the crevices, pooled, then spread out into the interconnected whirls of the design.

With the etched pattern filling with blood, the crimson lines stood out against the grey stone. Scarathar finally recognized the design. It was two interlocked dragons held in a three-clawed hand: the double dragon, the secret mark of Nithogar. Scarathar remembered a passage from the Annals.

The legacy of the dragon is guarded by the double dragon. The blood will open the way. But only once thou display the essence of the dragon will the legacy of the lord Nithogar be revealed.

As the final claw points of the design filled with blood, Scarathar heard and felt the rumble of stone scraping against stone. A large block detached from the wall and slid into the cliff, sending a shower of dust and pebbles to the chasm floor.

Arganoth pulled the dagger from Scarathar's wounded hand, sheathed it, and entered the doorway. Scarathar stared at the blood-filled etching while binding this latest wound. The mojh remembered another passage that it had read in the Annals nearly two weeks earlier and shuddered.

Instincts and emotions ingrained during a reckless and misspent youth resurfaced within Scarathar. The young mojh entered the secret chamber of Nithogar, knowing what waited within . . . and what must be done to fulfill the prophecies.

Once inside, Scarathar scanned the dark chamber. All was exactly as expected. It looked like another circular room—at least as far as Scarathar could see. The curving walls to either side bore writings as well as images depicting dragons and dramojh locked in combat. Black poles stood in a ring around the center of the chamber. Etched into the stone inside that circle was an intricate and familiar design.

Fear gripped Scarathar when this cursory scan showed no sign of the master. Was it too late? No. Scarathar knew the master had underestimated the young apprentice. It was time Arganoth learned how capable Scarathar truly was.

A pool of light flared from a candle set into a pole near the back of the chamber. The master's shadow on the far wall seemed to dance and taunt the apprentice. The master, now silhouetted in the candlelight, moved to the next pole, placed a candle on top, and lit it with the flick of two claws.

Ah yes. Tradition dictated that a ritual of this magnitude be conducted with a certain amount of ceremony and solemnity. Scarathar strode across the chamber to the master, bowed, and said, "May I help with the preparations?"

Arganoth nodded and handed the apprentice half the candles. While turning toward the next pole, Scarathar bumped the master, relieving the mojh of a single item, which the former thief secreted amid the candlesticks.

Apparently not noticing the theft, Arganoth moved toward the next pole. Scarathar watched the master while placing candles into the pole holders. Once Arganoth was opposite the apprentice, Scarathar tucked the stolen item into a belt pouch as flame flared in the master's clawtips.

Scarathar placed the last candle, then dutifully fell in step behind Arganoth as the master continued the lighting ceremony. As the final candle flickered into life, Scarathar stole up behind Arganoth and drove the stolen dagger into the master's back.

The claw dagger slipped through the master's thick hide like it was parchment. The angle of the attack ensured that the ten-inch blade, now embedded to the hilt, destroyed several soft organs beneath Arganoth's ribcage. It was a perfect strike. The old mojh gasped as Scarathar pulled the blade out, and nearly toppled to the floor while turning to face the apprentice.

Blood dribbled from the corner of the master's mouth. But instead of the wide-eyed, open-mouthed look of pain and surprise Scarathar had expected to see, Arganoth wore a slight, lopsided grin.

Arganoth extended a claw to the apprentice. Scarathar tensed, ready to strike again if necessary, but the master simply clasped the apprentice's claw and pressed something into the palm. Scarathar looked down to see the vial of dragon's breath. "Why?" the young mojh asked. "I don't understand."

"All that needs to be known is already written," the master wheezed, then slumped. Scarathar lowered the body gently into the center of the ring of light, then watched as the master's life's blood filled the crevices of the double-dragon design etched into the floor.

> Our Lord Nithogar nearly prevailed. If it were not for the untimely return of Erixalimar, the cabal and its dramojh warriors would have driven the foul metallics off this mortal coil.

> But even the powerful Erixalimar could not stand against the might of the great dragon's horde alone. Once again, the dragon king forged an alliance with beings not of draconic blood—the Lords of Denotholan.

> These so-called gods helped Erixalimar destroy our Lord's dramojh offspring and sunder his chromatic cabal. And for this service, the treasonous Dragonliege promised to relinquish the Land of the Dragons to the mortals. Those loyal to Erixalimar—and those who wished to live— followed him west.

> Those who did not bow to the rule of Erixalimar were hunted down . . . with the help of certain traitors to the cabal. . . .

* * * * *

The great dragon knew they were coming. He had precious little time to finish the ritual. The cavern was pitch black around the dragon. There were no more trees to burn in the hearth. His dramojh had, unfortunately, seen to that.

Nithogar winced as he remembered the conflagration and carnage. Entire forests set aflame. The land made black and barren by fire and foul magic. His dear Jelissican had been right. The dramojh were too hard to control. Now she was gone, too. But he would make it right. For her, he would make the land thrive again—if only he had enough time.

His tenebrian seeds were gone, but the great dragon still had a small horde of dragonstones. In addition to communication, the magical stones were known for their ability to heal life's energy. Nithogar believed they could also store this same energy. However, the ritual would be tricky . . . and costly.

A quick breath of fire into the hearth turned the charcoal remnants of several logs into hot embers. Nithogar reached into the hearth and spread the glowing ash across the pile of dragonstones while muttering mystical phrases.

The dragonstones glowed and pulsed from red to orange to black and back to red as the hot embers turned to grey ash around them. Still chanting, Nithogar mentally summoned his lone dramojh guard. The demon-dragon flapped its wings once as it turned and scuttled across the floor.

Nithogar snatched the dramojh around the neck as it neared, then quickly slashed open its belly. The dragon raised his former guard's limp body over the dragonstones. Dark blood flowed like a curtain from the creature, drenching the red-hot stones and completing the incantation.

It was done. Nithogar tossed the dead dramojh aside and sat back on his haunches to admire his work. The stones had been imbued with the essence of the dramojh. With these he could someday remake his army. And next time, he would find a way to control them. This battle was over, but he might still win the war . . . when the time was right.

For now, though, his work must remain hidden. Nithogar passed a claw over the pile of sizzling dragonstones. As he murmured one final spell, he watched the pile dwindle. The stones disappeared one by one from the dark chamber, magically transported to hidden locations all around the land to wait for him to come and begin again.

Some time later, the floor empty except for ash, Nithogar raised his red and black head. "I've been expecting you, Cridonag," he said without turning around.

The red dragon, moving less silently now, came up beside the former lord of the cabal. "I came as soon as I found out where you were, my lord."

Nithogar pretended not to notice the unstated lie. He turned to look into the toadying dragon's eyes. "How much time do we have?" he asked.

Cridonag wilted slightly under the icy gaze. "Our enemies are close, my lord."

"You mean 'my enemies,' don't you, traitor?" Before Cridonag could move, Nithogar slashed a single claw across the young red's neck, severing his vocal cords.

"I never had to worry about Sedonaral, did I?" continued Nithogar. "It was you all along. When the winds changed, you turned to protect your back." Weak from his ritual, Nithogar almost stumbled as he paced around the stunned dragon.

Cridonag lunged at Nithogar.

"Hold!" commanded the great dragon with the full force of his magical power. Weak he may be, but he still had enough strength to deal with one traitor. Cridonag stopped, unable to break the spell. "I have a task to complete, my foolish young friend, but first I need to find some dark dimension where I can rest and recuperate. . . ." *For several millennia*, he added to himself.

Nithogar sighed. "But Erixalimar will never stop hunting me until I am dead, no matter where I may disappear to," he said as he summoned energy into his claws. "So, I shall leave him a small present."

The great dragon waved his claws in front of the young red and muttered an incantation. The room seemed to fold over on itself, leaving Nithogar standing face to face with . . . Nithogar.

"Say hello to Erixalimar when he arrives, won't you?" asked

Nithogar. "Oh, right. You cannot, can you?" Nithogar started to laugh at his little joke, but a voice inside—a mere memory of a better dragon than he—scolded him for making light of death, any death.

Dearest Jelissican, he replied to the voice, *What I do now, I do for you. I have spread my legacy across the land. Now I must rest.*

With that, he disappeared from the dark chamber, leaving the red-and-black Cridonag to face the wrath of the king of the dragons.

* * * * *

Blood filled the double-dragon design, swirl after swirl. Scarathar stared at the dead mojh master. That damnable contented smile frozen on the elder's face mocked the apprentice.

The young mojh turned from the sight. Scarathar couldn't look at that face any longer. Was this the right thing to do? It had been instinct, right? A life-or-death reaction bred into his human self on the streets of Gahanis a lifetime ago.

No, There was more to this barbaric act than mere survival. Something had stirred inside the apprentice when the heart chamber opened. The answer had arrived with crystal clarity. At the end, Scarathar had felt the weight of destiny guiding the blade.

Scarathar looked at the vial containing the breath of the dragon. Had Arganoth known what would happen? What did it all mean?

A low rumble invaded the apprentice's reverie. The floor beneath Scarathar shook, and the young mojh fell to the ground. The apprentice turned to find the master and the double-dragon design gone. The entire center of the chamber had risen up.

As the dust settled, Scarathar saw a circular portico. Five stone columns carved with dragonscale motifs held a stone slab aloft above a central dais. Hundreds of gems were inlaid into the columns, a different stone on each: onyx, sapphire, ruby, emerald, and pearl. Above, the double-dragon design was etched into the underside of the slab—as if it had been carved straight through the rock floor.

A stone sarcophagus sat upon the dais. Scarathar climbed the steps to it. The sarcophagus was easily fifteen feet long and ten feet wide. The rounded stone lid was a foot thick; Scarathar could never remove it alone.

But it wouldn't take muscle to open the sarcophagus. Etched into the lid, a passage in Draconic read:

> *Herein lies the legacy of the dragon. Upon his return, our Lord Nithogar shall embrace this legacy, and from it shall spring a glorious future for the Land of the Dragons.*
>
> *Only one who displays the true essence of the dragon may unveil the legacy. If the essence of the dragon is within thee, the breath of the dragon shall open the way.*

"What does it mean, 'if the essence of the dragon is within thee'?" wondered Scarathar. The answer came unbidden to the apprentice. "All that needs to be known is already written."

Scarathar sat on the dais steps, leaning back against the sarcophagus, and pulled the Annals out of the pack. "Arganoth knew I would need the vial," the apprentice muttered, leafing through the pages. "But what is the 'essence'? We never even looked for that."

Hours later, the apprentice found the answer buried deep within obscure passages relating to Nithogar's prophesied return.

> *The essence of the dragon cannot be found where it has not always been, nor can it be hidden away. If the essence is within you, unveil the legacy and prepare for our lord Nithogar's return. Attune to the legacy. The heart knows how. The Lord will return to the chosen one when the time is right.*

Next to this cryptic passage—in the margin of the page—was scrawled a single sentence:

The apprentice shall become the master and complete the task, for it is written that the essence of the dragon is betrayal.

Scarathar dropped the Annals and stood before the sarcophagus. The mojh smashed the vial atop the stone lid. Black vapors poured forth from the shards, and tendrils of smoke enveloped Scarathar's claws.

The mojh took a step back and watched as the vaporous strands expanded into a billowing cloud that flowed across the sarcophagus. When the cloud cleared, the lid was gone. Scarathar stepped forward and gazed inside.

Inside the sarcophagus lay an enormous red rock—one of Lord Nithogar's dragonstones, secreted away until his return. Scarathar could feel its power, was drawn to it. But the mojh wasn't sure what to do next. What had it said in the Annals? "Attune to the legacy. The heart knows how."

Scarathar peered at the words and images scrawled on the chamber walls. There was much to read, but the new master had plenty of time. The first day of Twelfthmonth was weeks away. That left plenty of time to read the inscriptions; to follow the path laid out millennia before the young mojh's birth. Scarathar would attune to the dragonstone and await the return of Lord Nithogar. It was written.

BRUCE R. CORDELL

NOT ALL THAT TEMPTS

A spark of brutal memory bridged the gap between the figurine and the giant's finger, anticipating his approaching grasp. Na-Devaon flinched with something like pain. His oversized hand inadvertently knocked the figure off the display shelf, then his eight-foot frame crumpled, and he followed the fallen figure down to the hard floor. . . .

Grief blasted past his barriers, sending Na-Devaon's mind tumbling past the Four Principles—fire, air, earth, and water—and on into the ultimate ether: the akashic sea, in which all thoughts, words, and actions are recorded for all time. He tumbled past habitual moorings, accelerating into regions foreign to any that now lived. Never had he willingly ventured so far back into the akashic memory, so far beyond the sight of times and places with which he was at least passing familiar.

He glimpsed a horizon darkened by the wings of a dragon host, whose numbers the giant could not begin to calculate. Chromatic highlights glinted off flapping wings in the setting sun. Red, black, green . . . But at the center, there was no color—it was black, a pure darkness whose paucity of light was a presence unto itself. A name brushed Na-Devaon's consciousness: tenebrian seed. But the name was charged with fury as palpable as flesh. That anger slammed into him, flicking Na-Devaon from the akashic sea like a rowboat caught on the crest of a breaking wave.

As quickly as he'd succumbed, he was thrust out of his inadvertent reverie. . . .

"Easy, big guy. You all right?" The human shopkeeper squinted down at Na-Devaon, a vantage rare for the giant. Blinking, Na-Devaon sat up, rubbing his neck and attempting to gain his bearings. A litter of pottery, semi-precious stones, and tiny carved figurines lay around and under him. When he'd gone down, he must have clipped the display. Feeling around with his left hand, he found the figurine he sought.

This time, he was able to grab it without triggering another akashic episode. Looking up into the solicitous face, Na-Devaon said, "How much for this one?"

* * * * *

"So, what do you think?"

Dagath studied the brassy metallic figurine, turning it over in its scaled hands. Dagath, a magister and friend of the giant, rented a small apartment with attached study in De-Shamod, not too far from the shop where Na-Devaon purchased the tiny sculpture. Finally, the mojh said, "I can't detect any overt enchantment. If it is an item of potency, it must be purely psychic in nature." Dagath returned the object to Na-Devaon's waiting palm.

The giant closed his fist over the figurine, squeezing. "You didn't detect any sort of . . . affinity for it?"

Dagath cocked its hairless head at its giant colleague. "No. Why? It resembles a stylized dragon. Is that the familiarity to which you refer? Dragon, mojh—a little obvious."

Na-Devaon grinned. The mojh's sharp wit never failed. But despite the mojh's lack of affability, their bond of friendship shielded him from Dagath's most pointed comments. After all, had it not been for the mojh's change of heart a little over a year ago, Na-Devaon would have died from daily "questioning" by a chapter of the Fleshrune cult. Dagath had quit that cult, and the mojh's betrayal of the evil Master of Claw was a story all its own, though telling it overmuch only served to put the mojh in jeopardy—the surviving Fleshrunes had sworn vengeance on the magister. But Dagath had saved the giant despite the risk to itself, and from that act an enduring friendship was born.

The giant said, "When I first touched the figurine, it triggered an akashic vision of the time of dragons, dragons before even the coming of the dramojh, when the ancient drakes ruled all this land. And you being . . . what you are . . ."

Dagath waited, a quizzical look on its features. Then it shrugged, "Other than its shape, it means nothing to me. What distinguishes these visions from others you've had?"

The giant sighed and continued. "The power of them, for one. Also, the vision came upon me; I did not seek it. The figurine was a catalyst. That's never happened before."

The magister didn't seem particularly moved by that admission.

Na-Devaon persisted. "After I revived, I tried to use my abilities on the figurine to trace its lineage of ownership—it was surprisingly hard, despite my loresight. I did find the previous owner and asked her about it. The object had come into her possession accidentally, and she sold it to the curio shop. Anyhow, it turns out the figure comes from out west, from the mining town of Medaba. It is carved from a particularly rare mineral called orundum. In fact, from what Dolora tells me, orundum is mined at Medaba and no place else."

"Dolora?"

"A witch. She was the previous owner. She was very helpful—at first—but after I told her about my incredible vision, she wanted the figure back. Offered ten times the price I paid for it. But I figured I'd talk to you first." A pregnant pause ensued.

"All right, tell me more about the vision," Dagath said finally, when it had become all too obvious that Na-Devaon wanted to be asked. The mojh must be busy with another magical project, thought the giant. Dagath often failed to appreciate Na-Devaon's theatrics. Or perhaps the mojh was just being rude.

But Na-Devaon enjoyed telling his stories nonetheless. The giant described his akashic experience, determined not to rush through the retelling despite the mojh's slightly bored demeanor.

When the akashic mentioned the "tenebrian seed" portion of the vision, Dagath's eyes became saucers.

"What? What is it?" asked the giant, interrupting himself. Dagath wasn't usually given to emotional displays.

"You must journey to Medaba. The root of your vision lies there. I'm coming along."

* * * * *

The sweaty month of Pal-Henach was a warm time for over-land travel. The sun's unwavering gaze scoured the road. Heat mirages danced on the plain, forcing the ribbon of roadway stretching ahead to waver and tremble. Dagath advanced easily, using an ivory-white staff of magistry as a walking stick in one hand, clutching the figurine in the other. The mojh seemed untroubled by the heat, perhaps even happy in its stifling embrace. Na-Devaon wondered if heat tolerance was a trait shared by all mojh or was just a peculiarity of his companion.

For his own part, Na-Devaon was thoroughly miserable. The giant shuffled along, sweat running into his eyes and under his collar. The prodigious waterskin slung at his side was already half empty, but they had most of a day's trek yet before them. Behind, the pack horse followed along at the end of its lead, its head low. The foliage on either side of the road was not tall enough to shade their path.

They'd already been on the road for more than two weeks, which followed the three weeks that Dagath and Na-Devaon had required to set their affairs in order and prepare for the trip. During that time, Dagath had remained strangely reserved, even more quiet than was normal for the magister. Something was obviously spinning through the mojh's head, but on both occasions that Na-Devaon had questioned his friend, he'd been rebuffed with silence. It was beginning to get on the giant's nerves, and the day's unrelenting heat further embittered him.

"Dagath," called Na-Devaon. "Give me back the figurine for a moment."

The mojh stopped, turned, said, "Why? Have you remembered something of your vision? Something more about the . . . darkness?" A strange note of eagerness resonated in Dagath's normally calm voice.

"Maybe." Na-Devaon did not have any new insight, but the heat and his friend's manner had finally accomplished the impossible—the giant was irritable. He tried to clamp down on those feelings before he continued. "If you would explain to me what you obviously know, as I told you, I could attempt to enter a more directed akashic trance that would provide answers enough for the both of us. Why won't you tell me?"

Dagath tossed the figurine underhand to Na-Devaon, who snatched it out of the air. The mojh said simply, "I will disclose my conjecture when the time is appropriate—I need more time to get my thoughts in order. Perhaps tonight, when we reach Alrenburg."

The village of Alrenburg was a settlement of several hundred people, or so their expensive almanac claimed. Alrenburg was also the community closest to Medaba and, despite the village's small size, it hosted a market for items made from the ores unearthed in the nearby foothills—including carved orundum figurines.

"I'll hold you to that," promised the giant.

* * * * *

Bad news met the travelers in Alrenburg. According to the tavernmaster and owner of the Pale Pig Inn, where Na-Devaon and Dagath put up for the night, no trade had come out of Medaba for weeks.

"Worse than that," said the tavernmaster, his voice lowering, "we haven't seen anyone from Medaba. We used to get daily runners, and we'd send runners the other way, too. But when the last three we sent didn't return, we stopped sending them."

"Do you know the cause of the disruption?" demanded Dagath.

The tavernmaster shrugged. "Bandits, maybe? It happens out here on the fringe. That's why we've got extra men in the street. A strong militia'll keep bandits at bay. The cutthroats only go after the soft. Alrenburg's not soft, no sir." With that pronouncement, the tavernmaster moved off to fill the order of another customer.

Na-Devaon produced the orundum figurine from his pack. "That Medaba would fall silent just as we approach is too much for coincidence."

"Coincidence is merely the random concurrent incidence of two events that seem related only because of the short period of time in which they each occur," responded the magister.

"Right," the giant agreed, but the greater portion of his attention remained focused on the figurine. He'd gained no further akashic insights in all the time since his vision. He looked up then and caught the mojh's eyes with his own. "It's time you came clean with me, Dagath."

The magister cocked its head, curious.

"What is a tenebrian seed?" asked the giant.

The mojh sighed, fingered the shaft of its pale staff. Dagath said, "There is a story that the mojh know. . . ."

Na-Devaon nodded for the magister to proceed. Of course, as an akashic and something of a loremaster, he could delve into the matter himself. But he wanted to draw out the mojh. Perhaps if Dagath revealed what it knew, the magister would also divulge something of its intentions. . . .

"In ancient days, this realm was called the Land of the Dragons, for they ruled here. Dragons wield magic more aptly than any other creature, and it is recorded that one dragon was particularly blessed with aptitude for the art. This dragon, called Nithogar, discovered something called tenebrian seeds."

"So you did recognize the term," said Na-Devaon.

Dagath raised a scaled hand, asking for patience. The magister continued. "The tenebrian seeds were, according to rumor and tradition, used to engender the dramojh race."

"The demon-dragons!" spat Na-Devaon. "Why are you . . ." Then understanding came to him.

"Dagath, what is it that every mojh wishes?" asked the giant, accusation edging his voice.

"Na-Devaon, have you forgotten that I've renounced the Fleshrunes and their cruelty?" asked Dagath in turn, but the magister wouldn't meet the giant's questioning gaze. The Fleshrunes, obsessed with finding power at all costs, were too recent an affiliation in the mojh's past, or so it seemed to Na-Devaon.

Despite his question, the giant knew very well that every mojh desired, more than anything else, to grow in spirit and body as if a dragon itself. Any mojh would jump at the chance to find the fabled fount of dragon half-breeds. Never mind that those same dragon half-breeds, the dramojh, were tainted with demonic ancestry. Only the efforts of a group of deities, the Lords of Denotholan, ended the first dramojh threat, when the dragons themselves proved insufficient to halt the peril they had engendered. Later, after a second dramojh scourge claimed the Lands of the Diamond Throne, it was the power of the giants that proved the stronger, ending the dramojh threat once and for all. But, despite their vaunted evil, dramojh were also scions of the dragons.

"Whether a Fleshrune brother, cutpurse, or kind-hearted saint, any mojh would be tempted to find and use a dramojh-producing artifact, regardless of possible consequences. Or am I wrong?" challenged the giant, his voice rising.

"There is a difference between temptation and action, Na-Devaon. You taught me that." With that, Dagath stood, flipped a few coins onto the scarred tavern table, and retired.

Na-Devaon remained, sitting quietly, trying to quell the suspicion in his heart.

* * * * *

Magister and akashic reached the edge of Medaba a few days later. What was left of it.

The settlement was gutted. Hardly a roof remained unburned, and few were the walls that didn't lean or show dreadful gaps. Trash and debris blew in the street, and a terrible smell of putrescence clung to the ground despite a slight wind. Mercifully, the source of the odor was not apparent. Along the nearby ridge, great piles of tailings pointed at the sky, and many dark mouths plunged into the rock—the mines of Medaba.

"What happened here?" wondered Dagath aloud. The mojh turned to look at its friend. But Na-Devaon was already preparing himself.

The giant pinched the bridge of nose, as if pained, and plunged into the akashic sea. While others could see the light of the present, Na-Devaon could gaze into the past with akashic certitude. His loresight would reveal the atrocity that had occurred in Medaba. After only a moment, the trance was upon him.

A shadow bloomed. It blotted out the light. Its sinuous, feline shape flapped across the disc of the daystar, a silhouette of fear. A dragon descended upon Medaba.

Glints of red, gold, green, and black danced upon the beast's scales as it settled upon the ridge overlooking the settlement. It gave forth a great, booming roar of wrath—a hunting scream, it seemed, or a bawl of quintessential fury. Windows shattered, and people in the street cried out their fear as they scattered in panicked mobs. But the dragon came on, fire streaming from either side of its mouth, its eyes twin portals into Hell.

Na-Devaon gave his great head a quick shake, shattering the fearsome vision into disjointed and short-lived fragments. "A dragon! A dragon came to Medaba!"

The magister gasped, half-turning as if struck, at a loss for words. "A dragon…" Dagath looked around at the destruction, its eyes drinking in the damning evidence in light of Na-Devaon's revelation.

"Buy why? And where is it now?" finally managed Dagath.

"That is something we must discover. We must attempt to locate the mine records. The dragon's appearance has something to do with this figurine, or at least the mineral from which it was carved; I can feel it."

They entered the periphery of Medaba, eyeing the damage from a closer vantage. Too close for Na-Devaon's taste. A sworn pacifist, he didn't like to be reminded of those acts which he'd forever put aside. That was why he had aborted his akashic vision of the fiery dragon before its brutal conclusion. There were some things he simply did not want to see.

To distract himself as they made their way toward the center of the ruined community, Na-Devaon said, "The Lords of the Denotholan made a pact with the dragons—the wyrms ceded these lands and vowed never to return. Yet one has. Why?"

"Na-Devaon, I've heard other recent stories of dragon sightings, more than can be accounted as mere frippery. If what you saw is accurate, a dragon's advent here is not an isolated incident."

"How can that be?" The giant stepped over a burned-out cart, then backtracked when he realized that the pack horse couldn't clear the obstacle as easily. When he brushed the cart's side, fresh charcoal broke away and disintegrated as it fell. The destruction of Medaba couldn't have happened too long ago, the giant realized. Probably about the same time as the trade stopped coming into Alrenburg . . .

"I don't know," admitted Dagath. "The dragons made a divine pact with gods—I don't know how one goes about

34

breaking such a pledge. But it is now apparent to me that dragons have returned to our shores." The magister's tone was one more of reverence than dread. But of course, Dagath was a mojh. How else would a mojh feel?

"We must determine what brought it here," said Na-Devaon, squeezing the figurine as if to crush it. "We must establish what it is about this ore, orundum, that lured a dragon's fury."

After some time spent searching through shattered walls and broken windows, they found the structure they'd sought: the Mining Authority.

Unlike many of the other structures, the Mining Authority was built mostly of quarried stone and had withstood the burning far better than other buildings. Despite that, portions of the roof were missing, and doorways gaped enough to allow the giant and mojh to stroll right into the heart of the structure, though the giant paused first to tie up the pack horse.

"They must have kept records of all their activities, including their orundum mining," said Na-Devaon.

"If they are not burned," replied Dagath.

Na-Devaon quickly located the chamber where records were kept, aided by helpful signs. Despite the door that hung loosely on its hinges, the interior of the record chamber was unharmed. But a flurry of loose papers and overturned cabinets was the sight that greeted the giant and the mojh as they stood in the hall.

"Not very tidy for a records chamber," commented Dagath.

"Someone came through here looking for something."

The magister nodded. "Someone in a hurry."

The giant stooped and entered, his eyes roving across the mess. Dagath followed. Spread open on a central desk was a mine sketch clearly labeled "Orundum Vein A." It was a map indicating which cave mouth on the ridge outside the settlement held the orundum mine.

"And someone apparently looking for the exact same thing we are," concluded the magister.

Na-Devaon reached down and touched the map, his eyes closed to let his loresight reveal who had last handled the paper.

"I'm blocked!" said the giant, surprised. A potent magic shielded the map from his penetrating sight.

"Then we must enter the mine to find our answer," said Dagath, anticipation apparent in its voice.

* * * * *

The orundum mine entry extended nearly fifty feet into the ridge before its access was restricted by a metal valve on tremendous hinges. The valve was several feet across. "I suppose they were worried about opportunist mining," guessed Na-Devaon.

"They certainly wanted to guard something," agreed Dagath, whose staff-head blazed with light enough to illuminate the tunnel where they stood.

The giant shot the magister an exasperated look. "What if we find a tenebrian seed in here—what do you intend, Dagath?"

"It would be foolish not to study such an important relic of history," proclaimed the magister, swinging around to fully face its much larger companion, its grip white on its staff.

"Preparatory to destroying it, correct?"

"If warranted."

Na-Devaon poked a giant finger at the mojh. "Listen, Dagath, if you—"

Several silhouettes suddenly appeared in the open mine mouth from which they'd just entered. One of the silhouettes was as big as Na-Devaon—another giant. Magister and akashic faltered and ceased their heated discussion.

The smallest figure at the rear of the group of newcomers broke the stretching silence. "You know," spoke the figure, its timbre and intonation almost feminine, yet not quite, "if I had realized that I needed the figurine, or even recognized its significance when it originally passed through my possession, we could have avoided a lot of . . . unpleasantness."

The akashic squinted, then recognition broke across his face. "Dolora!"

The figures moved fully into the tunnel, close enough for Dagath's stafflight to render texture from silhouette. As Na-Devaon guessed, the smallest figure was Dolora, the witch who'd been the figurine's original owner, but who'd sold it as a mere oddity before its significance had been discovered in the akashic's vision. With "her" was a human male in dusty leathers who had a longbow drawn and aimed, and a giant wielding a dishearteningly large battle-maul carved from stone.

"When you spoke of your interaction with the previous owner, you failed to mention that Dolora was a mojh," noted Dagath.

"True," admitted Na-Devaon. "Perhaps that was an oversight."

Dolora laughed. "It seems I am not alone in my designs upon the alleged tenebrian seed." The witch waited for Dagath to respond, but the magister merely shrugged.

The witch continued. "It was an oversight on my part when I failed to take the figurine from you when I had the chance! I was too impatient—as soon as I left you, I gathered my friends and came to Medaba. We arrived three weeks ago. I had to waste a lot of time forcing the miners to tell me what I needed to know to get past this damned valve. Well . . . no, actually I rather enjoyed their extermination."

"Extermination?" repeated Na-Devaon. His stomach lurched.

"The dragon Na-Devaon saw with his akashic loresight didn't destroy the village; you did," stated Dagath, fixing Dolora with its gaze, challenging the witch to deny it.

Dolora spread scaled hands wide. "I can't deny it—if they'd told me what I wanted right away, I wouldn't have been forced to call down the fire."

"But I saw the dragon arrive . . . ," began Na-Devaon.

"And you apparently failed to follow the thread through to the end," finished Dolora.

The witch shook its head, mocking sadness. "The miners told

us about the dragon—it didn't attack Medaba. True, it made a frightening entrance, but it turned and made its way here, past this valve, into the orundum mine. For some reason, the dragon didn't need a key to get past this damned gate. But we need one. The figurine—or any object carved of orundum—will open these valves; we finally extracted that tidbit. Those cursed miners managed to hide their keys from me. After I finished off the last one, I couldn't find any orundum substitutes." Dolora smiled. "But now that you've come, I'll take my figurine back."

Dolora held out a murderer's hand.

Na-Devaon's eyes stung. Through his actions, death had come to Medaba. Images from the akashic sea suddenly burned through the ether and into his waking mind. Images of atrocities committed by Dolora. As had happened before to Na-Devaon, the giant's battle rage, a state called Chi-Julud, tempted him.

The Wardance welled in the giant's soul, sweet and hot and potent. He tensed. Rage ran as blood. If ever he was to break his pacifist oath, surely this was the time!

But the akashic was no oathbreaker. He'd proved that to himself when the agonies of Fleshrune torture had pushed him past limits he'd not known he could withstand. Instead, Na-Devaon managed to quell the rising wartide. "You cannot have it," he sighed.

"Wrong answer," declared Dolora.

The maul-wielder flung his hundred-pound weapon through the air as if it were a mere dart. Na-Devaon lightly sidestepped, and the maul smashed into the metal gate behind him, a rush of wind following in its wake. Despite being a pacifist, tapping into the collective memory allowed Na-Devaon to borrow many skills from the past, including those of defense. . . .

Except the arrow that slammed into his forearm still brought a cry of pain to his lips, interrupting his attempt to draw strength of mind from the eternal record.

Dagath, from a position beside Na-Devaon, raised its staff and pulled on lines of power threaded through the staff's pale length—power evident only to the magister. Dagath intoned, "Leave us, or be destroyed." The magister's voice rang with a strength born of magic.

The bowman looked uncertain as he drew back the cord for his next shot.

"Don't fall victim to the magister's ruse," sneered Dolora, executing in the air a delicate symbol, whose arcane configuration birthed a curtain of fire. With a delicate push, the witch sent the curtain rushing down the tunnel toward its victims.

Na-Devaon stepped in front of Dagath as the curtain swept forward. He screamed in pain as the fire burned but failed to consume him, though his clothes charred and smoked. Behind him, Dagath was only singed.

The giant warrior was upon Na-Devaon then, without the battle-maul; apparently, the brute had decided to merely squeeze the life from the akashic. The giant grasped Na-Devaon's shoulders and delivered a crushing head-butt. Na-Devaon was dazed, but he forced a smile. He, too was a giant, and could withstand many hurts. In fact, since the Fleshrune episode a few years ago, he had delved daily into the akashic memory, learning skills of avoidance, tolerance, and physical solidity. He willed himself to become a rock on which his attackers' blows could hammer, but not break.

The next arrow that struck Na-Devaon failed to penetrate his skin, and his smile grew broader.

"Hold him!" commanded Dolora to the other giant, who still grasped Na-Devaon's shoulders. The witch summoned to hand a slender, obscenely long lance of burning iron. Dolora grinned. "Now comes my favorite part."

Dagath stepped from out of Na-Devaon's shadow and said, "You were warned." The magister visibly drew power from its staff, attaining a dim body-glow that rapidly swelled to brilliance.

The giant wrestling with Na-Devaon loosed his grip, turning his attention to the magister. Another arrow whistled forward;

this time aimed at Dagath, but was deflected by a quick swat from Na-Devaon. The magister's glow illuminated the worried look that suffused Dolora's previously eager expression.

It was already too late.

The light streaming away from Dagath quickly narrowed into a beam that touched first Dolora, then the archer, and lastly the suddenly backpedaling giant warrior. When the light winked out, Dagath slumped against the metal valve, breathing hard.

The intruders each stood unmoving, held in place by the magic Dagath had wrought.

"How long until the magic fades?" asked Na-Devaon.

"Until I release them."

"Good. Thanks." The giant paused, then bulled on. "Then we have enough time to discuss the specifics of this tenebrian seed. I want to know what, exactly, you intend to do should we find one."

The magister wearily nodded. "I've been wrestling with that very question—you know me well enough to see that, I hope. Do I destroy it or use it myself to transcend my current incarnation and become truly akin to a dragon?"

The giant studied Dagath, new worries crinkling his burned brow. "So, what have you determined, my friend?"

Dagath sighed. "It was Dolora who decided me."

"In what way?"

"Dolora showed me that one would do well to be wary of temptation. I have discovered that temptation can lure one down proscribed corridors of the mind during the lonely hours of the night. The temptation of gaining the seed has engendered atrocities every bit as deplorable as those I've turned my back on in the cult. The seed should be destroyed. Not all that tempts should be accepted."

The giant clapped Dagath on the shoulder, saying nothing.

The two turned, facing the valve. Na-Devaon brought forth the figurine. When he touched it to the gate, the way into the mine opened.

* * * * *

The path led down an artificially straight grade, supported with occasional wooden struts. Five minutes of navigation was sufficient to see Dagath and Na-Devaon through to the edge of a natural cavern. The light of the magister's staff revealed the debris and scars mining had wrought throughout the cave. Most of the cavern floor's top layer was gone, strip-mined to a depth of three or four feet.

At the far edge of the strip-mined area, a bit of virgin cavern remained. Mojh and giant moved forward, tense with anticipation. Where was the dragon? What of the tenebrian seed?

The yet-to-be mined section of the cavern was studded with oblong, boulderlike nodules. They looked something like geodes, yet smoother. All the ones that showed up in Dagath's light were shattered, revealing a flashing core reminiscent of the figurine Na-Devaon carried.

"This is the orundum deposit," said the giant.

"I've never heard of metallic ore concentrated in such a unique fashion," mused Dagath. "These odd geodes remind me of something." The mojh scratched its temple.

It was then they heard the immense inhalation and saw the great shadow.

* * * * *

A dragon was there with them in the cavern, had been there all along. It was a creature like those ancient beings Na-Devaon had seen in his visions, yet unlike. It was of no definite color, but the giant somehow knew that its scales could reflect nearly any hue of the spectrum, depending on the dragon's mood. Currently, its scales were black as the bleak heart of a dead star.

Na-Devaon's breath caught. Did the dragon know it had visitors? He felt a hand on his arm: Dagath. The mojh leaned forward and drew Na-Devaon's head down to its own level. It

41

whispered, "Eggs. These 'orundum geodes' are dragon eggs."

The truth in Dagath's revelation hit Na-Devaon like a physical blow. Eggs! But yet unlike eggs—even those found buried after millennia—they were not so much fossilized as crystallized, as if caught in timeless stasis. A stasis that hadn't saved them from the Medaban miners' attention.

"Desecrated." The words issued from the looming shadow. "The Clutch is desecrated. I am the Seventh, the seventh in a sacred line of Clutch Mothers chosen to reinvigorate the ancient brood upon our return to these lands. But that reunion shall never happen now. The Clutch is lost."

The dragon loosed a roar that knocked Dagath to the floor and staggered Na-Devaon. This is the end, thought the giant, as he fought to regain his footing.

No killing blow followed. Instead came a forlorn cry of pain. The akashic sensed an ocean of grief, not rage. The dragon cried alone in the darkness for her slain ancestors.

While the echoes of the grief-stricken bellow still chased around the cavern, Na-Devaon remembered the figurine, which he still grasped. With the dragon's words, like keys, perhaps he could prize loose further understanding from the akashic memory. . . .

. . . The pact was not unmerciful in its dictates; it allowed the dragons some leeway, some grace in their exit from the lands they had ruled so long. They would leave, but not before assuring that some legacy of their presence remained behind in their ancient homeland. The Clutch was laid and placed outside time as a promise of rebirth to the dragons forced to abandon their lands. The best and brightest dragons of the age contributed to the Clutch. One dragon was selected to guard the knowledge of the Clutch and to pass that knowledge to one of her descendents every thousand years. Thus the brood was the legacy of the dragon-heroes of ancient days, a legacy that no giant or human tale even touches upon. . . .

Na-Devaon let his loresight fall away. The dragon was curled in upon itself, a mass of agony. Compassion bloomed in the giant, and with it, guilt for his earlier assumption that the dragon had razed Medaba. The dragon's sorrow seemed unbreakable, eternal. The akashic had a sudden intuition of the dragon dying here among the shards of its failed charge. He forced himself to move closer.

"I can't give you back your Clutch," said Na-Devaon, speaking loudly and addressing the darkness, "but I can give you this."

The giant akashic held up the sculpture and called upon his connection to the akashic realm of the eternal. The figurine already contained some essence of the dragon's lost brood; the ore from which it was smelted originated in this very nest. That connection served as anchor enough to attempt a greater working. The giant mentally pulled at the threads of akashic probability, weaving into existence something more than simple illusion—indeed, he attempted to imbue in the figurine the completed essence of the dragonlings that were lost to time—what they could have been, and what they could have accomplished.

It was an audacious task. Na-Devaon struggled with each of the Four Principles, seeking to weave his desire into existence. Halfway through, he faltered. The construct shivered, still imperfectly wed to the figurine, and threatened to unwind, but then the giant felt the touch of Dagath's staff. The magister aided him, fed him raw arcane might, which Na-Devaon desperately grasped and used to sustain his intent.

In the end, he fashioned a potent akashic working, a memorial capable of looking into a reality different from the present—it was a true shrine to the vanished Clutch, memorializing the legacy of the ancient dragons. Any creature that grasped the figurine and looked into its eyes would recall a special draconic heritage, seeing the dragonlings of the Clutch hatch and live as they would have done, had their nest not been disturbed.

Na-Devaon finished the working and slumped, exhausted. If Dagath hadn't helped . . .

The dragon stirred. Extending a prodigious claw, it took the insignificant figurine from Na-Devaon's grasp with a feat of delicacy astonishing in a creature so large.

"I accept your gift," the dragon whispered.

The Clutch Mother sprang from its curled position, vaulting over giant and mojh. Na-Devaon thought for an instant that the roof of the cavern was collapsing, but quickly regained his equilibrium when he saw the dragon exiting the chamber. "Come on," he urged, sprinting after the retreating tail. Dagath was already dashing forward, the mojh's face open and incredulous in the presence of a creature it had sought to emulate for much of its life.

They fled back up to the entrance. Outside, they found the dragon waiting, perched in the open air on the ridge above. It was gazing into the eyes of the figurine. When Na-Devaon and Dagath emerged, it blinked, and turned its gaze upon them.

Dagath gasped, "Great One, I beg—what has become of the tenebrian seed? Was there such a relic buried with the Clutch?"

The dragon cocked its head. It said, "The tenebrian seed's power was bled into each of the eggs, to keep them outside time's reach. All that remains of that seed was gathered by you and the giant, during your peculiar working, and is concentrated in this memorial. It was a mighty gift to return to me, and I shall not soon forget it."

Dagath blinked, at a loss for words.

Color gradually leached into the dragon's scales, as if sunlight slowly spilled across it from a new day's dawning. It roared once more. This time the sound was not laden with loss and pain, but instead, challenge and—perhaps—promise. The dragon took to the air, its wings spanning the heavens. It spiraled quickly up, and up, becoming ever smaller in the distance.

Dagath and Na-Devaon followed its progress, staring across the wide, cloud-speckled sky.

The dragon receded farther, becoming the smallest of blots upon the blue-hazed horizon . . . then it was gone.

ED GREENWOOD
THE MAD MOJH OF ONTETH

E very sunset brought on that moment when the stars were born. Thousands of tiny flashes all across the Crystal Fields, sparkling into sudden, brief life, as uncounted rock shards caught and mirrored the last light of the setting sun.

The two oldest men in the village of Onteth stood side by side in the familiar reek of the privy and watched the stars wink, flash and fade. They'd seen this beauty every day of their lives, but somehow, these last few seasons, it never seemed to last long enough.

The groundstars were fading already. Baerek shook his head at them through the window as he laced up his cods and spat thoughtfully into the trench beyond the belly-rail.

"I *said* that boy would be trouble," he growled, jerking his head toward the unseen tavern at their backs. At this distance, the mad mirth they'd left raging in it was only a faint keening.

ED GREENWOOD

Gnarled hands busy with his own laces, Oskul grinned at Baerek. Then, as always, he tugged at his grey remnants of a beard as if needing to loosen his jaw to start speaking.

"You say a lot of things, Old Sword—an' you must admit, Nalander provides sport for us all, talkin' of his mad plots an' spells and latest idiocies!"

Baerek gave his friend a dark look. "Aye, talk! And will we still be tongue-wagging and chuckling and whispering wild rumors, I wonder, when his madness brings him to blast our own roofs down on top of our heads with his spells—or turn us into what he made himself into?"

Oskul shrugged. "You worry too much, Baer—you always have. The gods want their entertainment, even if you don't. They'll see to it that Onteth'll still be standing around us next dawn . . . an' the next."

"Yes, but are the gods tired of *us* yet? Are these old limbs and unlovely faces 'entertaining' enough for them still?"

Oskul shrugged. "They haven't choked on Nalander yet, have they?"

"No," Baerek growled, "but I'm near to doing so."

Oskul chuckled as they started the long trudge across the muddy tavern yard to the back door of The Plough. Through it, as they strode closer, rose ever-stronger the gleeful cackling of Nalander—the Mad Mojh of Onteth.

* * * * *

Long and dusty were the cart-tracks to Onteth, and not much more than a handcount of merchants each season came all the bone-rattling way along them.

Wherefore Onteth-folk heard and laid eyes on fewer wonders of the wider world than they saw of weary crystal-delvers. Most of those were dazed, staggering men wounded and left to die by treacherous fellows or the desperate outlaws—and strange beasts—that lurked in the heart of the Crystal Fields.

46

Onteth looked down on the Crystal Fields from a ridge that bounded the village on the west. What passed for a main street in Onteth wandered along that ridge. The Plough, the slaughterhouse, the mill, and the cursed ruins of Nalander's tall stone house stood in an untidy row along the west side of the street, facing the workshops of the weavers and the cottages of those too old to farm. Lanes wandered between those cottages down into the farms that sprawled away east and north of Onteth. When sundown made work in the fields difficult or dangerous, folk were wont to either huddle close around their hearthfires or come trudging up to The Plough.

From the tavern one could see a long way west across the Crystal Fields. One could gaze southwest at the faint glow of distant Navael by night, or by day look northwest at the vast darkness of the Harrowdeep.

Not that most folk of Onteth had time to spare for standing and looking, with work beasts all too few and boreworms and the baking sun gnawing at the peppers and melons in the fields.

And too few traders brought work beasts for sale, their paltry visits brought too few jests and tales from afar to so remote a farming village—to say nothing of finecloth and good boots and baubles. Maps and books were things gossiped about more than seen, and few in Onteth had tongues supple enough to tell of their dreams, even if they'd wanted to risk being thought of as wanderwits.

Oh, men went mad, all right, and were found shuffling along slobbering and singing, knowing no one. There were feuds, too, and all that went with them. The tongues of the old women were honed sharp with spite and gossip. Daily they repeated old opinions but craved something more—and clucked disapprovingly when they got it.

Not half so much, mind, as they clucked at the curse of the gods upon the village: the Mad Mojh of Onteth.

47

ED GREENWOOD

* * * * *

Ambrin Nalander had been the richest trader in Onteth, a
man wealthy enough to own entire herds, and whole streets in
distant Navael, besides—and even have idle coins enough left
over to buy things of magic. He'd been lord in Onteth, of course.

He was a wise man, respected rather than hated through the
envy of his poorer neighbors, because Lord Ambrin thought
before he spoke. He tried to do his best and showed no
moonglimmer of pride.

He brought home a beauty from afar to be his bride, and if
the women of Onteth warmed not to her, well, that was only to
be expected. In due time Niashra smiled on the Lord and Lady
Nalander, and she grew large with child.

Then came the night of her birthing, and the dark laughter
of Mowren, the god who casts the dice of fate, was heard in the
streets of Onteth.

* * * * *

"If only Lord Ambrin's lady hadn't died birthing Zors,"
Baerek sighed. "Things would've been—"

"So different, yes," Oskul grunted, kicking aside something
bony but unseen in the dirt of the tavern yard, and reaching for
the back door. "Ambrin still alive, his son still sane . . ."

"Still *human*," Baerek growled.

The opening door spilled warm smoke and lamplight and
that insane, high cackling out into the night.

Clenching their remaining teeth in revulsion, the two old men
shouldered through the door to rejoin their neighbors. They all
sat in sullen, wary silence, tankards in hand, watching the tall,
scaled, reptile-headed *thing* capering atop the largest table: the
dragon-monster that had once been Zors Nalander.

* * * * *

48

It had surprised no one when Lord Ambrin Nalander had turned grim and thin-lipped at his wife's death and gone on long walks alone. In the end he'd been found one morning sprawled dead on the rocks at the end of the ridge.

However, it was still a matter of some debate in Onteth as to whether his heir, the boy Zors Nalander, had been born crazed or had gone that way after both his parents had been turned under by the plough.

Zors had a tongue more glib and wits swifter than his father's, with an everchanging mood to match and frenzied strength to boot. None knew what he ate or lived on, huddled alone in the house that had been his father's, but he did no farming—and paid no need to the decrees of the new Lord of Onteth.

The miller Dorlur had been chosen lord after Ambrin's death, and from that day to this had remained the same slow, stolid, careful man he'd always been. A stone set against the capering flame that was Zors Nalander.

Ambrin's son hurried everywhere, by day and night, striding purposefully through the fields or the village as if gods-driven, always talking to himself.

The only way to snatch his attention away from his self-debates was to smite him or speak to him of magic.

And that latter sort of talk always set his eyes aflame. In the words of old Ammada, ploughed under these ten summers gone, "Young Zors is obsessed with mastering magic, where his father was wise enough to merely collect it as an investment, to bargain for power."

Obsessed or not, Zors had walked to Navael six summers back, and farther than that . . . and back.

The dust kicked up by his boots had scarcely settled when strangers rode up to the tall stone house of Nalander with laden pack beasts—and departed back the way they'd come the same day, their beasts now barebacked.

Strange lights kindled and danced in the house that night and for several weeks thereafter, until the folk of Onteth took to muttering that something must be done—at least, someone should watch the house by night to see what was afoot.

Those mutterings ended the night House Nalander burned like a bonfire, roof roaring up into the sky. Its blazing beams tumbled, within, amid strange blue rushing radiances that kept the stone walls unscorched and whole. Through the crackle and growl of the hungry flames, Zors Nalander could be heard laughing: triumphant, gleeful mirth, that held no note of pain, loss, or madness.

Yet when bright morning had broken over Onteth, a tall, thin, reptile-headed thing had hurried forth from the ruins. Naked it was, with a tail, and lacking manhood. It hailed various Onteth folk by name, proclaiming itself "Zors Nalander no more! Behold me now: Zorlathar!"

The son of Ambrin had transformed himself into a dragon-creature—a mojh.

* * * * *

Eerie spell-sparks were winking into existence now, here and there among the mojh's widespread talons. Some folk in The Plough cowered at the sight, expecting magic to lash out and—

"Bah!" Baerek Hallowhand barked, bringing his fist down on the table before him with a crash. "This has gone far enough! You—Nalander! *Zorlathar!*"

The reptilian head snapped around to fix him with gleefully glowing eyes and hiss, "Yesss?"

"Back here you've come, all of a sudden, despite the stones we flung your way years back, to buy us quaffs these six nights, now—and all you do is prance and laugh like a madwit! *Why?*"

The mojh burst into a wild, high peal of laughter that set teeth on edge and made folk wince or even duck under tables, for fear of what might come.

When that mirth was done, the thing that had once been Zors Nalander ducked its head down like a snake sidling up to prey, grinning toothily, and hissed, "At lassst! I'd almossst begun to think you'd *never* asssk!"

* * * * *

The magic that had given Ambrin's son mojh-shape had seemingly touched his mind, too. The very day he'd revealed himself as the dragon-thing Zorlathar, he—no, *it*—had begun to give orders as if it were lord of the village. The folk of Onteth, of course, dismissed its attempts to order them around, declaring the creature mad.

Enraged, the mojh had raised its hands and cast a spell. Purple lightning whirled about its taloned hands to spit forth and send Lorglar the smith reeling and Lord Dorlur sprawling senseless.

Amid much shouting, the folk of Onteth took up mattocks and hoes and hounded the mojh out of the village amid a hail of hurled stones.

It fled before them until darkness came, loping east through the farms with stones bouncing from its scales, and turning betimes to lash its closest pursuers with magical flame and lightning.

The next day, the boldest young men of Onteth went forth in a great band, well armed with pitchforks and scythes.

Two nights later they returned to The Plough to tell excited tales of the mojh taking up a hermit's existence in a crumbling, long-abandoned keep in the beast-roamed Garlfangs, the nearest broken summits of the Bitter Peaks.

There was much fear in Onteth that this Zorlathar would creep back and work murder in this cottage and that, but the transformed heir of Ambrin Nalander was seen no more in the village that season.

More seasons passed, and sudden spell-glows kindled warningly, time and again, to keep folk from venturing into the ruins of House Nalander or carrying off its stones. Yet still the dragon-thing came not back, and some folk of Onteth took the view that Zors Nalander—or Zorlathar—was gone from the village for good, thanks be to the gods.

Yet there came a season when night after night was rent by strange flashes and rumblings from that distant keep, and the awakened folk of Onteth stood in the darkness gazing grimly east. Their dread of what the former Zors Nalander might do if allowed to continue working magic untrammeled warred with their fear of the spells the mojh commanded already.

Lord Dorlur would fain have let well enough alone, and said so, but the younger men of the village, swifter to anger and bright in their shoutings of it, were seized with the resolve to slay or drive out the mojh. They gathered in some strength with their bows and the best weapons they could muster, plus rope and torches and wineskins full of courage. They set forth in high spirits, and the older villagers watched them go rather sadly.

Long were the days ere their return—and at that homecoming, more than a handcount were missing. Those few who trudged back to The Plough shouted no more, but muttered of changes in the mojh's fortress.

Though they'd seen no one but Zorlathar therein—kneeling alone at a stone altar worked into the likeness of three rearing dragons—the keep stood taller, its many chambers bristling with deadly traps of falling blocks and hammers of stone, pits unseen that opened without warning beneath boots, and walls of sharp spears that slammed down with deadly speed.

So, in bloody surprise after bloody surprise, the younglings of Onteth perished—five falling in that innermost altar chamber, ignored by the kneeling mojh as they shouted, screamed, and died—and their fellows fled.

The folk of Onteth eyed each other and gossiped in fierce whispers. So Zorlathar had, it seemed, become even less human than before, and wild-witted enough now to worship dragons. In a word: mad, beyond doubt.

Lord Dorlur decreed that there would be no more forays to the abode of the mojh, not even to try to bring back the fallen for ploughing-under. His words met with no defiance this time.

Yet scarcely a month after that judgment, the former Zors Nalander appeared in the village, striding along almost jauntily with an old cart floating along in the air behind its tail—drifting with wheels clear of the ground and no beast in harness to pull it. Where the mojh went, the cart followed, though Zorlathar spared it barely a glance.

At first the mojh was shunned, but locked doors parted before it, and the dragon-thing took what it wanted from deserted counters, leaving behind fair coin. A few old women too slow or too quaking to run found themselves selling it crockery they'd otherwise not have parted with, and lived to tell the tale that night.

So it was that the mojh's next appearance in Onteth—but for the wary silences—was not much different from the shopping-forays of outlying farmers. As before, it bought sundries, paying fair prices, and went on its way.

Zorlathar came no more to Onteth that year, but it returned thrice the following season, and twice the year after. No one disturbed the mojh or refused to trade with it—not after it blasted Lardan One-Eye and his cottage to flaming dust for selling it poisoned wine, and after it transformed the drover Tarmtath into a toad for drawing steel on it.

And thus, Zors Nalander faded away, and the mojh Zorlathar took his place as an occasional—and dangerous to cross—visitor to Onteth.

So things continued, one harvest to the next, until now.

Now the Mad Mojh seemed to have gone even more crazy, if such a thing were possible. Its usual dour, menacing manner was gone, replaced by sudden stares, frequent cackles of glee, and even occasional caperings. In short, it seemed to be . . . gloating.

Every evening it came to Onteth, now, appearing in The Plough at dusk to buy drinks for all.

And the folk of Onteth ducked their heads low over their tankards to trade sidelong glances, not daring to ask it what they were all wondering: gloating about *what*?

* * * * *

Never taking its gleefully-glowing eyes from Baerek Hallowhand, the mojh sprang from one table to another to point at him . . . and then slowly turn to include everyone in The Plough in its triumphant answer.

"The dragonsss are coming! The dragonsss ssshall return to rule all, and the giantsss will be ssswept away! Then I ssswear you'll *rue* your mockery of me—your defiance of my rightful rule!"

There was a moment of utter silence, and then the amazed and disbelieving mutterings began.

"Hah!" Zorlathar cried. "Of *courssse* you don't believe me! But I have ssseen them, I tell you, flying hither. Not ssso far away are they, right now, on the far ssside of the Bitter Peaks!"

The mojh waved a scaled arm at the eastern wall of the crowded chamber, then ducked its head to hiss conspiratorially, "I can ssshow you them thisss inssstant, with my ssspellsss!"

It raised both of its taloned hands dramatically, as if to begin working magic—but Baerek snapped, "Save your unwelcome magic, son of Nalander. You can craft *any* image you like with a spell and claim to be showing us the truth!"

Rising growls of agreement sounded from the far corners of the crowded room.

The mojh's eyes glittered with rage, and its talons curled into rending claws. Some men shouted in fear, and others ducked under tables or started for the doors—but Zorlathar's softly menacing hiss sounded in their ears like a great war horn, spell-sent into the heads of everyone in Onteth.

"You *ssshall* be very sssorry, very sssoon. Yet ressst asssured: I'll do what'sss necesssary to greet the Great Onesss fittingly."

And then, without any fuss at all, the dragon-thing atop the table simply . . . faded away.

"Dragons," Oskul muttered in a daze. "Coming soon . . ."

"Worse than that," Baerek growled at him. "That madwit is going to 'greet them fittingly'! Gods know what that means!"

* * * * *

For once, it seemed, the gods were eager to share their knowledge with the folk of Onteth. The next morn Taraeye Longhair, the most beautiful maid in the village, disappeared on her way down to her spring-hut to bathe. By midday Malree Dorlur, Taraeye's rival in alluring looks and the Lord Miller's only daughter, vanished from the Dorlur outhouse, its door swinging wide to reveal—nothing but flies.

By nightfall, in like wise, the tall and tart-tongued tavernmaid, Lorndra, was gone—she flickered into oblivion in mid-step, right before the disbelieving eyes of the young brawnbrains and the old grizzled ex-tinker who served The Plough as its cellarers.

Magic, and doubtless the work of the mojh!

All Onteth was in an uproar, folk scouring the deserted ashes of House Nalander and then gathering in The Plough to hammer tables and shout until near dawn . . . when a white-faced drover stumbled into their midst to stammer that three great oval stone plinths had appeared—aye, as if by magic—in the market square.

Snarls of rage and fear rose, and the men of Onteth boiled forth to snatch spades and forks and hammers, intending to shatter the trio of massive, smooth-topped rocks. The three ovals stood inside a low stone wall that, like them, had sprung seemingly out of nowhere.

A wall emblazoned with the grainsheaf badge of Nalander.

"Runes and dragons," someone cursed, "The Mad One's building a new house for itself right here!"

And with a roar of rage and disgust, the men of Onteth swung their steel. The first ringing stroke had barely fallen on unyielding

55

stone when the grey of coming dawn erupted in flame.

Blue-white, blinding flames, snarling and leaping from plinth to plinth—wrapped around something tall and scaled and enraged. The Mad Mojh had returned to Onteth.

* * * * *

Zorlathar's talons writhed like snakes as its jaws hissed incantations.

"*Down,* Old Sword!" Oskul hissed, sprinting just fast enough to catch up to a bellowing Baerek—and shove his friend sprawling onto his face in the dirt. A trusted dagger bounced out of gnarled Hallowhand fingers as Oskul landed atop his friend. Baerek cursed feelingly as blue-white fire raged overhead with a deafening roar.

It faded fast but left flickering blue-white glows behind. Every one of the glows enshrouded a villager, frozen silent in mid-shout around the plinths, hammers and forks raised.

Behind those glowing, motionless figures cowered other villagers, some of them groveling on the ground not far from Oskul and Baerek.

"Son of Nalander," Baerek cried, as if fear were something he felt not, "*what* have you done?"

The mojh leaned forward to fix him with triumphant eyes, and hissed, "Sssaved them from themsssselvesss, Old Sssword. Limb-locked are they, and no more than that. The ssstonesss mussst *not* be harmed!"

"Oh? Why?" Baerek got to his feet, waving his hand imperiously behind him for Oskul to slap his dagger into it. "And what've you done with Lorndra and the others?"

"Aye," the cobbler Reldivar shouted. "*You* vanished the maids, didn't you?"

The mojh drew itself up and cast a swift spell, talons weaving in front of its face as deftly as the passes of the best village weavers.

Its next words roared out across the roofs and walls of On-teth, echoing back like thunder. "No time remainsss to you for anger and accusssationsss! The dragonsss come! The dragonsss *come!*"

Baerek felt the familiar heft of his dagger-hilt slap his palm and closed his hand around it furiously. If he threw just right . . .

The mojh seemed moth-eaten, or molting. Its skin was mottled with darksome blemishes, like the skin of a snake after a farm-dog's jaws had been at it. More than half of Zorlathar's scales were missing.

That should leave the dragon-thing's flesh unprotected against the bite of his steel, if he could manage to . . .

Baerek's eyes narrowed. Those missing scales hadn't cracked off or been eaten away—they'd been cut away, and the cuts seared shut with flame. Had the mojh injured itself? If so, why?

Zorlathar was pointing dramatically now, up into the dawn-brightening sky over the Bitter Peaks. "Sssee, you?" it crowed. "The dragonsss come!"

The rose-tinted clouds to the east were brightening by the instant as dawn melted away their night-purple. The folk of Onteth peered along the mojh's pointing talon and cried aloud in awe and fear.

High against the brightening clouds, two distant serpentine forms were beating great wings. Birds they might have been, if birds were shaped like snakes—and as large as barns.

The villagers shrank back, moaning in awe. Baerek forgot all about throwing his puny knife.

Atop the nearest plinth, the mojh threw back its head and cackled, its talons moving again in the passes and gestures of spellcasting. A glowing rune appeared momentarily in the air in the wake of one moving talon, and twisted into a second pat-tern ere it faded.

The purple stealing away from the sky seemed to bubble up like smoke in the air above the plinths, then vanish in a sudden puff to drift and fade in the wake of what it had brought: the maidens Taraeye, Malree, and Lorndra. Asleep they seemed, each one stretched out on her back atop a plinth, bound with wrists overhead to a spar that passed along her spine down to her trussed ankles. The maids wore nothing but strange splashes of something dark and crusted that seemed to be a kind of glue. At the heart of those splashes were the mojh's missing scales, stuck to their loins, flanks, foreheads, and breasts in untidy profusion.

"Behold these fitting offeringsss, lordsss!" Zorlathar roared in its spell-augmented voice, a great cry that smote the villagers' ears like hard blows and drove them, wincing, to their knees.

Blue-white radiance sprang from the frozen villagers. They collapsed like so many dolls, crashing limply to the ground with forks and hammers clattering. The lightning arced to the plinths, then flared up into the sky like beacons.

The mojh began leaping from plinth to plinth like a mad thing, touching each bound lass as it giggled and capered. When it had thrice visited each plinth, it stopped and started to cast a long and elaborate spell of half-sung incantations, shuffling dances, and glowing mid-air runes.

"We must stop this," Baerek growled, shaking off his fascination and raising his dagger. "We must—"

Oskul caught his friend's wrist in a stone-hard grip. "Not *now!*" he snarled. "If those—those *things* in the sky come down, what defender have we but the son of Nalander? Who can speak for us but him?"

Baerek turned his head to spit out curses of denial—and then stopped to stare. The mojh's spell was done.

The scales glued to the maidens were rippling and quivering, like the roilings made by a beast rolling in a mud-wallow. As most of Onteth stared, dumbstruck, those scales writhed and shifted over the smooth skin beneath them, darting hither and thither like pond-spiders!

The maidens trembled, their mouths opening and their breasts rising and falling in sudden, frantic breathing. Little lights seemed to rise up out of their bodies to race all over their hides among the moving mojh-scales, and become . . . tiny new scales!

Baerek swallowed in horror as he saw Taraeye's shapely fingers lengthen into long, spidery talons. They were all changing thus as Zorlathar danced among them . . .

As the trio of maidens arched and writhed, shadowy waves of scales seemed to wash over them, making them seem like three new mojh for an instant ere falling away again. The waves left behind the same patches of dark stickiness, and their own tangled hair, and . . . Zorlathar's scales stuck to them, now dwindling and smoking like tinder consumed by flames.

Trembling in pain, the three women sat up in shuddering unison, snapping their bonds like so much dried grass. Staring at the dawn with awakened, terrified eyes, they started to scream.

The mojh spread triumphant arms and drowned them out with a scream of its own—a scream of laughter.

Its crow rocked Onteth, high and long and shrill.

That shriek of triumph was laced by the horrified screams of the three maids—who sank down again under another surging shadow of scales, their human forms seeming to warp into snouted, scaled grotesqueries.

"Mojh," Oskul gasped. "More mojh!"

Zorlathar bent over one of the transformed maids to gloat at its work, and the arching, spasming dragon-thing that had been Lorndra Tlaggar spat at her tormentor and tried to claw him, snarling.

Whereupon the shadow of scales faded from her, leaving her as human as before.

"Look!" Reldivar shouted. "The mad mojh's spell failed!"

The mojh recoiled from Lorndra with something that was half a roar and half a shriek, leaping to the next plinth—but was greeted by Malree's raking nails, her scream just as fierce and hate-filled.

The mojh hissed right back at her, eyes flaring with rage and hatred.

"Hah!" cried old, toothless Narya, ragged sleeves fluttering as she pointed excitedly. "Zorlathar's magic is broken!"

The mojh jerked its head to glare at her—and then drew itself erect and stepped back, to teeter on the inside edge of Malree's plinth and work hasty magic.

The dawn darkened overhead as Zorlathar finished its spell—and the three maidens fell silent, their thrashings stilled, their jaws now soundless . . .

Baerek and Oskul frowned at them, and then at each other. Dawn *darkening* overhead?

They looked up together, saw what the mojh was already gazing at—and froze.

The dragons *were* as large as barns . . . and two of them were descending over the roofs of Onteth like a vast and solid second ridge, coming down to greet the familiar one the village clung to.

Before they could do anything more than mew and tremble, great talons opened to perch on The Plough, and one dragon settled onto the tavern roof as gently as a glimmering lands on a weed-head. The second descended onto the mill.

Both buildings promptly collapsed flat to the ground amid a groaning din of rending wood and billowing dust.

"Welcome!" the mojh cackled. "Behold my offerings, Great Onesss!"

Eyes as old and as wise as the moon itself gazed at Zorlathar and the three maidens, and then—without those great heads moving at all—examined Baerek and Oskul and the trembling and fainting villagers of Onteth.

One great taloned claw stretched forth almost lazily to the plinths. The mojh watched its approach and preened visibly, drawing itself up to strike a self-satisfied pose.

And those talons, each longer than the mojh stood tall, slashed down in disgust, dicing the former son of Nalander into red ruin in an instant.

Sparks of magic swirled briefly around the toppling carnage that had been Zorlathar. As they faded and winked out, the mojh-scales melted away from the three maidens.

"Is *this* what humans have become?" one dragon rumbled wearily, its voice so deep and rich that the very notes it reached shook Baerek and Oskul like leaves in a rising wind. "They had quick wits, swifter hands . . . so much promise. Yet I see no boldness, not even the will strong enough to stand and face us in a single one of them." Its voice trailed away into a growl of dismissal.

"We should have returned long ago," the other replied gravely, as the two old men flung themselves face-down in the dirt, in reverence.

Other villagers fled wildly into walls, or swooned, or cowered to the ground, weeping hysterically. The market square of Onteth stank with their fear.

"Get up," the second dragon added, disgust unmistakable in its rumble. "If you are to serve us, all of you have much to do in the time ahead."

JEFF GRUBB
ENVOY

T he sibeccai Janostis realized now that he should have
abandoned his plan long ago. He should have abandoned the plan when he first met the squamous lir. He
should have abandoned the plan when he found the enslaved
humans. He should have abandoned the plan when the chanting
started and the air turned cold.

But now the ground beneath his feet was turning to glass,
and he could see the squirming masses of lamprey-jawed,
spider-limbed slassans burrowing upward, and he realized that
it was far too late to abandon the plan.

At least he had the time to recognize that it had been a
stupid plan from the very beginning. . . .

* * * * *

It was a brilliant plan, Janostis the Facilitator thought when
he first hatched the concept, there at his small desk in his tiny

62

office in his nondescript building in the great granite-block capital city of De-Shamod. Great things were in the wind, if only one was sufficiently sensitive to pay attention. And Janostis, of the sibeccai race or jackal-men, was nothing if not sensitive—keen ears, sharp eyes, and a nose for opportunity.

The clues had been mounting over the past few weeks, as the reports and rumors came into the capital from all over Dor-Erthenos, the Lands of the Diamond Throne. Stories of great shadows passing over paddocks and fields at high speeds. Reports of missing farm animals. Strange appearances of burnt, frozen, or acid-scorched vegetation. Reptilian silhouettes in distant, dying sunsets.

At his small desk in his tiny office in his nondescript building, Janostis collected the messages, preparing reports for other minor bureaucrats to read and collate and pass on, until someone brought it to the notice of the giants. But Janostis realized what it all meant.

Dragons were back. Not in incidental sightings and lies told around the tavern hearth, but in large numbers. From Zalavat to the Harrowdeep the reports came in. Sightings. Testimonies. Descriptions of attacks or near-attacks. Droppings of unknown origins and excessive size. As a child he had heard the legends of the giants who ruled this land. As a youth, preparing for his service in the giant government, he had studied these elder eddas and epic poems. He knew what to look for, and what it all meant, at a time when others were fumbling toward the truth. He knew.

Dragons were returning to Dor-Erthenos.

And it would be only a matter of time before a dragon encountered a representative of the Hu-Charad, the ruling giants and masters of this land. Perhaps it would be a military outpost, perhaps a local official, perhaps a chance traveler. Someone somewhere would have to make that initial, true, official contact.

And Janostis the Facilitator—sibeccai, minor functionary in the greater giant bureaucracy—knew that person had to be him.

A peaceful contact between the giants and the ancient dragons would be a boon to all the realm. And if Janostis brought such a gift to the giants, his superiors would at last recognize his true potential. Recognize, and without a doubt, reward it. They would elevate him within the bureaucracy as they had elevated his people from savagery centuries before. They would improve his posting, promoting him in rank from Facilitator to Director, perhaps even Grand Director

He liked the sound of that. Janostis the Grand Director.

But Janostis the Facilitator's timeframe was incredibly small, a window more slender than that in a faen's front hallway—as soon as he sent out the reports that he had already gathered, others would come to the same conclusions. He could delay a day, a week at most. Any longer, and the sheer weight of new information would cause others to investigate.

So he seized the rhodin by the horns and hatched his plan. Boldly, he spread requests for information through the bureaucracy. Not asking about dragons, of course, but rather questions about odd sightings, animal attacks, or strange vegetation. He had most of the information already, but more importantly, he was *letting it be known* that he was asking. He requisitioned books from the library at Se-Heton, all the better to keep the knowledge to himself.

The purpose of all this was to drive anyone looking for similar information toward him. Anyone with a question on the subject. Anyone with a firm report or further information. Janostis could then position himself as a knowledgeable advisor and investigator. Perhaps even an ally for someone else with knowledge. And if the questioners were too powerful in the hierarchy, or too close to the truth, Janostis would be in a position to send them down a blind passage or two.

And at his tiny desk in his small office in his nondescript building, he reviewed the old legends and the musty tomes and discovered what the civilized world knew of the dragons.

The dragons were legendary creatures—they had contested with the giants at the dawn of the world, but were long gone from this land by time the giants arrived on these shores. They were alternately portrayed as great beasts, clever sorcerers, wise rulers, scaled tyrants, and collectors of gold or stories—sometimes both. They were not quite gods but seemed within spitting distance of them. The old poems talked of gigantic wings, foul and flaming jaws, and armor made of overlapping scales. And they had left this land behind, fleeing to parts unknown; "rarer than a dragon's scale" meant very rare, indeed.

Yet these mighty dragons, for all their physical power, also held great knowledge. They had created the dramojh—also called the dragon scions—the near-demonic creatures that had conquered the land, possibly driving the dragons from it (on this point the legends were conflicting and unclear). Janostis felt the short fur rise along his shoulders as he read over the tales of the dragon scions. The giants had come to this land specifically to battle the dramojh and free the captive peoples of the realm from their tyranny.

The dragons had passed along only a smattering of their knowledge to their hell-spawned heirs, yet that was enough to make the dramojh powerful in their own right.

It was the dramojh, heirs to the dragons, who had, in turn, made the spider-legged slassans, the serpent-tressed medusae, the keening lamia, the squamous lir, and other abominations.

Considering the growing reports, surely someone with concrete information on the dragons would come to him. The nature of the response surprised him when it finally came.

It arrived in the form of a nondescript young woman dressed in simple robes. Her voice was soft and sibilant, and she smelled like the desert at dawn. She appeared at the corner of his desk, and at first he was only vaguely aware of her.

"I am Orthac," she said.

"Sorry, I'm on break," said Janostis, his muzzle deep in the latest scrolls requisitioned from the Se-Heton library.

"You are needed," she said simply.

"On break," repeated Janostis. "Really."

"You are hunting dragons," she said, her soft timbre unchanged.

Janostis' head came up, and for the first time he truly looked at her. Yes, he realized, initial impressions were often the most correct. Nondescript. Would have passed her in a hallway without even remembering. Yet there was something about her that made the fur at the scruff of his neck go all prickly.

"You are needed," she said again, now that she had his attention. Her accent was unlike any Janostis had heard before.

"I am . . . a humble servant of our Hu-Charad rulers," replied Janostis, lowering his muzzle slightly trying to appear courteous. "I report to them. I facilitate. I meet with foreign delegations and trading companies. I negotiate on their behalf. Think of me as . . . an envoy."

"You speak for others?" she said, and Janostis was not sure if that was a question or not.

"I help the great and glorious giants in their wise rule. They rely on my advice." He paused a moment, then added. "Almost exclusively."

"I can help you find your dragon," Orthac said. "One will be in the Bitter Peaks, in the unsettled lands east of Mount Herrosh. Come with me if you want to meet it."

Janostis felt his ears standing fully upright in curiosity, but his eyes narrowed in suspicion. One did not rise to even the middle levels of bureaucracy without keeping one's wits about oneself. Was this some peasant with a wild fabrication? Or perhaps a colleague had discovered his plan and was seeking to distract him? Janostis said, "How do I know you are telling the truth?"

The human female placed a flat object on his desk, about the size of his hand. It had been darker shade, blue almost going to black, but had greyed slightly with age. Its surface was a branching pattern of raised veins.

It was a dragon's scale.

"You are sufficient," she said. "I will be at the North Gate at dawn." And she left, leaving the scale on the desk and her desert smell hanging in the air behind her. Janostis blinked at her departure. He looked at the scale, then at the empty space where she had stood.

Then he started to make arrangements.

* * * * *

Janostis met the woman Orthac at the North Gate at dawn. Janostis wore the dragon scale as a pendant. She did not comment on it, but seemed amused by the carriage he had hired for the trip.

"If you have other arrangements . . . ?" Janostis turned the unfinished statement into a question.

"It will be sufficient," said Orthac simply, and stepped up into the carriage.

After three days by carriage and two on foot, they had reached the foothills east of Mount Herrosh. Orthac was silent most of the way. Humans were like that, Janostis realized ruefully. They either chattered incessantly about everything or moodily pulled themselves into their cloaks.

Faced with a vacuum, Janostis filled the quiet with stories. Humans always liked to hear about others, he had discovered. He briefly talked about what he knew of dragons, seeking confirmation of his studies. When Orthac would neither confirm nor deny anything, he changed the subject to himself. He spoke of his own minor successes at negotiating with this merchant house or that giant clan. And if he rounded up a bit to reflect better upon himself, she did not seem to mind.

Indeed, by the time they had reached the foothills, Janostis believed himself when he said he was an envoy.

Yet the woman remained drawn in on herself, nodding only occasionally to show she was paying attention.

At one point, after an evening of cold rations around a small fire and a mostly fictitious account of a meeting with a verrik ambassador, Janostis asked directly, "Why did you choose me?"

"You speak for others," said Orthac.

Janostis tried again. "Yes, but how did I come to your attention? How did you end up in my particular office? You heard the rumors? You knew of my interest? Did someone send you?"

"You speak for others," repeated the slender human, "That is sufficient." And with that she pulled herself deeper into her traveling cloak, leaving Janostis alone by the fire with his thoughts and dreams of the giants recognizing his true potential.

* * * * *

On the sixth day of the journey they entered the foothills proper. There was little time for talk now, as Janostis seemed to spend most of his time trying to catch his breath.

"Is it much farther?" he asked, after a trio of steep switchbacks, barely visible to him but apparently obvious to the human female. His chest was heaving from the climb.

The woman stopped and pulled herself erect with a jolt. Janostis wondered if he had offended her in some way.

"This is the first gate," she said calmly,

Janostis did not see any gate, or any ghost of a gate, or fence, or a wall, anywhere around.

"I take it you are using a metaphor," he said, keeping his voice level, but his ears tilted backward, wary.

"You must know something before we proceed." Saying that, she dropped both her traveling cloak and her robe, and with it the spells that had kept her true form hidden. Janostis saw that his traveling companion was not human after all.

The creature was still slender, and could charitably be described as female, but now its flesh was dry and scaly. Its frame was reptilian, and it looked like one of the draconian mojh. Yet it was more than a mojh—taller, its head dominated by the great rill of spiky extrusions, and it had a sharp, pointed chin that looked like nothing less than a heavily-lacquered beard. Nictating eyes regarded him from beneath ridged protrusions, separated by a single punch-hole of a nostril, all above a lipless maw of erratic teeth. Deprived of her illusionary garb, the creature named Orthac was dressed in short cotton leggings and a long, open vest that draped to her lean knees.

Janostis' ears flattened fully along the top of his head and, despite himself, he took two steps backward, almost crouching. He could feel his lips pulling back in a snarl, but restrained himself. He recognized this thing before him from his own recent researches into dragon lore.

"Squamous lir," he said, trying not to bark out the words.

The scaly humanoid nodded. "I am of that race. This is the first gate. The first challenge. Do you wish to proceed, knowing what I am?"

Part of Janostis' mind, the part he always thought of being the earlier, more primitive part, untouched and unimproved by giant magic, wanted to flee at once, hurdling down the hillside for the safety of his small office and tiny desk and warm hearth.

Yet another part, the more civilized part, the part dedicated to the Hu-Charad and his own (ever-rising) place in the bureaucracy, restrained him. The squamous lir, the old books said, were experts in dragon lore. Indeed, many of the documents he had researched in the past week or so made it clear that the source of their information was from members of this very race.

The squamous lir, Janostis knew, were dedicated to learning more about the dragons. The squamous lir were not direct creations of the dragons. Rather, the dragons created the demonic dramojh, which in turn created such beings as the slassans and the squamous lir. It was little wonder that lir had information on the creators of their own creators.

The parts of Janostis' mind warred within him for a moment, as his reptilian companion regarded him, her eyelids blinking slowly like shutters in a soft breeze.

The fear rose within Janostis but was matched and then exceeded by his ambition. If anyone knew where to find a dragon, it would be the squamous lir. She was nothing less than a golden opportunity.

"My appearance frightens you," said the lir, and Janostis was unsure whether that was a question or a statement.

The sibeccai could still feel the fur prickling on his neck and back. He nodded, turned the motion into a theatrical shrug, and said, "What you told me in De-Shamod, that was truth? About the dragon, I mean."

"You want to meet a dragon," said Orthac, simply. "We want you to meet a dragon. There will be a dragon."

"I want to meet a dragon," agreed Janostis. "Let us proceed."

"It is not far," said the squamous lir, turning to continue the climb. Only after following a dozen paces did Janostis realize that the creature had finally answered his original question.

After an uncountable number of other switchbacks, they reached an upland vale cradled between two steep-sided mountains. They were high up at this point, in the rain shadow between the peaks. The brush grew scrawnier over distance and altitude, and was now reduced to scattered clumps of golden, dry weeds.

None of the brush, Janostis noted, was burned, or frozen, or curiously acid-spattered. He could catch only a wisp of smoke on the air. Nothing bespoke of dragons to him.

"There *will* be a dragon?" he asked again.

"There will be," she replied simply. "We are here. This is the second gate."

The sibeccai envoy crested a low hillock and stopped beside Orthac. Before them sprawled a huge open-pit mine carved into the vale between the mountains. The pit was as wide as the vale itself, and a long, curving path spiraled up its sides. A tent encampment occupied a wide spot halfway down the spiraled path. Small figures could be seen at the bottom of the pit, which looked to be a blue-tinged catch basin of runoff.

Janostis stood there, slightly bent, hands resting on his thighs, catching his breath from the climb, his tongue hanging to one side. Above the wheeze of his own laboring lungs, Janostis could now hear the sound of tools ringing against rock and human voices.

"So where is the dragon?" said Janostis.

"There will be a dragon," said the squamous lir. "This is the second challenge. You may turn back if you so choose."

Janostis regarded the open pit mine. It looked no different than a hundred similar operations along the Bitter Peaks. There was obviously no dragon present. He touched the dragon scale hanging around his neck, and shrugged agreement.

"It is . . ." he paused, "sufficient."

"Come," said the squamous lir, and Janostis followed her.

They reached the edge of the mine and started the long spiral down into the open pit. Janostis got a good look at both the miners and the overseers. There were other squamous lir here (Janostis counted four more) dressed in long vests similar to hers. All of them were directing the miners. None were doing any of the labor themselves.

The miners were human, all of them. They were at the muscular end of the human spectrum, dedicated to putting their backs into hard work. The inside of Janostis' muzzle tickled—in the elder days before the giants came to this land, the dramojh had enslaved the humans. The image of humans working while these reptilian creatures commanded them bothered him at a basic level.

"What are these people doing?" he asked as they arrived at the campsite.

"They are preparing for the dragon," said Orthac. She stopped at a large tent in the encampment. Another, taller squamous lir stepped out, one whose scales were tipped with yellow. (Older? thought Janostis. Male?). Orthac bowed to the taller one and said to Janostis, "I must prepare as well. Make yourself comfortable. You may stay or go as you see fit." And with that she disappeared into the tent.

There seemed few places where Janostis might be comfortable here, unless he chose to recline on the stone blocks themselves. Instead he continued to spiral down to the lake at the bottom of the pit.

As he neared the bottom, the sibeccai saw that what he'd thought was a catch basin was not a pool after all, but a mosaic like that in the Lady Protector's throne room, made of interlaced azure stones. It was lined but without any real pattern, a jigsaw spiraling crazily out in all directions, rising slightly in the center. The humans seemed to be most active at the edges of this blue surface, breaking up piles of rock and pushing it to all sides, revealing more and more of the azure surface.

The beetling human moved past Janostis again, carrying orders from one group of humans another. "Excuse me," he said, brightly.

"Excused," said Janostis, smoothly. The human seemed almost giddy. Enthusiasm was not an unusual human mood, but the human's degree of excitement seemed out of place in the sweat and toil of a mining pit. "May I ask a few questions?" said Janostis, falling in alongside the scampering human.

"No worry," said the human, "but you have to keep up." He headed toward a group of miners on the far side of the pit, fearlessly striding across the blue surface.

Janostis stepped out cautiously onto the azure mosaic. It seemed firm enough, and the sibeccai reached down and passed a hand over the surface. Cool, but pebbled, like a lizard's skin. The bulge in the center of the exposed area reminded him of bread fresh from the oven.

He loped after the human "What are you mining?" he asked.

"Mining?" Nothing," said the human, "Nothing yet. Though there is a good chance for gold, and we found some silver seams early on. No, no, we're *excavating*."

Janostis felt comfortable for the first time in days. This human was at least behaving like a normal human. Almost too much so. Talkative. Chatty. All of his emotions on the surface. Janostis paced along beside him. "Then what are you *excavating*?"

The miner looked at him, smiled, and then stamped his foot, hard, on the blue surface. Despite himself, Janostis jumped, expecting the jigsaw pattern to shatter. The blue surface didn't budge, and even the miner's dusty boots left no mark on its surface.

"What is this?" said Janostis.

"Dunno," said the human, "but it's what they brought us here to do. Promised good pay, if we can just clear it."

"Promised?" said Janostis. "You have yet to be paid?"

"Not yet, but they talked a good rate, and we get to keep digging after they get what they're after. As a mine, it looks very promising." When he said they, the human gave a head-shake toward the large tent where the squamous lir had retreated.

"But you don't know what they're . . . you're digging up?" said Janostis

"There are some ideas," said the human. "Some say it's a dragon's egg."

Janostis furrowed his brow. "It would be a very large dragon."

"Very large," said the human, "but I didn't say I believed it. It's just what some say. It could also be the roof of an old temple. A *big* old temple, with a dome. Part of a big city." He looked quite pleased with himself—he obviously was a big proponent of that theory. "From the lir's talking, we think the dragons are coming back. We're preparing the temple for them."

That made even less sense to Janostis. Did ancient dragons have temples, much less cities? Nothing in his books indicated that.

"So when will you finish?" the sibeccai asked.

"Almost done," said the human. "Almost wrapped up. That's why everyone is so excited. Excuse me," and with that, they reached the other group of humans. The miner gave a series of orders punctuated by hand gestures, then leaned in to help as the group started rolling away a particularly large rock.

The sibeccai watched them for a long moment. The enthusiasm of the miners troubled him. Surely humans would not react that way so close to the end of a difficult project? Happy to be done, yes, but wouldn't they be tired? And humans working on only the promise of pay? Plus, there were no shirkers in their numbers, another rarity. And these humans seemed unhumanly incurious about their work.

This place had the stench of magic on it. He knew he couldn't really smell magic, but it caught in his muzzle like acrid smoke and bothered Janostis.

Ensorcelled. These humans were ensorcelled, enslaved by spells. And that made the squamous lir the sorcerers.

Janostis strode back out of the pit, leaving the enthusiastic humans behind him. With every step he became more convinced that the lir were using these humans as little more than slaves.

He went back to the large tent and entered, unannounced. Orthac was there (he was surprised he could recognize her among the others), along with the elder squamous lir and the remaining four of the creatures. Orthac and the four were seated around the elder, who stood in the center of the circle. Musky, dusty scents drifted in the air, and Janostis fought the urge to sneeze.

The elder looked at him with a hard, inhuman glare. "You interrupt."

"I want some answers," said Janostis.

"Everyone wants answers," said the elder. Beside him, Orthac rose to her feet. Her eyes were blinking quickly. Irritation, wondered Janostis, or concern?

"Why do the humans dig here while the lir do not?" asked Janostis.

"They were hired to do so," said the elder, "as you were engaged."

"You've put spells on them," said Janostis. "You have enchanted them to serve willingly."

"We have gifted them with spells to boost their abilities and speed their steps, so they may complete their tasks more readily."

"You may leave if this offends," said Orthac. "This is the third gate."

"I am tired of gates," said Janostis, crossly.

"I thought you said this one was intelligent," said the older lir.

"He is the best that could be found," said Orthac.

"And he challenges us? He is nothing. You should dismiss him now, before he can make further trouble."

Janostis' ears flattened along his head and he snarled. "Dismiss me? Why would you dismiss me?"

"If you are insufficient," said the elder, "it would be for the best."

"Insufficient?" snapped the sibeccai.

"He may choose to leave at any time," said Orthac. She spoke to the elder, but her eyes burrowed into Janostis.

"No," said Janostis. He pointed to Orthac, "You promised a dragon. I hold you to that promise. No more gates. No more challenges. I demand you deliver on your promise."

The elder lir looked at him hard. "As you wish."

Janostis studied the squamous lir's face for a hint of a smile. Instead the elder looked past him and said, "Yes?"

The enthusiastic, wild-eyed human miner had appeared in the doorway. "We've cleared the last parts. We're ready for you."

"And so are we," said the squamous lir. The others rose to their feet and began to file out. To Janostis he said, "We deliver on our promise. You may still leave now."

"I wouldn't miss this for the world," sniffed Janostis.

Janostis and the human miner fell into line behind the six squamous lir as the reptilian humanoids descended into the pit. The other human miners had already retreated to the upper levels; they looked more like a crowd at a sporting event than a group of exhausted workers. The human miner stopped Janostis before the edge of the blue mosaic, but the rest of the lir moved out onto the floor, spacing themselves evenly along its edge. They moved with practiced, serious motions. Orthac walked across the mottled surface, then turned, facing him. Her eyelids beat sideways, as if blinking back tears.

A ceremony, thought Janostis. To break through? To what? Was this a dragon egg about to be hatched? Or was it a dragon temple? Part of a lost city?

Janostis shook his head. Whatever ensorcelment fell upon this land was affecting him as well. Dragons did not build temples, or live in cities, not that he knew of.

His studies *did* say the dramojh built cities, but the dramojh were all dead.

Yet their creations weren't. The medusae. The squamous lir. And the dagger-toothed slassans.

Suddenly Janostis realized just what they were breaking into. It was not a mosaic, or an eggshell, or a dome. It was a seal. A seal covering the legacy of the dramojh.

He took a step forward, but the human's burly arm reached out to restrain him.

"Too late now," said the human. "You'll queer the ceremony."

The squamous lir had already started chanting. It was a sibilant, buzzing chant that seemed to drive into Janostis' bones, with an overlay of an equally annoying whine that made the tips of his ears twitch.

The chant grew in intensity and pitch, rebounded off the close walls of the open pit, and redoubled in volume. The humans seemed to have taken it up as well. The air suddenly felt cold at the bottom of the pit, as if the sun had passed behind a cloud. Janostis let out a sharp breath and it fogged before him.

Janostis took another step forward, trying to reach Orthac and stop the ceremony, but the human's grip on his shoulder bore down harder, holding him fast.

The chant took another jump in pitch, and now it seemed

that the blue surface itself was reacting to the incantation, shimmering in response to the ceremony. Shimmering and clearing, turning translucent. Dark shapes now moved beneath the surface like great fish beneath the ice. Janostis felt as though his ears were going to bleed.

He struggled to step out onto the surface, but the human miner reached out with his other hand, pulling him back harder this time.

Janostis spun in place and bit the human, hard, just above the wrist. The human gave a frightened yip like a disciplined pup, and Janostis was suddenly free. He bounded across the mosaic toward Orthac.

And he felt the ground beneath him begin to crackle like ice breaking up in the first thaw.

Janostis looked down and saw that the bluish glaze of the mosaic was evaporating as the ceremony rose to a crescendo. The dark shapes were moving faster now and looked clearer as the last of the mosaic's surface turned transparent.

It was a nest of slassans beneath their feet, and the blue mosaic held it shut, like a seal on a letter, a shell wrapped around an egg. And burrowing up through the shell was a horde of the dramojh's fell creations. They were all claws and scales and jaws, a twisted combination of spider and eel. They ripped the ground beneath Janostis' feet, feeling at last the light above them, sensing the weakness of their prison, rousing from whatever nightmare dreams they slumbered within.

Heeding the call of the squamous lir.

And Janostis froze in place. All he could see was the quivering maws snaking up toward him, toward a weak spot in the shell, drawn by his presence, by the warmth of his body.

The ground beneath him cracked in a long fissure. He heard Orthac shout and something hit him hard, knocking him over. Something else, large and muscular, grabbed him by the scruff of his neck and pulled him to the edge. The strong-thewed

JEFF GRUBB

human miner dropped both him and Orthac, who had
knocked Janostis over, on the safe, solid ground.

"We have broken the seal," said Orthac weakly. "But the ceremony is a call as well. If that part failed, all is for naught."

Janostis gazed out over the blue expanse and ruefully thought
that the first part of the ceremony was a howling success. Already a half-dozen breaks were appearing across the crystal
mosaic, and the first serpentine heads were snaking out, reborn
after centuries of sleep, returning to the land of the living. The
other squamous lir had already retired to the safety of solid
rock, but they looked delighted by their endeavors.

But all Janostis could think was that his had been a stupid,
stupid plan, and he should have never been talked into coming
out here. Obviously, he was there for a sacrifice. He turned
toward Orthac to scream at her.

But the squamous lir was looking not at him or at the breaking seal of the slassan nest. Instead she was looking skyward.

Janostis looked up and saw them: three great shadows blocking out the sky. They were larger than any ship of the giants
that he had ever seen. As they landed, their huge leathery wings
kicked up thunderheads of dust, forcing the humans, the lir,
and even Janostis to back away from the pit.

The dragons had returned in the flesh—larger than anything
Janostis could have imagined. Great horned heads and huge jaws.
Ridges of spines along their backs and spurs at the joints. Wings
larger than the sails of a greatship. The smallest of the beasts
shone like freshly-minted gold coins, a second was as dark as
the night sky, and the third, the largest, was the color of blood.

The eggshell of the seal was now collapsing in on itself, and the
slassans were surging out of the pit, screaming in the new light of
day. The dragons returned the cry with a mighty roar, and Janostis
felt this would be the last sound he heard on this world.

And then the dragons began to feed. Their long, serpentine
heads lanced into the open holes and pulled struggling slassans

into their fanged mouths. The wriggling beasts screamed in pain from the strength of the grip, and each dragon raised its head in turn and swallowed a slassan whole. The great beasts dipped their heads again briefly, only to come up with another mouthful of the foul creatures. A few rough bites to quiet the screaming mass, then a raising of the head to slip them down the gullet. A shake of the head, almost like a feline worrying a rat, then an effortless swallow, and a return to the bounty.

Janostis didn't remember fleeing up the ramp, away from the dragons' feeding, but he was there, he and the human miner and Orthac and the others. He watched the feasting for longer than he knew. No one—human, sibeccai, or squamous lir, said anything. Any sound was drowned out by inhuman screams of the dragons' victims.

The dragons dipped deeper and deeper into the nest, and smoke now rose from the hole, along with the smell of melting things. The smallest dragon, the coin-colored one, had disappeared into the hole entirely, and when it hauled itself out, its belly was distended from its gorging. It pulled itself to the edge of the pit, curled in on itself, and promptly went to sleep, ignoring the ongoing slaughter.

The other dragons slowed only slightly. The night-beast came up from each grab with a struggling slassan more and more slowly each time, and finally it, too, was sated and curled up to sleep. The blood-colored dragon, its hide resplendent and shimmering from the slassan blood, finally slowed, yet it seemed to do so more from lack of prey than lack of appetite. It dipped in once, twice, and a third time. When it had cleaned its plate entirely, it pulled back and regarded the rest of the assemblage.

It sat on its haunches and regarded Janostis and the others with large yellow eyes. It licked its lips and grumbled in a voice a deep as the mountains itself.

"What do you want"?

Orthac was suddenly at Janostis' shoulder. "Now," she said.

"What?" said the sibeccai.

"It is your time," she said, "You are the envoy. You speak for others. Go speak for us."

"What?" repeated Janostis.

For the first time, the squamous lir showed an obvious emotion—frustration. "You speak for others. That is why we brought you here. You bragged of your abilities as we came here. You wanted to meet with a dragon. We want to meet the dragon as well. We wish to serve them, as you serve the giants. Introduce us to it."

"You don't know the dragons?" asked Janostis.

The lir snorted through its single nostril. "If we knew them, would we have had to summon them *here*? We knew the ceremony that would open the ancient nest and in opening it, summon them. And we believed they would have little love of their former minions, or their minions' minions. They would come and feed. We knew the ceremony of unsealing. All we needed was someone to speak to them on our behalf. You."

"Me?" said Janostis, feeling a cold, wet hand clamp around his heart. "You're smart. You're related. You can do it."

"We were made by dramojh, like you were made by the giants," said Orthac, "To them we are no different than the slassans, and no better. They already scent our origins in our blood, but they are curious, since we are here with humans, whom they know from earlier as slaves to the slassan, and you, who they do not know at all."

Janostis tried to put some steel into his voice. "And if I refuse?"

"This is the final gate. You may always refuse," she said simply. "But if you do, we will attempt to speak for ourselves. And they will destroy us as they destroyed the slassans, without a second thought. Then they will destroy the humans who were our allies. Then they may decide that they like how humans taste. And what will you tell your giant masters then?

The dragon let out a great catlike yawn, showing the cavern of its mouth and its long rows of fanglike teeth.

Janostis took a step forward, though it felt to him like the rest of the crowd took a step back. Another step. Surely, this was no worse than a hostile merchant, or an ambassador of the Verrik, or a rival bureaucrat. It was simply an identification of needs and wants. What do dragons want?

The dragon, for its part, regarded the sibeccai with bale-fire eyes. Janostis felt that it could see into his heart itself, and could weigh his words for lies.

"Who are you?" said the dragon. Its voice seemed to wrap itself around his bones and shake him, hard.

"I am Janostis the . . . Envoy," said the sibeccai. He opened his mouth to continue, but for the first time in his life did not know what to say. "I . . . speak for others."

The dragon cocked its head at him.

"Why did they choose you?" asked the dragon.

"I am an envoy," said Janostis. "I, um, speak. For others. For the squamous lir who provided you with this feast."

The dragon looked up at the collected lir and humans, and for an instant, Janostis thought he caught an expression of curiosity on the great creature's face. Then its heavy eyes were on him again. "Why you?" the dragon asked.

Janostis' mind whirled and, despite himself, he turned back towards the gathered others. Orthac looked worried, the humans scared, the other lir, unreadable and mute. Like prisoners in the docket, waiting for the judge to pass sentence.

He turned back to the dragon. "I am sibeccai. You know the race?"

"No," said the dragon, and for the first time Janostis allowed the cold hand around his heart to relax. He now knew one thing a dragon might want—information.

"My race was once rougher and cruder—unkempt, savage creatures. We were taken by the giants and made better. You

81

JEFF GRUBB

know the giants, from long ago. We, the sibeccai, were given the chance to reach our potential. Not given our potential, but given the chance. We were improved."

"This is important?" said the dragon, sounding impatient and vaguely hungry.

"You created the dramojh," started Janostis.

"I did not create the dramojh!" snarled the dragon, and Janostis had to step back from the blast of warm air.

"Not you," added the sibeccai quickly. "Not you personally. No. You as in 'you dragons'. The dragons created the dramojh. The dramojh in turn created other beings, like the slassans."

"Abominations," muttered the dragon. Behind him, Janostis could feel the lir draw in their breaths sharply.

"And they also made the squamous lir," said the sibeccai, "who offer you this gift, this collection of slassans long-buried, to call you forth. They call you forth to offer you their services."

"We need no new servants. We have many to serve us. We are dragons and we are mighty."

Janostis pressed his point. "I serve the giants, who are also mighty," he said, pausing to let the words sink in. Just the shadow of a threat. "The giants are mighty but still chose us to aid them in their work. So, too, do the lir, who have kept alive your draconic traditions, who have always sought you, wish to serve you."

Janostis paused a moment. If the dragons truly needed no aid, it would repeat the boast about its many servants. Otherwise . . .

"Why should the lir serve us?" said the dragon.

Janostis nodded. "They have long searched for your kind. They wish to show their dedication. They wish to learn from you, as my people have learned from the giants. That is why they tricked me into being here."

"Tricked you?" said the dragon, and the sibeccai could hear the curl of a smile in its voice. "They deceived you?"

Janostis was glad his fur covered his blush. "They . . . allowed me to become deceived. They told me truths—there would be a

82

dragon here. They needed someone who spoke for others. They allowed me to fill in certain blanks, and to leap to my own conclusions, to their advantage. They have shown themselves to be both honest and crafty. This land has changed since the last time you were here, and in this land the union of honesty and guile is very powerful. Let me tell you—they know this realm and would serve you well."

The dragon regarded the squamous lir clustered on the ramp. "They are not our children," it said at last.

"No, said Janostis, "but they have the potential to be."

The dragon paused for a moment, and then said, "Tell me more of how the squamous lir may serve us."

* * * * *

Night had fallen by the time they finished, and the humans had pulled back up to their camp to celebrate. At some point Janostis introduced Orthac to the dragon by name, and she, in turn, introduced the elder and the others. The conversation then moved into a language that Janostis was unfamiliar with. He retreated to the camp, where the humans were drinking and feasting and sleeping off the effects of the lir's spells.

The burly human miner insisted on describing in detail where they were going to exploit the silver and hunt for gold. He also tried to get Janostis interested a mug or three of mead, but the sibeccai refused, politely. Instead he just sat looking into the fire as the celebration swirled around him.

Orthac came up about an hour later, bearing a scroll. "This document," she said, "announces the return of the dragons to this land and recognizes the squamous lir as their servants."

"Servants of all dragons?" He did not reach out for the scroll.

"These dragons, at least," said Orthac, and Janostis thought he could detect bemusement in her voice. "This document also expressly thanks one Janostis the Envoy for his contribution, which was greatly appreciated."

Janostis held up a hand and growled. "So I was sufficient after all. After a few false starts."

There was a silence between them. "You are angry."

Janostis let out a deep breath. "I was scared. Absolutely, spell-brained scared. You know how I managed to pull it off?" He did not wait for her reply. "I realized you were no different than I was. Not that you were a creation of another, greater race. No, I mean you were willing to deceive to get what you wanted. And once I could see that, only then could I realize why the dragons needed you. That was why you really needed me. I could help the dragon recognize that you were crafty, and therefore useful."

"You convinced it."

"It was only when the dragon realized you were capable of deceit did it think of you as more than abominations." Now it was Orthac's turn to be quiet.

Janostis took the scroll from her and said, "I have what I came for. This will be a ticket to some plush position within the government. The Hu-Charad bureaucracy is large and sprawling, and I can find some safe corner far from enthusiastic miners and hungry slassans—particularly away from dragons that understand sibeccai all too well. I will be gone by morning. No need to accompany me. Good-bye."

* * * * *

It took six days for Janostis to return to De-Shamod, the last three on an oxcart. It took him another day to write up his report, as honest as he dared.

Then he went home and slept for a day. Upon his return, there was a summons on his tiny desk in his small office in his non-descript building, a summons from one of the giant stewards.

The steward sat on the low dais in his giant's chair, the squamous scroll in his lap. Janostis entered and knelt, rising only when the giant gave a guttural assent.

The sibeccai stood as the steward reviewed the scroll. Janostis was not as nervous as he thought he would be. Perhaps after being in the presence of a dragon, the prestige of a mere giant, one of the creators, was less awe inspiring.

The steward did not look up from the scroll but said, "You did this by yourself."

"Yes, Steward. I saw the opportunity and took the initiative."

Another grunt. The giant looked up, pale blue eyes sweeping over the sibeccai. "This is a good base. Not too solid, not too sweeping. It can be worked with. It refers to you here as . . . "

"The Envoy," nodded Janostis. "An honorific from the situation. Not a true title."

"It fits," said the giant, "and it reflects your performance. Yes, from this day, you are Janostis the Envoy, agent to the dragons within the Lands of the Diamond Throne." Behind him, Janostis heard a door opening and closing.

"I . . . am honored," said Janostis. He struggled to control his glee before the steward. "Should I arrange for an office, or . . ."

"No office, at least not for a while," said the steward. "You'll be spending too much time on the road. We're going to need to know as much information about the returned dragons as possible. I understand that you have been studying them of late."

Janostis stammered, "No office? But surely my duties. . ."

". . . will be primarily with the agent from the dragons of the Bitter Peaks."

"Who . . . ?" But he caught the wafting scent of the desert dawn and knew.

"I believe you know our new Envoy?" said the giant to the person behind Janostis.

"I know him well," came a soft, sibilant voice. Janostis turned to see Orthac behind him.

Her eyelids nictated, and she managed a humanish smile. "He will be . . . more than sufficient."

MARY H. HERBERT
OATHSWORN

re you feeling better yet? I have more water and some
soup too, which I think you should drink as soon as
possible 'cause you're really weak, and those burns are
bad." There were rustling sounds like the noises of softly-shod
feet on wet leaves, the voice went on again, quietly and calmly
with just a hint of a lilt.

"Why did you irritate that dragon? Don't you know better?
Some of them have really nasty tempers. Actually, in the stories,
most of them do. Can you believe it, though? A dragon! A real,
live, fire-snorting, wing-waving, tail-thumping dragon! I didn't
know dragons still existed. I wonder where they've been. I
wonder why they came back. They haven't been seen in these
mountains for thousands of years. And why did this one come
here? There's not much in these hills to interest a creature as ancient as a dragon. I remember our stories tell about dragons—
curl your hair, those stories would. Even yours." A pause and a

sigh. "Well, what's left of it. We should change the bandages. That burn on your shoulder is a bad one."

Ia-Keltior kept her eyes closed and let the prattle of words flow over her like the cold autumn rain that pattered down through the leaves of her shelter. He seemed to be talking to her, yet she wasn't certain who the speaker was, or what he was. Since she had awakened to his soft, light voice she hadn't had the strength to open her mouth, let alone force her eyes open. She didn't even know when he had appeared to take care of her. She wondered whether she would be dead by now if not for him. Of course, she could still die. She almost preferred the idea. Never in her young life had she felt so utterly devastated in body and soul.

Something delicate brushed over her forehead. She tried to reach for it, but her arm felt like a stone. All she could muster was a feeble flutter of her hand.

"Ah!" the voice piped up near her head. "The giantess moves at last. This is good. Do not fear, young woman. Your eyes are dark because I had to bandage them. Your face came too close to dragon fire."

A spurt of fear shot strength into Ia-Keltior's arm. She managed to reach up and feel the cloth wrapped loosely around her head. In spite of the warning and her own better sense, she tried to open her eyes. Her left eye opened to a fog of light seeping through several layers of fabric. The other eye opened to . . . darkness and pain.

She clamped her teeth over a whimper that tried to escape from her aching throat. She coughed instead, sending a searing jolt of pain through her head, lungs, and shoulder. Groaning, she rolled over to her left side and cradled her head in her left arm.

"You hurt, yes. You were badly injured and breathed too much smoke," said her companion. "But if you can sit up, I have something you can drink that will help."

Small hands lifted her shoulders with surprising strength and helped her lean back against a tree trunk. The wet bark seeped dampness into her filthy tunic. The smell of wood smoke, mingled with the odors of wet woods, filled her nostrils and reminded her bitterly that she was not home in her own house with her father working contentedly in his library. She savagely pushed that thought away.

She sagged against the tree. For a moment the light voice was silent, and she could hear the sounds of utensils scraping over metal, the crackle of a small fire, the steady patter of a light rain on trees. Then she smelled a rich, earthy scent and felt the heat of steam on her face.

"Drink this. Slowly. It's not tasty, but it will give you strength."

A small bowl was pressed to her mouth. She drank the hot contents as he suggested, ignoring the taste reminiscent of pine sap and dandelion tea. While her energy did not come flooding back, the drink eased the pain in her throat, settled her stomach, and gave her strength to stay upright. At least for now.

As her companion took the cup from her, Ia-Keltior reached out and touched his face. Her fingers spanned his entire head.

He stilled, waiting patiently while she traced his features and touched his chest.

"So small," she breathed. "Long hair, pointed ears. There is only one creature with those small manlike features and such a stature. You're a faen."

He laughed and ducked out of her reach. "A loresong, yes. Menien Trailsinger. And you are a giantess. A young one, I would say, for you look no older than a sixteen-year-old human I know, and you are only six feet tall." She could hear the grin in his voice. "A giant and a faen. Quite a pair, huh?"

"We're not a pair," she grumbled, knowing she sounded ungrateful and peevish.

"Oh, ho," he chuckled. "Shall I leave you, then? You can make your own way to De-Shamod, or wherever you came from."

She thought about her injuries and current events and sighed. "Mi-Theron. We came from Mi-Theron." There was a quick laugh and she heard the faen move away. "I'm sorry," she said quickly. "I owe you my life, and it seems I will have to depend on you a little while longer. Will you help me?"

There were more rustling sounds and noises from the fire, then he returned with the cup filled with soup this time. "Of course. It is a promise I made to Tomask, the god of injured travelers."

Ia-Keltior allowed a feeble smile. The faen were a deeply religious people who could find and recognize new personal gods at the slightest provocation.

She felt his hands rearrange her cloak on her upper body, then he moved away and she heard more sounds from the shelter around her. Apparently he was weaving more branches into the leaky roof.

"This rain won't last much longer," he announced.

The young giantess barely heard him. "How long has it been?" she asked quietly.

"It's been raining since yesterday. That's when I found you in the woods. You wandered a long way."

She said nothing, only stared into the darkness behind her eyes. Eventually she drank the soup and felt her strength come trudging back. But as the lethargy faded, she could feel her rage and grief kindle in its place.

Menien came back and retrieved his empty bowl. "I saw the dragon, you know." His lively voice was filled with awe.

Her hand shot out and grabbed the front of his heavy jacket. "Did you see where it went? When did you see it? Could you find it again?" Her voice was sharp and urgent.

He twisted out of her grasp and straightened his jacket with a jerk. "Why? Haven't you seen enough of it? I saw what it did to your group. I will take you back to the river. You can get a riverboat there to take you home."

Her hand slid to her throat; her injured eyes burned with tears. "No! I will not go home until I have righted this terrible wrong. I have to find that dragon!"

There was a long silence between the two while the rain dripped around them and the fire quietly burned under its shelter.

"Is this a vow? Are you oathsworn?" he asked at last.

Oathsworn. Now there was something she had never considered in her sheltered life. Oathsworn were the most dedicated and steadfast individuals in the land, setting their lives to fulfill a sacred vow. Did they feel any different from what she felt now? It was said that oathsworn began their careers alone, that they received their calling on a psychic level. She didn't know if what was in her heart was a sacred calling or not, but it felt every bit as compelling. She swore to her father's soul and to those who had accompanied him to the Houses of the Eternal that she would find the dragon and mend the great wrong she had done them.

"Perhaps," she said quietly. "I must seek the dragon."

"Well, that may be a problem," said Menien. "I only saw it in the air, flying at a great distance. I don't know where it is."

Ia-Keltior nodded once, rolled to her hands and knees, and crawled out of her shelter. Reaching out in front of her with one hand, she found a tree and pulled herself up the trunk until she was standing upright. The world rocked sickeningly around her, and she had to wrap both arms around the tree until the ground stopped pitching and the pounding in her head dropped to a mere throb.

"Where do you plan to go?" the loresong asked with interest.

Ia-Keltior held on to her tree and pressed her face against the cool, wet bark. "To a village called Waterglen. They were the ones who asked for help."

There was another reflective silence. Then she heard him move toward the fire, and she listened to the quick, light sounds he made as he tore down the shelter, put out the fire, and repacked his small traveler's pack.

After a while she pushed the bandages off her left eye and looked around at the blurry clearing. The faen in his green jacket and brown pants was a moving blob in a hazy, indistinct sea of yellows, greens, and browns.

"Does this mean you will come with me?" she asked hesitantly.

"That village is days from here," he said as an answer. "We have several more hours of daylight, which should see us well on our way. I'll cut a walking stick for you. That'll have to do for now."

Ia-Keltior closed her eyes against the painful light and leaned against the tree.

"Oh, Father," she whispered only to herself. "Forgive me."

* * * * *

It was that night that Ia-Keltior began to suspect they were being followed. She sat hunched by a small fire while the faen slept and added a stick or two when the flames began to die. At one point she looked up and saw a vague, indistinct figure standing in the darkness at the edge of their clearing. She squinted hard to see it clearly, but it had no solid form. It made no move to threaten her, and by dawn it was gone. She discounted it as a figment of her very tired imagination.

But she saw the shadow thing the next night and the next, growing larger and more distinct. It came when the loresong was asleep and moved silently around their camp, always vigilant and unaggressive.

She tried to approach it once, and it glided away and vanished as mysteriously as it appeared. She tried to waken Menien to show him the shadow thing, but by the time the faen awoke, it was gone. It never appeared to Menien and never came during the day. She puzzled over the odd visitation and wondered why it came only to her. Perhaps it was ghost or simply the hallucination of a brain worn by too many shocks and too much sadness. Perhaps when they found the village, the thing—whatever it was—would vanish for good.

* * * * *

For the four hundred sixty-third time in the three days since Ia-Keltior regained her senses, Menien broke into song. It was a weird ballad sung in a minor key in a language she did not recognize. It didn't surprise her, though. The faen had a fine tenor voice and a remarkable memory for every song he had ever heard—and he seemed determined to sing them all, from drinking songs to dirges to odd bits of poetry someone had set to music.

"You are well named, Trailsinger," she sighed.

He broke off his tune and turned around to grin at her. "Thank you. It's a nickname really. My real name is too hard for most Others to remember."

The giantess' foot slipped on a rock, and she fell forward to her knees. "Please tell me the village is around here somewhere," she groaned, climbing back to her weary feet. Her shins were bruised and her limbs ached.

His only answer was to return to his song and continue the long climb up the steep, rocky hill.

Ia-Keltior brushed off the mud and forced herself to follow. The way was difficult even for a climber with two good eyes. There was a path of sorts, but it had been made by feet much smaller and harder than hers—the feet of creatures who were not intent on going anywhere in a hurry. It straggled up the hillside like so many other paths she had already struggled up. Was there no "down" in these mountains?

The Elder Mountains were well named, being ancient weathered summits whose sheer, jagged walls had been worn down in the passage of millennia. But while they were not nearly impassable ramparts like the towering Bitter Peaks to the west, they were rugged, rock-strewn mountains whose stony heads rose sluggishly out of a cloak of heavy vegetation.

Ia-Keltior thought she knew the mountains from her excursions into the southern hills near her home. Now she realized she was literally a babe in the woods. If it weren't for the faen, she would not have made it this far.

She planted the staff in the rocks and climbed slowly after him, feeling her way with feet, hands, and stick. Her left eye was still uncovered and although her vision remained blurred, she could see shapes and shadows and outlines. Her right eye was still bandaged.

Upon reaching the summit of the hill, they crossed a broad, open meadow and came to a place where the ground dropped gently into a rounded valley dotted with boulders and copses of slender trees.

Menien stopped so abruptly, Ia-Keltior bumped into him.

She was about to apologize to him when a gust of wind whisked up from the valley, carrying a stench of old burn and decay. Her body went numb; her mind turned to rage.

"Where are we?" she demanded.

Menien's voice came back to her, soft with sadness. "We had to pass by the place where your party was attacked. I thought . . . maybe . . . you'd want to say goodbye."

"No!" The denial came out as sharp and defiant as a wolf's snarl. "Not yet." The stones ground beneath her heels as she turned away.

"They're just over there." He pointed toward a thin cluster of burned tree trunks that pointed to the sky like grave markers. Surrounding the dead trees was a large patch of charred grass where the huddled forms of burned bodies lay scattered.

"No!" she cried again, her voice strained to the breaking point. "I must be forgiven first."

"Forgiven for—" His question abruptly cut off, and she heard him step hurriedly away from her. "Stay here!" he called.

A host of emotions and worries swarmed through her mind. What did he see? What was out there?

"There on the high hill," Menien cried. "There are radonts up there watching us."

Ia-Keltior's head snapped up. Try as she might she could not see them, but the coldness in her heart eased just a little at the thought of their presence. A memory, raw with pain, focused in her mind with stark clarity: her father's small delegation, dismounted, holding the reins of their mounts; the ebon horses taut with fear as the dragon swept overhead.

Was it possible some of them had survived?

"Be still. Be patient. Let them see you. I will try to call them," Menien said. He climbed up on the rock beside her and, throwing out his arms, burst into a rollicking wild song peppered with thundering bass notes, tenor trills that filled the ears like the neighs of excited horses, and high-pitched whistles. His long hair blew in the cold wind, and his cheeks turned red from his effort.

The giantess turned to listen, amazed. "What song is that?"

He paused, his dark eyes fixed on an open meadow just ahead. "It is a song a radont taught me once when I helped her."

"But radonts are not telepathic with two-legged people, only horses and other radonts."

"But I am. I have learned to talk to other intelligent creatures. Radonts are easy."

Her one eye widened. "Are you an ollamh lorekeeper?"

The ollamh lorekeepers were faen teachers, storytellers, poets, historians, singers, and judges rolled into one. They were the repositories of all faen lore and history and the masters of faen wisdom.

"Would I be out in this forsaken wilderness if I were?" he replied. "Some day I hope to be. When I am allowed to return to my village."

His short tone and his words struck through her own self-pity, but before she could ask another question, she heard a muted tattoo roll down from the mountain. She straightened, tilting her head to hear. The sound grew louder and more distinct, and suddenly it clarified into hoof beats. She saw two large black shapes approaching at a canter.

Her breath sucked through her teeth in a quick gasp of pleasure. The two radonts came to a stop, their heads turned toward her. The giantess did not move, frightened of scaring the horses away. She waited nervously while Menien bowed low. He said nothing out loud, but he seemed to be communicating with them, for one radont stomped a hoof and neighed several times in response to some sort of prompting.

"One is a wild radont who came to investigate the attack on your party," Menien supplied for her. "He found the other, a domesticated radont, nearby. One of yours?"

Ia-Keltior held her breath. She squinted with her one eye, wishing she could see the magnificent animals more clearly. Radonts were huge—large enough to carry a full-grown giant—with thick sturdy legs, ebony coats, and the regal bearing of the Lords of Horses. She moved slowly to get closer to them, to see them better with her one eye. But the mare nickered a welcome and thrust her warm muzzle against the young giant's face. Ia-Keltior gave a cry, "Tirrana," and buried her face in the radont's mane.

"I have told the stallion of your search for the dragon. He wants to know the reason for your request," the faen said aloud to her. "You should tell him. He might help you if he knows your cause is just and your oath is truth."

"Can't he see the truth around him?" she snapped. Then she bit her tongue hard and used the pain to fight back the sudden rush of tears. She didn't want to tell them everything, only her driving need to find the dragon. Surely the rest of it was unimportant. But wild radonts were highly intelligent and considered themselves to be allies and equals of giants, partners in any endeavor they chose to perform with one of the Hu-Charad. If she tried to lie to this stallion, he would sense it and leave her here in this desolate place. And yet, she worried, if she told him the whole story, he—and Menien—might reject her completely.

She began slowly, halting over her words, hoping she could gloss over the worst. "There is a village in these mountains somewhere. I don't know where. It is called Waterglen. They have been suffering depredations from something they haven't seen. Their herds are stolen, people disappear, tracts of woods are burned or trampled flat, the crops are ruined. They thought the damage could be caused by a dragon, but the notion seemed so far-fetched, they didn't want to raise a warning. Finally, in desperation, they sent word up the river as far as Mi-Theron, asking for help. The steward sent them to my father, who used to be a Knight of the Diamond." This order was known throughout the realm for enforcing the laws of Dor-Erthenos, the Lands of the Diamond Throne.

Her voice caught and she put a hand to her heaving chest. Her emotions rose like a storm surge, and she could not draw breath fast enough to keep up with her words. Once started, they flowed from her unchecked, like blood from a torn vein.

"My father suspected the truth, for we had heard rumors that dragons were returning to the land. But we didn't know! When the elders of Waterglen came to him and begged for help, he agreed to go and try to negotiate with the dragon. He brought me to help him and learn his ways." A bitter sound escaped her throat. "To help! Do you know what I did? I panicked. I saw that monster fly overhead—it was just looking at us—but I could not control my fear. My father yelled at me to put my bow down. I couldn't! I couldn't stop myself. I raised the bow and, in my terror, I fired an arrow at the dragon. I didn't kill it, of course. I don't think I even hurt it. But it took the arrow as an attack, and it veered around and flamed us. My father died trying to protect me. The others in our party didn't survive. . . ." Her voice trailed off. Abruptly she flung herself to her feet, her stick held out before her like a pike. "I have to find the dragon. I must finish my father's vow and right this terrible grief I have done."

"Your father's vow, or yours?" Menien asked quietly.

"His blood is my blood. His voice is my voice. He watches me and guides my way. I will finish what he started," she answered.

The slender faen nodded once. "The Horse Lord wants to know what it is you wish to accomplish?"

To kill it! screamed her thoughts. But giants were not supposed to be vindictive killers. Out loud she answered as levelly as she could, "To stop it from raiding and terrorizing the people." Which was true, from one perspective.

Weary and drained beyond measure, she dropped back to the stone and sat with her head in her hands. Menien said nothing but stood beside her and patiently waited. She didn't dare ask him what he would do if the radont condemned her. She didn't think she could bear it if he left her.

She heard a sudden commotion, and a huge black shape moved into her limited vision. It stamped a massive hoof.

"He asks if you are blind," Menien said.

She lifted her bandaged head toward the radont stallion, and her lips twisted into a wry grimace. "Am I blind to what? The danger of facing a dragon? The stupidity of trying to find the ancient beast with no weapon, only one good eye, and a faen who sings the entire repertoire of his people at the top of his lungs?"

"I do not," Menien interjected indignantly.

"No, I am not blind to my chances." She raised her hands imploringly. "But I have to try. It is a promise I made to my father."

Menien tilted his head toward the stallion and said, "He says he can heal you if you are willing."

The words of agreement pounced to her lips, but she cut them off before they could escape. "Not yet," she whispered. "I will bear this a little while longer as my penance."

The loresong crossed his arms. "Don't be rock headed. You are hunting a dragon. You will need command of every faculty."

A snort from the stallion emphasized the faen's words.

Ia-Keltior bowed her head in acceptance. She did not move as the radont dipped his head and touched her gently with the velvet softness of his muzzle. In silence his spell was formed, and power from his own magic poured into her mind and body. It laved her face with warmth and touched her with the blessed release of pain. Her eyes tingled and suddenly she realized the grass she was staring at had changed from a golden blur to a finely detailed image of grass stalks, dried leaves, dead mulch, and the tiniest clump of mountain star flowers she had ever seen.

She pulled the bandage off and smiled up at the stallion in gratitude and humility.

He snorted once and neighed to Menien.

"He says he must go to report to his herd. He thinks you would be wise to negotiate a truce of some kind between the village and the dragon. Seek a peace between them. The dragon may be searching for something. Perhaps you could learn what it is and help him find it."

She ground her teeth and tried to smile. She could not tell them that the only resolution she wanted was the dragon's death.

The wild radont neighed and stamped his hoof again. Giving a snort of farewell, he cantered away, leaving the mare, Tirrana, in his wake.

The remaining radont stepped forward and dipped her muzzle to Ia-Keltior's face. Each inhaled deeply of the other's scent. The giantess smelled warm horse, cold mountain air, and the pungent odors of crushed herbs and grasses. She was so relieved and so tired, she drooped forward and rested her forehead on the radont's thick-coated leg. Domesticated radonts did not have the intelligence of their wild brethren, but they had the same strength, loyalty, and will.

A small hand took her fingers. "She says she is glad to see you. She is willing to help. You should ride and save your knees. The mare has agreed to carry us both."

Ia-Keltior looked up and saw his delicately handsome face clearly for the first time. "Us?" she asked gratefully. "You are still coming with me? You know what I am attempting to do."

"Of course. We can help each other." He paused and added, "Wait."

Startled, she watched him hurry over to the dead patch of grass and burnt lives. When he came back, he was carrying a long, heavy staff. He pressed it into her hand, and her fingers closed instinctively around its sooty circumference. Her vision blurred with tears.

"He would want you to have that," Menien said.

She didn't ask how he had known. Emotion overcame her. He was right. Her father's magister's staff had been his pride and joy. Now it was hers.

With the aid of a handy rock, Ia-Keltior managed to climb up onto the radont's back and pull Menien up behind her. The radont was so large, the faen had to sit crosswise and hold onto the giantess' cloak. Warmth from the radont's broad back seeped into their damp clothes and chased some of the chill from their bodies.

Tirrana moved smoothly into a slow lope along the road to Waterglen. Menien grinned and launched into his four hundred sixty-fourth song. Unhearing, Ia-Keltior turned to bid farewell to her father. "I will return to speed you to the Houses of the Eternal," she murmured. "When I have avenged you."

* * * * *

That night the shadow came into camp. It came late when the others were asleep and Ia-Keltior tended the fire.

The giantess saw the slight movement among the trees and tilted her head to see the figure standing at the edge of the firelight. Strangely she felt no fear, only a resigned curiosity that this thing, whatever it was, seemed to be following her.

"What do you want?" she called softly.

It drifted closer. Even with her restored vision she still could not see it clearly. The figure stood upright, about as tall as she, but she could see no detail of its clothing—if it had any—or its face.

"Who are you?" she demanded, raising her father's staff between her and the shadow.

You do not recognize me? The words formed in her mind like small flames licking at tinder.

"Should I?"

If you don't, you will soon.

"What do you want?"

To be near you.

"Why?"

You seek revenge. The words hissed and sizzled in her brain.

"Against the dragon? Do you know the dragon?"

It destroyed what we loved. It ruined our lives.

Ia-Keltior rubbed her temples to ease a throbbing ache growing in her head. Fear grew with it and left her skin cold and her hands shaking. What was this thing? Trying to be surreptitious, she nudged Menien with her boot. "Why don't you kill it?" she said to the shadow, nudging the faen harder.

I cannot do it alone.

The form drifted closer, its features still indistinct to the giantess. She peered harder at it over the fire and could just make out a dark mass on the shadow creature's back.

You swore an oath, it went on. *And I have heard. The dragon must be destroyed.*

"The radont suggested I try to negotiate with it," she said, testing its response.

The being bent toward her, and the mass on its back suddenly spread out and arched around it. It was a massive pair of wings. *The time to negotiate is past! The dragon dies! It is your oath.*

The shadow's voice beat into her mind like a firebrand, burning the words on her soul. Pain seared through her aching head. Her voice rose in a terrified shriek.

Menien and the radont snapped awake even as the shadow vanished.

"What?" cried the faen blearily. "What is it?"

"Didn't you see it?" she cried through her tears. "The figure, there by the fire!"

Tirrana neighed and trotted around the small camp to look, but there was nothing to find.

Menien put sleep aside and built up the fire. He brewed a kettle of bark tea and gave a bowl of it to Ia-Keltior. "When was the last time you slept?" he asked, his small face filled with worry.

"I saw it, Menien! I am not imagining this," she insisted. She drank the tea, grateful for its warmth and the terrible taste that helped distract her from the pain in her head.

"The radont tells me she can smell nothing unusual. There are no footprints or sign of anything."

She wiped her face fiercely on her sleeve and stared into the darkness. "I'm telling you, there was a figure standing right there. It was tall and it had wings. It spoke to me telepathically. It must have been doing something to you two as well, because I couldn't wake you up!"

The small faen shrugged. "There is nothing in my lore that fits that description." He moved gently around her, refilling the bowl.

There was nothing in Ia-Keltior's memory that fit that description, either. If she hadn't seen it several times before, she would perhaps believe it had been a dream. But the creature had come to her every night since she woke in the clearing, and its effects on her felt all too real.

If only her father were with her. He had read vast numbers of books and ancient scrolls in his lifetime and studied the incredible wealth of knowledge in the world of Serran. He could have helped her understand what was happening to her. Her grief returned, sharp and poignant, and she covered her head and wept.

* * * * *

The village of Waterglen was in a shambles. No, Ia-Keltior amended that, it was in a ruin. Many of the houses and out-buildings were smashed or trampled, and several barns had been burned. The streets were empty of any life except for a rat that scuttled out of sight when Tirrana walked warily on the road past a deserted livestock market.

"Stop," demanded Menien. "Listen."

The three froze in place and strained to listen for a sound, any sound that might tell them something still lived in this scene of devastation.

Somewhere, not too far away, they heard an odd whistling noise and a muffled rumble of something heavy being moved.

"Perhaps we should get a better view of things before we go riding blithely into the square," suggested the loresong.

The radont turned on her heel before Ia-Keltior could protest and cantered back out of the village. She turned up a high hill that overlooked the sheltered valley where the settlement lay. In the cover of a thin copse of trees the mare stopped, and the three companions stared down at the village below.

It had been a prosperous place, from the look of the stone houses and shops that lined the two intersecting streets. Besides a livestock market, there was another market in the common, an inn, and a dock beside the narrow river that flowed around its western edge. Almost all of it was smashed to rubble now.

They did not have to look far to find the culprit—and the source of the odd noises. In the center of the village, where the common had once gathered people together, a huge mottled form squatted over the scorched grass. It had crushed a building aside and was digging industriously into the side of a gently mounded hill.

Ia-Keltior felt her heart race. A red haze filled her mind, and her hands clenched into fists. Terror and fury together stormed through her. It was the same dragon. She would recognize that strange mottled brown and gold color anywhere. Neither metallic nor chromatic, it had aged into its own mysterious patina.

"Look!" the faen pointed downward toward the village. "There are still people down there."

The giantess shook her head hard, not listening. Her only desire was to find a weapon and kill the dragon. "Maybe I can find a sword in one of the houses," she mumbled.

Tirrana flattened her ears and squealed.

"You'll do no such thing!" Menien said, horrified at the suggestion. "That beast could crush you with its tail before you got within twenty feet of it. A sword! Don't be ridiculous. Whatever we do, we have to find a way to rescue those people."

"What people?" she cried, angry that they were trying to thwart her, angry at the conflict in her heart.

"The dragon has hostages. They're in a corral just there by the edge of the common."

"Hostages or supper?" she snapped.

"We shall have to go talk to it," Menien replied.

His head was held high, but Ia-Keltior could feel his small body trembling against her back. That sign of Menien's fear cooled her rage as nothing else had and brought her thoughts back to other considerations. She had sworn to right a wrong, to fulfill her father's oath. He had not promised to kill the dragon, only to help the villagers. He had made no specific plans or promises, only an offer to protect them. As much as she wanted to slake her need for revenge, perhaps she should slow down and plan ahead. Yes, she could go charging into the village without a sword or a bow or even a dagger, and Menien would be right. She would be crushed with one swing of the dragon's heavy tail, or mashed beneath a foot, or burned to a pathetic pile of ash. Perhaps a modicum of reason would be a good idea. Her people believed in service, after all, not blind vengeance.

She blinked rapidly in the pale sunlight. What had her father said once? The only cure for grief is action. He had quoted that shortly after her mother died, and soon thereafter he had retired from the knighthood and plunged himself into an intense study of magic, law, and history. Whether it had cured him or not, Ia-Keltior never knew.

She steeled herself and said as calmly as she could, "Very well, we will need a white flag for a parley. If you two wish to avoid this meeting, you may stay here."

The faen stood up behind her and stared over her shoulder at the distant dragon. "He doesn't seem to be the sort of dragon who negotiates."

"Oh, you noticed," the giantess said, her voice edged with irony. "Then we shall just have to rely on his sense of tradition."

She kept her voice cool and distant, as if the coming confrontation meant little to her. But she could not control the tremors in the pit of her stomach or the anger cresting in her head. She had never taken a formal vow to be an oathsworn, had never received the training, had never even experienced the intensity of emotions that she felt now. Yet she did not question her motives, She had to face the dragon and face her fear, or her father's death would be meaningless.

The radont shook her head, sending her long mane flying, and snorted a great gust of air. She cantered back down the hill and entered the village on the east side. They paused long enough to find a white linen shift in an abandoned house. Then the faen and the giantess remounted, and the mare walked boldly up the wagon road toward the common.

Ia-Keltior felt the tremors in her belly spread out like ripples until her entire body trembled. Her hands turned to ice and her heart pounded.

"People would understand if you turned around and went away," Menien murmured behind her. "You can't be expected to deal with a dragon alone."

"My father wouldn't understand," she responded sharply. "You knew I had to do this. Why are you coming with me?"

He was uncharacteristically silent for a long moment while Tirrana picked her way among the rubble and debris in the road. "Our lorekeeper sent me away," he said finally in a voice so soft she could barely hear him. "He told me not to return until I had learned compassion and the willingness to serve others. I can memorize songs and tales better than most, but a lorekeeper must be more than just a singer."

"Have you learned anything?"

"Not to take up with young giants on suicide missions. I'll never get to be a lorekeeper that way."

Ia-Keltior's mouth spread wide in a grin, and all at once she began to sing a giant's song of battle, one of her father's favorites. Giants relied heavily on music and ritual in their lives, and often used songs for important ceremonies. She wished she could stop and perform the Chi-Julud, the Wardance, which transformed a giant's normally patient personality to a more warlike and deadly mien. But the ritual needed other giants to be effective, and all she had was a radont and a faen. She would have to make do.

Without hesitation Menien joined his voice to hers and their song rose above the wreckage of Waterglen. The powerful tune may not have had the same effect as the war ritual, yet it helped hide their fear.

Several bangs and crashes and the sound of splintering timbers came from up ahead, and something heavy crashed to the ground. There were words, too, in a language none of them knew, spoken loudly and angrily by a voice amplified by a long throat and a deep set of lungs.

The radont passed the last mangled house on the road and stepped into the open space of the common. The human prisoners saw them immediately and swarmed to the fence of their prison pen. The giantess' song died into silence.

Holding the white shift high on her staff, Ia-Keltior glared at the dragon, who was digging busily around the foundation of another house at the foot of the hill and paying no attention to the approaching radont.

The black mare changed that with a ringing neigh.

With a snort that sounded a little surprised, the dragon twisted around and flattened his body to the ground. His snakelike head lowered to glare fiercely at the new intruders. He spied the white flag, and his eyes narrowed to mere slits.

"What is this?" he growled. His taloned foot raked the ground.

"It's a white flag of parley," Ia-Keltior stated the obvious. "Surely dragons haven't been gone from the land so long they have forgotten the traditions of parley?"

"We remember, but it is meaningless. I have no desire to talk."

"You're doing it now. We just wanted to ask what you were looking for."

His nose dropped lower until Ia-Keltior was looking up the dark pits of his nostrils. "Who said I was looking for anything?" he snapped, a little too quickly.

"I am making this place my lair."

"But this is already a home to a population of humans," the giantess said reasonably. "Have you paid them for their land? Or their ruined crops? Or the destroyed houses? I thought dragons were more civilized that mere brigands."

"We are ancient and wise beyond your feeble measure. This was my forefathers' lair thousands of years ago. This land is mine. It is not my business that puny humans decided to build this village on top of it." He curved his head toward the large hole he was digging into the mounded hill. "My ancestors were forced to leave before they could move their most valuable treasures. There is a relic of great power buried somewhere around here. I want that relic. Now go!" he roared. "Parley is over."

Ia-Keltior wasn't ready to give in that easily. "I wish to negotiate a peace with you. Perhaps we could help find this relic."

The dragon peered down his long nose at her. "I know you. I recognize your scent. You were part of the raiding party that was coming to steal my treasure."

Ia-Keltior stiffened. Any calm or cautious tendency she had fled into the darkness behind her memories of fire and shame.

"We were not coming to steal anything. We had come only to talk, and you murdered them all!" she shouted.

"Obviously I was sloppy, since you have returned to pester me."

"It is said in our lore," the giantess spoke with cold fury, "that if an injury is done to a man, it should be so severe that his vengeance need not be feared."

The dragon's response took even the radont by surprise. Smoke rolled from his nostrils, and his eyes flared with a red light. "I said, go!" and he whipped his tail around into Tirrana's broad side.

The powerful blow knocked the black mare to the ground. Ia-Keltior and Menien flew off her back to land in a pile of dirt and rubble. Winded and stunned, the young giantess lay on her back, gasping for air. Her blackened staff lay unseen several yards away.

"Father, please," she whispered. "Help me."

Frantic screams suddenly yanked her upright. She saw the prisoners screaming and pointing at the dragon, who had pinned the radont to the ground. His head dipped down, his lips lifted over a set of wicked teeth.

Ia-Keltior staggered to her feet. In that instant she saw the shadow creature standing beside her. Its form was indistinct even in the light of day, but its features looked vaguely familiar, and the great wings spread out on either side like sails.

I am with you. The words formed in her mind, framed with love and reinforced with knowledge.

* * * * *

She looked at the waiting shadow, and understanding exploded with incandescent light in her mind. Her fear vanished. There was only her oath, the promise she had made to her father. The shadow sprang at her, it wings forming a cloak around her. Opening her arms, she welcomed it into her mind and body in a symbiotic joining that united the two into one.

Power she had never felt before flowed through her muscles. Energy as hot as flame burned in her veins. Images of things she had never known raced into her mind and gave her the weapons she needed. She spread the great wings on her back and sprang into the air. They had tried negotiations; now she would do it her way.

Taken by surprise, the dragon reared his head and spouted a stream of flame at her.

Without thinking about what she was doing or how she could do it, she lifted her hands, gathered the dragon fire into a ball, and slammed it back at him. The fireball struck him on the side and burned a hole in his wing vane. The dragon roared in pain and fury and charged after her, the radont forgotten.

Blowing more flame, he jumped upward and took wing to gain height on her and destroy her from above.

The giantess, unencumbered by his great weight, flew faster. Gathering his fire, she sent more fireballs blazing back at him, each time aiming for his wings. In moments, the dragon could no longer stay aloft. With a shriek of rage, he spiraled down and landed heavily on the burned grass of the common. Ia-Keltior dove after him.

He crouched down, and his tail lashed up toward her wings.

She veered frantically out of the way and looked desperately for another weapon. While the dragon's fire worked well on the thinner skin of his wings, it did not penetrate his scales well. She needed something faster and more effective before he overwhelmed her with sheer size. But there was nothing at hand. He came at her again with tail and teeth, forcing her to fly up to a safer distance.

Around and around the open common of the wrecked village, the dragon and his winged opponent fought a deadly dance of fire and magic. Soon Ia-Keltior's muscles began to ache, and the burn on her shoulder hurt with an almost blinding fury.

Desperate for help, she spotted Menien. Heedless of his own danger, the loresong ran toward her carrying her staff. Just as the dragon spotted him, he skidded to a halt and heaved the staff at her like a javelin. She caught it with one hand and turned on a wingtip just in time to catch the fire aimed at the faen. Menien fell flat on the ground, his arms over his head as she heaved the fire back at the dragon's head, forcing him to duck.

Instead of diving for cover or making a run for it, Menien scrambled to his feet and ran closer to the dragon. The old monster's head swung around and dropped to snap the faen into pieces. But before the great mouth opened, Menien lifted his hands and began to sing. His melodious voice rose above the dragon's racket and abruptly silenced it. The old creature stopped in place and stared at the young faen, mesmerized.

Swiftly the giantess beat upward, carrying the charred staff. It was not a sword, but it might have its purpose. Her father had given up the sword and exchanged it for this staff, the tool of a magister. Perhaps she could remember one of the spells he often practiced in his study. But she would have to think of something quickly. The mesmerizing spell Menien was using was simple magic taught to beginning lorekeepers. That he could make it work on something as old and cunning as the dragon was impressive. Unfortunately, it probably wouldn't last long. Already the dragon stirred restlessly. Menien raised his voice and sang harder.

Winging overhead, Ia-Keltior stared down the length of the staff. The end had been worn to a point of sorts by the rocks and rough terrain she had climbed over. The length of the staff was scorched black and hardened by dragon fire.

Then her father's voice echoed in her thoughts, and the words she needed came to her: a simple spell, one of her father's favorites. She had heard him practice it so many times she could repeat the words in her sleep. The "Spell of True Flight," he called it. Placing both hands on the staff, she began the chant she knew so well.

"Faster!" Menien shouted between the words of his song. "I'm losing him!"

Her great wings swept into a downbeat; the words soared from her mouth.

On the ground, the dragon rolled his eyes to look at her instead of staring in rapt attention at the faen.

She felt the staff begin to tingle in her hands, and then it was done. She flew up higher, tucked in her wings, then swept downward like a diving raptor.

The dragon wrenched his head up, opened his mouth, and . . .

Ia-Keltior threw the staff like a spear, with all the grief and all the power of her oath behind it. The staff flew straight and true into the dragon's open mouth. The length of the staff caught the leading edge of his flame, burst into fire, and, still burning, stabbed through the dragon's skull and into his brain. The dragon stood poised at the brink of life, blood and flames spewing out of his mouth. Then he slowly collapsed, his body sagging into the stillness of death.

The instant the dragon died, Ia-Keltior felt something change. The power drained from her limbs, the strength wilted from her mind. She felt weak and bereft and, worst of all, she felt the wings shrivel on her back. Her companion of the battle was gone, disappearing as surely as her father's lifeforce.

"Menien," she cried, trying to backwing as she began to fall.

"This way!" the faen cried.

She made one last desperate flap with the wings before they were gone to force her falling body over the corpse of the dragon. Below her, she could see Menien and Tirrana grab one of the perforated wings and pull it out beneath her like a large blanket. She had just enough time to hope it would hold her weight before she crashed into the dragon and rolled onto its wing. Sliding and rolling down the wing vane, she landed in a heap at the radont's feet.

All at once she was surrounded by humans laughing and crying and shouting. Menien broke into a song of victory, and the radont neighed her own tidings. The young giantess could only sit where she had landed and lean back against the corpse of the dragon. Tears trickled down her face.

"That was incredible!" shouted Menien. "How did you do it?"

"I asked my father for help."

"That shadow thing was your father?"

She laughed. She was utterly spent and drained, yet she felt elated. "No. That was part of me. It was the power of my oath and the strength of my love. It took form somehow and, when I needed it, my father's spirit helped me to understand and use it."

"Was your father a great mage?" a strange voice asked.

She turned and saw an elderly man kneel by her side. He was battered and bloodied, but he had an indefatigable stubbornness in his eyes that Ia-Keltior liked.

"No, he was training to be a magister, but he died before he could finish his rites."

"Well," said the old man. "He must have had talent, which he passed on to you. That was the most exciting thing I have seen in a long while, young lady. As an elder in this community, I would be honored to have you stay with us as long as you like."

She looked around her at Waterglen and saw the people had already started to spread out through the ruins to search. They would rebuild and perhaps make use of the dragon's scales and bones to help pay for the tools and materials they could not make themselves. There was also the dragon's relic hidden somewhere in the rounded hills of the valley. She had a feeling it would not remain hidden much longer. Why not? she thought to herself. After all, she had given her oath to protect this village.

She reached out and touched Menien's green jacket. "Lorekeeper, how many more songs to you know?"

"Hundreds," he grinned, propping himself against Tirrana's leg.

"Enough to last until I heal. Will you stay that long, and help me lay my father to rest, before you return home?"

He bowed. "Only if I am allowed to write a ballad about the young giantess and the dragon. It will be my gift to your father."

PRIDE

Ramthor could smell the dragon's stench all over the Swift-foot tribe's hunting grounds, long before he and his hunters scattered the hyenas and buzzards from their scavenging. The birds were cleaning the last strips of flesh from a kill with dragon tracks all around it.

On this trip, Ramthor had led seven young litorian hunters after hill goats in the foothills of Mount Herrosh, hoping they would be lucky. After all, he figured, the dragon might avoid the gullies and scrub forest of the mountains. Ramthor's luck held steady: just as bad as it had been all summer. They found two hill goat carcasses surrounded by dragon spoor on the third day, and another the next morning.

Despite that, they found two goats of their own and brought them down after patient hours of stalking. After the kill, the scent of blood sharpened his hunger and drove caution from his mind. He set the youngest hunter, Talesh, to take watch, but the dragon swooped out of low-hanging clouds. Talesh had just enough time to bark a warning, and Ramthor's proud warriors scattered into the brush like antelope. The kill lay where it had fallen, but it was no longer theirs.

The dragon's wings snapped as it landed beside the hill goats. It roared once, echoing among the gullies and down the hills to the Central Plains. That roar was becoming as familiar as the beast's stench.

Ramthor gathered the others quickly, silently, padding over the ground and pulling the pack together with a few gestures, baring his fangs, and tossing his mane to emphasize his point. They couldn't stay to watch the dragon feed. The finest pack of hunters on the Central Plains slunk into the twilight, driven off their kill.

* * * * *

That night, beside a tiny campfire hidden in a gully, Ramthor patched a cut Talesh had gotten as he fled the dragon and listened to the rumble among his companions. Nunchot, the eldest whitemane still on the hunter's path, complained, "My neck hurts from looking up at the skies. How many kills has that beast taken from us?" A low mutter of agreement rippled through the hunting party.

"Too many," said Jossla, a broad-shouldered litorian with an excellent spear-eye. "I miss the taste of water bison. And ground sloth. And horse. And today, I miss the taste of hill goat."

The wood in the campfire popped and shifted; they had no meat to cook, but the fire's warmth was welcome. Ramthor knew that, if not for smaller animals they could carry slung over their shoulders, the gazelles and antelopes, the tribe's hunger would be even worse. When his hunters complained of empty bellies, a challenge for the leadership might not be far off.

"Ulyovar's tribe went to De-Shamod, to swear fealty to the giants," said Talesh. He squirmed away from Ramthor's attempt to bind a cloth over the bandages. Ramthor placed a heavy, clawed hand on the youngster's shoulder to steady him. Talesh kept talking. "The elders say Ulyovar's people were tired of the Black Beast taking all their best kills."

"We don't have to leave our hunting grounds. We won't go anywhere," said Ramthor. "We'll hunt at night. That dragon can't see every kill."

* * * * *

The Swiftfoot hunters slept late the next day and prepared themselves for darkness by blacking their metal spearpoints with grease and ashes, to avoid a telltale glint. They brushed their reddish-brown manes and cleaned the dirt from their claws to give themselves a better grip on their spears, javelins, and bows. Broad in the shoulders and muscled like oxen, the hunters gripped tiny bone needles in their scarred hands and mended leather garments, repaired quivers, and checked the trail bags holding their supply of jerky and nuts. Nunchot lavished time on a suit of boiled buffalo hide, made of a triple thickness of hide, all polished and painted. Nunchot was not as quick as he once was. Most of the hunters touched their amulets and ancestor tokens. Ramthor did not believe the amulets gave a hunter much help, but he didn't share his skepticism with the others. The simple amulets scratched from bone or made from tooth and claw restored their spirits and kept the hunters dreaming of success rather than hunger.

That night their luck did improve; even in the dim starlight it was impossible to miss the hand-deep hoofprints of a water bison, their favorite prey. In one way, the night hunt was easier: the bison didn't see them coming, and it had poor night vision, blundering into a tree when they rushed it from one side. That moment of confusion was all Ramthor needed to swing the fatal blow. The water bison fell slumped against the tree, pushing the trunk and rattling the leaves. Ramthor worried that the dragon could hear the sound, then shook his head.

The hunters ate all they could, stripping the skin off the carcass, devouring easy meat raw, and packing large cuts in salt and hides to take back to the hunting camp. It was the first large kill they had lingered over in months, and Ramthor knew they had until dawn to make the most of it.

Perhaps this would be the way for them from now on; it had worked, and there was no arguing with success. But night hunting presented its own difficulties: Talesh, spear-eyed Jossa, Nunchot, and even keen-nosed Bandortat couldn't find their prey as easily, as the night air dampened the scents. Worse, a wounded antelope, gazelle, or plains horse could still run and would be tough to track through the tall grass at night. Ramthor knew litorians were better daylight hunters. Or at least, so it had been for his father, his grandfather, and a thousand fathers before them.

* * * * *

A week later, the others complained of just the difficulties Ramthor had foreseen. He listened as if it were the first time the issues had occurred to him.

"It's not enough," said Nunchot. Ramthor's heart shrank to hear the whitemane's scolding tone. "We skulk in the dark, and the tribe eats a little, but who are we now? Night-skulking mojh? Worthless raiding rhodin? Nothing more than scavengers at our own kills? This is not the Swiftfoot tribe of my father." He spat on the ground, then stepped back into the shadows.

Bandortat stepped forward into the firelight, taking up the conversation, bowing slightly to Nunchot. "We have to do something bold. The dragon keeps us starving. It's time we took it down through sheer numbers." Nunchot and the others were silent. The pause stretched out as the hunters considered the size of the task. The campfire crackled and shifted. The smoke filled Ramthor's nostrils, blocking out the damp smells of night.

Keen-nosed Bandortat spoke for the others, and no one contradicted his rashness and folly. Nunchot at least should have known better. The tribe had lost half a dozen hunters in his grandfather's time to a nightmarish shadow troll, and the Swift-foot had never quite recovered their former glory. Attacking a dragon was pure foolishness.

Ramthor had toyed with the idea himself in the first weeks of the black beast's arrival. Every litorian warrior dreamed of such a moment: prey worthy of a song, a kill that every tribe on the Central Plains would envy. But the Swiftfoot numbers were not great: six hunters in their prime, one boy still learning, one whitemane overdue to retire to the winter lodge with the old women and chew mush. Ramthor wanted the kill, but it was not a practical dream. Tribal hunting chiefs who sought only glory might win it at the cost of their tribe. In his mind he knew that, though his heart still yearned to seize the chance of a spectacular kill.

Ramthor rumbled, a close-mouthed growl. "It's a dragon, not a water bison," he said. "Yes, it would bring us great glory to defeat it, but if only one or two of us survive the struggle, our people will suffer and our children will scatter among our neighbors. This is not glory. It's barely even victory." He looked around, catching the eye of each hunter in turn, beginning with Nunchot and ending with young Talesh.

Ramthor picked up a stick and stirred the fire. "I have a better plan. We must leave our territory, find better lands. The hills have always been difficult hunting."

"Where would we go?" said Nunchot. His voice was shaky with age, but deep. He shook his mane, looked away into the dark toward the smudge of grey on the eastern horizon. "The Spotted Hide tribe has already been driven away. We hunt their riverbed, yet it does us no good to find more prey we cannot feast on. More dragons fly to the west, and the stragglers from the southern tribes tell a story we already know."

"We'll find someplace," said Ramthor.

Nunchot snorted. "No place is safe; every tribe is hungry. Perhaps it is not the same beast everywhere, but the dragons are all hunting on our plains. If we do not defend our lands, the giants certainly won't." Three of the young hunters—keen-nosed Bandortat, heavy Grunfess, and spear-eyed Jossa—all growled agreement. Light-maned young Talesh, Nunchot, clever Agemtat, and fat Ennerung were silent. Ramthor could see that Talesh was more nervous than eager. Unusual wisdom in one so young.

Ramthor considered a journey to a safe refuge without cares or hunger. He'd been dreaming of it every night, but the visions never showed him where to go, only taunted him. Better to make a stand while the others still respected his leadership. "Very well," he said. "We will choose our ground, ambush the beast, and make sure it never flies again." The young hunters roared and shook their spears, and even fat Ennerung was caught up in the moment.

Nunchot, Agemtat, and Jossa did not roar. They had hunted large and deadly monsters before, and they knew what kind of risk this would be. Nunchot was the only one to speak it. "This is not a hunt for prey. If we make any mistake, it will sense our intent. We must treat it as if it were an armored river horse: Move quickly, strike carefully, and overrun it in a rush. If we fail, the Swiftfoot tribe is no more."

The young hunters looked at one another. They did not contradict their elder.

Ramthor said, "Nunchot is right; this dragon will probably catch one of us in its claws before a spear finds its heart. We must scout the ground to give ourselves every advantage. Be ready to leave before sunup."

Ramthor walked off quickly and prepared himself to tell Old Elemarra, the akashic wise woman of the Swiftfoot tribe, of the hunters' plans. Elemarra, her old gossips, and the female chiefs would tell the others. The lorekeeping woman would not like the news, but the young warriors were bitter with their own failure. Only blood would slake their rage.

* * * * *

Ramthor prepared everything he could; he chose a site along a riverbank, a place where the river slowed to a crawl, with the shelter of trees to hide it from the sky. He hid their spears and the tribe's single crossbow in the brush, and brought Old Elemarra, their best shaman, along for luck. Early in the morning, the hunters caught a fine plains horse on the edge of the grasslands, ran it up the gorge to the riverbank, and brought it down just outside the trees. Visible from the sky, but within a spear's throw of the bushes. A small ambush ditch allowed the litorians to crawl up close to the horse carcass without disturbing the grasses and without leaving a scent trail in the wind. The perfect site.

Of course, after that, things didn't quite go according to plan. They waited for hours. That was normal for an ambush hunt like this. Ramthor sat hidden in a muddy overhang along the river bank. He let his hunters eat their fill instead of conserving their meager supply; no sense in dying hungry.

Jossa and Talesh's young eyes saw it first, a small black spot in the sky, circling. It slowly grew closer and larger, then it made its usual scouting pass. Bardortat and Jossa staged a false, panicky retreat to the trees, leaving the plains horse half-eaten in the sun. The dragon fell out of the sky like a storm, scattering leaves and dirt.

The beast looked like a small hill in the sun, a glittering pile of mottled violet, brown, and black scales, with eyes as deep as any watering hole. Its black wings cast a huge shadow as it dived and whirled. Its claws were the size of axeheads, and the white spikes along its back made any killing leap behind it dangerous. Ramthor remembered thinking that perhaps shredding its wings would be best. Then it spoke a shattering word of power that deafened them all; the syllables hung in the late afternoon air with a buzz, then silence. Ramthor realized that he could no longer hear; none of the Swiftfoot could hear one another's cries or signals.

Heavy Grunfess and Talesh threw their spears too soon, before Bardortat and Jossa had fully recovered their breath from sprinting back from the kill. Worse, they threw just as the dragon looked directly toward the tribe's ambush ditch, a semicircle of woven grass that made it easier to get close to prey. The dragon ignored the spears, which bounced off its hide, and instead saw Bardortat and Jossa's stealthy charge coming. If those two had been just a little faster, perhaps. Or if the spears had caught under a scale. If only.

The rest was not worth remembering, but Ramthor couldn't help himself. He hadn't seen the dragon's claw strike, but he had seen Jossa's head roll back to the riverbank. Bardortat was gutted almost right on top of the plains horse carcass. Talesh, foolish youth, threw his axe and closed with his spear, just in time to see the beast pull its head up and let loose. Talesh was burnt to cinders where he stood, and Ramthor's eyes saw him turn from flesh to shadow to ashes, outlined by the violet white fire of the beast's breath, brighter than sunlight.

Ramthor ran for the riverbank and hid among the reeds. He hid there until his hearing returned and he could hear the dragon methodically crunching Jossa's bones.

Ramthor was not the only coward that day. The rest of the hunters had scattered, been eaten, or fled; the leader saw none of them down by the reeds. Ramthor spent the twilight hour searching for survivors but smelled only death. His stomach turned when he found heavy Grunfess, gutted and with all his choicest flesh eaten. He recognized him only because patches of his reddish mane were still attached to his skull. He found light-maned Talesh's bones and ashes, Bardortat's fly-crusted remains, and spear-eyed Jossa's skull. At each spot, he spoke the ceremonial words as quietly as he could, to give their spirits rest.

After midnight, he found Nunchot, clever Agemtat, fat Ennerung, and Old Elemarra, each too old, too wise, or too slow to take foolish risks. Ramthor joined them under the cover of brush, patient enough to wait for dawn. When it came, together the remnants of the Swiftfoot tribe lived up to its name. They returned to the hunting camp and found that it, too, had been raided by the beast; the younger women and older boys had survived, but the dragon had burned many elders and infants in the camp tents, or had run them down in the tall grass of the plains. Somehow, the dragon knew they were members of the same tribe as the hunting party, or perhaps in its rage it merely destroyed the nearest litorians it could find. Of thirty proud-maned Swiftfoot, young and old, only fourteen survived—and just four of them hunters.

Ramthor gathered what remained and the Swiftfoot fled to De-Shamod, the fortress capital of the giants. As he placed one foot in front of the other, he muttered under his breath. No one heard him, but he swore his vengeance against the Black Beast of Herrosh.

* * * * *

Once within the barren walls and muck of the city, the women, children, and elders grew silent; the tribe had never visited a city quite so large. The walls reared like cliffs, the streets spread as wide as a river and twice as busy, and above all, the confusing welter of food smells and jabbering noise. They all looked to Ramthor for food, for solace, and for answers. Ramthor had none. How could he explain why any thinking creature would live in its own filth when it could live free on the open plains instead? To ease their minds, though, he asked the Swiftfoot to remain together in the company of the White Claw, an allied tribe. Perhaps the White Claw could explain city customs to his people.

Ramthor had other tasks and spent hours trying to navigate the stone streets. While walking in the tanner's quarter,

Ramthor saw a group of a dozen litorians, all well-fed, heavily muscled, and clad in scaled armor. "Who are you, and why does your tribe flourish when others starve?" he asked, too surprised for tact. Their leader laughed and shook his head.

"You and every other refugee should do as we did," said the mercenary. "Go see the Speaker Malethar. He speaks for our people to the giants, and he hires our best warriors for their armies."

Ramthor had heard that litorian mercenaries were popular and commanded high prices for their service. But he had always considered the mercenaries less pure than the Central Plains hunters, somehow tainted by their city lives and penned meat. But the mercenary was half a hand taller than Ramthor, well armored in steely scales and a helmet that gathered his mane into a topknot flowing out through a narrow ring at the top. He carried a gleaming broad sword and a punch dagger with a hilt set with amber. His fur was clean, his leggings embroidered with giantish patterns. This was a wealthy warrior, indeed.

"Where would I find the speaker?" said Ramthor.

"In the city center," said the mercenary. "But bathe first. You have the dust of the outlands on you still. And maybe fleas!" He guffawed and walked off with his friends down the street. Ramthor's claws twitched, but he had sworn vengeance against the Black Beast. A slayer's oath would tax all his strength. On the plains, Ramthor never left a challenge unanswered, but here in the giant city, what use was it to fight a stranger over a trifle? He had a plan to kill the beast. Nothing else mattered.

Perhaps he was learning city ways after all.

* * * * *

Ramthor traded untanned water bison hides, plus their teeth and horns, to one of the furriers in De-Shamod's great market for enough golden queens and silver deuces to keep him, the children, and his elders fed and sheltered for a few days. The remaining hunters settled in at the sign of the Fish and Ferry, by the river water where the giants' deep voices rang all day along the docks. Ramthor and the elders groomed themselves and donned sets of the overrobes worn to audiences in the giantish court. The White Claw assured them that the Speaker for the Litorians, Malethar, listened to anyone who visited and did not demand bribes the way some other speakers did. Many litorian refugees in the city had pleaded with him before for food, shelter, and new hunting grounds. So far, Malethar seemed to have listened a great deal and spoken rather little.

The audience day was Waday, beginning at dawn and going until the last litorian left the hall. Ramthor, Nunchot, clever Agemtat, and Old Elemarra went to the Speaker's Hall, leaving fat Ennerung to watch over the rest of the tribe. They strode in, their claws clicking on the cold marble, and asked to add their names to the list of supplicants. No one opposed them, and a small sibeccai clerk politely wrote down their names and the name of the Swiftfoot. Ramthor swelled a little with pride. His people would stand before the speaker, as good as any other tribe. Better, perhaps, for they had faced the beast and could tell the speaker how to defeat it, how many of the litorian mercenaries in their silver scales it would be best to send. The Swiftfoot would be the eyes and scouts for the sword of the giants' army. Ramthor's grin at the thought was not a pleasant grin. He could almost taste the sour dragon flesh between his claws already.

The meaning of the list soon became clear, though. Many other tribes had come to complain. Each told of hunting grounds thinned by the flying threat of hungry dragons. Some sounded like the Black Beast, though others called it the Pass Dragon, or the Demon of Mount Herrosh. Others were clearly different animals: the scarlet-orange dragon called the Hound of the Verrik in the distant southern plains, the greenish-yellow-brown beast called the River Drinker ranging along the Ghost-wash, the pale white Moonlight Rustler devastating the cattle herds of Gahanis. Three tribes asked the speaker for food, gold, and shelter; he granted this to one of them, whose members were clearly starving. Two other tribes asked to join the giant's legions; all were told that both male and female warriors would be accepted and granted giant-forged armor and weapons, but their children must be fostered to other tribes. Their tribal names would end, and the litorians would take on legion names. One tribe agreed; the other found the price too steep.

"Ramthor, hunting chieftain of the Swiftfoot tribe, approach the speaker and state your case," said the clerk, his high voice ringing to the rafters.

Ramthor stepped forward; he did not need to look back to know that Nunchot, Agemtat, and Old Elemarra followed him. He opened his arms wide and bowed to Speaker Malethar, looking up to find the black-maned litorian watching him with dull eyes. The lazy hours of talk had made Malethar sluggish. Perhaps Ramthor could turn this to his advantage.

"Mighty Speaker, I am Ramthor, the hunting chieftain of the Swiftfoot, son of Fellthor and Smilara, and latest victim of the Black Beast of Mount Herrosh." Ramthor straightened up and pointed toward the mountain. "For all of the spring and summer, it has stolen our kills, just as it stole the kills of the Three Stripes and the White Claws, who have already spoken here. We ask for no gold, no food, no shelter."

"Then what do you want, Swiftfoot?" asked Speaker Malethar.

"We are a hunting tribe, not a city tribe, though our numbers have been cut in half and we have had no time to grieve. We ask for vengeance."

The speaker's eyes cleared as Ramthor spoke. His nose wrinkled as at a bad smell. "The beast you speak of is a dragon, Swiftfoot. It and its kind have sent emissaries and seek an understanding with the giants of the Diamond Throne. They may agree not to attack the people of the giant lands, as long as they are left unmolested in return."

"And they may not agree!" said Ramthor.

"If your tribe is half-dead, chieftain," said the Speaker, "look to your own foolishness and mend your ways."

"The beast kills us slowly by stealing the meat from our mouths. To allow it to starve us this way is shameful," said Ramthor.

Speaker Malethar sighed. "I have heard this pride before, and it accomplishes nothing. To seek vengeance against the dragon is to seek your own destruction."

"With the help of a company of litorian warriors, the thing is done! Surely it is not wrong to want to keep one's kills, to feed the children and the whitemaned elderly? Why do you side with this monster against your own people?" Ramthor's voice rose.

"The giants have forbidden it. Reprisal against the dragons is more than a tribal matter; it could drag us all into war. A war we are in no wise ready for." The speaker's eyes narrowed. "With your rage, you would be better served to join the legions, Ramthor. Your people's skills are known, their scouting and cleverness. Join the legions defending De-Shamod, instead of bringing ruin upon the giants and our people alike. I can grant you a captain's rank, if your warriors and shaman join with you."

Ramthor almost snarled, but caution held him back. He bared his teeth and spoke in a roar. "It is not to serve the giants that we came! We seek our lands, and if you will not help us keep them, we will defend them ourselves!"

"No, you will not, for I forbid it in the name of the giants' kingdom," said the speaker. He half-turned away to face his clerk, as if the conversation were already over.

"It is not my kingdom you speak for, then," said Ramthor. "My kingdom is found in the tall grasses of the plains, not the stone and the river and the sea. If the giants will do nothing to help me, then I likewise owe them nothing."

The speaker turned back to face Ramthor, his lips pulled back from his bright fangs. "You have already said half your tribe lies dead on Mount Herrosh. Do not be a fool and throw away the other half as well."

Ramthor hesitated only a moment. "The Swiftfoot can hold their own." He thought he heard a snicker from the sibeccai clerk or one of the waiting petitioners, but his gaze stayed fixed on the speaker. His blood ran hot. "A tribe that does not defend its territory is no tribe at all. You are nothing more than sibeccai jackals—scavengers." He heard the sharp intake of breath from the sibeccai and human members of the audience.

"You insult the giants and their friends. Begone, and do not return," said the speaker, gesturing to brush them away with one heavy clawed hand.

Ramthor laughed. "Insults mean nothing; actions are the measure of a warrior. I thank you for listening to our plea, speaker. We will find new hunting grounds without your assistance." It was a lie, but the giants would lock him up if they knew what was really in his heart.

Ramthor turned and left, his knuckles white, his heart pounding.

* * * * *

The meeting had failed. The elder women would have been furious, but few of them had survived the dragon's assault. Ramthor left his tribemates, avoiding Elemarra the akashic, for the cagey old woman always asked sharp questions he did not want to answer. No one should know all his plans before he was ready.

Ramthor immediately made the rounds of the Swiftfoot's closest friends and allies, then other drifting refugees and tribal remnants. Some greeted him with hands on hilts, suspicion in every twitching whisker, but most were pleased to hear of a dragon hunt. It was unheard of, bold—a thing of sheer bravado that any litorian thought a noble cause. Most were too polite to mention that it was likely suicide.

Nine hunting chieftains pledged their support when he approached them at the city wells or taverns; four of those came slinking back to the Swiftfoot and White Claw encampment carrying their elders' denials between their teeth. A few singers even began telling the tale of the Black Beast in the taverns, though they all sang it as a tale of tribal death foretold, a tragedy that simply hadn't come to fruition yet.

Several times he saw a grey-cloaked sibeccai merchant following him from the taverns to his quarters, but the man never approached him. Let him report to his giantish masters, let him lick their boots and spin his tales.

Some of the work was haggling. Usually the Swiftfoot visited the outskirts of De-Shamod at the end of the hunting season to trade for salt, spices, cloth, and jewels. This time, Ramthor and Nunchot gathered all the axes and boar spears they could, as well as a shield for each warrior, wood and iron thick enough to turn dragon fire. He traded their light hunting crossbow for a heavy crossbow able to punch through black scales as thick as a litorian wrist. Again Ramthor spotted the grey-cloaked sibeccai, though this time he seemed to be purchasing some needlelike throwing daggers. Perhaps the giants and their servants did not approve of his warlike talk or of uniting the tribes for a hunt.

That night, Ramthor was stopped by the city watch and asked a few sharp questions: "Why are you buying shields for war? Are you a rebel against the Diamond Throne? Why have you not left town as you said you would?" Ramthor had no answers, and spoke meekly. It didn't help; two members of the city watch pinned his arms as their captain barked in his face and finally beat him with truncheons until it became clear that Ramthor was simply going to remain silent. He crawled back to the small house favored by the White Claws, who took him in and made a fuss over his bloodied fur. The next morning, Ramthor began using messengers to do his bidding, asking others to visit him instead of showing himself on the streets.

By the full moon, Ramthor was almost done with his efforts to gather new strength for his venture. He had decided not to question just the hunting chieftains, but also to recruit among the young warriors, those with the hottest blood and sharpest taste for revenge. Even among the elders he found a few sympathetic ears, refugees who smiled all the way to their fangs when he suggested that a dragon could be killed, if only there were enough hands and enough spears. The akashics of the city spoke their secrets to Elemarra. Every litorian hand turned to help Ramthor's scheme, but still he worried. He had never hunted with these tribes before. Sheer numbers could help, but could also just get in each other's way. He wished for something greater, a weapon or a witchery that would guarantee victory. He shook his head sadly; he was old enough to know no hunter was ever guaranteed a kill. Sheer courage and thicker shields would have to do.

The next morning, a note arrived from Speaker Malethar asking him to appear and explain his intentions at the court. Ramthor ignored the summons but stopped leaving the tribe's quarters alone: Nunchot and some of the White Claws became his constant companions. Not everyone hindered him; some meant well. Even the litorian guards who had insulted him in the street took the time to find him and warn him off, saying that his arrest was certain unless he left or stopped agitating for a dragon hunt.

Though nine tribes claimed they would help, in the end just five other shattered tribes joined them on the trail north and west from De-Shamod. Outside the city gates, they met seven tribeless young bravos, males with thick manes and (perhaps) empty heads. All told, there were Ramthor, Nunchot, clever Agemtat, fat Ennerung, and twenty-nine warriors of the White Claw, Sunsnake, Blackmane, and other tribes. They left early, before the dawn. By the time the morning mist had burned away, they were miles away, loping steadily through the chest-high grasses, eating up the miles.

* * * * *

Two days outside the city, it was clear that the giants were pursuing them, as an enormous Hu-Charad captain leading two dozen swift, jackal-like sibeccai paralleled their course. Some of the scouts reported that a grey-cloaked sibeccai witch of some kind led them. Ramthor growled low; they would be shadowed every step. He had hoped not to waste time putting the giants off the scent outside the city, but he had no choice. He turned and led the tribes south, away from their territories on Mount Herrosh, toward the grounds of the Blackmanes where the Spiral Stone stood, a place of good omen. As soon as the giants and their sibeccai were convinced that they were not going back to Mount Herrosh, they lost interest, and one morning they were simply gone.

Ramthor didn't quite believe they'd give up so easily. In the end, the tribe spent a week at the Spiral Stone. Elemarra sought out Ramthor the first night. "I have not been idle while you gathered our strength in the city. The other elders and akashics believe that this stone holds a great secret of the dragon times of old."

"What makes you think so?" said Ramthor. Like the others, he had touched the gritty warmth of Spiral Stone for luck as they arrived, but did not give it another thought.

Elemarra said, "I have sought answers from the akashic memory, and I am close to some of them now. Others are too far from recent memory to capture, even with a mind as old as mine. The Spiral Stone is an akashic node. It makes it easier to reach into the past, and easier to hold your kill."

"Well, good," said Ramthor. That was plain enough to understand. "So work your hunt and tell me what you learn."

"It's not something I can do alone. I need a hunter's mind and a hunter's understanding of what I learn."

Reluctantly, Ramthor agreed, although the akashic's ability to consult the memories of the ancestors made his fur stand on end. Elemarra gave him a mixture of herbs and bitter roots, sweetened with honey and spiced with cloves to hide the taste. He held her hand to anchor her as she slid into the akashic memory. Elemarra lay on soft furs atop the Spiral Stone, whispering secrets in a voice not her own. Sometimes she stayed silent for long minutes, but again and again she spoke.

"The dragons have driven the litorians from the plains many times." A long pause. "Our ancestors fled south." Another pause. "But the dragonslayers of the Red Axe tribe found the three Great Strikes."

Ramthor's ears perked up. "Tell me, Elemarra, what are they?" he said. "What do my hunters need to know?" She seemed not to hear him, but snuffled into the furs. The old woman shifted left and right, as if buffeted by spirits around her. She mumbled again, louder.

"What? You must tell me!" Ramthor hoped that the akashic memory could pull something, some distant ancestor's blessing, from the mists. He had never really respected the elderly woman before, but he swore silently that this would change if only they could grant him this secret. He wanted to shake her old bones, but feared breaking her trance. The minutes crawled by. Elemarra began to drool. Perhaps the old akashic was reaching too far into the past? When had dragons last been seen in this land? Could she be lost among the ghosts of their ancestors? Ramthor worried that she might not come back.

Nothing had ever sounded so sweet as Elemarra's thin voice, quavering, "The wing lock, the eye strike, and the pale throat scale."

"Tell me more," said Ramthor, softly. And she did. She spoke though the whole of the deep night, ever so slowly, carefully, and bloodcurdlingly filling his ears with the hunting secrets of litorian dragonslayers ten thousand years dead.

That night, Ramthor dreamed of his father, his grandfather, and ancestors so ancient he could only tremble before them. Over and over, he pictured the strikes Elemarra had described to him, felt the leap in his legs, reached through scales with a steel edge that was his own right hand. Elemarra had spoken of hundreds of dragonslayers who had died, describing each fall in bloody detail. He would not fail his people. He could not. Such a thing must not be.

* * * * *

In the days that followed, the combined tribes of litorians moved over the grasslands, not bothering to hide themselves from the dragon. Indeed, they made their campfires more numerous, left their droppings clustered close together, the scent trail strong. Let the dragon come; they had dared attack it and they would not live in fear. And indeed, the dragon often flew along the horizon, but it left them alone.

A week later, the scouts found one of the dragon's favorite watering holes. It was nesting season for the flightless axebirds, and the dragon killed and ate dozens of them and their young by the waterhole, feathers and all. The scouts approached the nesting grounds a few times, but they fled whenever the dragon roared or made a scouting pass. The dragon grew accustomed to seeing the hunters flee.

They fled half a hundred times until one day, the dragon again saw the grasses and savannah shrubs by the waterhole, and the body of a striding axebird, and four litorians hunkered over their kill, just as the hunters had intended it should see.

The dragon landed heavily beside the waterhole, half a bowshot from the axebird's carcass, its wings stirring up a few feathers and a scattering of dry grass. Its veined, bluish-black wings quickly folded back, and the dragon raised its neck, trumpeting its arrival with a sound loud enough to shake the dust off its back. But the four litorians at their kill did not scatter, as they usually did. Instead, they picked up their spears and turned to form a line abreast between the dragon and the raw reek of fresh blood.

The dragon did not hesitate. Roaring, it gathered itself, a mountain of black and brown mottled scales, hints of violet flesh at the joints and eye sockets, a crest of pure white spines. Its fangs dripped with hunger, and its eyes darted from one litorian to the next.

The dragon's charge was very, very quick, and its neck darted forward even faster. Ramthor barely had time to shout and raise his pike from the dust; Nunchot and Agemtat were faster, and the young Sunsnake volunteer the fastest of them all. All four pikes splintered under the dragon's charge, but one of the pike heads had struck home—the dragon's own weight had driven it onto the blade. The dragon held the young Sunsnake in its jaws for a moment, then bit him in half. Ramthor, Nunchot, and Agemtat fled before it could choose another victim.

They would not have made it but for Old Elemarra's enchantment, which had concealed their true numbers, obscuring fifteen Sunsnake and White Claws under a haze of heat shimmer and sun glare. From every side, Ramthor saw the roaring litorian warriors emerge out of ambush, booming their battle cries that they could not hear, for they had sealed their ears with wax to protect against the dragon's roar.

To one side, he saw the White Claw chieftain signal, "Now!" followed by the satisfying thwack of crossbow quarrels. Four scratched the scales but slid off, but one buried itself deep in the dragon's haunches. Another buried itself in the creature's wing, pinning it to its side. The dragon hopped to its right, away from the volley, and raised its wing, tearing a bloody hole in the black surface where the quarrel had been.

Ramthor felt the beast's inrush of breath and saw its neck rear back. Its tail swept a handful of White Claw warriors aside like dolls, and one of the White Claws landed head-first against a stone. Two dead already, and the battle only joined for a few heartbeats.

Ramthor remembered light-maned Talesh, turned to ashes before his eyes, and he threw his spear as carefully as spear-eyed Jossa, with all the speed and muscle of heavy Grunfess. Every one of his father's fathers was in that spear-cast, every blessing of the elders, and yet the spear itself felt as light as a clump of fur, shed and drifting in the summer haze. The spear flew straight and high, into the dragon's left eye, an eye the blue of summer horizons. The beast choked, its blue flame coughed up into the air instead of down onto the hunters.

Clever Agemtat stepped forward with his axe while the beast was still clawing at an eye, and hacked at the injured wing. If the beast got off the ground, it might still recover and return to exact a heavy price from hunting camps for hundreds of miles around. Agemtat struck at the wing joint with a full swing and connected, but was himself knocked sprawling when the huge wing twitched in response. The axe flew from his hand, and he did not get up.

The dragon whirled, knocking down seven or eight litorians all along one flank, but there were too many, and its wing was too injured. Agemtat's axe seemed to have done its work. The injured wing scraped across the ground, stirring up the dust and hampering every move the dragon made.

For a time, the hunters circled to stay on its blind side, hoping the dragon's exhaustion and pain would do their work for them. But the beast was cannier than Ramthor suspected. The dragging wing, the blinded weak side, none of it was as bad as the wyrm pretended. The three boldest hunters rushed it, trying to finish the beast quickly. Roaring, it folded the wounded wing back along the length of its body with a snap in the air and rushed to meet their charge, catching the leading hunter in its claws. Reaching down, it snapped the spine of the second with a bite, and it caught the last with a blast of violet fire as he turned to run.

The older hunters reloaded the crossbows, and others stood their ground with spears set to defend them. Six dead already, and yet the beast was still strong enough to chase them, bold enough to roar its challenges. The old hunters loosed the second volley, but their aim was shaky from fear and rage. Ramthor thought that the hunters' numbers would tell in the end, but they were losing those numbers much more quickly than he'd expected. Again the beast unleashed its blazing fire, and Ramthor rolled away barely in time. Others were not so quick.

Ramthor stepped to the opposite side, turning his head away from the blazing light and concentrating on the pattern of its throat scales. If the akashic whisper was right, the weak point was so high that only a leap could reach it. Even the length of his war axe might not be quite enough to reach if the dragon's head reared up. He moved in and out, trying to get close when the dragon's head darted down to strike. Behind him, he heard a hunter turn and run.

Keeping his concentration was difficult, as the dragon struck sharply at anyone close and kept turning to lash along its sides with tail and wing. Wherever the dragon turned, the litorians struck from the off side, leaping over its lashing tail and one striking wing, darting in to throw a javelin at point-blank range or to slip in low and strike at the underbelly.

Slowly, slowly, like a giant ground sloth, its blood drained away and its reactions slowed. But not fast enough. It had already killed at least ten hunters, and wounded eight more so they could not continue. The hunting party was coming apart. Ramthor looked and saw Nunchot, Elemarra, and three elder White Claws with crossbows. Only fat Ennerung and five Sun-snakes and Blackmanes were still at close quarters with the beast. They'd all be dead in another minute.

Still Ramthor waited, watching the steady rhythm of the hunters and their prey, the same rhythm he had seen at the akashic node. Without thought, he saw his chance, saw the pale scale at the dragon's weak point, and charged forward in a rush. His arms and legs, tired from constant movement and the long grinding fight, felt as light as puffseeds on the wind. He planted his feet and leapt for the beast's throat, axe already swinging.

The dragon saw his charge, but was engaged with two Black-manes trying to gut it. Somehow it pulled back its scaly neck and struck out with a claw, cutting Ramthor's fine steel scales like the skin of a fish. Ramthor's thigh burned as the claw ripped it open, but then his axe struck home. The dragon's neck twitched in reaction, and Ramthor was thrown to the earth with the crack of broken ribs.

The ancestors had not lied, and Old Elemarra's faint whispers from the akashic memory had been right. The pale throat scale lay shattered to prove it. The death throes were hard to see; the beast moved in a quick circle and threw up dust in all directions, scattering the hunters in fear of a last charge. When the dust settled, Ramthor saw that its wing lay twisted on the ground, and the dragon's neck was sprawled in the dirt. No one could believe it was dead, and yet it lay there, unmoving. Ramthor rushed in close and saw that the beast was paralyzed, its neck broken but its breath still rasping. He stepped up, raised his axe to the heavens, and struck the death-blow, sepa-rating its head from the body and tumbling the head with its one remaining heaven-blue eye into the dust.

* * * * *

In the end, the hunters lost fully fifteen of their number, and nine were injured, the chieftain of the White Claw among them. They counted it a price worth paying for the loss of their com-rades, children, and elders, the months of starvation, the shame that the beast had wrought on a hunting nation. More than that: Clever Agemtat had lingered among them for long minutes before his cracked skull killed him, and he kept saying the same words as he lay dying: "I am proud to have taken my death-blow here, with you, today." Perhaps he could not hear their answers; the dragon's roar had deafened many despite their precautions.

Ramthor was the first to open the dragon heart vein, gather-ing the drops in a wooden cup and offering them first to Old

Elemarra, then to whitemane Nunchot and fat Ennerung. The blood tasted foul, but to Ramthor it was sweet as giantish wine, and surely as intoxicating. Ramthor and the others each ate a handful of the dragon's uncooked flesh, reptilian and gamy. Their names would be remembered. Every hunt was a tally of small victories and small defeats, this tally mark cut a little deeper than most. No sibeccai, no giant had believed in this hunt, no domesticated mercenary or scavenger would share in its feast. Every year when the winter rains came, the shamans would tell the tale around the campfire. Surely it would be told to his children and grandchildren: the tale of the dragon hunt, and the return of the Central Plains hunting grounds to the litorians.

In days to come, the giants would hear about this battle, and the taste of hot blood and the joy of victory would fade. The giants would declare them outlaws and promise severe reprisals against the Swiftfoot, Blackmane, Sunsnake, and White Claw. The giant's patrols might find them, tracked by sibeccai noses and sorcery. Other dragons might seek to collect a blood price, chasing litorians and killing their youngest and oldest. It didn't matter; worrying wouldn't change the truth. The land was theirs. Ramthor and his hunters had triumphed over a dragon. Even if their tribes were scattered and destroyed, their names would live on, in the akashic memory and in litorian legend. They had silenced the dragon's roar and soon would teach others to do the same. They had fought together, and won together, not as separate tribes but as one pride, and one people.

Ramthor bellowed his victory call, a blood-dark summons to eat from the hands of the hunters. No one was going to push him and his brothers off this kill. No one would dare.

RICHARD LEE BYERS

VOWS

At first, intermittent flares of yellow light illuminated the tunnel. Then Dathred ran around a bend, and all was darkness, though he could still hear the roaring and scuttling. He raced blindly onward, upward, stumbling, banging his toes against stalagmites, until the clamor of battle faded.

Finally, panting, the warrior—a short, sturdily built man in his middle years, with auburn hair just beginning to go white—stumbled to a halt. Standing still made it easier to invoke his abilities. He asked for light and felt a sudden stab of fear that none would appear. That he was now unworthy to receive it. But a ball of pearly glow flowered in the air and floated along before him as he resumed his flight.

He had to squint when he reached the mouth of the cavern, because the afternoon sun still shone outside. It was difficult to believe he'd descended into the earth such a short time ago.

He staggered into the brightness and twenty yards farther, then slumped down on the ground, spent. *It's over,* he told himself, *and I only did what I had to do. What I vowed to do.*

* * * * *

The sheep ran back and forth, but their plight was hopeless. Springing, its prodigious bat wings beating, the gigantic reptile repeatedly bounded over them, planted itself in front of them, and slaughtered more, with a snap of its jaws, a swipe of its talons, or a puff of fiery breath.

Watching from a stand of oaks, Dathred knew the dragon was a wonder and could even see that, with its glittering scarlet scales and pale golden pinions, it was beautiful. But he didn't care. He was too sick with anger. And guilt.

"You're the village champion," said Mabbor, the stooped, wizened shepherd. "Do something!"

"There's nothing I can do," Dathred said. "Not alone. I sent to Navael for help."

"Which will take weeks getting here, if it comes at all," Mabbor said. "By then, that thing will have destroyed all the livestock, torn up all the crops, and most likely started killing people when it needs a new amusement."

The dragon pulped the last ewe with a flick of its serpentine tail, then leaped into the air and flew away without even eating any of its kill.

"I'm sorry," Dathred said. "Truly. If I thought I had one chance in a thousand of defeating a wyrm . . ."

The old man made a sour face. "It's all right. Everybody knows you're no coward, and no one wants you to throw your life away."

Forgiveness only made Dathred feel more useless.

For the rest of the day and into the night, he walked the hills and moors, pondering, and, when his wits failed him, even asking the gods for help. He'd never placed any stock in such beings, but if dragons still walked the earth, maybe deities were real as well.

Perhaps one of them even whispered the scheme that finally popped into his head, though it seemed unlikely a god would conceive of anything so hare-brained.

* * * * *

Dathred hummed a marching song as he traversed the heath where the dragon went to rest. He didn't want the creature to think he was trying to creep up on it.

In fact, it was the reptile that surprised him, suddenly rearing up from the grass, where it seemed impossible that anything so immense could lie unnoticed. The yellow, slit-pupiled eyes glared from the wedge-shaped crimson head with its crest and frills.

Badly startled, Dathred nearly summoned his sword and shield of light into his hands as a reflex. He caught himself just in time, though, and bowed instead, as he'd once bowed to stewards, speakers, and nobles in the more populous lands to the south.

The wyrm just kept on staring, until he feared his nerve would break beneath the pressure of its gaze. At last it said, "What do you want?" Its voice, though deep, was higher and softer than any tone he would have expected from such a long, enormous throat. Its breath smelled of burning.

"To bargain," he replied.

Though a dragon's mouth was formed differently than a man's, the wyrm demonstrated that it could nonetheless manage a sneer. "For your life?"

Dathred swallowed. "For the life of Rosehill—my village. You kill our animals and trample our crops. Just for sport, as far as we can tell. We can't survive if you destroy our food."

The dragon flipped its golden wings in a gesture like a shrug. "What do I care? You're not my kind. If you can't live near me, move elsewhere."

"We'd rather pay you to go away."

The wyrm snorted. "With what? Goats? Cabbages? A wattle hut?"

"Gold and jewels." The legends said dragons lusted after treasure. Dathred could only hope they spoke true. "Obviously, my friends and I don't possess them ourselves. But I can show you where to get them, because I know where the wyrms of old made their lairs, before you all flew into the West. It's said the ancient drakes left much of their hoards behind."

"And you humans know where this wealth can be found, but in all the centuries since, no one has bothered to plunder it?"

It was a shrewd question. Dathred felt himself start to sweat. "The stories tell of a curse. But you needn't fear it, because you won't come as a thief. Your ancestors' wealth is rightfully yours."

The reptile's eyes narrowed. "I suppose it would be. So, you'll lead me to a place where dragons dwelled, and if we find treasure there, I'll leave the farmers and their chattels alone thereafter. Is that the bargain?"

"Yes."

The creature stood silent, considering, until Dathred thought the waiting would make him scream. At last it said, "I take you for a knight, or something comparable."

"Something comparable, yes."

"Then swear on your honor to be my true and faithful guide."

Dathred felt a pang of dismay. In point of fact, he was a champion of light, pledged to uphold goodness and truth. In consequence, though he might on occasion employ trickery to mislead a foe, his actual oath was sacred, and he'd never broken it.

Yet he'd also vowed to protect Rosehill, come what might, and surely that promise took precedence over any pledge extorted by a heartless monster. He drew the broadsword hanging at his hip, pressed it to his heart, and swore as the dragon bade him.

This isn't a real vow, he insisted to himself, just a ploy. I'm only swearing on a piece of steel, not my sword of light. Still, it was hard to force the words out.

When he finished, the dragon said, "Since we're to travel together, what do I call you?"

"Dathred."

"And I'm the lord Sjakrinshyamandalac."

"Sja . . . Sjakrinkee . . ."

The dragon spat a wisp of smoke. "Don't tie your tongue in a knot. In your speech, it means 'Amberwing.'"

* * * * *

Even Amberwing seemed surprised by the edge of the Harrowdeep, by the hugeness of the mossy tree trunks, the density of the brush, and the sudden dimness when the foliage overhead blocked out the sun. "It will be slow going," he said.

"We'll find trails farther in," Dathred replied.

"Still, when I think how easily we could fly over it . . ."

"I told you, I couldn't locate the cave from the air. That's not how I'm accustomed to finding my way, and the branches are too thick to let me spot landmarks on the ground."

The dragon grunted. "Lead on, then."

Oh, I will, Dathred thought. He'd lead Amberwing in circles as long as he dared. It would buy time for the soldiers from Navael to reach the village.

They hiked without speaking for a while. Considering his size and weight, Amberwing's progress through the undergrowth and over dry, fallen leaves was miraculously, eerily quiet. The thought of his false oath wore at Dathred like a stone in a shoe. He tried to dismiss it and concentrate on watching for dangers, which the vast forest possessed in abundance.

Eventually, Amberwing jerked his head to point to a delicate pink blossom adorning a vine. "What's this?"

Dathred blinked in surprise at the question. "Maidenblush. Doesn't it grow where you come from?"

"No. Nor does this." The dragon pointed a curved, gleaming talon at a bush with dark, furry leaves.

"That's sourroot. The healers brew it into a nasty tea and make you drink it when you have a cough."

"Interesting."

Dathred couldn't imagine why. It seemed too humble and homely a matter to interest a horror out of legend. "Do dragons get the catarrh?"

Amberwing made a rumbling sound. It alarmed Dathred for an instant, until he recognized it for a chuckle. "No," the reptile said. "I just have a . . . curiosity about this land. Since I'm going to make my home here from now on."

"Why? Is it better than the place where you drakes have spent the last however many ages it's been?"

Amberwing grunted. "It's supposed to be."

"Because if it's not, what's the point of returning and troubling the folk who never left? I mean, if you have a country all your own—"

He heard, or perhaps only sensed, a surge of motion at his back. He tried to pivot to face it, to defend himself if possible, but he was too slow. Claws as long as scimitars seized him and slammed him to the ground. Amberwing lowered his head to glare at him. Smoke fumed from the wyrm's nostrils and maw.

"Your folk mean nothing to me," the reptile said, "and I'll settle where I please."

"Evidently I've offended you somehow," Dathred wheezed. The drake was squeezing and squashing the breath out of him. "But if you kill me, you'll never find the treasure."

"I . . . don't mean to hurt you," said Amberwing. He released Dathred and stepped back, giving the human room to stand up. "But stop prattling about matters you can't understand."

"As you wish." Dathred hesitated. "Shall we continue on?" When Amberwing agreed, the champion found it required an effort of will to turn his back on his titanic companion once more.

After a while, the drake asked, "How do you name the white birds with the brown spots on their wings?"

* * * * *

On their fifth night in the forest, Amberwing said, "You keep watch for once." He lay down, curled into a ball, and the lids drooped down over his feline eyes.

Dathred's heart beat faster, for it was the first time Amberwing had sought to sleep. Dragons evidently didn't need it as often as men, and the warrior had nearly abandoned hope of gaining such an opportunity.

He waited until the wyrm's breathing became slow and shallow, then rose silently to his feet. Now was the time to summon his sword of light. Because, while he had no hope of besting a dragon in anything approximating a fair fight, he just might be able to kill a slumbering one.

But his heart rebelled at the thought of using his sacred gifts to strike such a foul blow. He eased his steel sword out of the scabbard instead. Poised it to thrust. Balked.

Because he didn't want to be a traitor and oathbreaker.

He told himself his reluctance was ridiculous. His pledge to the dragon was no true vow, and in any case, he'd started violating it the instant they sealed their bargain. It was days too late for qualms and reservations.

By the moon and stars, he had to take this chance! Otherwise, he truly was false: to the village. To his genuine oath and allegiance.

But he couldn't. Not with his mind muddled and divided. He needed to clear his head, and it would be difficult to do it standing over Amberwing. The spectacle of the dragon's vulnerability, the trust manifest in his willingness to sleep in his companion's presence, made Dathred feel vile and ashamed.

He crept some distance away, then stood steeling himself for the task at hand, breathing hard as if performing some arduous labor. Until the stone whizzed out of the darkness and hit him in the head.

Only his helmet kept the blow from smashing his skull, as his brigandine somewhat blunted the impacts of the volley of rocks that followed an instant later. He staggered, and shadows rushed him. They were half again as tall as a man, gaunt and long-armed, with noses like spikes or hooks. Trolls!

Dathred's head rang from the knock it had taken, and he struggled to shake off the shock of it. He dropped his mundane weapon and evoked his sword and shield of light, both shining as if formed of curdled moonlight. Then the first of the man-eaters shambled into striking distance.

The troll clawed at him. He defended with the shield and slashed open its belly. It reeled back, but now, from the corner of his eye, he glimpsed another on his flank. As he pivoted, it bobbed its head down to bite. He met the attack with a stop cut to its spindly neck. The blade sent its head flying, and the body fell . . . then started sluggishly groping about, seeking what it had lost, for that was the way of trolls. They were hellishly difficult to kill.

Dathred crippled a third creature, maimed a fourth. Then something hit him in the back of the head. He pitched forward onto his knees, and the trolls swarmed onto him.

A prodigious roar split the night, followed at once by a plume of flame. Kneeling, Dathred flinched from the heat but remained untouched by the actual fire. The trolls clustered around him were less fortunate. The flare charred their flesh and set their manes of snaky hair ablaze.

The attack killed several of them outright. The survivors bolted. Amberwing looked about, making sure the skirmish was over, then stalked up to Dathred. "Are you all right?" the dragon asked.

Dathred checked and found he was, more or less, although the trolls' raking talons had torn his brigandine in several places. "Yes."

"You're lucky the commotion woke me. What were you doing, wandering off alone?"

Still rattled by his narrow escape, the champion fumbled for a serviceable explanation. "You don't want me pissing in the middle of our campsite, do you?"

"I suppose not."

"I . . . was lucky you were here. Thank you."

Amberwing grinned. "You said it yourself. If I lose you, I lose the treasure."

That was it, of course. He'd rescued Dathred for purely selfish reasons. Still, the champion knew that even if another chance presented itself, he wouldn't have the stomach to kill the dragon in his sleep.

The realization brought a surge of guilt. He strained to quell it by telling himself such an attack was a stupid notion anyway. What if one stroke failed to dispatch such a formidable creature? Then Amberwing would rise up, tear him apart, and then, for all he knew, massacre the whole village in retribution for his treachery.

No, surely it was better to continue as he was. Give the soldiers time to come, and, when he felt he could stall no longer, guide Amberwing to the cavern. One way or another, somebody or something would slay the dragon.

* * * * *

"So," said Dathred, pushing aside a low-hanging branch, "the princess slipped away from her minders, out of the castle, and down to the river, stole a boat, and rowed out into the center of the current. There, she summoned a water spirit—"

"Wait," said Amberwing. "The princess knew magic?"

"Yes."

"You should have mentioned it before. You don't know how to tell a story."

"I never claimed I did. Look, you've made it clear you don't care about humans. Why do you want to hear these old tales anyway?"

"To get a sense of things."

"I don't understand."

Amberwing spat a wisp of smoke. "How could you? Why don't you tell me a story from your own life. Maybe you can keep that straight."

"I've never done anything that would make a good yarn."

"You're brave, an able swordsman, and wield some sort of magic, too. I saw the glowing blade and shield you conjured to fend off the trolls. You could be a captain in a great host, or some lord's personal champion. How, then, did you wind up the protector of a small hamlet on the edge of the wild?"

"Well . . ." Dathred brushed a gnat away from his face. "When I was still a boy, I heard the call to become a champion of light and fight for what's worthy and true."

Amberwing cocked his serpentine head. "You mean, some knightly order announced it was seeking recruits?"

"No, nothing like that. I simply felt an urge. A need. So I pledged myself to the ideal and started learning the sword and lance. Much to the dismay of my parents, who wanted me to follow their path and become a merchant. In time, my champion abilities began to emerge, and when I was ready, I offered my services to the Lord Protector who ruled in those days." According to tidings that had only recently reached remote, isolated Rosehill, a Lady Protector had now succeeded him.

"Because your monarch was the paragon of everything 'worthy and true?'"

Dathred bristled at the irony in the dragon's tone. "The Lord Protector's rule was just and compassionate. My duties gave me plenty of opportunity to uphold the good."

"Peace, human. If you say it, I believe it. Go on with the tale."

"In time, a crazy magister named Cosinda led an uprising against the giants. Since only a few malcontents supported it, it had no chance of success, but it caused a lot of needless misery and destruction before we soldiers broke its back. Cosinda and her surviving followers fled north, and my comrades and I pursued. The rebels dispersed and, resolved to hunt down every last one of them, my company split up, too.

"The problem with a situation like that," Dathred continued, "is you can wind up chasing a band of fugitives as big or bigger than your own, and they can stop running and set a trap for you. That's what happened to my friends and me. We fought our way clear and even put the rebels to flight again, but not before I suffered an ugly wound." Beneath his brigandine and tunic, the long scar on his chest itched at the memory.

"Everyone assumed I'd die. Even if they'd believed otherwise, they could neither tarry with me nor carry me along with them. They had to keep chasing the enemy. So they left me at a nearby settlement."

"Rosehill," said Amberwing, "where you evidently recovered."

"Yes, thanks to the care the villagers gave me. It took months, though. Time enough for me to start feeling like a part of the place, and to observe how my new friends suffered when goblins and their ilk came raiding out of the wild. They fought back courageously, but none of them was a trained warrior. It struck me that even one such could make a difference in their lives."

"Thus you decided to stay."

"Yes. It felt right, just as it had once felt proper to offer my sword to the Diamond Throne. I asked permission to make a permanent home among them, and we broke bread together. That was their ritual to welcome and adopt me as one of their own." He shrugged. "I warned you it wasn't much of a story."

"No," said Amberwing, his tail dragging over a rotten log, "it's not. But it almost makes me envy you."

Dathred glanced quizzically at the reptile. "Are you mocking me?"

"No. Before, you wondered why dragons have returned to these lands."

"Yes. I'm still curious."

"Different wyrms have different reasons, I suppose. For my part . . . Well, dragons are magical creatures. Manifestations of the vitality of the land. We're meant to feel a bond with it, like the love you hold for your wretched village, perhaps, but stronger. We're supposed to be as one with fields and forest, water and sky."

"But you weren't?"

"No," Amberwing sighed, "never in two hundred years of life, and eventually, I imagined I'd inferred the reason. It was because I was living in the wrong place. My connection was to the homeland of my forebears. So naturally, when it became possible to return, I did."

"From your tone, it hasn't been what you expected."

"No. My ancestors claimed—and loved—this territory, but to me, it's just another patch of ground." The dragon hesitated. "Why do you think I slaughtered your animals? I'm disappointed. Bored. Frustrated."

It almost sounded like some veiled approximation of an apology. Dathred told himself the arrogant drake couldn't actually mean it as such. "I wish I knew the answer to your plight."

"But you did, or at least I hope so. Did you really think I'm making this journey just for treasure? Oh, I'll be happy to claim it, but the real point is to visit the actual lairs of my ancestors. Perhaps there, at long last, I can feel what they felt, and fill the hollow place inside me."

Dathred's jaw clenched. Amberwing's explanation made him feel even baser and more treacherous than before.

Curse it, he didn't want to feel sympathy for the dragon. He couldn't afford it, and neither could Rosehill. He'd delayed long enough. It was time to head straight for their destination.

* * * * *

The ground rose, and then they came to it: a great arched cavity in the hillside, with brush blurring the edges. The passage within descended into darkness.

Dathred pulled the torch from his knapsack, reached for his belt pouch to extract flint and steel, then jumped when Amberwing set the length of dry wood alight with a puff of flame. Had the dragon's aim been off by even a little, he might well have set his companion on fire also. Dathred glowered, and the wyrm replied with a grin of impish excitement and good humor.

They headed into the cavern. The torch hissed and crackled in the cool air. Shadow oozed at the edge of the wavering light.

Dathred's heart pounded, and his mouth was dry. Tangled emotions ground together in his head: shame, and resentment of Amberwing for compelling him to break his oath. An eager resolve to see his task completed, even if it was at the cost of his own life. And, of course, fear.

After a while, Amberwing said, "I see no sign that dragons ever laired here."

Dathred groped for a reassuring answer and couldn't think of anything at all, certainly nothing likely to stop the wyrm from turning back prematurely.

"But then, we might not, not after all this time, nor this close to the surface," Amberwing continued. "My kind don't like the entrances to our caves to look like anything out of the ordinary. We don't want foes and robbers knowing where we live."

He stalked onward. Dathred let out a sigh, then followed. A few minutes later, the darkness sprang to life around them.

Dathred had expected something to happen. The cavern was an entrance to the Dark Depths, domain of the abominable slassans and their slave creatures, and surely they kept it guarded. But even so, the sudden movement caught him by surprise. The subterranean dwellers must have used spells of concealment to creep so close undetected.

From the corner of his eye, he saw a shaft of violet light streaking at him. He wrenched himself to the side, and it missed by a finger length.

At the same time, a whole barrage of magical effects erupted, whining, sizzling, and banging through the air, filling it with flashes of colored light and vile stenches. Fortunately, though, the enemy had aimed the rest of its spells at Amberwing. For after all, a single human was a paltry threat compared to a dragon.

A splash of hissing acid blistered Amberwing's scales. An ear-splitting screech made him lash his sinuous neck like a whip. A bright, sparking form like a living lightning bolt sprang into the air, caught hold of his leathery wing, and tore at the folds of hide.

Amberwing roared and spat a gout of fire. Probably it incin-erated some of the hostile spellcasters. But plainly not all of them, for more magic battered him. Stones exploded from the floor to hammer his head and chest. A prodigious mass of ice abruptly congealed around his neck, shoulders, and forelegs, immobilizing him like a drunkard confined in the stocks.

Dathred cast away his torch. Underground dwellers could see in the dark, but even so, prey carrying a light was more likely to draw their attention. He turned and ran. Amberwing bellowed his name. Something twisted inside him, but he didn't break stride.

The slassans' slave warriors weren't all concentrating on the dragon. A pair of stunted, flat-faced goblins scuttled out of the dark to block Dathred's way. For an instant, he considered in-voking his champion's sword, but that would shed light, and he could only use this ability a few times each day. Instead, he yanked out his steel blade, parried a spear thrust, and cut into his attacker's neck. The sword stuck in the wound, and the second goblin lunged to spit him on its lance. He released the weapon's hilt, dodged and shifted forward simultaneously, and punched the creature in the mouth. Jagged fangs broke against his knuckles, and the goblin collapsed. He freed his sword and ran on.

* * * * *

Dathred watched the cave mouth to see if Amberwing would follow him back out. It wasn't impossible. Slassans were a byword for terror and power, but so were dragons.

Still, no one and nothing else emerged. Dathred tried again to dredge up the elation of victory. What came instead was an-other pang of self-loathing.

Which, in turn, made him angry. It was neither fair nor sensible that he should have to despise himself simply for doing his duty. Especially considering that now it truly was too late for second thoughts. Amberwing was already dead.

Or was he? Slassans were notorious mages and slave takers, and Amberwing was an arcane wonder the likes of which no one had seen for centuries. It seemed plausible the abominations had attempted to capture him alive, to study and exploit.

Dathred gave his head a shake, trying to break the chain of thoughts he didn't want to think. He resolved to get up and march away, put distance between himself and the cave, for surely this was a perilous place to linger after nightfall.

In the end, though, that wasn't what he did.

* * * * *

Dathred would be helpless without light, yet had no hope of making a stealthy advance with any sort of illumination shining in his vicinity. Accordingly, he skulked back into the cave, groped his way through the blackness for as long as he dared, then summoned another hovering ball of phosphorescence.

From that point onward, he shuffled and staggered, whimpering occasionally, even falling a time or two. He was trying to look like a man so sorely wounded he could barely cling to consciousness, so addled he didn't even know how to find his way back to the mouth of the tunnel. Maybe the rents the trolls had clawed in his brigandine would foster the illusion.

As he'd expected, he didn't see the four goblin sentries until they scrambled from their hiding places to accost him.

When he and Amberwing had reached this point before, the guards had obviously scurried deeper into the cavern to warn their masters, who had then arranged an ambush capable of overwhelming even a dragon. But Dathred was no drake, just a lone and seemingly crippled human. The goblins were confident they could cope with him by themselves, and that way, they wouldn't have to share any plunder, or the meat they'd strip from his bones.

Hooting and jeering, they spread out to flank him as they advanced. That was a potential problem, but he had to allow it if he was to lure them in close before abandoning his pretense of helplessness. He stood swaying and moaning until the goblins were almost near enough to strike, then whipped out his sword. It was the steel blade once again. The sword of light only lasted a few minutes before dissolving, and in all likelihood, he'd face more formidable foes later on. He sprang and cut.

The first of his enemies dropped with a split skull. He pivoted, parried a slash from a scimitar, and hacked open his attacker's belly. Sensing danger at his back, he knew he had no time to whirl and defend. Instead, he leaped forward, nearly flinging himself onto a spear point but managing to stop short.

The goblin with the lance tried to drive it on into his chest. Dathred knocked the weapon out of line and cut into the creature's torso, parry and riposte a single arc of motion, then spun back around to face the warrior behind him.

The goblin's eyes widened in dismay as it realized it was the only one still on its feet. As it started to back away, Dathred charged it, and it swept its scimitar in a horizontal stop cut. The champion beat the curved blade with his own and knocked it out of his adversary's grip. He pulped the goblin's nose with the heavy brass pommel of his sword, then booted its legs out from under it, dropping it to the ground. Panting, he threatened it with his point. Supine and disarmed, the creature cowered.

"Answer my questions," Dathred said in the subterranean tongue called Undercommon, learned during his service to the Lord Protector, "and I'll let you live."

"Yes," his prisoner moaned. "Anything. I tell."

"Did you and your comrades capture the dragon alive?"

"Yes."

"Where is he now? A slassan city?"

"No. City's miles away. Couldn't drag anything so big that far. Dragon's still at outpost."

"Outpost?"

"Camp. Place where we guard the path up to the forest."

Dathred frowned, pondering, then asked, "Do your masters keep human slaves there?"

"Just a couple," the goblin said. "Humans are too much bother. Can't work without a torch or lamp."

"But there are a few?"

"Yes."

"Go. Up to the Harrowdeep, and don't come back. Even if I don't kill you, your masters surely will, for failing to slay or capture me and for giving away their secrets."

The goblin fled. Dathred watched it for a moment, then turned to inspect one of its fallen comrades, a creature mewling and shuddering in agony. He ended its suffering, then appropriated its helmet with the distinctive scalloped crest and dark cloak embroidered with a pair of pale, twisted glyphs.

A goblin was smaller than any full-grown man. But at least Dathred was short, and he doubted the slassans took any great pains to outfit their slaves in garments that fit properly. If he was lucky, the creature's trappings might just serve to disguise him. He jammed the helmet on his own head, wrapped himself in the cape, and trudged onward.

The slassans had established their outpost at a point where the passage expanded into a complex of interconnecting chambers and side galleries. Smoke from cook fires scented the air. Bedrolls lay on the ground, and hammocks hung between stalagmites.

To Dathred's surprise, a celebration of sorts was underway. Goblins, trolls, and other slaves chattered, laughed, and sang, tore at hunks of roasted meat, enormous mushrooms, and slabs of fungus, and swilled raw spirit from bowls. Evidently their masters had opted to reward them for their part in Amber-wing's capture.

The commotion made it relatively easy to pass unnoticed. The creatures were too intent on their pleasure to pay Dathred any mind. He skulked along peering into the various chambers, looking for the dragon.

He didn't see him. But eventually he did spot a sentry—a rhodin with curling horns, caprine head, and hairy, manlike body—guarding the arched opening at the end of a passage long enough and high enough to accommodate a wyrm.

Dathred ambled toward the creature. It glared and bared jagged teeth. Perhaps having to stand watch while the other thralls enjoyed themselves had put it in a foul humor. "Clear off," it snarled.

Dathred tried a friendly smile. "I just want—"

"To peek and poke at it, like everybody else. Well, you can't. The masters say nobody goes in."

"What if I bring you a drink, and food from the feast? It's not fair, everybody else stuffing themselves while you go without."

The rhodin hesitated, then shook its head. "If the masters catch you inside, they'll make us both drink acid."

"Oh, come on. They wouldn't be as angry as all that . . ." As Dathred nattered on, he eased his hand toward the hilt of his sword, gripped it, yanked out the blade, and thrust it into the rhodin's breast.

The creature died instantly. Dathred caught the corpse as its knees began to buckle and heaved it through the opening into the next vault, where nobody in the central chamber could see it.

But had anyone seen him kill the rhodin? Heart hammering, he peered back the way he'd come. Everyone was drinking and gorging, the same as before, which meant he was all right so far. He'd just have to hope nobody would notice—or, failing that, care—that the guard was no longer at his post.

Dathred slipped warily into the next cave. It was another large chamber with a high ceiling, spacious enough for Amberwing to lay with tail, neck, and wings stretched to full length on the limestone floor.

The dragon shook and jerked, and Dathred could make out at least two causes for his distress. Several plump, pale, grublike things, each a yard long, clung to Amberwing, nuzzling at him, apparently either eating his flesh or drinking his blood. Moreover, the wyrm's captors had pressed his limbs down onto sharp stalagmites, then used magic to swell the points of the rocky spikes into bulbs, effectively nailing the colossal reptile to the floor.

"Amberwing!" Dathred said, keeping his voice low. The drake didn't answer. Evidently enchantment or simple agony had plunged him into delirium.

Perhaps if Dathred freed him from his torments, his wits would return. He reckoned now was the time for the sword of light. He called for it, and it shimmered into existence. While it endured, it could cut virtually anything, even rock.

He moved to the length of bloody limestone impaling Amberwing's right forefoot. One of the huge grubs clung farther up the leg, and when he lifted his sword to chop the stalagmite, it abruptly reared, exposing a ring of gory lamprey teeth, and struck, the violence of the action hurling it through the air like an arrow.

The worm's leap caught Dathred by surprise, and he barely managed to twist aside in time. It smacked onto the floor beside him and instantly lifted its eyeless head for another attack. He hacked completely through its boneless softness, splitting it in two just beneath the circular maw. The body collapsed and flopped.

He turned. The other grubs were crawling toward him, might all be on top of him already if they hadn't needed to clamber over the immense contours of Amberwing's body to reach him.

Dathred summoned his shield of light, then darted back and forth, obliging them to change course repeatedly, denying them the chance to converge on him and attack all at once. They made that final explosive spring one at a time, and he killed them that way, until none remained.

He started breaking Amberwing's restraints, freeing his forefoot. The dragon didn't stir. "Come on," Dathred pleaded, "wake up. I killed the worm-things. I'm cutting you loose. But I can't carry you out of here, and we're running out of time. Nobody was in here with you when I arrived, but that luck can't hold—"

Then, as if his own words had summoned it into being, he sensed a presence behind him. He spun around.

Considerably larger than a man, the slassan scuttled on eight segmented legs and possessed a bulbous, spidery body armored in dark chitin. Its long neck, however, was serpentine, and its head a hideous fusion of reptile and human.

Dathred called on the power of the light once more, heightening his strength and vitality, and charged. He wanted to close before the slassan started using its magic to tear him apart at range.

He didn't quite make it. Baring its scores of needle fangs, the slassan glared at him, and pain exploded inside his skull. He stumbled, nearly collapsed, forced himself onward. He cut, and the sword of light slashed a rent in the creature's torso.

It screeched, struck like an adder, raked at him with the barbs on its two front legs. Its teeth and claws alike glistened with venom. Dathred's shield rang as he blocked the blows. The impacts knocked him reeling backward.

Having opened up the distance once again, the slassan used more of its magic. Force flared from its bulbous eyes, and, partway to the target, became hurtling grit, as blinding and choking as the fiercest sandstorm. Dathred twisted away and cowered behind his shield as best he could, but the stuff battered and scraped him even so.

The slassan charged and nearly trampled him and shredded him with its talons before he came back on guard. He cut it across the chest, but again, not deeply enough to stop it. The creature's carapace absorbed the force of his strokes.

The slassan struck. He lifted the shield an instant too late. The abomination's fangs stabbed into his shoulder. At once a wave of weakness and numbness flowed from the wound through the rest of his body.

The slassan lifted its claws to finish the spastic human half dangling from its jaws. Dathred struggled to draw breath enough to bellow a battle cry, another technique for channeling the power of the light. Rather to his own amazement, the shout boomed from his lips, and its virtue cleansed the venom from his veins. He flung himself backward, jerking clear of the slassan's fangs.

So the fight would continue. But only, he suspected, for a little longer. Because he was overmatched, and, though no longer poisoned, the wound in his shoulder throbbed and bled profusely. Despite the supernatural augmentation to his strength, it was difficult to hold up the shield.

Then, conscious once more, Amberwing roared and writhed. Perhaps the war cry had roused him. Alas, it wouldn't matter. The stalagmite nails still held him at too many points along his body. If only Dathred had managed to destroy a few more!

But he hadn't, and now must simply acquit himself as best he could for however many heartbeats he had left. The slassan took a retreat, and he scrambled after it. Straight into the spider web of blue light that sprang into existence around him.

The glowing strands felt solid as the stoutest rope and sticky as glue. Dathred strained but couldn't break free or bring his sword to bear to slice the cords. The slassan laughed and lifted a barbed claw.

At which point Amberwing heaved up from the floor. Unable to work his limbs off the stalagmites with any care or finesse, he'd simply ripped free all at once, tearing open his wounds in the process.

The pain must have been ghastly, but it didn't slow him. He sprang across the cavern and bore the slassan down beneath him. Talons slashing, jaws snapping, he tore the abomination apart.

Once it was dead, the dragon turned, regarded Dathred for a moment, then spoke a word of power. Hissing, the web dissolved.

Something scuttled. Dathred and Amberwing looked around. Another pair of slassans had entered the chamber. The wyrm spat flame at them, but the flare fell short, and they scurried out of view.

"We'll have to fight them all, slassans and slaves alike, to get out of here," Dathred gasped.

"Good," said Amberwing.

"Are you sure about that?" The drake bore dozens of bloody injuries, from his torture and the ambush that proceeded it.

"Entirely sure. They took me by surprise before. It kept me from using my own sorcery. This time they'll see what a dragon can actually do." Amberwing snarled an incantation. A mass of roaring flame sprang up in the chamber entrance, then surged after the fleeing slassans and toward the central cavern like a wave racing for the shore. Screams echoed down the passage.

"Fair enough," said Dathred, hefting his sword. "They'll try to get around behind you. I'll guard your back."

* * * * *

A few stars shone through the thick foliage overhead. Dathred took a moment to look at them and wondered if it was for the final time.

If so, he deserved to die. He'd failed the village. Betrayed it, even. Betrayed everyone and everything before he was done.

"Now," Amberwing growled, smelling of flame and blood as well as his normal dry reptilian scent, "we finally have time to talk. My kind never laired in those caves, did they?"

"No," Dathred said. "That was just a lie to draw you away from the settlement. To give a company of soldiers time to arrive and prepare to fight you, and, if possible, to lead you into harm's way."

"As you did. But then you came back to rescue me. Why?"

"I wish I knew. Because I vowed to guide you truly, perhaps, or because you saved my life. Please, since I did return for you, grant me one favor. Take your revenge on me alone. Leave Rosehill out of it. My friends had no idea what I intended."

Amberwing sighed. "I did promise myself I'd kill you, once we escaped the caves. But I seem to have expended all my anger on the slassans."

"That's . . . more generous than I could have expected."

The dragon shifted his wings in a shrug. "I enjoyed our time traveling together. Listening to your tales and lore, I sometimes felt easier in my skin, as if I actually was starting to become a part of this land." He grunted. "It was just yearning playing tricks in my head, I suppose."

Dathred frowned as a thought struck him. "You know, I wonder."

Amberwing cocked his head. "What do you mean?"

"When humans feel at home in a place, it may be partly because they fancy the particular blue of the sky or green of the meadows, but mainly, it's because of community. Ties of affection and loyalty to their neighbors. Maybe a dose of that is what you need to anchor you to the country hereabouts."

"Well . . . perhaps." The reptile scowled. "If I hadn't already made myself a pest. A hardship. A menace."

"If it's true every drake keeps treasure stashed away somewhere, you could make restitution for the damage you did, and pledge not to cause any more. In which case, I'd speak for you." Dathred grinned, his heart suddenly light and full of hope. "Even after such a rocky start, I think I could persuade people of the advantages of having a dragon around. You'd certainly give the raiders something to think about, the next time they appear."

Amberwing peered at the man, almost as if he suspected a joke at his expense, then bared his rows of immense ivory fangs in a smile. "If you're serious, I'd like a chance to know your folk, and see if it changes the way I feel. In fact, I'd like it very much."

"Well, I told you we villagers have a welcoming ceremony. Let's see if I have any bread left in my knapsack."

THE SAND VEILS

By midday, the scimitar curve of the horizon was a breath-taking orange, the tint of exotic fruit and jungle flowers. By dusk's approach, the orange stretched high and wide along the bridge of sky spanning the north and south. And it sparkled like starlight. Truly the desert was beautiful . . .

. . . for those unfamiliar with its dangers.

Evening came, and with it, the sandstorm's opening yawn overtook the desert, blinding travelers caught in the open plains. A few hours later, the storm raged full pitch, the strongest winds carrying tiny darts of rough crystals in their fists. Anyone unprepared for this moment was dead, his exposed skin flayed and his mouth crusted with blood from each lungful drawn from the razor air.

* * * * *

Mradin moved quickly through the soft valleys between towering dunes, pressed on by urgent matters. The storm raged about him, curling sand from the tops of banks and covering him under more dust, but it was of trivial concern. He was well protected from the biting winds, a heavy brown cloak upon his thin shoulders and an eyeless mask of camel bone shielding his face. It was a trick of the verrik bedu who often navigated such blinding storms through their active senses and a keen understanding of their lands.

Beyond wearing their clothing, Mradin acted with the skill of the bedu; a long staff to probe the ground for sinkholes, the ornamental mask protecting his face, and his unerring sense of direction steered him through dune valleys as though they were marked by road signs.

A flutter in the wind caught Mradin's attention. He stopped, listening for the rustling fabric. He heard it again and moved more quickly toward the noise, stumbling on fatigue-numbed legs. He was almost upon the village, with its tents and animal-hide lodge. It was a hundred feet away, he knew, but something behind him snarled, a deep, sinister growl. It was about forty feet to his back and running fast. Mradin sprinted for the safety of the village. . . .

* * * * *

The lodge was well insulated against the sands, but a prevailing dust haze still found its way inside. The black-robed bedu slept together tonight, their snores whispers against the roaring winds outside. Along each tent wall sat two bedu, men and women with closed eyes, their skin the hue of redberry stains, their legs folded beneath them. They listened to the wind, seemingly lost to the trance of their vigil.

Outside, a howl was cut short. One of the guards, her eyes still closed, snapped her fingers lightly. The other guards were on their feet, by the sentry's side, listening to the winds, curved sabers in their grip. Their eyes remained closed; no need to open them when there was nothing to see. Instead they listened

intently and heard more snarls. Five of the bedu warriors
moved to the entrance flap, nimbly stepping in the empty
spaces between the sleeping bodies with practiced familiarity.
They stepped out into the storm, affixing plate-masks of bone
or toughened palm-hide to their faces.

The winds inflicted the occasional gash to exposed flesh and
thin fabric from large, storm-propelled crystals, delivering
death by a thousand cuts to those who remained in the storm
long enough. The bedu intended to be quick, however. They
navigated their way to the noise, catching the snarls and grunts
that were not swept away. Only when they arrived, mere yards
from the skirmish, did they open their eyes and lift their masks,
the wind pushing at their backs.

The stranger dressed like a bedu, but wore fabrics and
pouches of strange materials. In his grip, a sword made of lightning and crackling flame danced with the flick of his wrist and
elbow. His movements were economical, never more than they
needed to be, and his steps were light. Not once did he remove
his mask to see. He fought blind.

The three beasts darting around the stranger were likewise
exotic. The bedu had never seen anything like them. They were
like boars, with long lizard snouts, two tusks that curled up
from their lower jaws, tails much like spiked chains, and manes
of thick bristles. Despite their mass, they were nimble and
smart—using one another to feint and trick their quarry. The
stranger, however, seemed to anticipate their darting movements, attacking where they would be, moving from where
they would strike.

One of the bedu held out her hand and the others stepped
back. This was not their fight. They would not interfere with
the outcome.

The stranger cut one beast, cleaving its flank open, but
earned its claws across his arm. He knew the blow was coming,
but it was necessary to draw blood for blood. He decapitated

the second beast with little effort, the sword stroke clean and sharp, but the third creature was upon his back, scrabbling with its claws for lethal purchase, forcing him down into the sand. The blade disappeared from the stranger's grip, evaporating on the wind. The female bedu waited for the creature to bite its prey's neck, to snap the spine or tear out his throat. It was the way of all desert cats.

Instead, the beast opened its mouth and screamed. Pain, like ice-cold daggers, stabbed through the skulls of everyone present. They staggered about, the mental wail an anguish unlike any they'd ever felt. The stranger, while afflicted, up-ended the animal and rolled atop it, a fiery dagger manifest-ing in his hand. The stranger struck down, pushing the blade into the beast's chest with both hands before the blade van-ished.

The bedu regained their footing in time to see the stranger fall to the ground, unconscious and wounded.

* * * * *

Mradin awoke, sensing someone about to lift his mask. His hands shot out and grabbed a pair of wrists. That was met with its own response . . . two blades drawn and brought to either side of his exposed throat. He didn't let go, however.

"You fought well," a woman said, likely the one whose wrists Mradin held. "It'd be a pity to see you die so carelessly. You're the guest of the Bnahzra. By the Codes of the Vrmassat, I wel-come you. Does that make you feel better?"

Mradin hesitated, his senses growing stronger. He smelled the hannyha that spiced last night's meal. He heard the un-quenched storm and, beneath that, the quiet breath of many. A window opened in his mind, forming shapes like dust motes caught in a beam of light. He saw the people around him . . . recognized them. They knew him in return, and touched his face. He was safe for now.

Once Mradin released the woman's wrists, the two blades lifted from their perch on his collarbone.

"Thank you for your offer," Mradin said, lifting his mask, "but I cannot accept." As he suspected, he was inside the communal lodge on a wood cot, surrounded by familiar faces. "This place is already home."

The elderly woman sitting at his side touched his face. Her name was Aujmana, and her hair was black, like ravens' feathers, though Mradin didn't remember her having so many streaks of blue; she was certainly older. Her burgundy skin was dark, her eyes two stones surrounded by a ripple of wrinkles on her face.

"Mradin?" Aujmana asked, caressing his cheek with the back of her hand.

Mradin offered a weak smile in response, then tumbled back into the whirlpool of darkness, his strength spent. He blacked out, the name *Trylith* on his breath.

* * * * *

Cool water touched his lips and dribbled down his parched throat. Mradin awoke, guzzling and choking at once.

"Easy," Aujmana said, seated by his side. She put the water bowl at her feet.

The other bedu gathered nearby, watching. Some struggled to remember him, but Mradin knew it would be difficult. He had aged some, certainly, but he looked different as well, his sanguine face cut in marble and dappled like a butterfly's wings with equal patterns of light red splotches and white freckles.

"Hello, aunt," Mradin said.

"You've changed," Aujmana replied, studying him carefully. She glanced to a stooped woman whose age outstripped her own by decades. Her name was Vrkassna, the tribal akashic.

"As have things here," Mradin said, ignoring the way Vrkassna studied his markings. "Where's your husband?"

"Knassro died four summers ago. I lead now."

163

"You're better off without him," Mradin said, hoisting himself up on his elbows with a grunt. Pain shot through his body, his muscles cramping. He ignored it, though his face told the truth in its knots and scowls.

"So I've been told. What are these markings?" she asked, tracing the contours of his blemishes with her fingers.

"A story for later," he said.

"And those beasts you fought?"

"They don't concern you. I dispensed with them. They no longer matter."

"Mradin," Aujmana said, withdrawing her touch and leveling an even stare. "Are you here as a member of the Bnahzra, or as my guest?"

Mradin hesitated and followed the argument through its natural course. As a guest, he would be well treated, but kept at arm's length as an outsider. When he felt better, the bedu would send him on his way. As a member of the tribe, however, he belonged to a family that respected and followed Aujmana's leadership.

There was a third option that proved more appealing. He could challenge Aujmana for tribal leadership. *Why not*, he thought. *I am far superior to her. In fact, she should beg me to assume leadership. She is old, and they would be lucky to have me!*

Horrified, Mradin quickly swallowed those last thoughts. They were unworthy of him and of what this tribe once meant to him.

"I am part of the tribe," Mradin said, struggling hard with that allowance. "And the beasts that attacked me do concern you and everyone here for as long as I remain."

"What are they?"

"Drakyn-hounds. They were sent to kill me."

"Kill you? What did you do?"

"Why do you assume the fault is mine?"

"I did not lay blame, Mradin. But someone chases you. Therefore you must have done something, whether it was for the right or the wrong reasons."

"I—am indentured to someone. His name is Kyrophage. I escaped his service."

Aujmana raised a thin eyebrow. "You broke your word to this Kyrophage?"

"Yes, but the terms of my service were unfair."

"Did you understand those terms before entering into them?"

Mradin thought about lying, but he he'd taken too long to answer by a heartbeat. Anything he said now was suspect.

"Yes. I understood them."

"Then I am disappointed. You were either foolish for entering into this bargain, or untrustworthy for escaping your obligation. Either way, you were shortsighted."

"Aunt, I—"

"Enough for tonight," Aujmana said, standing up. "Rest. We have a long day tomorrow."

"Aunt, wait," Mradin said, his vision swooning under his hurting head. "What of Trylith?"

"She suffers the Curse."

"May I see her?"

"Tomorrow. Your sister needs her rest."

Mradin didn't argue. His head grew heavy and he fell back into his cot. His vision wavered, but his faculties remained sharp enough. He closed his eyes, aware that Vrkassna studied him carefully. Now that he had failed to satisfy their curiosity, they would send Vrkassna. As tribal akashic, she could tap into the collective memories and emotions of anyone living or once alive. Likely, she would also invade his thoughts.

But he would be ready.

* * * * *

The beast was in pain, the sharp, harrowing ache from his bandaged flanks searing him awake. His forked tongue flicked out, dancing across his tusks before tasting the air. The acrid tang of incense and burning dung greeted his tongue, while outside the small tent, the winds howled their chorus. The beast peered around his sanctuary, his vision adjusting to the frail lamp light, but hurting still from the storm. A woman sat watching him in the dark corner of the tent. He tried moving, to see her better, but the pain was too great. He collapsed again, gasping in heavy, shallow breaths.

"Don't move. You'll reopen that wound," the woman said. "It's only been a couple of days."

"You share words with I?" the beast asked, struggling through the Common tongue. Speaking scratched his throat like grating sand; it felt alien to him.

"Yes," the woman replied. "You may not remember, but you asked for mercy when I found you. I was curious why a beast was capable of speech."

"I evolved!" he said proudly.

She moved closer to check his bandages. He craned his neck to see her face, but she pushed his head back down, mindful of his sharp bristles.

"You not fear I teeth?" he asked.

"You're too wounded to move, much less kill me and escape this storm."

The beast grunted. "Yes. Newborn weak. But I not spill blood," he said with a growl. It was hard not to slip into snarls and hisses; she wouldn't understand his words or intentions if he did. "I repay your mercy."

"Are you so sure it's mercy?" she asked.

"No."

"What are you called?" she asked.

"Skaraph."

"Skaraph," she repeated. "You're a drakyn-hound, yes?"

"You know I people's name?" Skaraph asked.

"Through the man you fought."

"Mradin here?" Skaraph asked, trying to rise to his feet. He fell instead.

The woman kept her hand on his flank, steadying him.
"Why are you after him?"

"My master, Kyrophage, want him."

"For breaking his covenant with your master?"

"Yes."

"Does he want Mradin dead?"

"No. Return honor to broken handshake."

"To honor his word. I see. And do you know the terms of
that agreement? What kind of man is Kyrophage?"

"No man," Skaraph said, almost reverently. "Kyrophage
walks not upon two legs."

"Tell me more," the woman said.

* * * * *

Mradin waited at the bottom of the wide marble stairs.
Behind him, a building loomed, tall and impressive with its
spiral quartz columns and walls of engraved onyx. It was the
sole feature in a blasted, devastated landscape of burnt brush
and sand-melted glass. A woman appeared, frail by age, but not
broken by it.

"Hello, Vrkassna," Mradin said to the akashic. "Come to
probe my memories, have you?"

Vrkassna looked around, awed by this place. It was obvious
she'd never seen its like. Mradin smiled and waited.

"Where are we?" she asked.

"It is my domain," Mradin said. "And you can't imagine the
worlds I hold within my mind now. Imagine… each thought a
kingdom. Each memory a new realm to explore."

"How?" she asked.

"Your akashic abilities are an echo of what we once possessed
as a race."

"Your markings," she said, nodding to his face. "My memories speak of our forebearers as Sanguine Butterflies. Are you
Vnaxian?"

"If you wish to ask me such questions, do so in the flesh. You are unwelcome in my thoughts, Vrkassna. Leave!" Mradin said. He dismissed her with one hand, a gesture that discorporated her body into a wash of sand.

* * * * *

"What have you done?" Aujmana screamed. She was on the lodge floor of hardened dirt and dark rugs, holding the vacant-eyed Vrkassna in her arms. The other bedu clustered around the pair, uncertain, except for four bedu with scimitars drawn and pointed at Mradin. He ignored them, instead exploring his thoughts for some recourse. In his mind, he saw arguments and a blade fight that ended badly for him. In all of them, however, a young girl in the crowd stepped forth in his defense.

"She'll recover momentarily," Mradin said, "and before you blame me, I suggest you question your own actions first. Did you not instruct her to search my memories?"

"We doubted your words."

"You know little about me, now, yet you know enough to call me a liar? Fine, then. As your guest, I'll depart."

Mradin extended his hand to the young girl in the crowd, the one from his visions. She was in her late teens, with dark-wine skin and short white hair. Her left eye had calcified into crystal, and her left arm and leg were likewise riddled with exposed bone spurs of quartz and torqued flesh. Soon, Mradin realized, the Curse would completely transform her into crystal. All verrik suffered the affliction, but for most, it only manifested as an unease that other races felt around their kind. For others, their bodies grew twisted in reflection of their psychological quirks. A rare and terrible few, however—like this young woman—would crystallize. It was more prevalent within the Bnahzra tribe. Soon they would take the girl's inert body to the verrik capital city of Yrterot, where she'd serve as a living memory stone for the akashics.

"Come, Trylith," Mradin said. "We're leaving."

"No, brother," Trylith said, stepping forward. "I'm staying."

There was no pretense to their conversation, no happy embraces. He'd promised to return, and he did. "I came for you," Mradin said, moving to meet her. Two bedu interceded, stepping in his path with drawn blades.

"As simple as that?" Trylith asked. "You give me no say in my own future?"

"Your destiny, as it stands, provides nothing you could want," Mradin said. "But I offer you something better. If you come with me."

Trylith hobbled past the guards, her movements slow and pained. The crystal growth had overtaken her joints, Mradin realized, calcifying them and inhibiting her movement. Her left foot and shin were fully crystallized, the Curse further along than he expected.

"Vrkassna?" Trylith asked, shuffling up to Aujmana.

The old akashic blinked, then stared at Mradin, her eyes widening. She muttered and clawed at Aujmana's lapel. "Vnaxian," she said. "He's Vnaxian."

* * * * *

Vnaxians. The verrik's ancestors who, evolved in the mental disciplines, eventually eschewed their flesh in favor of existing as pure thought. Vnaxians. The last of their kind to remain physical was Xyphon, who ruled the verrik, then cursed them when they cast him out. . . .

Mradin paced inside the lodge under the watchful eyes of five bedu guards. The tribe was outside, tending to flocks and repairing the storm's damage. The tribal mothers, however, conferred elsewhere, debating Vrkassna's claims.

This is ludicrous, Mradin thought; he'd even told them so earlier: *I am no more Vnaxian than you are litorian, old woman.*

Mradin regretted his sharp tongue and the tone of his voice. That sounded far more pointed than he had intended, but it was hard to control his temper. The others, including his sister, had stared at him in shock. Aujmana, however, looked ready to gut him.

Mradin sat down on his cot and rubbed his head, sulking. *I'm sorry,* he remembered saying. *My temper frequently escapes me.*

But the damage was done.

The tent flap lifted and Aujmana returned, helping Trylith back inside. Aujmana was angry, but Trylith spoke to avert a confrontation.

"If you're not Vnaxian, as you claim," Trylith said, "what are you?"

"Elevated," he said. "I'm stronger, and my mental disciplines are unrivaled by any other verrik." Again he cringed at his own words; it was so easy to treat others as insignificant.

"Yes, you have changed," Trylith said, "but not for the better. You barely control your anger, and your words are beneath you."

"The metamorphosis hasn't been easy."

"Was that the bargain?" Trylith asked. "The service you struck with Kyrophage?"

"Yes," Mradin said, lowering his head.

"Explain," Aujmana said, "before your tongue gets the better of you again and I lose my patience. Who is Kyrophage?"

Mradin sighed. "A dragon. Kyrophage is a dragon."

* * * * *

"He elevated your species?" the woman asked.

Skaraph acknowledged with a grunt. He still had difficulty seeing, but his strength was returning quickly.

"How?"

"Tenebrian seeds. Kyrophage masters them. Turned I people away from cave floors and gave us words," Skaraph said proudly. "Us no longer beasts. Us evolved. Us serve Kyrophage in thanks."

"And Mradin?"

"Mradin shatter word. Mradin betray oath to serve with honor. Not like I."

"And what service was demanded of him?"

"Matter not. Him bound to Kyrophage by oath."

"Did Kyrophage abuse him?"

"No!" Skaraph growled. "Kyrophage raise only voice in anger, never claw. Us precious to Kyrophage. Us children."

"All of you?"

"All who him touch with seeds." With that, Skaraph raised himself to his feet, and stood on steady legs. He paced around the tent, testing and stretching his limbs.

"You've healed quickly," the woman said, surprised.

"Blessing of master. Gift from seed. You still unafraid."

"Yes," the woman said. "You promised me mercy. I believe you."

"Good," Skaraph said with a barking laugh. "You honor I with trust. I leave now, with thanks."

"Can you let Mradin be?"

"No. I oath bound or I become the thing I hunt."

"I understand. Mradin was wrong to break his oath. But allow us two days, please."

Skaraph considered the matter a moment. "Two days. Yes. After, I return."

"Before you leave . . . did Kyrophage elevate Mradin with the tenebrian seeds?"

"Yes. Do you wish the same?"

"That depends. What did Mradin become?"

* * * * *

"I've become perfect," Mradin said, savoring those words. The tribe had returned, so that they too could hear his tale. Mradin's chest swelled when he spoke of his own glory. He couldn't help it.

"Perfection is fallacy," an old bedu said, his body gnarled by age and his flesh twisted with the spiral knots of the Curse.

"Perhaps, but I, too, suffered from the full blossom of Xyphon's Curse. My innards slowly turned to crystal, my very bones stabbing me as they grew rampant like a thicket of thorns. I even sought the path of the crystal warrior, to master their skills, but their crystal weaving abilities could not save me."

"You're free of the Curse?" a young bedu with stringy black hair asked, a thousand doubts in his gaze.

"Yes," Mradin admitted. "But I'm not Vnaxian."

"Do you know how to perform this ritual?" a bedu shepherd asked, stepping forward eagerly.

"No," Mradin said. "It is not within my power to perform it."

"But you said you could save me from the Curse of Xyphon?" Trylith said.

"I know who to approach. He'll perform it."

"For all of us?" Aujmana asked, her question acrimonious enough that she already suspected the answer.

"All of you? My only concern is my sister. What happens to you . . . ." he said with a shrug.

"We all suffer from the Curse," a middle-aged mother cried.

"No," Mradin said, "you suffer from fear of the Curse. What you have is trivial . . . a dispassionate sense of things, an unease that others feels in your presence. So what? Few here will endure it as my sister and I have. Most of you will never know its fullest touch. Am I supposed to grieve over that blessing?"

"Mradin, please," Trylith said. "We're all family. You do for all, or you do for none. I cannot accept your offer otherwise."

Mradin shook his head. It would've been easier stealing her in the night as he'd planned a few evenings ago. To save her and her alone was an acceptable sacrifice. But for everyone to receive the blessing of the tenebrian seeds grated on him in rough strokes.

Why do they deserve such gifts? They did not earn this!

The thought struck Mradin with thunderous volume. He wasn't perfect; it was just the lie he spoke in moments of arrogance. He was still cursed, his affliction transformed, but . . . but at least he could endure this new burden. It wouldn't alienate him, or twist his flesh, or slowly calcify him till he was nothing but a resonating stone for the akashics.

"The transformation carries its own price," Mradin said.

"I thought you were perfect?" Aujmana asked, a sneer on her lips. "Or is this a desperate lie to keep the power for yourself?"

"The tenebrian evolution carries a darkness, yes, but it is a far cry from what the Curse of Xyphon offers its most damned."

"And what is this darkness?" Trylith asked.

"You've seen its touch upon me already," Mradin said, barely maintaining his patience. "You remarked on my temper? My intolerant and harsh manner? The tenebrian seeds instill a measure of arrogance, impatience . . . anger, even. It makes it far easier for me to discount you as inferior. And you haven't seen its full extent. But, I will spare you my fury. Just know that my patience, my measure of compassion, wilts like a rose in the open desert."

"I would take that chance to be free of the Curse," the old bedu with twisted skin said.

"As would I," others said, adding to the chorus.

Mradin shook his head. "I thought the same as all of you, at first, but I was wrong. I didn't realize how difficult that struggle would become. I was a fool, and Kyrophage encouraged this well of darkness now consuming me. I fight it in my every word, in my every action!"

"And yet you wish that for me?" Trylith asked.

"It pales to the agony awaiting you. But not to the benign Curse most verrik endure."

"I cannot accept Mradin's gift," Aujmana said.

"You are wise, aunt."

"Don't presume you understand my reasons, nephew!" Aujmana snapped. She studied the other bedu. "Have you forgotten that he is hunted? That he has stolen his new life from his benefactor?"

"Kyrophage wanted me to kill and steal for him, like a common cutthroat."

"But you knew this going into the bargain, didn't you?" Aujmana asked.

"Yes, but—"

"Did Kyrophage warn you about this tenebrian curse?" Trylith asked.

Mradin shook his head. He wouldn't lie to his sister. "Yes."

"And he told you about the terms of your service? As assassin and thief?" Trylith said, pressing forward.

Mradin didn't answer. He remained quiet and let the silence speak for him.

"Then you knew," Aujmana said. "Going into the bargain, you were already planning to break your covenant. You had no intention of carrying through with your contract."

"No." Mradin said, drawing to full stature, his chest jutting out with a monarch's bearing, his head raised in imperious fashion. "I had no intention of fulfilling my part of the bargain. At first I felt guilty for my deceit, but I knew that if I was suffering, then so was Trylith. And after becoming elevated, those feelings of guilt vanished. I now possess clarity. I did what was right for me and her."

"And was the cost worth it?" Trylith asked, her comment one of pity.

Mradin, however, would not be deterred. "As an akashic, each tattered, dusty memory I once scrounged for is now a kingdom that I can explore for years," he said tapping his head. "The knowledge I draw upon is unrivaled, forgotten by all but the most ancient of creatures. And the treasures I've found . . . my Flamebolt sword and dagger discovered in a forgotten crypt that only I remember. I once respected Vrkassna's abilities to draw memories from the great oceans of time. But now, I know

she's nothing more than a small child stirring the shore waters
with a twig!"

"At least she's not drowning as you are, sweet brother."

"Sharks never drown in the sea, sweet sister."

"Enough!' Aujmana said. "Mradin, you are no longer welcome among the Bnahzra. Leave us immediately and never
return, upon punishment of—"

"Spare me, old woman," Mradin said. "My only concern is
my sister. Trylith, come!"

Several bedu drew their blades, ready to attack Mradin for
his insults. He in turn opened his hand; a wickedly curved
scimitar of fire and lightning leapt forth from the bone ring on
his middle finger. Trylith nearly stumbled, interposing herself
between the tribe and her brother.

"No!" she shouted. "No blood will be spilled on my account!"

Nobody moved, no blade was sheathed. Desperate, Trylith
turned to her brother, her expression one of profound sadness.
"Brother, leave," she said.

"Not without you."

"I won't go. Aujmana's right. I will not contribute to your
shame by sharing your theft."

"No, no," Mradin said. "I know of another dragon who can
perform the ritual. A rival to Kyrophage."

"Another secret earned before you betrayed Kyrophage's
trust?" she asked.

Mradin said nothing.

"I see. Go, brother. I would prefer to serve the akashic as a
memory stone than live in shame."

"The shame will vanish. You'll see—"

"No," she said. "No, I won't see."

* * * * *

Skaraph sprinted across the desert, his legs aching and his feet
hammering the sand faster than his own racing heart. And he felt

joy, running unbridled till his flanks hurt and his breath skipped in shallow beats. He stopped a moment, listening, panting.

A cold, gentle nudge touched Skaraph's mind. Skaraph welcomed Kyrophage's presence as the wyrm coiled and nested inside the bowl of his skull, communing with him under Zalavat's hot sun. Off in the distance, more drakyn-hounds approached.

* * * * *

The stars were plentiful in the tranquil night, with neither cloud nor Serran's moon to diminish their luster. Mradin moved quietly, skirting wide the black tents to approach his sister's home. The sentries were fewer tonight than the nights previous. The Bnahzra believed him gone, having tracked him for two evenings. When he was certain his escorts had returned home, Mradin doubled back.

He slipped through the tent flap with barely a rustle; Trylith was meditating upon a diamond-checkered carpet, cross-legged and uncomfortable from stiffening joints. She opened her eyes, but Mradin found no surprise in her expression.

"You knew I'd be back," Mradin said.

"The man I remember kept his word."

"Perhaps my love for you is the last true thing of me that remains," Mradin said, kneeling before her. He stroked her cheek.

"You cannot ask me to leave," Trylith said, her eyes cloaked in miserable sorrow.

"I'm no longer asking."

"I'll scream," she said.

"They'll kill me if you do. Or they'll die trying. Regardless, I doubt you want to assume that guilt."

"You cannot carry me across the desert."

"I don't have to," Mradin said, sweeping his sister up into the cradle of his arms. "Wild camels still drink from the local oasis, do they not?"

"Please," she said. "Don't do this."

"How can I watch you die?" Mradin said; he shouldered his way through the tent flap.

* * * * *

Mradin stumbled through the sand, nearly upending himself and Trylith as they scaled the back of another mammoth dune. She said nothing but studied Mradin intently. They were barely halfway to the oasis.

"I know what you're doing," he said through labored breaths. "You're limp. You're making this more difficult."

"Leave me, then. I can make my way back."

"And I can reach the oasis. I can be just as stubborn as you."

Struggling through the sands, Mradin finally reached the apex of the dune. Below them, an ocean of static waves spread out to meet the dark horizon. Trylith gasped and grabbed her brother's shoulder. He turned in time to see a drakyn-hound pack moving up a neighboring dune, away from them.

"They're heading for the village!" she said.

"They won't find me there," Mradin replied, making his way down the dune's slope. "And when they track me to the oasis, we'll be far from there, safe."

"But the tribe—"

"I'm past caring for them," Mradin said.

Trylith slapped Mradin, hard enough that he fell back into the dune's face with her in his arms. She'd never raised a fist against him, even as a child. Trylith escaped his grasp and scrambled back up the slope.

"Damn you, Mradin," she said, fleeing.

Mradin crawled after her, grabbing her cold, crystal ankle.

"This isn't about you!" she cried. "Are you so blind you can't see that?"

"I'm trying to save you!" he said and pulled her down harder than he'd intended.

Something cracked, like the sharp whisper of broken glass.

Trylith cried out, more shock than pain, and Mradin backpedaled, horrified by his own brutality . . .

. . . horrified at the deep cleft across her crystalline ankle.

"I'm sorry!" he cried. He reached out, but he couldn't bear to touch the wound. "We can heal this. Please, let me try—"

But Trylith said nothing. She wept heavy tears that turned to mud from the sand on her face.

"I'm sorry," Mradin whispered, embracing her. He held her, gently, her head against his chest. "I'm sorry," he repeated, rocking her gently. It was only in such moments of horrible clarity that Mradin realized how much he'd truly changed; how much the darkness had consumed his heart. Finally, Trylith wiped away the muddy tears and stared at her brother.

"I love you, Mradin. Your gift is a wonderful promise," she whispered, "but it is not yours to give. Go, please."

"I can't leave you here, like this."

"You must. Aujmana will track me as soon as she realizes I'm missing. But, as a favor to me . . . stop the drakyn-hounds from attacking the tribe."

"I—" Mradin began, still uncertain.

"If the drakyn-hounds attack the Bnahzra, then Aujmana may not find me for days, if she even survives. And I wish to return home."

Mradin said nothing at first, and though unable to meet her gaze, he nodded. "Stay in the slope of the dune," he said. "The shade will protect you till late morning."

"They'll find me by then," Trylith said. "Be well, brother."

"And you," Mradin replied, walking over the dune crest. "Remember me kindly."

"I'll try," she whispered.

* * * * *

The drakyn-hounds were within sight of the tents when they quickened their thundering pace, but a sharp whistle behind them drew them to a skidding stop. The drakyn-hounds exchanged glances and returned back the way they had come, running low to the ground and outflanking their verrik prey.

Mradin, however, stood his ground, his hands extended. He held his bone ring between two fingers.

"I surrender," he said. "Take me back to Kyrophage."

"Trick!" one of the drakyn-hounds said with a sharp hiss.

"No," Mradin said. "I'm tired of running. I'll return with you. No tricks." With that, he dropped the ring into the sand.

The drakyn-hounds looked at one another before the pack elder snapped its jaws twice. "Walk," it said. "That way."

Mradin nodded and walked away, the drakyn-hounds surrounding him except for one that scooped up the ring with its tongue. Only once did Mradin pause, to look back to the distant black tents. Only once did he wonder if the Bnahzra appreciated what he was doing for them.

* * * * *

Aujmana and the other bedu scrambled over the dunes, following the wind-brushed footsteps and the broken peaks of someone's passage. They moved quickly, for their path took them to the oasis where wild camels grazed. From there, tracking Trylith would prove impossible.

Over one dune to the next, Aujmana and her trackers were surprised when they almost stumbled over Trylith in the shaded slope, a drakyn-hound lying next to her.

"Skaraph," Aujmana said. "We're surprised to see you so soon."

"You know I?"

"It was Trylith who convinced us to spare your life. We brought you to her tent. Did he fight off Mradin?" Aujmana asked Trylith, nodding to the drakyn-hound. "We recognized Mradin's tracks."

"No," Trylith said. "Mradin departed to right his own mistakes, as it should have been. Skaraph has kept me company since he found me a few hours ago."

"Return compassion," Skaraph said.

"Why are you here, Skaraph?" Aujmana asked. "We know your pack was near our village this morning."

"Yes. But seek only oath-breaker."

"And you?" Aujmana asked.

"Kyrophage send I to offer deal. Elevate you and other verrik. Save you from Curse."

"Mradin spoke of a darkness that afflicts him," Aujmana said. "A malevolent anger and arrogance. Does it affect all elevated?"

"Yes. But I fight its call."

"How?" Trylith asked.

"Greater trumpet is duty and oath."

"Even though that duty may ask you to kill?"

Skaraph shook his head. "I kill as beast. Not new. You kill as warrior. Not new. If duty and oath to your word is stronger than personal desire, then you fight Curse."

"I've heard Kyrophage's offer," Trylith said.

"And?" Aujmana asked.

"I will undergo the ritual."

"Even after turning away your own brother?" a bedu asked.

"It's not the same. It was not Mradin's place to make the choice for me, and he offered me a gift that was not his to begin with. But he was right in one thing. It is better I choose my fate than suffer under a crueler affliction. And if I am to serve Kyrophage, perhaps I can save Mradin as well."

"I respect your decision," Aujmana said. "Come then, Skaraph. Let the members of the tribe hear Kyrophage's offer and let them make their own choices."

The other bedu helped Trylith to her feet while Skaraph took his place between her and Aujmana.

"I glad," Skaraph said.

"And perhaps," Trylith said, "we can offer all verrik the choice."

"Yes," Skaraph said. "Master would like that."

THIS LAND IS IN OUR BLOOD

"Hurry!" Daelyn shouted. He held open the door of a small, squat building whose moss-covered roof hung bare inches above his bushy black hair. "Get in here! Get in quickly!"

The building stood halfway up a grassy hill above a crossroads. Covered in vegetation as it was, you had to look carefully to notice that it was more than just an overgrown shack—in fact, it was merely the front few feet of a bunker built into the side of the hill. The bunker was nearly impossible to spot unless you knew what you were looking for. But, like all his neighbors, Daelyn knew it so well that he could find it blindfolded on a moonless night. It was built on land that had belonged to Daelyn's family for generations so, as usual, he was the first to arrive. Now he was just waiting to see who else would show up.

From every direction Daelyn could see men, women, and children running toward him. The crimson and orange wisps painting the western horizon were all that was left of the day, so it was impossible for him to make out details of the approaching faces. But so few people lived in this region of Thartholan, it was easy to identify your neighbors by their gaits alone.

Paet and Jul were the first to come running up. Somehow, even with three young children in tow, they still always managed to be among the first to arrive at the bunker—or perhaps it was because of the children. Nothing puts spring in your step like fear for your child's life.

"Is Babba Hespyr here yet?" Jul asked. She clutched her infant daughter, Sari, to her chest while Paet herded their two young boys, Naen and Byrn, through the door and down the stairs.

"You're the first ones tonight," Daelyn said. He peered out over the landscape and pointed to the approaching silhouettes one by one. "I see Cariss and Fern, and I think that's Kael, but he's moving funny. Maybe he threw his back out again."

"That's all?" asked Jul. A few strands of straw-colored hair fell out from below her white bonnet and stuck to the perspiration on her brow.

"I think so."

Jul gazed anxiously to the north, in the direction of Hespyr's farm. "Are you certain?" she asked.

And even though he was sure, Daelyn shaded his small, brown eyes and looked again. Only one shape was moving across the fields—the one he'd just identified as Kael—lumbering haltingly closer. There was no sign of anyone else.

"I'm sure," he said. "Why? What's wrong?"

Jul turned her head to look away to the west. Although there was nothing to see, a dry, relentless, unearthly chittering sound echoed over the hill. It had grown noticeably louder even as they stood there talking.

"Babba Hespyr didn't sleep a wink last night," said Jul. She held Sari closer and rocked the baby soothingly. However, since the little girl had slept soundly despite the panicked race across the fields and the rising cacophony of chittering, the motion seemed intended more to soothe the mother than the child. "When I checked in on her this afternoon she was pale and shaky. I don't think she can make it here by herself tonight."

Daelyn looked to the north again. Maybe she simply hadn't heard the chittering—her hearing was getting worse by the day. Even at a dead run it would take ten minutes for him to get to Hespyr's cabin and, presuming he found her alive, fifteen more to carry her back. There certainly was no longer enough time to let the old woman walk the distance. Daelyn ran a tanned hand through his hair. Considering his options, he worked his jaw back and forth behind pursed lips.

"What are you doing?" demanded Cariss. Not a single gray hair strayed from under the kerchief tied around her head as she marched up the hill at a pace most folk would find difficult to maintain over flat land. Cariss was solid as the hills and seemed to be built from the same mud and granite, so Daelyn felt it when she poked him in the chest with the tip of her walking stick. "Shouldn't you be inside making sure everything's secure?"

"Paet is in there," said Daelyn. "And everything is just the way we left it this morning."

"Paet!" Cariss spat the name out like it was a curse, either not noticing or not caring that Jul was standing right in front of her. "He can barely handle those ruffian sons of his. Do you really think he is the best choice to secure our only protection against—"

"Babba Hespyr hasn't come yet," said Jul.

"Sh-she h-hasn't?" asked Fern as she finally reached the bunker. Although twenty years younger, she seemed to have only half her mother's energy. Curly blond hair billowed around her face as she approached, her expression a mixture of apology for Cariss' brusqueness and worry over their missing neighbor. "Perhaps we should send someone to see if she's all right?"

"I don't think there's enough time," said Jul. She had to raise her voice to be heard above the building noise.

Daelyn was about to start down the hill when Cariss poked him in the chest again, this time more forcefully.

"Kael has her," she said. "Honestly, don't you fools have eyes?"

Daelyn looked down to the crossroads. Kael was just stepping off the path and starting to climb the hill. Despite the failing light, it was now obvious that he wasn't hobbling because his back was sore, but rather because of what he carried upon it.

Babba Hespyr had her arms wrapped around Kael's neck like the collar of a cloak, and he held her legs to provide balance and support to them both as he marched across the uneven terrain.

"At least one person was thinking about someone other than himself," said Cariss.

"All right," Daelyn said, "you'll have all night to tell us what horrible people we are, Cariss. Right now, let's get inside."

While the others ambled through the door and down the stairs, Daelyn waited. "I see you brought a date tonight," he called out when Kael was close enough to hear him over the din of alien chirping.

The other man barked a short laugh.

"Yeah," he said in a raspy voice as deep as the lines in his care-worn face. Kael was only ten years Daelyn's senior, but he looked like he'd lived a lifetime longer. "I have a thing for older women, didn't you know?"

"Well it's just your bad luck that I don't like immature men," said Hespyr. Her voice was so thin that it was almost impossible to hear her over the chittering. The two men helped lower her to the ground and then down the bunker steps where Jul and Fern waited.

"Damn, they're louder than ever," said Kael standing up and looking to the west. There still was nothing to see, but the noise kept rising and moving closer. "How much worse can it get?"

"Never ask questions you don't really want the answers to," replied Daelyn.

Kael shook his head and cracked a craggy grin. "I suppose

you're right," he said. "Is everyone here now?"

"Almost," said Daelyn. "We still haven't seen Aevyrt."

"That makes what, three days?" asked Kael.

"Four," answered Daelyn. "I know he has a cellar at his cabin, but we'd better check on him in the morning."

"We have to make it through the night first," said Kael. He barked another short laugh as he started down the stairs into the bunker. "C'mon, let's get in and lock up."

If you'd asked Daelyn why, he couldn't have answered, but instead of following immediately he stole one more look at the western horizon. The last wisps of color were nearly gone from the sky, but they still provided enough light to see a pair of silhouettes coming toward the crossroads. They weren't insectoid shapes, skittering and crawling over the land—they were human, one about twice as tall as the other, and they were walking down the road. No, they were strolling down the road, hand in hand, calm as can be.

"Hey!" Daelyn shouted as loudly as he could. He had to find some way to attract their attention over the blaring noise, so he jumped up and down waving his hands as he continued to shout. "Hey, you two! Up here on the hill! Look!"

The pair stopped and looked directly at Daelyn, as though they had no trouble hearing him.

He stopped jumping.

For a very long moment none of them did anything but stand stock-still staring at one another. The oddity of the situation made the skin prickle on the back of Daelyn's neck—and, living in this valley, that was no mean feat. Were they unaware of the danger they were in? Did they have no idea what was about to come swarming over the hill? Or were they insane enough to simply not be afraid?

It didn't matter. Daelyn couldn't go inside and leave them to their grisly fate.

"Get up here!" he called to them, beckoning with a wave.

The taller figure picked up the smaller one in a single arm and began walking up the hill. Walking! Daelyn couldn't believe his eyes. "Hurry up!" he yelled. "They'll be here any minute!"

The larger figure doubled the length of his strides, but never moved quicker than a stately, military march. By the time he was close enough for Daelyn to see their faces, the others inside the bunker were screaming for him to come in and close the door.

"Just a second," he said. "They're here."

They were indeed human—a man in the prime of life and a boy on the verge of adolescence. If they were not father and son, they were closely related. They had the same dark hair, ruddy skin, and narrow sunken eyes, and both their faces bore identical stony expressions. They looked at Daelyn calmly but quizzically, as if to say, "Yes, good man, why did you call us off the road?"

Clearly, as impossible as it seemed, they had no clue what was about to happen in the valley.

"You're lucky I saw you," Daelyn said as he moved through the door and down the half-dozen stairs into the bunker. "Come in."

The man set the boy on the ground and the two of them stepped up to the threshold, peered in, but did not yet enter the bunker. Daelyn stepped aside so that they could see what was inside—a single room with three cots, a dozen chairs, two tall water barrels, and walls covered with shelves bearing dried and preserved food, blankets, and other items one would want in times of emergency.

"For Niashra's sake, Daelyn," called Cariss, "shut the door!"

"Mother!" said Fern. "They're strangers. You can't expect them to just trust us."

"Well, you can't expect us to stand here with the door open until the scourge comes swarming in just because they're too dim to realize we mean them no harm."

"She's right, y'know," said Kael. "We gotta close the door."

"Mister, no one here's going to hurt you or your boy," Daelyn said, doing his best to ignore the bickering going on behind him.

"In fact, we want to save you from a whole mess of trouble. But we're about to close this door. And once it's closed we don't open it up for anyone or anything until the sun comes up."

The stranger looked at the neighbors huddled in the bunker. They were ordinary folk, dressed in plain clothes covered with stains from mud, grass, and the sweat of a hard day's work. He took his young companion by the hand, and stepped inside just as Daelyn was about to give up. He helped close and secure the door. The walls were insulated by enough earth to cut the clamor outside to a distant thrum.

The stranger turned to stare stoically at the group again. He and the boy were dressed in traveling clothes—tunic, breeches, cloak, and boots—but rather than simple, sturdy cloth, they were fashioned from silks, satins, and velvet dyed in bright shades of purple, yellow, and rich royal blue. They might have looked like nobility except that they had a coarse, brash, almost defiant air about them. Nobles could be arrogant and confrontational, in Daelyn's experience, but always in a refined, sophisticated way.

"What is 'the scourge?'" the stranger asked. Despite his gruff demeanor, the stranger's voice was almost musical. To be certain, it was deep and commanding as well, but melodic was the first word that sprang to Daelyn's mind—like a tune played on the lowest keys of a cathedral's organ.

"'What's the scourge?' Is he kiddin' me?" chuckled Kael. "Mister, did you hear that racket out there?"

"Indeed I did," said the stranger. "Is that what you call kikrikki? 'The scourge?'"

"If they have any other name, we've never heard it," Paet said from the corner. Naen and Byrn sat in his lap, which in itself was unusual. Generally they were crawling all over every inch of the bunker, but tonight they were silent as mice. They simply sat there and stared at the strangers, especially the younger one. But whenever the young stranger looked their way, the boys buried their faces in their father's chest.

"They've been coming to the valley since before I was born," Hespyr said in her shaky, frail voice. "We call them 'the scourge' because they destroy whatever is in their way, and when they swarm, *everything* is in their way."

"Remember the time they ate the Thousand Year Oak?" said Jul. Most of the adults nodded or grunted that they did, but she turned to the stranger and continued. "They didn't just eat the leaves and strip the bark, they ate the whole tree. All that was left in the morning was the very core of the trunk, gnawed on like an old dog's bone."

"And this happens often?" asked the stranger.

"Nah, not often," said Kael. "Only once or twice a year. We count ourselves lucky it's just *after* a harvest rather than just before one."

"Well, it used to be only once a year," said Fern. "But it's been happening a lot lately."

"But they hadn't swarmed since last summer," said Cariss. "And I don't think we saw them at all for two whole years before that."

"You can't talk about averages," Paet said. "That's meaningless. All we really can say is that it's been happening a lot lately."

"But it's still not as bad as five years ago," said Hespyr. "That was the worst I've ever seen in all my years—once before the spring harvest and again before the fall harvest. That was a long, cold, hungry winter for us all."

"Paet's right," Daelyn said. "All that matters is how bad off the swarms leave us. If this keeps up the way it has since the Day of Exodus, this will be the worst year ever. We won't have enough food to get through the autumn, let alone the winter."

They all nodded in agreement.

"What is the Day of Exodus? A local festival?" the stranger asked. While the others were speaking he was completely, almost unnaturally still. He seemed to even cease breathing so he could better hear what they were saying.

"No. It happened about a fortnight ago," said Daelyn. "We opened our doors one morning and thought the world had ended. Instead of a sunny day, or even a cloudy one, it was dark outside."

"Mostly dark," said Cariss. "Tell the story right."

"It was dark," Daelyn continued, "except that beams of sunlight were passing over the land like lights from hooded lanterns. We looked up to see—"

"Dragons," Jul interrupted. "The sky was filled with dragons flying east. They blocked out the sun for the whole day."

"It was only for a few hours," said Cariss.

"'Only,' you say!" added Kael. "'Only a few hours.' Do you know how many dragons it takes to fill the sky for a few hours?"

"No I don't," said Cariss. "But neither do you."

"It's a lot," said Jul.

"A hell of a lot," said Kael.

"It was an omen," said Hespyr, "an omen of change."

"You keep saying that," muttered Cariss, "but it doesn't mean anything. 'An omen of change.' What sort of change? Change for who? Change of what?"

"Omens are funny things," Hespyr answered. "You never can tell what they mean exactly until it's done."

"Then what good are they?" asked Kael. "What good does it do us to know that something is different if we don't know what *it* is? We can't prepare to welcome it. We can't guard against it. We may not even be able to recognize it when it arrives."

"Oh, we'll know when it's here," Hespyr assured them.

"But how, Babba Hespyr?" asked Jul. "How will we know?"

"It will come out of nowhere and fill the air," the old woman said. "It will be something that no one expects, but everyone must accept. It will be like a bolt from the blue or thunder at night."

At that exact moment the air was split by a loud series of thumps—fists pounding and feet kicking the door so hard that it rattled on its hinges. From the hillside beyond came a panicked voice.

"Open the door!" it said.

For a very long moment no one moved.

The thumping continued, increasing in savagery.

"It's me," the voice continued. "It's Aevyrt! For pity's sake, let me in!"

"Aevyrt, you fool, what are you doing out there?" called out Kael, though he stayed a good dozen paces away from the door. "Why aren't you in your cellar at home?"

"It collapsed last night," Aevyrt answered. "I thought I was a goner for sure, but they couldn't get to me through the rubble before the sun rose. It took me all day to dig my way out of there. Now let me in!" All the while he continued to punch and kick at the door.

"You know the rule, Aevyrt," shouted Paet. "Once the door is closed, it doesn't open until morning."

"The hell with the rule!" Aevyrt screamed. "I'm telling you, the scourge hasn't come over the hill yet. Open the damned door!"

"It's dark out there," said Cariss. "He can't be sure that there aren't any of those damned bugs anywhere nearby."

"We can't just sit here and do nothing, Mother," Fern said.

"We most certainly can," Cariss replied. Her voice was as solid and unyielding as the barrier against which Aevyrt was pounding. "If we open the door, it won't take a whole swarm to wipe us out—one or two will do."

"The rule is there for a reason," said Kael.

"Oh sweet Niashra!" cried Aevyrt. "I can see them now. They're just coming over the hill—the whole hill, as far as I can see. There's never been so many. Open the door. They won't be here for a minute yet. In the name of all that's good and right, let me in." As he spoke his voice faded from a shout down to just normal speaking tone, barely enough to be heard over the insectoid noises that were now piercing even the thick walls of the bunker. The violent pounding lessened to a token few thumps. "Please let me in."

"Screw the rule," said Daelyn as he shouldered past the others. Before anyone could stop him, he stepped up to the door and slid back the bolt. In a swift single motion Daelyn pushed the door open only the slightest of cracks, reached out, and pulled in a thin, sun-parched man with several days' growth of beard that accounted for just about all the hair on his head. Aevyrt collapsed on the ground at Daelyn's feet.

As the door slammed shut under its own weight, Kael and Fern leapt forward to bolt it again. Paet looked as if he wanted to, but he was still pinned beneath his unusually calm children.

"You told me that once the door was closed, you wouldn't open it for any reason," said the stranger, who had been standing still and silent as a statue during all the excitement. "You said it was 'the rule.'"

"And it is!" bellowed Cariss. "You had no right to do such a foolish thing, Daelyn. If one of those things had—"

"But it didn't," Daelyn interrupted. "You know those things can't do anything quietly. There wasn't anything on the other side of the door but a frightened friend of ours."

"That's not the point," said Kael. "The rule isn't complicated, it's not hard to interpret. In fact, it's simple for one reason—so that it's easy to follow. What if you were wrong? What if there was just one quiet bug out there?"

"That's a chance I was willing to take," Daelyn said. "I couldn't live with myself if I didn't do everything in my power to help a neighbor in need. And if it had been you on the other side of the door, you'd be glad I felt that way."

"It wouldn't be me on the other side of the door," said Cariss. She stood, squared her shoulders, and stared down her nose at Daelyn. "I'd know better."

"That's all well and good to say," he answered, stepping up to look her dead in the eye. "Perhaps we'll remind you of that next spring when the rains turn the fields to mud and it takes you an extra ten minutes to get here, or in the winter when the snow is so deep that you have to snowshoe here without the aid of your walking stick."

Cariss made no reply, but she did not lower her gaze. The two stood there toe to toe, simply glaring at one another.

"Why do you stay?" said a small voice from the back of the room.

The neighbors all turned at the same time to see that it was the stranger's companion who asked the question.

"If things are so desperate, why do you stay?" the boy asked again. His voice was as musical as the stranger's, but higher and more airy. "Surely there are better places to live. Why don't you move somewhere where there is no scourge?"

The neighbors all laughed.

"Leave?" said Kael, his gruff voice softened by the humor of the moment. "Why should we leave? The land's fertile, there's plenty of fresh water, the weather's mild enough that we can farm ten months out of most years, and the giant stewards never made it this far west, so they never bother us. We're free to live our lives the way we like."

"There's nothing wrong with the land," added Jul, "it's just some of the wildlife. And even that isn't really natural. If we ever figured out a way to close down the portal on the western ridge, we'd have no problems at all—the scourge'd be stuck forever on the other side, wherever that is."

"Besides," Cariss said, "we can't let them chase us off our land. We were here first."

The boy cocked his head and raised an eyebrow—the most emotion either of the strangers had shown since they arrived. "But the old woman said that the kikrikki have been visiting this valley since before she was born."

The neighbors laughed again.

"Son," Kael said, "eighty-five generations of my family have lived on and farmed pieces of this land. We were here before the scourge, and we'll be here long after they've been run off."

"It's the same for all of us," said Daelyn. "My great-great-great-great-grandfather built this bunker because he was tired of having to ride around the valley just to be certain that Aevyrt's great-great-great-great-grandmother was all right after every time the scourge swarmed. Everyone in this part of Thartholan knows everyone else. We have to—our families have been here so long, there's hardly anyone who isn't a distant cousin or in-law of one sort or another."

"But no one knows you, stranger," Cariss added. Rather than sitting on a chair or cot, she was leaning against one of the water barrels with her arms crossed. She'd been staring at the stranger and the boy for most of the time since they came in.

"Come on now, Cariss," said Aevyrt who, having finally gathered his wits, was getting off the ground and dusting himself off. "Just 'cause you're mad at me, don't take it out on these folks."

"No, that's not it at all. She's right," said Kael. "We don't know anything about these two. Hell, we don't even know their names."

The strangers seemed completely undisturbed—practically unaware that they were suddenly the topic of discussion. They simply stood where they were, side-by-side about five paces away from the stairs, listening intently to the conversation. Their eyes darted from face to face, following the conversation, but other than that, they hardly moved a muscle. They were so quiet and still that at times they seemed not to be there at all—quite a trick, in a small room crowded with neighbors.

Now, though, an uneasy tension was filling the bunker. Even Fern, who never had anything but a smile for everyone, cast suspicious eyes toward the newcomers. Daelyn could sense, even if the strangers couldn't, the others growing restless and shifting into more aggressive postures. As ridiculous as it seemed, they somehow felt threatened by the strangers and were on the verge of doing something about it.

"That's easily solved," he said. "I don't think we've been properly introduced. I'm Daelyn, and this is my place." He

193

extended an open hand and smiled his best smile first to the older stranger and then to the younger one.

The young boy ignored Daelyn completely, instead turning his head to stare up at his companion. The older stranger looked down at Daelyn's hand as though not sure what to make of it. His eyes were wide and his mouth was taut.

Every eye in the room was on them.

"I am Goedaer," the stranger said eventually. "My son is Toi."

Goedaer did not shake Daelyn's hand, but he did close his eyes and give his host a short, formal bow. Toi did the same.

Daelyn lowered his hand and smiled.

"There now, that wasn't so hard, was it?"

The others relaxed—some more than others—and introduced themselves. Fern's warm smile returned, but Cariss' wary scowl remained. Kael began to offer his hand to Goedaer but seemed to think better of it at the last moment. Naen and Byrn climbed off their father's lap and stepped up to Toi, staring at him the way they did tadpoles in a pond (except that unlike the tadpoles, Toi stared right back with an equally curious gaze).

Suddenly the chittering sounds that had been a steady but distant thrum somewhere beyond the bunker's walls rose in pitch, volume, and proximity. It was as if the size of the scourge swarm had doubled, and all of the horrible creatures decided to clamber over this hill at the same time. Once again a loud thump resounded against the door. This time, however, it wasn't the solid, meaty sound of a fist or boot on the wood. This was a much more powerful blow, as though the door were being struck by a falling tree or a battering ram or a giant insectoid limb.

The blow was hard enough to rattle not only the bunker's door but also the entire front wall, causing clouds of dust and dirt to rain down from the ceiling. This was immediately followed by the sound of dozens, perhaps hundreds, of tiny limbs scratching against the wood as though they were trying to tear it down one sliver at a time.

Naen, Byrn, and Sari all screamed and clutched their parents tightly. Paet and Jul did what they could to comfort the children, which proved to be very little. Kael, Daelyn, Aevyrt, and Cariss threw themselves against the door in hopes of providing the entry with even a fraction more stability. Fern ran over to the cot where Hespyr sat and threw her arms protectively around the old woman who, quite understandably, mistook the gesture for one of abject terror and wrapped her arms around the teenager saying, "There, there, dear. It will be all right. You'll see."

Only Goedaer and Toi were unfazed by the commotion. They continued to stand in the same spots they had since arriving. But now they turned their heads curiously this way and that, following the panicked activities carefully.

Another blow struck the door, knocking Daelyn and Kael two feet back and sending Aevyrt and Cariss sprawling onto the floor. They leapt back to bolster the door again, but no further attacks were forthcoming. The creatures hadn't left; the neighbors could hear them on the other side of door clicking their mandibles and climbing all over themselves in a writhing mass of insect fury.

The cocoon of earth surrounding the bunker no longer provided any respite from the inhuman noise the scourge made. The horrible sound filled the space, but it was mixed with a new sound: a scraping, scrabbling, scratching noise that could be felt deep in the bones as much as it could be heard.

"What the hell is that?" asked Kael. No one could provide an answer with any kind of certainty.

"I've never heard anything like it," said Paet.

"Is the scourge making that sound," asked Jul, "or did they bring some new kind of bug with them?"

"A new kind?" Cariss said. "After all this time, why in the world would they do that?"

"An omen of change," Hespyr called out from the cot. "The only thing you can be certain of is that nothing will be the same."

Goedaer began to chuckle, a deep, reverberating sound nearly as alien as the chattering of the scourge. He stopped when it became obvious that everyone else in the bunker was staring at him.

"What the hell was that about?" growled Kael.

Goedaer looked at him as though he had no idea what the man was talking about.

"What was so funny?" asked Daelyn. "We all really could use a good laugh about now."

"I thought the old woman was joking," Goedaer said. "It has been my experience that, omens or no, omens, the only thing you can *ever* be certain of is that nothing will remain the same."

"Who *are* you?" Cariss said. "Really, I think we deserve to know. Who are you, Goedaer? What sort of man comes wandering down the western road just at sunset—trailing his son along behind him, no less—knowing nothing about the scourge?"

Goedaer gave her the same neutral look he'd worn in response to nearly everything the neighbors had said.

"I am a traveler," he said.

"A traveler from where?" she demanded. "You couldn't possibly have walked from Balatosh in a single day, not with a child. But lately the scourge has been swarming every night, so you couldn't have just camped by the roadside. How did you get here? What sort of 'traveler' are you?"

For the first time, Goedaer looked slightly perturbed, as though he did not like having the truth of his statements questioned. He narrowed his eyes and fixed Cariss with a withering stare. After a few moments he said, "My son and I are sorcerers of a sort. We were able to protect ourselves from the kikrikki. We would have done so tonight as well if you had not invited us to share your shelter. I must say that we are glad for the company, but if you regret allowing us in, we can leave any time you like."

"No!" barked Kael. "No one's opening that door again!"

"As you wish," Goedaer said.

"Are you really sorcerers?" asked Fern.

Goedaer pondered the question before finally replying, "Yes."

"Well, what are you doing here?" Cariss asked. "Why in the world would a sorcerer and his apprentice come here? No one just visits this valley."

"Toi is my progeny, not my student," said Goedaer. "And we are not visiting. We have come here to live."

For a moment none of the neighbors made a sound—they almost seemed to stop breathing. The next moment they all burst out laughing.

"You *are* crazy," said Kael.

"Why would anyone in his right mind bring a child here?" said Jul.

"No one 'comes to live' in Thartholan," said Paet.

For the first time, Toi actually became physically agitated. He put his hands on his hips and cocked his head to the side.

"What's so funny?" he said. "You just finished telling us what a wonderful place this is and how you would never think about living anywhere else."

"Yes," said Daelyn. "But our families have lived here for hundreds of years. We belong to the land as much as it does to us. We can't help but love this place—it is in our blood. But it's been generations since anyone moved here of their own choice. Thartholan just isn't someplace that you learn to love."

"We know," Goedaer said. "This land is in our blood as well."

The assembled neighbors uttered a series of half-formed questions and grunts of disbelief.

"That can't possibly be," said Cariss. When Goedaer gave her another piercing glare she added, "What I meant to say was, if that's true, then we must have heard of your family."

"Perhaps," said Goedaer, "but they left a very long time ago, when my grandfather was not yet as old as Toi is now. He loved this land, and it broke his heart to leave. In all the years that followed, he never forgot. Grandfather was always telling stories about the rolling hills and the grassy plains, about the warmth of the summer breeze and the bitter cold of the winter wind. He said that this was the most perfect place the gods ever created, and we believed him. Nothing would have pleased him more than to return, but his master would not allow it. Still, the longing never left his heart, and he passed that devotion on to his son—my father—who passed it on to me. And since the day Toi came into the world I have been telling him tales of this magical land."

Toi looked at his father and rolled his eyes—a normal enough expression that somehow looked completely unnatural on this strange boy's face.

"When the opportunity to return arose, I seized it—seized it for me, for my son, and for all the dreams my grandfather never surrendered," Goedaer continued. "This land is in our blood. And it touches my heart to see that the people living here feel the same way about the land and about each other."

"It sounds like your grandfather was a good man," said Daelyn. "I'm sorry that I'll never get to meet him."

"Where did he live?" Hespyr's frail, wavering voice called out from where she sat on the cot.

"Excuse me?" said Goedaer.

"Your grandfather," the old woman said. "Where did he live? My father was a traveling merchant, and I spent most of my youth riding from town to town in his wagon. Perhaps I knew some of your kin."

"I think that is unlikely," Goedaer answered. "From what I understand, they lived in an extremely isolated area."

Daelyn thought the stranger was being exceptionally careful with his words, particularly for such an innocuous subject.

"I don't think there's a corner of Thartholan that I haven't been to," said Hespyr. "Was it in the Venthal mud flats? That's actually where I met my husband, gods rest his soul. He wandered out of that desolate waste just to find me, can you believe it?" She turned to Fern. "Did I ever tell you that story, dear? It's the most romantic thing you've ever heard."

"We've all heard that story, Babba Hespyr," said Cariss. "Let's hear our new friend's answer. Where *was* your family from, Goedaer? If not Venthal, was it Southsands? Or Redcliff?"

"Yeah," Kael chimed in. "We all have friends and relations spread out across Thartholan. There's a good chance one of us will know someone from your hometown."

While Daelyn was not pleased with the accusatory tone the conversation had taken, he had to admit to his own curiosity. Why would Goedaer be so effusive about his love for Thartholan yet so secretive about his family's roots?

The newcomer stood as still and as stoically as ever, yet somehow his stance seemed to express resignation.

"I do not know any of those names," he said. "In fact, Grandfather rarely called any place by name—he said they never capture the true essence of the land. But I believe that others called his home Drohthal."

The silence that followed was made more pronounced by the fact that it drew attention to the chirping and scratching noises from outside the bunker. Daelyn imagined that they were growing louder again, but perhaps they just seemed that way in the strained bunker air.

"The Dragon Hills?" said Paet finally. "Does anyone actually live there?"

"Certainly," Hespyr said. "There are dozens of tiny villages in the woods on those haunted hills. But they live according to traditions older than the hills themselves—from before the coming of the dramojh—and they don't welcome strangers. Some of them are even said to practice cannibalism."

The others gasped and again turned their gazes suspiciously on Goedaer and Toi.

Daelyn was now certain that the sounds from outside had grown noticeably louder, particularly the scratching noises—they seemed to be coming from every direction at once. No one else was paying the least attention, though.

"Those were never my grandfather's ways," Goedaer said calmly. "And they are certainly not mine, nor my son's. Do we look askance at you because your ancestors used to burn strangers at the stake for fear that they were demons in disguise?"

"No one has done that for centuries," said Cariss. "It's ancient history."

"My point exactly," replied Goedaer.

This was the time in most arguments where Daelyn stepped in to make sure it didn't get out of hand. Both sides had had their say, and it was becoming more and more likely that people were going to say something that they would regret later. Yes, this was when Daelyn usually called for cooler heads to prevail, but this time he didn't.

Part of it was the fact that he himself was uncertain about Goedaer and Toi. He had invited them into the bunker, but he was no longer sure that had been the correct thing to do. He didn't think they were cannibals, but they could still be dangerous.

"That's not the point at all," said Kael. "We still don't know a damned thing about you. You say your grandfather came from the Dragon Hills and that he left at a very young age, but he filled you with tales of the plains and the deserts. You say you've brought your son here to return to your ancestral home, but you're hundreds of miles from Drohthal and headed in the wrong direction."

"You arrive in the middle of the worst scourge swarm we've seen in years," added Cariss, "but you hardly even seem to notice or care about the bugs. You say you can protect yourself from them, but you huddle here in the bunker alongside the rest of us. You claim to be a great sorcerer whose family comes from a land of barbaric cannibals."

Another reason Daelyn didn't step in was that he felt on the verge of understanding it all, of figuring out who this newcomer was. A grandfather who was forced to leave, love of the land, stories passed from father to son, Drohthal, sorcerers—it all fit together somehow, and Daelyn could almost see the pattern.

"Mister," Kael said, "I don't know if a single word you've told us is true, but I'm getting real tired of guessing. Give me one good reason why we shouldn't just throw you out the door and let the scourge take care of you?"

Goedaer seemed completely unmoved by the ugliness and violence in the threat.

"Because it would break the rule," he said as calmly as ever.

Daelyn's eyes opened wide. He raised his hand, finger sticking straight in the air as if to point to the revelation he was about to make. Before he could say a word, though, the bunker erupted into bedlam as the scourge renewed its assault. This time it was not against the door and front wall. This time the bugs threw themselves against the side walls and ceiling.

"How?" cried Paet, covering Naen and Byrn to protect them from the clumps of earth that were raining from the roof. "How did they get up there?"

"They burrowed!" Kael yelled. "The bugs learned a new damned trick. They burrowed to get at our soft sides."

"It's worse than that," said Daelyn shielding his eyes with one hand and looking up. The bunker's roof wasn't much to speak of, just a series of planks to prevent the dirt from collapsing in during the rainy season. Sometimes the scourge hit the front door hard enough to cause pebbles and dust to sprinkle through the cracks—every once in a while they hit it hard enough to knock a plank loose. Right now every plank in the roof was shaking and dirt was pouring down into the room. Through the cracks, Daelyn could see black chitinous limbs, iridescent segmented eyes, and here and there even a patch of star-speckled sky. "They're digging. They're digging us out of the earth!"

For a long moment all the neighbors seemed to be frozen by this revelation. They stood there as still as Goedaer and Toi had been. Then icy fear and red-hot panic jolted them back into action.

"Merciful Niashra, what can we do?" cried Jul as she clutched the screaming Sari to her chest.

Fern ran back to Hespyr's arms, but this time the old woman had no soothing words for her.

"I don't know about the rest of you," said Cariss, "but I don't intend to go without a fight." She clutched her walking stick at the short end and waved it around as though it were a spiked warclub instead of a simple tree limb.

Kael reached into the back of one of the shelves and pulled out a blanket wrapped around a heavy bundle. With a single tug the contents clattered to the ground—three rusted swords, a machete with several nicks in the blade, and what looked like part of a fence post with a length of chain nailed to one end. He gave the makeshift flail to Aevyrt, Paet (who had pushed his two boys into his wife's arms) took the machete, while Kael handed a sword to Daelyn and kept one for himself.

Then Kael turned to Goedaer and offered him the final sword.

"You would trust me with a weapon?"

"We can argue about the small stuff later," Kael said. "Right now, I figure we can use all the help we can get, neighbor."

Goedaer took the sword, but it was clear from the way he held it that he was not skilled in its use. He looked at the blade, at Kael, and then at the faces of all the other neighbors. He smiled.

When Toi saw this he smiled, too. The boy began to wave his hands in a strange pattern and mumble words that Daelyn and his neighbors couldn't understand. But Goedaer placed a hand on Toi's shoulder and simply shook his head no.

"What?" said Kael. "A little magic would be a big help now."

Three gargantuan insects smashed against the rear wall, collapsing the back of the structure. Dirt cascaded into the bunker.

"We cannot," said Goedaer. "Not here."

"Why not?" cried Daelyn.

The stranger looked at him calmly.

"It's against *our* rule."

An arm ending in a chitinous claw burst through what used to be the rear wall and swung wildly, narrowly missing Fern and

Hespyr. Aevyrt and Paet leapt forward and struck the limb as hard as they could, but they barely scratched its insectoid armor.

"You've got to be kidding," said Kael. It was unclear what was more shocking, the unprecedented attack or the stranger's answer.

"No," said Goedaer. "In any case, you wouldn't like it if we used that spell here—we couldn't protect you from the side effects."

"We're about to be eaten by giant bugs!" Kael said. "We're not worried about a few side effects."

"How would you feel about being crushed under a four-ton weight?"

"I'll take my chances with the bugs," said Kael, then jumped in to help Aevyrt and Paet with the slashing limb.

Goedaer reached down and took Toi by the hand. "It is time for us to leave," he said and walked over to the bunker door.

"What are you doing?" shrieked Cariss. "Don't open that door!"

"Tonight your rule failed to protect you," said Goedaer.

"The hell with the rule," said Cariss as she used her walking stick to shore up a plank in the eastern wall that seemed ready to snap. "Just *listen* to them! We might be able to handle a few of the scourge coming through the walls, but if you let a thousand of them in the door, we're doomed."

"None of them will get through the door."

"But how can we be sure of that? How can we know you won't just run out, cast some spell to protect you two, and leave us?"

Goedaer stopped and turned to face her.

"Would you rather Toi and I wait here until your fate is met and then leave?" he asked.

"No," said Daelyn. "We trust you. Go do what you need to do." When it looked like Cariss was about to object again, he added, "I'll bolt the door behind you."

"Be sure that you do," said Goedaer. "And no matter what, no matter what you hear or what happens in here, this time you must stick to your rule. You must not open the door until morning light fills the sky."

"I understand," Daelyn said. Giving his best imitation of the bow Goedaer had done earlier, he gave the pair a knowing smile and said, "I trust you."

"Good," said Goedaer as he unbolted the door. "That may yet be your salvation." He took Toi's hand, pushed the door open, and ran out into the chittering night.

Daelyn immediately rebolted the door, then turned to help the others fight the encroaching insects. But before he could take two steps, the invading limb withdrew of its own volition. What's more, the limbs and mandibles pushing against the roof and walls also retreated.

The bunker was suddenly free of attack. On the other hand, the neighbors could now hear the sound of the scourge moving down the hill in the direction that Goedaer and Toi had gone.

"It was them they were after?" said Kael.

"We should have thrown them out when we had the chance," Cariss muttered.

"Well, perhaps you'll be able to tell them that in the morning," said Daelyn.

"There won't be enough of them left to bury by the time morning comes," Cariss said. "At least they had the common decency not to drag us down with them."

Suddenly two violent jolts shook the earth, causing what little dirt was left above the bunker to shower down through the roof.

A deep, menacing growl filled the air, only to be followed by a second, nearly identical but less powerful growl. As if in response, the chittering of the scourge spiked in volume.

Then the air was filled with two sounds that none of the neighbors had ever heard before. The first sounded like a winter wind mixed with the crackle of a summer thunderstorm. The second, which followed immediately, was clearly the scourge screaming.

As the screams echoed into nothingness, the neighbors strained their ears to hear more, but there was nothing left to hear. In fact, the only noise they could discern was an insectoid thrum that they found oddly relaxing—the chirping of crickets.

* * * * *

When Goedaer reached the point where the road went over the western hill, he turned and looked back at the bunker. Although the hill all around it had been dug out and shafts of lantern light shone through the gaps in the walls and ceiling, it looked secure. None of the kikrikki bodies scattered across the hillside showed any sign of motion—they were all dead.

The same could not be said for the half-dozen tremendous black insects that came racing over the hill. They skidded to a halt when they saw Goedaer, then turned to run in a different direction, but their hesitation proved fatal. With a rush of icy wind they were suddenly engulfed by a thin fog that smelled of ozone. Delicate patterns of frost formed on the kikrikki carapaces. Then the insects began to pop and sizzle as electric arcs played across their bodies, frying them from within.

"Did you see that, Father?" said Toi, wagging his mighty tail as he trotted on all fours up to where his father stood. "I got 'em!"

"That you did, Son, that you did," said Goedaer. It was doubtful that Daelyn or any of the others in the bunker could hear them, but even if they could, the conversation would sound like a series of reptilian growls. He doubted very much if any of these farmers had ever heard the Draconic language, let alone studied it. "And I'm proud of the way you waited until you had them all grouped together. You should always use your breath to its maximum effect."

"I know," Toi answered with only a hint of annoyance. Like most children, he desperately wanted to learn everything his father knew, but despised taking instruction.

The two dragons sat on the hilltop and stared across the valley. The pale moonlight played across their iridescent scales in a cascade of rainbows.

"My grandfather was right," Goedaer said quietly, not wanting to disturb the beauty of the rolling, grass-covered hills before them. "This may well be the most beautiful place ever. But why did the humans have to call it 'Thartholan?'"

"I guess he was right about place names, too," said Toi.

"He was right about a great many things," answered Goedaer.

They sat for a few moments in silence.

"Do you think they knew?" Toi asked when he could take the quiet no longer.

"Do I think who knew what?"

"The people," Toi said. "Do you think they knew we were dragons?"

His father thought about it for a moment.

"No," he said finally. "We're much too clever for them."

Toi considered this answer, then said, "I think they knew. Well, I think some of them knew. They're a lot more clever than you think, Father."

"Perhaps," said Goedaer. "But they always look for the simple answer."

"Yeah, but they'll know for sure when they come out and see us sitting here."

"If they do as they're told," said Goedaer, "they will not come out until morning. By then I'll be able to cast a spell to transform us back into human form, and we won't have to test your theory."

"What if they come out sooner?" Toi asked.

"We'll deal with that problem if it arises," answered Goedaer. "I hope we'll be able to forge strong ties with these humans before we are forced to reveal too much. It will make things so much easier. This land was in our family's blood since before their kind ever walked the world. But in a strange way, they are as much a part of this place as the hills, streams, and fields. We could certainly kill them or force them off, but that would leach the land of a great deal of its beauty and nobility."

"Yeah," said Toi. "I like them, too."

KRISTINE KATHRYN RUSCH
MANIPULATORS

The wind blew cold through the mountain pass. Maalar crouched between two snow-covered boulders, study-ing the pile of wares on the blanket before him.

The human behind the blanket looked miserable. Wrapped in furs, with a fur-covered hat over its head, the human looked colder than Maalar believed possible. Ice had formed on the human's beard just below its mouth, and its lower jaw trembled.

"A fire would be nice," it said in the Common tongue.

"A fire would be nice, wouldn't it?" Maalar replied in the same language. "The sooner we finish here, the sooner we can return to our hearth and home."

The human's lower jaw trembled even more. "Fifty gold pieces. For the lot."

Maalar resisted the urge to roll his eyes. Gold pieces. Humans had no concept of true wealth. "I'm not sure what you've presented me is worth any price."

He lifted his right forepaw and pushed at the skull with his claw. The skull rolled against a pile of scales, and knocked them all over the blanket.

"That skull is made of some other kind of bone, put together with a kind of glue. It is not a dragon skull." He let the contempt he felt fill his voice. "Neither are these things scales, at least they are not dragon scales. They are too small, for one, and not sharp enough, for another."

The human's eyelashes had snow on the edges. It crouched even closer to Maalar, crowding him even though he knew the creature was trying to get out of the wind.

"You promised me gold if I brought you relics," the human said.

"So I did," Maalar said. "But these are trash. Except . . ."

He paused, let out a small breath, with just enough heat to melt some of the snow on the nearby rocks. It wouldn't be enough to help the human, but it would give the poor thing an illusion of warmth. While the human moved closer to the rocks, Maalar leaned toward the blanket, squinting at one item near the corner.

The item was large, the size of his own forepaw, and had jewel-encrusted claws. It smelled faintly dusty, like a relic that had been too long in storage, or a dragon who had mummified in his lair. A hint of power floated off of it—old power, power that had once lived and was now dead.

Maalar didn't want to touch it, but he did, pulling it toward him with a single claw. He flipped the thing over and saw tendons and the hint of bones beneath dried skin, bones so fine that they couldn't be reproduced by the same crude method that had produced the skull.

He sniffed again, feeling hot anger flow through him. He clenched his teeth together and didn't let the anger out.

"Where did you get this?" he asked the human.

"I told you." The human's entire body was shivering again. It looked like a painful jarring, as if the creature wasn't in control of its body at all. Warmbloods. They suffered in weather like this, instead of letting their bodies cool to match the air, like dragon bodies did.

"Tell me again," Maalar said.

"In Omset," the human said. "A store there specializes in relics. Dragon relics. For religious purposes—and magical ones."

Maalar didn't care about the reasons, only the relics. He knew that unless humans had developed a preservation process he didn't know about, they didn't have the skill to keep an actual dragon forepaw for more than a thousand years. And this one hadn't come from the dramojh. They hadn't had some of those tiny bones in the foreclaw, nor the vanity that would make them embed jewels into their own flesh.

"Where did this Omset get this so-called relic?" Maalar asked.

"Dragons have hidden in these mountains for centuries." The human rubbed its hands together, its eyelashes fluttering. "Even before you came back."

"You know this because?"

"The stories," the human said. "Omset was once called 'Home of the Dragon Slayers.'"

* * * * *

Treyna huddled in the cellar of the closed store. Outside the winter wind howled. The store was cold, even this deep underground, but she didn't dare start a fire in the hearth.

She had heard that the dragons had finally come to the Bitter Peaks, and it would only be a matter of time before they found Omset. Omset and the followers of Dragonslore.

She had placed a lantern on a nearby table, and farther away, she had lit a few candles against the darkness. When her father died, she had wanted to close this place, but her mother had argued against it. Her mother liked the power that being a small part of the religion gave her, but she liked the money more.

The shop had made the family wealthy, at least by Omset standards, and her mother was reluctant to part with even a fraction of that wealth. When word of the dragons' return to the Lands of the Diamond Throne came through the Bitter Peaks, brought by travelers through the Ghostwash river valley, Treyna's mother refused to believe the news.

Not until the priests of the Dragonslore urged believers to hide their relics in safe places and not talk of the religion to any unbelievers. Business at the store dropped significantly. The only items that sold in the last few months were traditional ones, things usually found in a witchbag, like tindertwigs and gossamer strands of spider webs.

Then, even that small business quit, as more and more people in Omset grew worried about the shop's reputation. Dragon fear had lived in this place for centuries. Now that living, breathing dragons were so close, it seemed only natural for that fear to grow.

Treyna blew on her chilled fingers. She packed glass beads into pouches, careful not to place those used in divining spells next to those used for cursing. Most of the magical items worked. The Dragonslore pieces, so far as Treyna could tell, were sold to the gullible for their make-believe religion.

But her mother wouldn't let her simply close the shop and be done with it. No. Instead, the inventory had to be packed and housed in special storage places until the dragon threat passed.

As if it would pass. The dragons had returned, and no matter how much Mother wanted to deny it, they wouldn't leave again.

* * * * *

The cavern was deep and wide, hidden in the bowels of the Bitter Peaks. Stalactites dripped lime from overhead. Lumps that were too small to be blessed with the name stalagmite looked like human-sized chairs on the cavern floor. A stream ran through this place, filling the air with droplets of moisture and giving it a mildewy smell that Maalar found exotic. Passageways branched off this main cavern in all directions, many of them too narrow for even a young dragon like Maalar. Dragon-laid fires dotted the entrances to all the passageways, adding light and keeping the cavern warmer than the wintery outdoors.

He hated this room, hated this so-called shared lair, and could scarcely wait until this group of dragons had its own palatial home, as Kooplar had promised.

Kooplar was the head of this clan, an ancient and extremely large male who claimed he had lived in the Land of Dragons before, claimed even that he had known Erixalimar, the greatest of the dragons.

No one believed Kooplar, but that didn't stop anyone from following him. When he declared that this clan had to move east, no one thought of contradicting him, although about half the clan found family reasons to remain in Pallembor, their western home.

Maalar would have stayed as well, if it weren't for Kooplar's greatest granddaughter, Wolar. Maalar had thought her the most beautiful dragon he had ever seen from the moment she hatched from her egg. He had found her attractive from their childhood on, but as they aged, he realized how stunning she was. Stunning and intelligent, the perfect mate.

He was still too powerless to ask for her. To court her, he would need Kooplar's permission as head of the clan, and Kooplar was much too protective of his great-granddaughter.

Still, this discovery might make all the difference.

Maalar set the wizened front paw on the flat-topped rock that served as the dragons' meeting stone. He had paid the freezing human all the gold the creature had asked for, even though it had only brought one relic of worth. That single relic was more than Maalar had believed the human capable of.

Dragons bestirred themselves from all over the cavern. It looked, as it had since they had come to this cold and lonely land, as if the very boulders themselves were coming to life. This clan of dragons seemed greyer than they had in the past, less full of the richness of dragon life. Or perhaps it was the natural sluggishness brought on by the chill.

"You have no right to call a meeting," Kooplar said as he picked his way across the stream. He hadn't flown since the trip to the Bitter Peaks. His wings looked thin, as if he had worn them into nothingness.

Maalar did not answer. Any dragon had the right to call a meeting in an emergency. And if the humans were strong enough to take on dragons, this clan needed to know of it.

Wolar extended her wings. She yawned, revealing perfect teeth. Maalar liked their brown sharpness better than the whiteness he had seen in other families or the jewel-encrusted vanities of the southern clans.

Then he glanced at the jewel-encrusted claws before him, and wondered if the tradition of pressing wealth into the scales had come from this land instead of the one in which he had been raised.

"What is that?" Kooplar said, nodding toward the mummified forepaw. "It reeks."

It did have a stronger smell in here, now that the wind wasn't blowing the stench all over the mountain pass.

"This," Maalar said, "if we are not careful, could be our doom."

He hadn't meant to be so dramatic, but his words caught Wolar's attention. Her green eyes met his across the cavern floor. She raised her lids ever so slightly in a sign of surprise.

"Doom?" Kooplar sat in front of the table. His three henchmen filled the remaining space so that the dozen other dragons, heads of their families all, couldn't see the relic.

"I got this from a human," Maalar said. "It claims this came from a dragon killed after our people left. I have examined it. It's not dramojh. Nor is it fake. He brought me many other fake relics. This is the only one that's real."

Now he had his clan's attention. Kooplar let him speak, and Maalar told the story, down to the city of dragon slayers in a valley just outside the Peaks.

As Maalar spoke, Kooplar picked up the paw and examined it. He passed it to his henchmen, who then passed it from family head to family head, so that the entire clan could view it.

"Disturbing," Kooplar said when Maalar was finished. "You are right that this is dragon and it is not old enough to come from a dragon that existed before we left for the West. It is not young enough to come from a dragon recently returned."

Maalar hadn't even thought of that. His chilled blood cooled even more as he realized how foolish he would have looked if the forepaw had come from a recent kill.

"And," Kooplar said, "there is truth to the human's story. The forepaw was severed at the bone, using one of those smooth blades the humans fashioned from metal and fire. At best, there is a dragon living in these mountains without a front paw. At worst, the humans have become powerful enough to slay us with little more than meager weapons, which we used to scoff at thousands of years ago."

"Only one dragon?" Wolar's soft voice echoed through the cavern. Technically, she had no right to speak, since she was not the head of a family, but her great-grandfather indulged her.

The heads of the families turned toward her; they appreciated her mighty intelligence. She still crouched near the stream, her wingtips in the icy water. The chill made her seem even more silver than usual, and the green that occasionally laced her scales was missing.

"If one stayed behind," she said, "why not many?"

"Very few stayed," Kooplar said. "Staying violated the treaty."

"But our clan travels in family units. Perhaps others lived that way in the past." Wolar sounded sure of herself.

Kooplar shook his head. The weight of his body made the ground rock. "We would have known. Entire families missing? Erixalimar wouldn't have allowed it. He made an agreement to rid the land of dramojh. Erixalimar kept his word."

"Surely some escaped it," Wolar said. "Families—"

"Families could not have, " Kooplar said. "An individual or two, perhaps. Families, no."

And even if Wolar's suppositions were true, Kooplar would not allow the speculation. Which, of course, closed down much of Maalar's argument as well.

"We must find the truth of this matter," Kooplar said. "We must learn if the humans are in any way threatening to us. You say they have used dragon parts for magic? Has this magic given them more power than they had in the past?"

The last dragon placed the claw back on the meeting stone.

"I don't know," Maalar said. "I brought this to the clan the moment I left the human."

"Why did it come to you?" Kooplar asked.

"Because I promised it payment." Maalar could not resist a dig at his leader.

Kooplar did not answer that. Instead he stared at the mummified claw. Then he pushed it, as Maalar had when he first saw it. The claw rolled on the stone, the jewels clinking on the surface.

"We must find the truth behind this." Kooplar's voice was unusually quiet. "Our first mission is to find the dragon. He is clearly male—no females decorate their claws like this, not even in the Rroaresh clan—but I cannot tell you how old. The heads of the families will spread out and search. You will look for a dragon who no longer knows how to be social, or the body of one."

"If it hasn't been cut up for parts," Wolar mumbled. Her words carried.

Her great-grandfather turned to her, his lips raised in disapproval, his time-flattened teeth lacking the menace they once had.

"You speak of horrors you don't understand."

She raised her wings enough to bring the tips, dripping, out of the stream. "And you expect a reasonable search. The humans have already showed you that they are not reasonable. If they have taken a claw and made fake items, as Maalar said, then they will take a true tail tip or a wing or even a snout."

Maalar dipped his head slightly, pleased she had said his name. He also wanted to keep his gaze away from Kooplar's.

"Perhaps you should let those who are interested look," Wolar said. "After all, it was not the heads of the families who brought this to you. It was Maalar, and he did so out of goodness and concern for our people, not because rules guide him to do so."

The entire clan looked at him. Dragon eyes glittered in the flickering light. Maalar had never before caught the attention of every one of his family and friends.

"I would like to go," said Epsila, one of Wolar's close friends.

"And I," said Salotar, who usually did not deign to speak to Maalar.

"Me, too," said Ugusta. Her wings wrapped around her front in a self-satisfied hug. "Like Maalar, I speak the local languages. Perhaps I could find out what we need to know by talking with the humans, just like he has."

"I will not send our entire breeding stock out of the mountains." Kooplar glared at Maalar, as if Maalar had started this revolt, not Wolar, then shook his head again. "But I will allow two from each family to search. It is up to the heads as to which two. I will not argue it."

Wolar tilted her head, her eyes sparkling as they found Maalar's. He did not tilt his head in return. He didn't want her to leave the lair, and he knew she would.

Her great-grandfather would not stop her. No one could when she put her mind to something. No one, not even the dragons she loved.

* * * * *

The crowd inside her mother's great room was a motley one. Treyna noticed the stench of bear grease and unwashed bodies the moment she entered.

Trappers and traders circled the hearthstone fireplace, their hair braided and tumbling down their backs, their clothing unchanged since the winter began. None had shed their fur cloaks since coming inside, and their fur-covered boots left mud-tracks along the usually clean stone floor.

Treyna couldn't see her mother, but she heard her voice, muttering some sort of spell.

Treyna pushed past a group of men she recognized only from the market. She shuddered as her shoulders brushed against cloth so filthy the dirt tumbled onto the floor behind her.

Finally she got to the front of the group. A man lay before the fire, his face blackened, his nose nearly gone, his beard dripping with wet. He wore the same costume as the others, but someone had opened it, revealing white flesh the color of fish bellies. His right hand, blackened at the fingertips, was clenched into an impossibly tight fist.

Treyna's mother shook her head. She was a slight, grey-haired woman who claimed to have the gifts of a minor akashic. Her gaze met Treyna's, but her mother didn't acknowledge her. Instead, her mother wiped her hands on her robes and looked up at the dozen or more people surrounding her.

"He's been dead too long," she said. "We cannot revive him, even if one of us had the skill."

"But we need to find what killed him," a woman across from Treyna's mother said. The woman was tall and broad, her features cut from bones as sharp as knives.

"You know what killed him." Treyna's mother used her calming voice. "He is still frozen. No human survives the winds of the peaks, not wearing the thin layers that he has."

"He wasn't a fool!" The woman looked at the rest of the people around her.

"No one says that he was," Treyna's mother said.

"But only fools go into the mountains dressed for valley weather." The woman's voice broke. Then she fell to her knees beside the body and touched the bare skin. Her hands pulled away as if she had been burned.

"See?" Treyna's mother said. "Frozen."

Treyna crossed her arms, uncertain why this crowd had come.

"He was off the path, and he was alone," one of the men said. "He had been left for wolves." The implication was that he had been murdered and left so that no one would recover the body.

"Nonsense," Treyna's mother said. "If he'd been left for wolves, you never would have found him. The wolves aren't starving this season. They don't prey close to the paths."

The man shook his head. "I know Nyret would never have gone alone into the mountains. He had to have had a traveling companion, and that companion left him for dead. There is no other explanation."

Treyna sighed. Her mother repeated herself a third time. This was why her mother did not lead, why the villagers had stopped coming here except for medical knowledge and in search of items to help with their potions. Her mother lacked the skills to influence others, and that was what was needed now.

Trappers could get violent. They were loners, but they valued each other. They felt the villagers hated them, and they blamed every human-based problem on the village, not on themselves.

The interesting thing was that Nyret was not a trapper. He was a rebel from the First Family of Omset, the nominal leaders of the village, and as such, a distant relation of hers. Nyret had tried to make it on his own, but his travels and battles had not worked for him. Instead, he had come home and done his best to disrupt the First Family, finding ways to pull at their power without adding to his own.

"Was he alone where you found him?" Treyna asked.

Her mother winced, obviously not wanting Treyna involved. The others looked at her as if they hadn't realized she was there.

One man tossed a bundle in front of her. "He had this."

The bundle looked light. Treyna crouched, grabbed the leather string, and pulled. The blanket fell open, letting loose a wisp of mold and ancient dust.

Relics clanked against the stone floor. A dragon's shattered skull, a collection of scales, and a dragon's tail tip—so sharp a customer had once cut his fingers on it—were the first things she noticed.

She ran her fingers through the wares. All of the items were relics for Dragonslore. She did not believe in the religion, but her mother did. So did most people in Omset.

Treyna looked over at her mother. Her mother's face looked as bloodless as Nyret's belly.

"I did not sell these to him," her mother whispered, a sound meant only for Treyna. "He does not practice."

If the shop were still open, Treyna would have ground the skull into powder for prayer enhancement. She still had vials, all stored in a safe place, of dragon's breath, dragon smoke, and ashes from a dragon-caused fire. She had purchased most of the items before her, thinking them all junk.

In those days, no one had ever seen a dragon, although Omset was supposed to be the home of dragon slayers. That was how the Dragonslore religion had started; a group of champions had come here, the legend said, to slay the dragons remaining in these mountains.

Over time, champion after champion died here. An akashic named Daagown, trained in the old ways, found dragon bits in travel all over the mountains. Dragon parts, and dragon scales, dragon scent all had mystical powers, or so Daagown had said. Other akashics Treyna had met in her short lifetime claimed these items had no such powers: They were scams for the easily fooled.

Treyna had never seen the magic of Dragonslore work. Neither had anyone else. Yet most everyone in town believed in it. She had no idea why.

She did not believe. She never had.

She also had never expected the stock to appear before her like this, scattered and ruined. If her mother hadn't sold it, and Treyna hadn't either, then Nyret had stolen it. Not a surprise, given how he had conducted his life these last few years.

The surprise was that he had stolen these items before the shop closed. She had noticed that stock was missing weeks ago, changed the policy toward allowing customers to examine the merchandise, and made certain that either she or her mother was in the relic room at all times.

She hadn't really cared that these cheap items had gone missing. But one valuable item had disappeared as well: a jewel-encrusted claw that had been in the shop as long as she could remember. It looked so real that she was loath to touch it, and yet the jewels always winked at her as if they were sharing a secret.

"What's in his hand?" Treyna asked.

Her mother shook her head slightly.

"We need to know, Mother. What's in his hand?"

"It's not thawed yet—"

"Of course it is," Treyna said. "It's closest to the fire."

Treyna's mother didn't move, but one of the men stepped across the body, grabbed the arm, and forced the fingers open. Gold pieces tumbled onto the stone, making everyone gasp.

Including Treyna. She hadn't seen gold like that since she was a child, and then only because a trader from Verdune had found a buried pile of treasure that he swore had been in the lands near the Unknown West for millennia.

The gold coins came from a time when humans roamed the lands freely, before the dramojh became a scourge, killing everything. Ancient money, a missing dragon's claw.

Treyna shivered despite the heat of the fire.

"What is it, child?" her mother whispered.

But Treyna didn't answer. She had never told her mother the story of the ancient gold nor of her fear of the dragon's claw. She had revealed her belief that Dragonslore was a false religion.

She kept everything to herself.

But she now knew that this couldn't keep. Nor could she speak of her suspicions in front of every trader and trapper who worked this part of the foothills.

Her silence, however, was worthless. The man next to her picked up one of the coins, bit it, then studied it as if he hadn't seen anything like it before.

"By Malleus' Beard," he said, his face filled with awe. "Dragon's gold."

The words "dragon's gold" were repeated in whispers throughout the room. One by one, the believers among the traders fell to their knees and covered their faces with their hands. A few remained standing, looking stunned.

Treyna's mother looked stunned as well. "We're rich."

"No," Treyna said softly. "We're doomed."

* * * * *

Maalar had flown these mountain passes before. He liked the way the chill winds created currents that seemed like eddies in a powerful stream. He sometimes played here, alone and unwatched, searching for a hideaway of his own, one he could make into the perfect lair, a place to bring Wolar if he ever achieved wings-match with her.

The other dragons were searching through caves he had already visited in his drive to explore this place. All of those caves he knew to be empty: no dragons, no dragon bones, no hint of a previous lair. The searchers hadn't listened to him, though— not even Wolar, who had left with her female friends despite her great-grandfather's objections.

In fact, all of the searchers through the passes were young dragons. Which made Maalar suspicious. The old ones were up to something. He wanted to see what.

So when the column of dragons appeared in the skies long after the searchers had left, he was not surprised. He kept his distance, hiding among the mountain peaks as the heads of the families flew toward the east.

Toward the east and the humans. Toward the east, and the place where the relic makers dwelled.

* * * * *

Treyna wrapped a cloak around her, a scarf across her nose and mouth. The winter winds seemed even colder than usual. Ice hung off the buildings like daggers, and the ground was slick with fresh snow.

The streets were empty. The traders remained in her mother's house, arguing over the body, the dragon's gold, the relics. No one else shared Treyna's fears.

No one else seemed to understand what they all faced.

Summer travelers through the Ghostwash river valley claimed they'd seen more than a hundred dragons in the skies, circling, looking for places to live. The story made her argue with her mother to close the shop.

Now Treyna checked the sky repeatedly as she hurried through the village streets. The clouds hung low. They were dark grey, pregnant with more storms, waiting to unleash them at the worst possible moment for the villagers below.

The First Family's compound stood at what had once been the center of the village. The First Family had a dozen buildings, all ancient, all stone, and in the middle of them, where the village square used to be, they had built a tower that overlooked all of Omset.

At the western edge of the village, where the foothills started to grow into impassable, craggy peaks, she pushed open the door of a massive stone home. The home had been added to, month after month, year after year, decade after decade. Most in Omset had no idea where the home began and where it ended, and how much of the surrounding stone crags it consumed.

As usual, the interior was dark and smelled of decay. She used a tindertwig to light a nearby candle. She did not call out as she walked, instead ducking as she went through doorway after doorway, past decades of discarded clothing and blankets and gifts.

The decaying smell grew the farther she went, until she reached a central room located deep inside the neighboring hillside. The air was humid and warm here.

The man in the middle of that room did not look up as she entered. He kept his head bent over a small bit of wood, which he was shaving clean so that it looked worn by time and weather.

"Grandfather," she said, "tell me the truth about something."

He looked up, startled, his blue eyes the only live things in a face that had fallen in on itself. His white hair looked as though it hadn't been combed in a year; if mice had nested within it, no one would be able to tell.

"I have a pile of goods," he said, swinging his knife-hand toward a knapsack near the door. "You haven't come in days."

She had no idea how he would know how many days had passed, since his windows were covered and he never ventured outside. If it weren't for his network of friends, all of whom were as eccentric as he was, he probably wouldn't have known what year it was.

"I told you," she said. "We closed the shop."

"The priests still need their wares. Religion does not quit because you do, girl."

"It does when the dragons return."

His eyes twinkled. "You have told me that story before."

"It's not a story. It's true."

He looked at the wood in his hand, then began to whittle again. "What is so urgent you arrive without a gift?"

She hadn't brought food or payment for the work he had done. His mind seemed to wander often, but it never wandered from money.

"You have to tell me where you got the claw," she said.

"I have told you." He smiled at the wood, as if it were his granddaughter. "Time and again. You were a child then. You liked to sit at my feet and listen to stories. Then you weren't so judgmental. Then you believed—"

"I need to know if it's real."

He stopped. He set down the wood and the knife, and stood. His body seemed as thin as the knife's blade, but he still had an imposing height, one that made his head brush the stone ceiling.

"We don't talk of these things." He no longer spoke in his old man voice. This was the voice of the man who had started the shop, the man who had run his family with an iron will until an obsessiveness trapped him here, in the only home he had ever known. "If the priests find out—"

"The priests are the least of our worries, Grandfather. The *dragons* have returned."

He stared at her, his eyes clear. It was as if he heard her for the first time. "You believe this."

"I know this. I've seen them flying in the skies above. If you left this building, you would know it too. The dragons have returned to the Lands of the Diamond Throne. They want to reclaim it."

He glanced at the corner of the room, in a place he called "his stash," a place he let no one else near, let no one else touch.

"What of the priests?" he asked.

"The priests are worthless, Grandfather. They have believed this nonsense for so long that, when they learned the dragons had returned, you'd think they thought something horrible had arrived. The priests believe that a vial of dragon's breath gives them enough power to rule their followers for half a year. By that token, imagine the power the dragons themselves wield— large, intact creatures, filled with breath."

He sank into his chair. "So that is why you have not come."

She had been there since the dragons returned, but she did not contradict him. "I've closed the shop, hidden the wares, and destroyed many of them. I never wanted word to reach the dragon lairs of what they could find if they approached Omset."

He closed his eyes, and rocked back and forth. Then he seemed to gather himself again. "You came here to ask me a question."

She nodded, trying to hang onto her patience. "I need to know if the dragon's claw is real."

His withered face was sad as he said, "It's real, child."

"I always thought so."

"I always told you so."

"You always told me everything was real, even when I watched you glue skulls together from bits of a dozen different creatures."

That was why she had never believed. Dragonslore claimed to draw its power from relics, and yet her grandfather made the relics. The religion was false, and she knew it as clearly as if she had invented it herself.

Her grandfather smiled a little, then shrugged. "You sell better when you believe."

"I have never believed, not in Dragonslore, not in anything. But I have stayed here because this is my home, and now I need to know, old man, where you got that claw."

"It was on my last hunt—"

"The truth," she snapped. She didn't want to hear the old story again. She hadn't believed it when she was tiny, and she didn't believe it now. "I need the truth."

He closed his eyes and whispered, "From the last room in the back, as far into the darkness as you can go."

It took her a moment to understand exactly what he meant.

* * * * *

They circled the village, their big dragon bodies blocking what remained of the light. They looked huge as they flew over the tiny buildings, like things that had fallen out of the clouds.

Maalar was too far away to see the villagers. He hovered over the last foothill, ready to duck behind it if the leaders looked in his direction. But, oh, his people were magnificent: powerful and unyielding, they swooped around the village as if it belonged to them.

One by one, they landed, extended their wings, and touched the tips, a maneuver he had been taught but had never used.

The maneuver blocked fleeing prey, blocked it on all sides. He slid between two of the elders, who looked at him in shock. One of them winked, and he was accepted.

The dragons waited. The winds whipped around them, the snow picked up, but they knew the villagers saw only them.

* * * * *

She saw the drawings first, etched onto wood that lined up against the stone walls, as if someone were trying to get details right. She recognized the style as that of her grandfather, his use of charcoal and ash to create thin lines. Some of the drawings were simple things—a claw, a tooth—but most were of the creature itself, mighty, terrifying, and stuck back into the corner like discarded laundry.

She couldn't believe such a great thing hid in the back of her grandfather's house. Finally, she gathered her courage, and pushed open an iron-framed wooden door.

The smell came first, that stench of decay that had always belonged to this house, as long as she could remember. Without lighting the torch that her grandfather claimed he kept beside the door, she knew that the creature inside was dead.

She used her candle to light the torch. Bit by bit, as the flames extended around the torch's top, the room revealed itself. Not a room, exactly. A cave, hollowed out by time and water, and crumbling stone. The ceiling looked like it still crumbled sometimes; the water, however, was long gone from this chamber.

She set the candle on a holder carved into the wall. She took the torch off its peg and moved closer to the large frame in the back. There was no corner, only a hollowed-out shape that was the end of the cave.

It had come there to die. She could tell just from its posture, hunched and defensive. Even if it weren't missing its front paws, cut neatly by a blade, it would seem defenseless. Its teeth were ground almost to powder, its eye sockets black

and frightened holes, its hoary spine a mere shadow of its terrifying self.

But the real problem was the wings. They were shattered as if
the dragon had fallen on them and crushed their fragile bones.

That was why she never got anything but wing-tips from her
grandfather. He did not know the real structure of the wings.
He could only guess.

The rest, she understood completely. Her grandfather had used
the dragon as a model, building replicas of its frame and form,
using them to make a fortune off the believers in Dragonslore—
believers who, for decades, still thought they had power even
when the "magical" items they used had none.

The wily old man had fooled everyone, including her. He
had made a mockery of everything on which this village was
based, everything that it stood for.

She eased out of the room, put out the torch, and replaced it.
She was happy to leave the stench; it had lingered long after the
decay that caused it had ended. Most of the dragon had mummified. What was left seemed like a shadow of its former self.

When she reached her grandfather, she asked, "Was it alive
when you found it?"

He shook his head. "I don't even know how it got in there. I
built the hallways you used. When I found the dragon, I crawled
through passages smaller than you are, tracking down the stink."

"Did you know what was there?"

"I thought it was a bear. A dead one. I planned to sell its
parts to the people south of here."

"Were you surprised?"

He nodded. "Until I found the wider opening that led into
the Bitter Peaks. I blocked that off, so no one else could find
the body. Then I brought out the first paw. It was good enough
to convince the Dragonslore priests that I had slain a dragon.
The second paw was mine. I had once hoped to sell those
jewels and leave here, but . . ."

Even the tales of the dragonslayers were false. She shook her head slightly. Her grandfather had helped to create a religion, using its relics to bilk the people of Omset.

And she had helped him from the time she could stand upright.

He was watching her. She wondered if he had been truly lucid these last years and hiding it, as he had hidden everything else.

"But?" she asked.

"But I could not leave the creature," he said quietly. "Its essence had crept into me. I am part dragon now, and I must hide here, lest the priests carve me up. So I sell fake parts and protect myself, just as you should do."

No, he wasn't lucid. But she had heard truth in all of his words. She thanked him, vowed to bring him food soon, and left, feeling shaken to her very core.

* * * * *

The villagers lined up dozens deep. They wrapped themselves in furs and blankets and stared at the dragons. Maalar felt the wind beneath his scales, slowing his blood and making him even more sluggish than he had been. When the whispers came from behind, he almost didn't hear them.

He turned his head and saw Wolar.

"How did you know about this?" she asked, and there was awe in her voice. Many of the other young scattered behind her, watching. Obviously they had seen the gathering from the sky.

"I figured there was a reason they had sent us away. They don't want the young ones harmed. We're the future," Maalar said.

"Apparently, my great-grandfather is frightened there will be no future," Wolar said. "He wants Ugusta to speak to the humans, but your Common tongue is so much better than hers. I think you should talk to them."

"No," Maalar said.

"I made Ugusta fly back to the lair. You'll have to." Wolar was as wily as her great-grandfather.

"You'll have to tell him."

"I know the messages. I'll speak for him. He's occupied."

Suspicious, Maalar looked around and saw that Kooplar was intent on studying the gathered humans. Somehow the young dragon felt this was a trap. But it was a lovely trap, the first time he'd ever really been the object of Wolar's trust.

"All right," he said cautiously.

"Tell them to bring all of their dragon relics to us. We won't destroy the village if they cooperate."

Maalar grimaced. "If they can defeat us, threatening them will make them angry. They will attack."

Wolar nodded. "That is my great-grandfather's plan. He believes they can kill one dragon at a time, but not dozens."

"He gambles on our lives."

"He did so when he brought us here." Her eyes glinted in that familiar way. "That's why he leads us, because his gambles work."

Maalar took a deep breath, felt the fire in his belly warming him like an eternal flame. The warmth helped; he was alone here. He could say whatever he wanted and the other dragons wouldn't know.

Not even Wolar.

But he would do as she said. He wanted her to trust him.

"People of the village!" Maalar said in Common. "Listen to me!"

Several humans crowded forward. He repeated Wolar's words. The humans made a squeaking sound, and several of them ran toward the buildings.

The warmth in his belly faded. Had they misunderstood? Were they going to attack?

He glanced at Wolar, and her face reflected his uncertainty.

He didn't dare look at Kooplar, across the way. He didn't dare see the disapproval in Kooplar's eyes.

* * * * *

Treyna emerged from the home into chaos. People ran past her, their faces filled with terror. Others ran in the opposite direction, clutching blankets against their chests or vials she recognized, vials of air she had labeled dragon's breath.

She was buffeted by bodies until she saw what had caused the panic: dragons, large and alive, their wings spread, surrounding the outside edges of the village itself.

For a moment, she simply stared. They were such magnificent creatures, their scales reflecting the light of a hundred candles held by people who couldn't move, people who watched the dragons like the dragons watched them.

She recognized those people as well—all of them believers, all of them petrified by the power of the creatures before them.

Even the First Family watched, from their place inside their tower. She could see silhouettes against the lighted windows, the protectors of Omset letting their subjects protect them.

"Cowards," she whispered.

More people ran around her, slamming into her, pushing her back and forth. The snow trickled down, as if it couldn't decide whether to storm or not.

She grabbed the arm of a passing man and yanked him toward her. "What's going on?"

"They're going to destroy us if they don't get the relics. They want the relics."

Because they had seen the claw. Because they knew there was a dead dragon somewhere near Omset. Because they believed the humans had killed it.

A chill ran through her. She realized then that she had let go of her furs, that her coat was open, and she was shivering from both fear and the chill.

She glanced back toward her grandfather's home, but it was lost in the running bodies, the dim light, and the trickle of snow. Her grandfather wouldn't come out, not even if she begged him. He hadn't come out in two dozen years.

She swallowed. She hadn't let go of the man's arm. He stared at her like he expected her to give him instructions.

"How do we know what the dragons want?" she asked.

"One of them speaks Common!" He sounded like a man who had just discovered that his gods not only existed, but that they were angry and bent on destruction.

"Which one?"

He pointed.

She let him go and walked in the direction he pointed. Perhaps her gait kept others away from her. Perhaps her determination. Or perhaps it was the way she had set her face, willing it to show no fear.

Finally she stopped at the edge of the building, before one of the smaller dragons, its eyes an amazing emerald green.

"You are the leader?" she asked.

"I am the speaker," it said.

"You want to know where the claw came from."

A hush fell around her. People stopped running. Everyone stared at her as if she were as crazy as her grandfather.

"We want to know how you slew our brethren. We want their bodies returned, not defiled in your unholy rites."

She swallowed again, only this time there was no moisture in her mouth. The swallowing hurt. "There is only one. We didn't slay it. Its wings were crushed. It died, alone, in a cave that my grandfather has hidden."

Gasps around her, and not from the dragons. Someone whispered, "Blasphemer," and someone else moved toward her, only to be stopped by yet a third person's hand.

"Show us," the dragon said.

"I'm not sure I can," Treyna said. "My grandfather blocked the passages."

The dragon made a guttural sound, and the tip of a flame emerged from its mouth. Its teeth were different from the remnants in her grandfather's house, large and brown and very sharp.

Other dragons made noise as well, and she realized then that they were considering what she said.

"Are these passages wide?" the dragon asked her.

"Not wide enough for you," she said.

Its wings collapsed against its body. They were intricate, and beautiful. No wonder that poor creature in the cave hadn't flown. It hadn't been able to.

"Show me," the dragon said. "Show me or die."

* * * * *

Maalar did not believe he would fit inside the human dwelling, but somehow he did. And he knew from the moment that he stepped into the tiny place that a dragon had died here.

He recognized the smell, the smell of ancient death. The dragon had done as dragons were trained to do, find the farthest, most secret hiding place, and wait for the wounds to heal. Only this dragon's wounds hadn't healed.

The human had explained what it knew of the dragon as it brought Maalar to the dwelling. The human had also apologized for creating false relics, saying as a justification that its grandfather had done so to prevent more destruction of the dead dragon.

Maalar saw the grandfather only briefly. It looked like all other humans, only wizened. It took one look at him and collapsed, as if all of its bones had broken all at once.

The other human squeaked, and ran to the grandfather. Maalar followed the stench on his own.

His wings pressed against his body, and he would have known, even if the human hadn't told him, that the other dragon had not come this way. He would later discover the other passage, and use it to show his people this place of death.

But he found the door made of wood and iron, as the human had told him. The stench was eye-dripping here. He lit a little flame, saw the corpse of a long-dead cousin, one whose wings had been crushed, just as the human said, and he intoned a poem of mourning.

He would have burned the corpse, but he felt it best not to, not yet. He needed to show Kooplar and the others, to prevent them from destroying this desolate place.

Maalar wasn't sure why he wanted to keep these human creatures alive. He didn't like them. He hated the way they had desecrated this helpless dragon before them, even if the dragon's life force was long gone. But he had learned, in his travels from the Unknown West, that he was not fond of random killings.

He believed more in life than he did in death.

He let the trickle of flame build into a small stream, and touched it to the wall beside him. It glowed red, and in the edges of the stone, he saw the faint outlines of a blocked passage.

It took only a moment to pull the stones aside. Air poured into the room, taking with it some of the decaying stench.

He followed the tunnel out, the tunnel last used by the long-dead dragon, saw the markings the dragon had used to record his final journey, and knew the truth would be revealed soon enough.

* * * * *

When the dragon did not return, Treyna left her grandfather and walked through the silent hallway. Scales littered the ground like gemstones, and her grandfather's drawings were shattered—not intentionally, but by the dragon's body as it squeezed through the narrow corridor.

Even before she reached the door, she knew what had happened. She felt the chill wind.

The dragon had found the sealed passageway and opened it.

She went inside the room, near a wall still glowing with heat, and waited. When the other dragons came, she would explain that, while her people were stupid, they were not malicious. They had only learned superstition from radical priests and had meant no harm.

232

Surely they had meant no harm.

After a while, her revived grandfather joined her. He sat beside her and said, with an awe she had never heard in his voice, "They are so much more magnificent than I had ever imagined."

"Yeah," she said softly. "They are."

They were. They truly were.

* * * * *

Kooplar reserved the right to burn the body, destroying it according to the clan's custom and ritual. But he did so as his last act as leader.

The heads of the families had chosen Maalar to guide them through this strange new world they found themselves in, a world that looked nothing like the place they had left millennia ago.

His first act was to order them all to learn the Common tongue. His second was to ask Wolar to match her wings to his.

For a breathless moment, he thought she wouldn't accept. Then her eyes glinted.

"Of course," she said, loud enough for all to hear, and then her gaze met his again, a gaze filled with warmth and laughter, and maybe—he dared hope—love.

Months later, Kooplar claimed in a moment of weakness that he had never ordered anyone to speak to the villagers. Wolar denied to the entire clan that it was her idea and swore that Kooplar had issued the order.

Maalar stayed out of the dispute. He already knew what had happened. He had known from the moment she crawled from her egg that his mate was strong enough to manipulate an entire clan.

He was profoundly stunned and grateful that the first time she had used her powers, she had done so to be with him.

He would do his best to be worthy of her.

He would do his best to be worthy of them all.

LORESIGHT LEGATION

Katay pushed windblown strands of her short red hair back under her hat. Her green eyes were blurring from tears caused by the stinging cold. She flicked the water away, returned her chilled hands back under her armpits, and glared back down at the mojh village at the base of the cliff. "Nothing. No movement for hours," she muttered. "Everyone's inside, out of the cold. Everyone but us spies."

"Somehow I thought spying on a village of dragon worshippers would be more interesting. Or at least not as dull as watching you stare at broken pottery for hours," Manda chirped.

Katay gave a little snort in response to the spryte's comment. She wished she were back at the Silver Creek akashic node, staring at pieces of broken pottery instead of freezing her fingers off on this Bitter Peaks mountainside at the behest of the authorities in Gahanis. "Damned giants, always getting us little people involved in their problems," she groused.

"Little!" Manda giggled. Her blue eyes sparkled in the sunshine, and she fluttered her gossamer wings forward and backward about her slender body. She shook her ponytail of silver-streaked black hair so that she seemed to glitter when she laughed. Katay, who was shorter and wirier than most humans, still stood nearly four times the spryte's height and was twenty-five times the spryte's weight. Sometimes Katay felt like a graceless cow beside the tiny creature.

"Anyway," the spryte said, "you're not here because the steward of Gahanis wants to know about this dragon," she chided. "You're here because of that ring."

Katay reached her hand into her pocket and fingered the turquoise ring that had compelled her to seek out the mojh of this village. A skilled hand had carved the blue stone into the shape of two circling flicker fish each about to swallow the tail of the other. The fish's eyes glinted with tiny ruby chips. It was hardly a thing of beauty, but it held a lot of meaning for ten akashic students. "Akashic knowledge is like the flicker fish," Master Beile always said. "You must know where to look, then bring it in with a net."

Save for being just a little larger, the ring was identical to the one Katay wore on her right hand. Master Beile had gifted them to his last class of students the spring before he'd been mauled to death by an akashic seeker. There had been ten students that year. Katay had left Gouby at Silver Creek wearing his ring just two weeks ago. Doravi had been buried west of the Bitter Peaks beneath an avalanche of scree three years back. Katay hadn't seen the remaining seven since the night after Master Beile's funeral.

Which one of them had lost their ring? she fretted. How had it come to be hanging from a platinum chain around the neck of a kobold? And who killed the kobold and dumped its corpse in a miner's cave near Gahanis?

Katay squeezed her eyes shut as if she could block out her memories. She recalled the faces of the miners, pale with fear that the kobold's battered, decaying body would bring them bad luck. She remembered how the city steward's giant hands clenched with anger that a creature so tiny had been harmed in his territory. Worst of all, she could not bury the vision that her loresight had revealed—how the creature had been tortured to death. That was the problem with akashic training. It made it impossible to forget.

"Katay!" Manda whispered in an alarmed tone. "What's that?"

Katay's eyes flew open. Manda's tiny finger swung wildly, pointing out a fast-moving shadow that raced over the vista below, then circled around and moved back in their direction.

"Not good," Katay growled, squinting up into the sun at whatever had cast the shadow. "It's really big, but I can't make out any detail."

Something big hit the mountainside with a thud somewhere uphill from them, then another something crashed beside it, sending loose dirt and rock skittering around Katay's feet. Manda took to the air with a squeak. Katay turned about, sighing.

Two large reptilian creatures stood blocking the trail leading up. They stood upright, each just a little taller than Katay, the scales of their hides a blue-green. Their great batlike wings bore scales just a shade paler than those covering their body. They glared at the intruders with glinting red eyes that reminded Katay of the ruby eyes of her turquoise flicker fish rings.

The shadow of the creature in the air swept over them. Without looking up, Katay counted the moments it took to pass by. Manda landed on Katay's pack.

Behind them, someone cleared his throat politely.

Katay turned back in the direction of the village. A third reptile creature stood at the cliff's edge. This one had a darker blue hide, though, with black eyes. He was taller than his fellows, with an even greater wingspan. He was probably a more graceful flyer, too, Katay thought. He'd landed so softly she hadn't even heard his arrival.

Manda whispered, "Aren't they kind of small to be dragons?"

"The dragon is still in the air," Katay replied. "These are dracha. Warrior servants to the dragon."

"You are correct, lady," the blue dracha answered. "I am M'kald'r. First warrior of Lord Hardolis."

Katay bowed her head politely. "Katay Bracken, akashic scholar. My companion is Manda Lightsword, my bodyguard." Manda launched herself from Katay's shoulder and landed just in front of the akashic.

The dracha behind them made a sort of wheezing sound that Katay assumed was laughter. Manda bowed to M'kald'r, pointedly ignoring the pair of smaller dracha who obviously underestimated her prowess.

"Lord Hardolis would know your business in his lands," M'kald'r said.

"I'm here to see a mojh about a kobold," Katay explained.

"You missed the trail to the village," M'kald'r noted.

"I noticed that," Katay replied smoothly. "I was just going to suggest that Manda scout out where I went wrong."

"We will guide you down," M'kald'r said.

A statement, not an offer, Katay realized. "Thank you," she replied.

So they followed M'kald'r back to the trail they had left behind to spy on the camp, with the smaller dracha herding them from behind. It would have taken the dracha and Manda all of a minute to glide down to the village. Escorting Katay down the steep trail took an hour, a delay full of agonizing anticipation. Katay was just grateful that none of the dracha had suggested they pick her up and fly her down.

The akashic kept her attention focused on the bigger dracha, quizzing him on his own background. He'd adventured with the other two warriors throughout the western land of Pallembor, discovering many riches, but left that life behind when, paying them great honor, Lord Hardolis had bid them enter his service. They'd been here a year, keeping the tiny mojh community secure at the behest of his lordship. Lord Hardolis had rewarded M'kald'r by enhancing his physique in a ceremony involving something called a tenebrian seed. That explained not only his greater size, Katay realized, but also his more graceful landing.

M'kald'r's polished manners were, the akashic concluded, the result of his supreme confidence. He had a stillness at his core completely impervious to fear or doubt. Which meant he was unlikely to harm them—unless Lord Hardolis ordered it.

At the base of the cliff they passed through the mojh village, about fifteen small cottages and a community hall. Mojh almost always lived apart from the other races, even humans, the race they were born into before they underwent the mojh transformation. Not, Katay knew, that most humans would welcome them. Most people found the idea of mojh metamorphosis uncomfortable, even treacherous.

The community hall abutted the cliff face. Farther up the cliff was a great cave opening, which they would have never been able to see from the top of the cliff. The dragon and the dracha must have issued forth from this exit just before dawn and been spying on the spies ever since.

The dracha led them inside the hall, which was curiously empty, and then Katay realized why they'd seen no sign of life since breakfast. The back of the hall opened into a second portal into the cliff face, this one considerably smaller. All the mojh were in the mountain all morning, just under her feet.

M'kald'r stepped into the cave. Katay hesitated, her eyes unable to pierce the darkness beyond.

"Excuse me," M'kald'r said. "I had forgotten you would need light."

"That's okay," Manda replied. "I'm never without." She chirped the Faen word for starlight, and a glowglobe as big as her head appeared by her belly. With a gesture from the spryte, the ball of light began hopping along the cave floor like a lost frog.

M'kald'r led them along a passage with numerous side halls, excavated by nature and smoothed out with tools or magic.

They could fit an army in here, the akashic realized.

They climbed a long set of stairs, five hundred thirty-one steps by Katay's count. As they climbed, the air grew noticeably warmer. Then two things assailed her senses at once: the stench and the node. All the vast knowledge of a long dead, but once thriving community tangled and clotted in this place, creating a mystical akashic node of great strength. Katay's gift was the power to sense that knowledge, so she recognized the smell almost immediately. In the ancient past, the people who had lived here had dwelled alongside a dragon, and they all knew the dragon's scent. For the long dead it was the scent of home, but for Katay it was not so reassuring a smell.

The stairs opened on a vast cavern. Manda's glowglobe was completely incapable of illuminating the walls or ceiling. The spryte flew excitedly into the expanse, taking the light with her, leaving Katay to stand in the dark with the dracha. Then suddenly the light was extinguished.

"Hey! Who did that?" Manda demanded. "I can't see where I'm going. *No!* Let me go!" the spryte squeaked.

M'kald'r called out, "My lord Hardolis, I present the akashic Katay Bracken and her bodyguard, Manda Lightsword."

A few feet away a brazier blazed up, then another, and another, until a path of twenty lights showed the way into the cavern. Katay moved along the path to the last brazier.

Manda came rolling like a ball across the floor into the pool of the braziers' light. Katay reached down and steadied her.

Manda, glaring into the darkness, stood and took a defensive posture in front of Katay. Lord Hardolis apparently was not about to reveal his greatness to them. Katay knew better than to ask.

As Katay's eyes adjusted, she saw they were surrounded by mojh, twenty of them. They were all taller than Katay, and, like all mojh, possessed gangly limbs and prominent fangs. Their scaly hides glittered in the brazier light, and their tails twitched curiously as they stared at the nonmojh. The two smaller dracha stood to either side of Katay. M'kald'r had disappeared into the darkness, no doubt to stand beside Lord Hardolis.

"My people," a booming voice rumbled in the darkness, "these outsiders have come to discuss a kobold."

There was a shift in the circle of mojh. One mojh pressed forward, the others moving aside for it. "I am Phenilac," the mojh whispered. "Tell me of this kobold."

Katay bowed politely. "Ne-Chardath, steward of Gahanis, asked me to bear this sad news to your people. The corpse of a kobold was discovered two weeks ago in a mine near his town."

There was a shudder among the mojh, and the one called Phenilac lowered its head.

"My loresight revealed that the creature came from your village," Katay explained. "It wore a token about its neck. Perhaps you can tell me its origin." The akashic pulled the ring on the chain from her pocket and held it out to the mojh.

Phenilac's shoulders slumped; the creature shook visibly as it reached for the ring.

Katay closed her hand about the ring. "Please, first tell me how this ring came to the kobold," she insisted.

"The kobold was my own. I gave the ring to it as a charm to hunt for fish," Phenilac explained.

"And how came you to this ring?" Katay demanded.

"Master Beile gave it to me when I was the girl you knew as Jeddina," the mojh replied.

Katay stepped back as if she'd been slapped. Stunned, she let the ring drop into the mojh's hand. Jeddina. Beautiful, brilliant Jeddina. She could not be this creature.

Phenilac placed a hand on Katay's shoulder. "Please, Katay, tell me what happened to my mojhborn."

Katay looked up into the mojh's green eyes. Jeddina's eyes, with the same speckles of brown. "Rickest, the kobold's name was Rickest," she said, revealing another bit of loresight knowledge she'd gleaned.

Phenilac nodded.

"A mojh tortured Rickest until it died," she whispered, choking back tears from some newly realized bitterness. "It lived for hours until it knew the peace of death."

An angry murmur rippled round the circle of mojh.

"You are lying," another mojh declared.

"No," Phenilac snapped. "She is not." The mojh who once was Jeddina straightened and strode out of the pool of light, into the darkness. Katay could hear its claws clicking against the stone floor as it tried to flee from this evil news.

The other mojh backed into the darkness.

M'kald'r stepped into the light. "My lord bids you spend the night as his guest, while he considers your news more carefully," the dracha said.

Katay shrugged. Ordinarily the invitation to spend the night in a dragon's lair would be disconcerting, but at the moment she was too stunned to summon any emotion.

M'kald'r led them through another corridor to a room lit with more braziers and left them alone. Two nestlike pallets covered with the hides of wolves lay in the corner. Beside the brazier sat a low table of ebony black wood inlaid with a mother-of-pearl design of clouds and flying dragons. Katay knelt on the sheepskin rug laid out on the floor by the table and ran her hands along the pattern. The table was as old as the culture that birthed this akashic node. Perfectly preserved, undoubtedly, with some enchantment.

Manda buzzed about the room, as she always did in a new place, searching for exits and hidey-holes. When the spryte began to flit about the ceiling like an unhappy fly, Katay realized the only exit from the room was the door M'kald'r had closed behind him.

"Manda, please, settle," the akashic said.

The spryte circled around the room one last time before she thudded into the table and skidded across the surface into Katay's lap. She scrambled back up onto the table and sat down on a mother-of-pearl cloud.

"You're as graceful as those two dracha on the hill," Katay said dryly. "You really need to practice more. You've had those wings over a year now."

Like Jeddina, Manda had also transformed from the shape she'd been born with. When Katay first met the mage blade, she was a quickling faen, a creature nearly twice as big as a spryte, but without the wings. Then one day Manda announced she wanted to fly, walked into the wood and came out a week later transformed. Am I the only person in this place satisfied with the way I was born? Katay wondered. No, she realized, Lord Hardolis was probably glad to be a dragon.

A kobold brought them roasted flesh of some large bird that Manda declared was good eats, but Katay could not stomach the thought of food.

"This is wrong," she muttered. "I should be with Jeddina. She just lost her child."

"It," Manda corrected. "Your friend isn't a 'she' anymore. That kobold wasn't really a child, either—they kind of bud out of the side of the mojh. It's really kind of interesting."

"Not a 'she' anymore—that's ridiculous. How can she just not be what she was? Jeddina was always doing crazy things trying to find the meaning to life. When she wasn't in a deep despair because she hadn't found it."

"You knew mojh didn't come from cabbage patches," Manda said. "Sometimes humans start worshipping dragons and become mojh."

Katay rolled her eyes at Manda's oversimplification. Humans had to perform a complex magical ritual to become mojh.

"You weren't bothered when I became a spryte," Manda pointed out.

"You wanted to fly," Katay retorted.

"Maybe Jeddina wanted scales," Manda said.

"Why would anyone want scales?" Katay hissed.

"Or to live longer. Mojh live longer," Manda reminded her. She yawned. "I think I'll take a nap." She flitted over to one of the round pallets, and snuggled into the fur with her wings wrapped around her, leaving Katay alone with her thoughts.

Katay found herself wondering if the mojh transformation was something Jeddina had done in one of those frenzied moments when she was sure she was about to unlock the secrets of the universe. At those times, her fellow akashic had seemed almost luminous—ideas flowed from her like a geyser. Jeddina's link with the akashic memory was stronger than anyone's around her. She was full of energy and joy. Then there were the dark times, when Jeddina couldn't concentrate even in an akashic node, when all her thoughts encompassed some unseen misery. Sometimes the misery grew so strong that Jeddina seemed like a mortally sickened animal, unwilling to eat or comb her hair or change her clothes. It was just as likely, Katay realized, that Jeddina had performed the ritual in one of her dark moods, hoping to lift herself from despair before she lost her mind, a fear that constantly haunted her at those times.

When her anxiety grew so great thinking about Jeddina that her pulse began to race, Katay knew she needed to distract her thoughts. She began with a still meditation to empty her mind, then the ritual moving meditations. Beside her Manda gave a chirping snore.

Knowing that she was still within the akashic node, Katay concentrated a long while on Lord Hardolis, the dragon who lounged in the darkness with a court of mojh and dracha. Hardolis had promised his current servants greatness, but they knew very little about him. It was easier to tap into the long-dead knowledge of the people who used to live in what was now his lair.

A vast community, thousands of years old, had thrived here, co-existing with a dragon named Tallispan. They were renowned for their skill at crafting jewelry and enchanting it with great powers. The dragon lit huge bonfires to celebrate their weddings and cremate their dead. The caves echoed with their music day and night.

Katay let the little motes of knowledge drift through her mind, giving her a sense of an ancient culture that had absolutely nothing to do with her current worries.

The grueling three-day climb into the mountains and the constant exposure to the bitter cold finally took its toll. Katay stumbled over to the other sleeping pallet and was soon fast asleep, granting her mind a respite from the stress of wondering how long they would remain "guests" of the dragon, and her heart refuge from the grief of her friend's loss.

She awoke feeling confused and anxious. In the cave complex it was impossible to tell night from day, so she had no idea how long she'd slept. Her anxiety over Jeddina-now-Phenilac came immediately to her mind, like a painful tooth.

"What's wrong?" she heard Manda ask, and realized as she climbed into consciousness that Manda was asking someone else that question.

M'kald'r stood in the doorway. Even Katay could see the reason for Manda's question. The dracha's wings slumped, and his expression was grim. The akashic wondered briefly if Lord Hárdolis had decided to eat them and the dracha felt bad about it. She sat upright, waiting. Manda stood by her side.

"It is I who must bring you bad news now," M'kald'r said.

Instantly Katay sensed what he would say before he said it. She closed her eyes as if she could shut out his words.

"Phenilac took its own life last night," the dracha whispered.

Manda gasped. "Why?"

"We do not know. It left no note. It locked itself into one of the rooms within the akashic node—"

"She swallowed poison," Katay stated.

"How did you know that?" M'kald'r asked.

"It's how she always said she would," Katay explained. "Drumflower seed. It's supposed to be completely painless. First you fall asleep, then your brain stops, then you don't breathe, and then your heart stops."

M'kald'r nodded. "So Phenilac had these dark moods as a human, too?" he asked.

"Never so dark that she went through with it," Katay said. "She should never have joined the mojh. I can't believe she thought that might help her."

"You cannot think that it did harm," M'kald'r stated coolly.

"She wouldn't have been living with mojh, one of whom murdered her mojhborn," Katay snapped.

"And human women never despair when their children are harmed by other humans," the dracha replied sarcastically.

"This doesn't make any sense," Manda interrupted. "It just found out someone killed its mojhborn. Phenilac should be looking for the killer. Why commit suicide?"

M'kald'r bowed his head in the spryte's direction. "You have posed the question that my lord Hardolis asked," he stated.

Katay pressed her fingers against her temples. What was the point? Even if Jeddina hadn't done it because she was crazy, whatever the answer was, it would never bring her friend back.

"We are blessed with a surfeit of magic, but Phenilac was the only one in our community with the skills of an akashic," M'kald'r explained. "My lord Hardolis requests that you use your loresight as you did with Rickest and bring to light whatever you learn."

Bring to light. An odd choice of words for a dragon who ponders in the darkness, Katay thought, but she nodded her consent.

M'kald'r lit a torch at the brazier and, by its light, led them from the room and down the corridor. He stopped before the very next door. Katay tensed with anger at how physically near her friend had been to her when she had died. Why hadn't she come to talk to her, seeking solace or strength?

Manda hung back from the door, which was unusual since she was almost always first into any room offered her. "I'll guard here," the spryte announced, taking up a stance to the side of the door.

Katay followed the dracha into the room. Phenilac's body was laid out on a low bier fashioned from sheep hides stretched over a frame of cedar limbs. M'kald'r set the torch in a wall sconce. The only furnishing in the room was a low desk holding a journal. A small kneeling rug lay before the desk. Katay guessed the room lay in the center of the akashic node, which would explain the sparseness of the furnishings. The living and their daily hubbub weakened the strength of a node. A well-trained akashic left a node as undisturbed as possible and discouraged the clutter that made a room livable.

"This is where Jeddina—Phenilac studied?" she asked M'kald'r. The dracha nodded.

"I'd like to be alone with—" Katay could not bring herself to verbalize the word "it." "With my friend's body," she said, moving to stand beside the bier.

M'kald'r nodded. "I will return in an hour," he said, and, closing the door behind her, he left her alone in the room.

Katay reached out and fingered the soft wool of the hide beneath the mojh corpse, trying to remember the feel of the thick, dark hair that had covered Jeddina's head before she had transformed into this creature.

Katay peered down at the journal on the desk. It was covered in Jeddina's precise, flowing handwriting, but the mojh recorded its thoughts in Draconic. Katay flipped through the last few pages. They contained her friend's account of what she had learned meditating on the ancient people of this node, but nothing describing her despair.

She reached out and stroked the scales on the mojh's brow. If she had harbored any doubts, they fled with the certainty of her loresight. Her friend had swallowed a vial of oil seasoned with crushed drumflower seeds. But the vial had not belonged to her. It had been left in this room. Phenilac had discovered it. The mojh's death was a suicide of opportunity. Who had provided the opportunity? Katay stroked the cool chin. The mojh's sense of determination to take its life struck Katay like a blow. If someone had not provided the vial of poison, Phenilac might have found another way, painful or not.

* * * * *

Outside in the corridor, Manda stood in the darkness. There was something about that room that made her wings twitch. It wasn't the corpse. She'd seen plenty of those. Made several people into corpses, for that matter. Really, though, there was no reason she couldn't bodyguard Katay just outside the room. Rather than create light and call attention to herself, she unsheathed her athame, her two-handed sword that Katay often described as a shiv. Focusing on the athame, the spryte summoned up magical darkvision. There was a ledge across the corridor about eight feet up. She flew up and perched on the edge, keeping watch.

* * * * *

In the room, Katay leaned against the wall, trying to stop the sobs that wracked her body. Reaching deeper with the loresight on the mojh's corpse was more emotionally difficult than uncovering the truth of the kobold's death. Jeddina's affection for Katay had not dimmed upon her transformation, yet before death, the mojh felt Katay's absence as a betrayal. Jeddina had often felt betrayed by everyone around her, for no reason, when she was in her darkest moods. It was part of her affliction. Despite this knowledge, Katay could not overcome a futile sense of guilt that she had not been part of Jeddina's life. The human woman felt as if a vise was crushing her heart. She might have kept Jeddina from transforming to a mojh. If not, she might have been there to help protect the kobold. At the

247

very least she should have insisted on following Phenilac yesterday and stayed with her through the night.

* * * * *

Up on her ledge, Manda could hear Katay's sobs. The spryte was just screwing up the courage to brave the disturbing feeling the room gave her in order to comfort the human woman when a mojh came around the corner. The creature paused at the very door Manda was guarding and reached down for the door handle, muttering something in Draconic that Manda could not understand. She clenched her fists about the hilt of her athame, but a moment later the mojh moved on without opening the door. Manda might not have given the creature a second thought, but there was something about it that made her wings twitch, just as the darkness in the room behind the door had. Not a coincidence, she decided, and launched herself from the ledge to fly after the mojh.

* * * * *

Katay, barely composed, reached out to touch the mojh's corpse one last time. She drew in a deep breath and touched its eyelids. The last person her friend had spoken with was another mojh. Not surprising, but with her loresight Katay instantly recognized this mojh as the same one who had tortured and murdered the kobold. Katay had failed to discover the murderer's name the first time. The kobold had not known it, but Phenilac had—Brenner the magister. Brenner had come to Phenilac last night before the akashic mojh could discover the magister's secrets.

Katay pressed her eyes closed to hold the vision, stretch it out through time, bring to light all Brenner's secrets.

"You killed my Rickest for your dark magic," Phenilac accused.

"Your kobold was a useless thing until it brought me power over the Dark," Brenner declared, setting a vial down on Phenilac's journal.

"The dracha forbade you to follow that path," Phenilac whispered.

"The dracha are cowardly fools, jealous of the mojh's magic. They forbade it because they knew I would win Lord Hardolis' favor with such acts. We cannot come to the greatness the dragon has promised us without sacrifice and daring."

"My sacrifice and your daring," Phenilac hissed, raking her claws across Brenner's chest. Brenner fell back with a snarl.

Even before transforming into a mojh, Jeddina could use her akashic ability to call upon the knowledge of great warriors. She was a deadly foe in combat. Katay expected Phenilac to press the attack. She hoped her vision would show her Brenner's death, too.

But Brenner uttered the word, "Feed," and darkness poured down from the walls like a waterfall and pooled at Phenilac's feet.

Phenilac gasped and fell to the ground, grasping her arms around herself as if to keep warm. The darkness lapped at the akashic's body like an incoming tide.

Katay's eyes snapped open. Just as in her vision, darkness was pouring down from the walls and pooling at her feet. In another moment the flowing darkness extinguished the torch that M'kald'r had left for her. She stood in utter blackness. Her memory of the space remained accurate, however, and she paced the number of steps back to the door. The handle would not turn. Katay shouted for Manda.

* * * * *

Following the strange mojh, Manda had just reached the dragon's lair. To her delight she heard voices, including the dragon's booming one. Then, annoyed, she realized they were speaking Draconic. *How rude,* she thought. She spat on her athame to make the ancient tongue comprehensible.

"It would appear so, my lord," M'kald'r replied to something the dragon had just asked him. "Yes, what is it, Brenner?" the dracha asked the strange mojh who had just entered the chamber.

"I thought you should know, I looked into the room where Phenilac is laid out. The nonmojh is in there performing a ceremony upon the body," the mojh Brenner said.

"She is using her loresight as Lord Hardolis requested," the dracha replied.

"No. She is using oils and words of magic to animate the dead," Brenner declared. "I recognized the spellcraft. I took the precaution of locking her in so she could bring no further harm to us."

Without thinking Manda blurted out, "You big liar!"

The mojh and the dracha whirled about, startled by the spryte's outburst as well as her presence.

"There're no dead bodies being animated in that room. Not unless—" Suddenly Manda remembered that when Brenner had paused at the door, the mojh had muttered something before it locked Katay in. Perhaps it had summoned something undead. Which meant Katay was in danger.

"Grab her! Grab the spy before she escapes!" Brenner ordered the dracha, but Manda was already speeding back to Katay as fast as her wings could beat.

* * * * *

Katay stopped hollering for Manda. She took a deep breath to steady her nerves. Normally she was not afraid of the dark, but there was something unnatural about this darkness. It was what had eaten away at Jeddina's spirit until she had swallowed the poison in the vial.

She needed to keep calm and wait for Manda. Wherever the spryte had gone, she would return and open the door. From the center of the room came the sound of claws clacking on the stone floor. The bier stood in the center of the room. With a jolt of horror Katay realized the mojh corpse was moving toward her. Something had animated the corpse. Katay had heard tales that black streams of negative energy could do that in the places where they pooled.

Would the undead mojh be as deadly as she could be as a living akashic? It hardly seemed to matter. Katay was no fighter. That was Manda's job. Dealing with a foe in the dark was bad enough, but the thought of stabbing at the corpse of her friend, even transformed, revolted Katay.

A chill breeze stirred up from the floor, numbing her feet and legs. *This mission was doomed from the start,* Katay thought with resignation. She would join her friend in death, though her death would be nowhere near as painless as the mojh's suicide had been.

* * * * *

Manda gave a screech as she rounded the corner of the corridor, banging her elbow in her haste. Katay was right; she really needed more practice flying. She flew right past her goal. She landed on the floor in a tumble and turned to go back. Every muscle in her body twitched now, as if to warn her away from the room behind the door.

"Katay, what have you gotten yourself into?" the spryte muttered. She focused a spell and smacked her athame against the iron bolt securing the door. The bolt slid back and the door creaked open four inches. *Thank the gods,* Manda thought. *Brenner didn't use some annoying magister spell to hold the door closed.*

An icy chill poured from the room. Manda took a deep breath and plunged across the threshold. The room was filled with an unnatural darkness that Manda's darkvision could not penetrate.

"Katay!" the spryte shouted. "Where are you?"

The room seemed to echo with the sound of claws clacking on the stone floor. Manda set her athame out before her. The tiny sword shone ever so slightly; then Manda realized the darkness was moving away from her blade. In a way that was good, but in a way it was bad. Her athame was a Greenblade, infused with the power of life; any darkness it cut away was not simply magical darkness, but an evil, life-devouring Darkness. *Only one thing to do,* the spryte thought with a sigh. *Have at it.*

With a yell that would have done a banshee proud, the mage blade launched herself into the air and flew directly toward the sound of the clacking claws.

Her sword sliced through the black and thrust into something solid. The Darkness settled lower to the ground, uncovering the torch M'kald'r had placed in the sconce on the wall. Now Manda could see the creature she'd struck. It was Phenilac's dead body, walking around as it ought not to be.

Phenilac's corpse took a swing at the spryte, batting the tiny creature aside. Momentarily stunned but unwounded, Manda flew to the ceiling and spied out the battlefield. Katay was nowhere to be seen. She might be lying beneath the Dark that still pooled near the floor.

The spryte made another dive on the walking dead mojh. She struck the creature's arm, but she had little practice with aerial combat and fell to the floor after her blow into the icy Dark.

The Darkness swirled away from the spryte as if repulsed.

Manda picked herself up and took a defensive posture. Some instinct prompted her to speak to the Dark, not the undead. "Might as well leave now. I have lots of stamina. I can stab at you all day with the power of the Green," she threatened.

The Dark grew still. Then, like a receding tide, it pulled away from one side of the room. As it withdrew from Phenilac's dead body, the mojh corpse collapsed to the ground.

Manda stepped up and poked her athame at the pool that remained. "Beat it," she snapped.

The Dark drained away into the floor, leaving no trace. Katay was still nowhere to be seen.

Then the spryte spotted the other door. She flew over and yanked on the handle. Beyond was a very small closet; Katay was curled on the floor.

"Katay, have you thanked Sigornee?" the spryte teased.

Katay looked up at Manda. Her face was splotched and covered with tears. "Who's Sigornee?" she snuffled.

"Goddess of people who need a closet to hide in."

"Right," Katay replied, pushing herself to her feet, and drawing upright with as much dignity as she could muster.

M'kald'r entered the room. Katay had not heard his approach.

"Are you all right?" he inquired politely.

The akashic nodded. She looked down at the mojh's corpse. "This is Brenner's work. Phenilac realized Brenner was using darkbond magic. Torturing Rickest to death was part of Brenner's ceremony to draw the Darkness. There's a phenomenon called black streams, negative energy of the Dark. I don't know if the streams pool naturally in this room or if Brenner found a way to bring them forth, but that's what he used to overwhelm Phenilac. The Dark drove her to her death. The black stream pooled back in here while I was using my loresight. That's what animated her—the corpse."

M'kald'r nodded thoughtfully. He bent over and picked up Phenilac's corpse and laid the mojh's body back on the bier. Then he turned back to Katay and bowed. "My lord Hardolis is grateful for your services. I will report your findings to him."

"What's going to happen to Brenner?" Manda asked.

"My lord Hardolis will judge the magister and deal with it accordingly," M'kald'r replied.

"We want to leave now," Katay insisted.

"As you wish," M'kald'r replied with a nod.

Katay reached out one last time and stroked the scales on the back of the mojh's hand. Then she turned and left.

* * * * *

Once they'd collected their gear, M'kald'r escorted the human and the spryte out of the mountain, to the edge of the mojh's village. The sun was still climbing toward its zenith.

"Farewell, Katay Bracken and Manda Lightsword," the dracha bade them. His wings spread out with a whoosh, and he sprang into the air.

They watched him soar upward until he disappeared into the cave set in the cliff over the mojh village.

"Well, that's the end of Brenner," the spryte said, brushing imaginary dirt off her palms. "Your friend's spirit can float down the Ghostwash in peace."

"I hope so," Katay whispered.

"Why wouldn't it?" Manda asked.

"The dracha did not approve of Brenner using the Dark, that I saw with my loresight. Brenner, though, believed the dragon might not disapprove."

"M'kald'r seemed like a fine fellow," Manda pointed out.

"The servant is not the master," Katay reminded her.

"That's silly. Why would the dragon let us go if Brenner were right?" Manda demanded.

"Because he knows we will take that news back to the steward of Gahanis."

"You don't really believe that, do you?" the spryte insisted.

"I don't know what to believe," Katay replied. "Unless you want to volunteer to go back and twist the dragon's arm for me until he reveals the truth."

"Not part of my bodyguard duties," Manda replied. "You wouldn't be so suspicious if you weren't just depressed by your friend's death and because you took a bath in the Dark."

"I hope so," Katay whispered again.

"Race you back to Gahanis," Manda offered and began tripping down the mountain trail.

Katay followed in the spryte's wake with less enthusiasm. She had come to the mountains determined to discover all about Jeddina's ring, with no concern for the steward of Gahanis' interest in the dragon. Now, she realized, it might have been better had she learned less about Jeddina's life and death, and more about the dragon.

MONTE COOK
MEMORIES AND GHOSTS

When Re-Magul found the master dragonstone, he sat down upon it. After a while, he stood again, drew *thu-terris* from its sheath, and resumed his position with the bared blade lying across his lap. The stone was red, although patches of a dark lichen grew on its surface. Its top rose up from the ground about five feet and was about seven feet long.

He waited.

When Re-Magul's jaw began to hurt from being clenched in anger, he stood and performed an ancient giantish ceremony, taught to him by his father, designed to calm the spirit. While the rite did not grant him serenity, at least it gave him something that some might call patience. Others would say that "patience" is too gentle a word. "Grim determination," they would say, or perhaps just "tenacity."

On the third day, a rainstorm rolled in over the Bitter Peaks and drenched the area surrounding the hill where he sat, a

255

place the locals called Draconhill—although none of those Re-Magul had spoken with knew why. The giant warmain appreciated the rainwater, which replenished his own dwindling supply. He caught the big, heavy drops in his helmet to refill his leather waterskins.

When the rain ended, he waited some more.

* * * * *

Nithogar had departed from the host three weeks ago. He had not needed to give them a reason why, but he did mutter something to the elders about checking some of the ancient sites. Which, of course, was the truth.

"A useful tool, the truth can be," he had once told his lairmate, Jelissican, "but that is all it is—a tool. Not an ethic. Not a goal unto itself."

She never liked it when he spoke that way, so he learned to avoid doing so. Of course, that was lifetimes ago. Dragon lifetimes. When Nithogar had lived in the Land of the Dragons.

When he—and the other elders of the Conclave—had ruled it.

His survey of the ancient sites had borne no fruit. He felt despondent at the sight of so many places his people had once revered and used now fallen into ruin. In fact, "ruin" was not a word that performed its job adequately in this case. The ancient dragon sites were no longer sites at all. They were nothing. An anonymous spot in the woods here, an unnoticed end of a ravine there. Even the topography had changed in the time the dragons had been gone. Rivers had carved new courses, mountains had toppled, and even the coastline had taken a different curve here and there, like the face of a long-lost love, now held tightly in the talons of age.

Nithogar was a stranger to age. The sight of even the land itself changing upset him greatly. He had dwelled upon the world for more centuries than had passed here before his birth. Yet, he had spent most of that time away from this, his ancestral home. There was a crime in that—and, worse, those of his kind who still lived no longer remembered this place. To them, the Land of the Dragons was a tale told in the hatchling dens and dreamed of in monthslong slumbers deep in subterranean caves and high in floating castles. And Nithogar knew he was to blame. But truth was not a goal unto itself, and thus dwelling upon it served no purpose. Guilt was an emotion for lesser beings, a pitfall to be avoided by those with the power and intelligence to reach for the stars.

There were still great deeds to be done, and only those with the will to persevere could accomplish them. He had been granted—no, he had earned—immortality, or something very close. It was not something to squander in regret or remorse. The threat of future regrets was no barrier to stop one such as he.

It had indeed been dragon lifetimes since he had been to this realm. Jelissican's lifetime, to be sure. Thoughts of her urged him onward.

Nithogar drew upon the power of the land around him. It felt warm and familiar as its essence flowed into his outstretched wings. After a savoring moment, he channeled that power into his tired muscles to grant himself speed. There was one more site to visit. It was perhaps the most vital, and thus the most dangerous.

* * * * *

At first, it was just a black spot in the sky. Re-Magul had no doubt as to what it was. He kept his seat upon the reddish stone atop the hill. His shaggy black hair showed tufts of grey, both on his head and in his beard. His helmet lay on the ground next to the rock, but the rest of his towering form was shod in articulated armored plates—except for his hands. He eschewed gauntlets so he could hold *thu-terris* with his bare flesh. That was the way he had entered battle since landing at Khorl, some five hundred years ago.

His steely eyes focused on the ever-growing shape as it approached. Its form grew steadily more distinct, but its color remained black. Wide, sweeping wings were visible propelling the thing at great speeds. Soon, its long serpentine neck and terrible reptilian head became clear.

A dragon.

Re-Magul resisted the urge to stand. This was what he had been waiting for.

The dragon flew directly toward him, or, perhaps more accurately, toward the master dragonstone upon which he sat.

The huge creature circled Draconhill in a wide arc, its head turned inward as it rounded him, studying the giant. Its shuddering black wings and back, covered in black scales tipped with red, glistened with rainwater. It made the dragon's scales gleam as if they were metal, a dark reddish bronze. It kept its four massive legs tucked loosely under its massive torso as it flew, its belly scales showing more red than black, though its claws were ebon. Of its entire body, easily one hundred feet from nose to tail tip, only its pale teeth and fiery eyes—the color of the hungry desert sun—were something other than black or red.

Finally, the dragon descended, landing quietly in the grass on the side of the hill that the giant warmain faced. It folded its huge wings and took a few steps forward with its head low—right at Re-Magul's eye level, in fact.

"I know who you are, worm." Re-Magul said through teeth clenched so hard that his jaw again ached, but the pain helped him focus his anger. His deep voice sounded weak from disuse.

The dragon cocked its head slightly. "I have no idea who you are, giant," it—or rather *he*—replied with a gravelly voice that, while soft, betrayed its ability to become louder. Much louder. It was as though he were speaking to a child.

Re-Magul could not resist the urge to stand in the face of the creature's obvious contempt. He gripped *thu-terris* so that his knuckles showed white. He arched his back so that he stood at his full eighteen-foot height, stiff bones crunching loudly in his back as he did. His massive chest, like the prow of a mighty ship, thrust toward the dragon. "I am Re-Magul, warmain in the service of Lady Protector Ia-Thordani; oldest of the Hu-Charad; slayer of the dramojh fangmaster Villithiss at the Battle of the Serpent's Heart; commander of the Knights of Diamond; and wielder of the Blade of the East: *thu-terris*, the sword-that-severs-with-icy-flame-as-it-dances."

Nithogar stared at him in silence, without the twitch of a draconic muscle. Eventually, he spoke. "I have no quarrel with you, giant. Remember what your grandfathers must have told you of the ancient pacts, of which their own grandfathers must have spoken before them."

"I have no wish to speak with you of pacts," Re-Magul said, still gritting his teeth.

"I would think not. Those ancient pacts made between your people and my own lord Erixalimar, the dragon king, forbade you from even coming to this land. Yet here you stand."

Now Re-Magul only stared, his eyes narrowing.

"And it is my understanding that you have been here for some time."

"We came here," Re-Magul took a breath, then continued, "because this land was in peril. A peril you had wrought, then fled from."

The muscles around the left side of Nithogar's wide mouth twitched.

"You said," the dragon said, raising its head higher, "that you knew who I was."

"Oh yes. Perhaps you thought that such lore had been lost, but the akashics have made sure your crimes would always be remembered. I know who you are, Nithogar the Wicked. Nithogar the Hated. Nithogar the Despoiler."

"These are epithets I must have earned after I left."

"Then how about this one, dragon: Nithogar, creator of the dramojh." Out of habit, Re-Magul spat as he said both "dragon" and "dramojh."

Nithogar flexed his wings. "You know nothing of it, Hu-Charad."

"Nothing?" Re-Magul's eyes flared. "You are ancient, it is true, but I am no mere youth. I was there when the stone ships arrived on these shores, one of the first off the boats. I remember the battles with the dramojh—the so-called 'dragon scions.' I battled their dark sorcery and demonic powers. I saw friends and relatives die in their claws and teeth. They scuttled out of the shadows and they raped this land like nothing before them or—thank all the singers in the Houses of the Eternal—since."

"So your kind dealt with the dramojh. I am aware of that. And you were some kind of leader in your campaign against them. What do you want from me? Gratitude? So be it. Thanks to you, giant, and to all your kind."

And with a sneer, he added quickly: "Now be on your way."

Re-Magul recoiled. No one had ever spoken to him like that regarding the hated dramojh.

The dragon pointed to the east with a long, sharp claw. "Your ancestral home lies in that direction." He lowered his talon and added, "I trust your vaunted sailing craft still work."

"I know where my homeland lies, beast! I left everything and everyone there to come here to deal with the chaos you left."

"Really, giant. Is that so? And what made the dramojh your problem? I recognize that they were an abomination, but why do you, hailing from across the boundless sea, care about such matters?"

"We are the wardens of the land!"

"We *are* the land!"

The shouted words of both giant and dragon echoed dully across the landscape. Each could feel the fevered breath of the other. Re-Magul trembled with anger, while the only change in the dragon's demeanor was an intensity of color growing behind his narrow eyes.

The dragon's words were not without their own truth, Re-Magul knew. This was once the Land of the Dragons, and the creatures held a mystical tie to it that even today sages wondered at.

But that was no excuse for their crimes, particularly not this dragon's crimes.

Nithogar spoke again. "You came here because we had gone, and you assumed we would not return. You saw a chance to rule yet another land, under the guise of your vaunted stewardship."

"Lies!"

"You serve the land. You protect all who live in it—as long as they submit to giant rule, is that not so? You are the guardians of all, as long as they obey the will of your sacred Diamond Throne!"

"I'll kill you where you stand!"

"You think you can do what time itself cannot?"

This gave Re-Magul pause. He raised *thu-terris* so that its point—a full twelve feet from its pommel—pointed at the dragon's neck. "Why *are* you still alive, worm? Even dragons grow old and die. Why have you not? Are you so base, so vile, that you have given into the Dark? Have you succumbed to undeath?"

"There are secrets to magic that you cannot comprehend, giant."

Oh, how he hated dragons. Re-Magul had always felt so, for as long as he had been aware of their existence. Dragons were arrogant, self-serving monsters with no concern for how they might affect the land around them. So powerful and yet so careless with that power. How could he not despise them and all they had wrought?

Especially what they had wrought. Especially what *this* dragon had wrought.

"Like the secrets of magic that allowed you to give birth to the dramojh? That's a secret I don't want to comprehend, monster. That's a secret that resulted in the deaths of thousands and the enslavement of many more. Your actions brought this land to its knees. And yet you claim ties to it. If that's so, why were you not ravaged as it was?"

"Impudent giant. Do you really think the failure of the dramojh did not harm us? *We left our homeland because of them!*"

"You fled in fear of your own creation. You took no responsibility for your actions. You— "

"Enough!" The dragon's roar, issued from his upraised head far above the giant's own, shook Re-Magul's very bones, but he fought not to show it. It resonated through the silence that followed, drifting amid the stones that littered the surrounding hills.

Nithogar's gaze fell upon the red master dragonstone behind the giant.

"How . . ." he began, lowering his head. "How did you know I would be here?"

Re-Magul smiled mirthlessly. "Perhaps there are secrets to magic that *you* do not comprehend, dragon. Do not think that your scaly kind has a monopoly on arcane lore and magic spells. Your coming was foreseen by our magisters, and your presence by those who have bonded with the Green. True, not many had the power and insight to see it, but some did, and when I learned of it, my path was clear."

"Your path?"

"I am here to kill you, Nithogar. *Thu-terris* does not leave her sheath lightly."

* * * * *

Nithogar studied the giant standing before him. It had been centuries since the dragon had engaged in physical combat. And even then, he was used to fighting creatures far smaller than this giant. True, in the past, there had been reason for dragon to struggle against dragon, but those days were long gone and better forgotten. Re-Magul was large, even for a giant. The sturdy warrior held his blade in a way that suggested not just skill, but intimate familiarity. And Nithogar could see the arcane power seething within the sword as easily as he could see that it was made of finely tempered steel. The sword had all the markings of something giant-made and ancient. Probably something the giantish armies brought with them from their own homeland across the Great Eastern Sea. Maybe something brought by Re-Magul himself. He claimed to be that old, but Nithogar had not known that giants were so long-lived. There was much he did not know about giantkind. Why would he? For so long, they had simply been the folk of distant lands, of little concern to him and his kind after the pact wrought by Erixalimar ensured that they would never come to these shores.

But now they were here, entrenched in the ancestral homeland of all dragonkind. They had broken the pact. Perhaps they had done it in the name of what they saw as a good cause, but that was irrelevant—particularly now.

"You have threatened me with death twice now, giant," Nithogar said softly but without a mote of gentleness. "I can look at you and tell that you are prepared to stand behind your words. You want to slay me with every fiber of your being. So why address me at all? Why not await me here with an army to sling stones and arrows into the sky at my approach, with a phalanx of your so-called warmains ready to charge when I land?"

How much could he know? The folk of the realm seemed to have forgotten the ancient sites of dragon power, each centered around one of the magical, reddish dragonstones. Perhaps not all had been forgotten. But did he know the significance of this site above all the others?

As if he had read Nithogar's mind, Re-Magul responded, "Before you die, I want to know why your kind have returned." He took a step backward and pointed his sword at the dragonstone. "Does it have something to do with this?"

Nithogar could not help betraying his dismay with a gasp.

"It's of obvious value to you, dragon. But is it why you have returned?"

Nithogar regained his composure, reminding himself that surely the giant's blade could do no harm to the magical stone. "You don't realize it, giant, but you ask two questions, not one."

Re-Magul stared back at the dragon without a change to his angry countenance.

"You ask why my kind has come back, and the answer is simple. This is our land. Our time of self-imposed exile has reached its end. The Dragon Conclave is composed of different dragons now—except for me. Those who led us out of this land are gone and, in fact, even their children are gone. Time has a way of . . ." Nithogar readjusted his wings uncomfortably, "changing things.

"But," the dragon continued, "you also ask about the stone, and why I have come back. That is a very different question with a very different answer."

Nithogar examined Re-Magul for any sign that might betray what he knew about this particular site, then said, "And it is an answer I have no intention of granting you, if for no other reason than you threaten me with your paltry weapon."

The insult seemed to shake Re-Magul, but he clearly possessed more self-control than the dragon had given him credit for.

"You asked me why I did not bring an army with me," the giant said. "I could ask the same of you. Where is the draconic host that, I have heard, darkens the sky with its numbers? Why are you here alone? Is it because this place—this rock—has something to do with the creation of the dramojh?"

Was he really asking, or did he already know? Nithogar mused.

The dragon sighed. "I wonder," he said, "will every dragon find a giant with a sword wherever he goes in this land? Must there be war?"

"Answer my question, dragon."

"Perhaps, after you answer mine. Why are *you* here alone?"

Re-Magul ran a hand through his beard, letting the tip of his sword almost touch the ground. He worked his jaw slightly.

"No. War is not inevitable. I do not speak for all giantkind. I do not even speak for the Lady Protector in this instance. You are the progenitor of the dramojh, Nithogar. I cannot abide you in the land I struggled and bled for. I came here, alone, of my own will and no other's. You are the root of virtually all this land's shadows. I could perhaps permit the dragons to return. But not you."

"Permit?" Nithogar spat. "I called you impudent before, but I was wrong. That is arrogance. Misplaced arrogance. We are dragons. This is our land. You permit or deny us nothing."

"Things have changed, dragon. This *was* your land, but you abandoned it. We are its stewards now. Were it not for us, it would be a wasteland: barren of life and broken forever from the Green."

Nithogar raised a massive claw, blocking the rays of the setting sun as it sank to tops of the distant Bitter Peaks. Re-Magul was cast in shadow. The giant responded by raising his sword with both hands above his head.

With a roar that shook both the warmain and the hill upon which he stood, Nithogar brought his talon down upon the giant. Re-Magul called upon the power within *thu-terris,* and it flared with blue flame. With a mighty swing, he deflected the dragon's strike and cut into the scaly flesh of the claw.

Nithogar did not utter a sound with the wound, but he did rear his head back in surprise.

The giant stood his ground and gripped his sword tightly, holding it low to the ground in a hunched, defensive stance.

"I wondered how long it would be before you came to blows," a voice said.

Both dragon and giant turned toward the sound. Standing on the north end of the hill was a reptilian creature covered in scales: yellow-gold on its back and brownish-copper on its belly and limbs. It was not as large as Nithogar, but it was thick and broad where he was thin and snakelike. And the new creature bore no wings on its back.

Another dragon.

* * * * *

Re-Magul was ready to fight one dragon, but two? His hopes for surviving until nightfall diminished to nil. Still, he stood firm.

"Afraid to face me alone, Nithogar?" Re-Magul taunted. His mind raced for some strategy. Perhaps angering the dragon further might buy him some time.

The black dragon ignored him, however, and spoke to the newcomer in Draconic. Re-Magul had studied the ancient language of dragons, however, and understood the words: "Who are you?"

The yellow and brown dragon's voice was gruff, sounding almost like stones rattling around in an iron bucket. "You don't remember me, I'm sure. I was very young when you left. My name is Cohalisaram, or . . . it was. No one has had cause to use that name in five thousand years or more. Yes, Nithogar, I am one of those you left behind, and I still live. There are a couple of us still here, and a few children and grandchildren of those who stayed when the dragon host left. I may not have the power of the tenebrian seeds to give me long life, but there are other means."

Then Cohalisaram turned to Re-Magul and spoke in Giantish. "Greetings, Hu-Charad. I have taken great pains never to meet one of your kind in person, until today of course."

"How—" Nithogar began.

"—did I approach you," Cohalisaram interrupted, "without your seeing or hearing me?" The dragon gave a gruff laugh. "I'd like to say it was because the two of you were too busy posturing for one another's benefit, but the truth is that—like those few others of our kind who remained in this realm—I have adapted to a life of secrecy. I have learned to step between the moments. I hide within time itself."

Re-Magul had no idea what that meant, but it was nonetheless true that a dragon like Cohalisaram, who must weigh at least one hundred tons, should not have been able to approach this hill undetected without the aid of some kind of magic.

"And what," Nithogar said, "is your business here? Have you come for the stone?"

"I have had millennia to access this stone. Why would I come for it now?"

"So you have come here because of one of us," Nithogar stated, cocking his head to one side ever so slightly.

Re-Magul stood tall and held his sword before him in a new but still fully defensible stance.

"Both of you, actually," Cohalisaram replied.

"Explain," was all Re-Magul could manage. He reflected back to his ceremony of calming to keep his rage in check. His hatred for dragons made it difficult to concentrate on their words. And he had not come here to talk.

Cohalisaram took a few steps closer. "I suppose, in the tales of old from the Denotholan, I would be the threat that provides a reason for you two enemies to work together. That, however, is not my intent. I have no desire to enter combat with either of you. Frankly, I have no doubt that either of you could best me. I have spent eons perfecting ways of avoiding fights, not winning them."

Re-Magul shook his head with distrust.

Cohalisaram turned his attention to the giant. "You knew Nithogar was coming, and you knew who he was, but do you know his purpose here? Do you know the stone's significance?"

Nithogar gave a low growl.

"This specific stone?" Cohalisaram asked.

The answer was no, but the giant did not care. His mind was focused only on slaying the dragon he had come here to slay and avenging the dead he had come here to avenge.

Cohalisaram did not explain further. Instead, he turned his wide head back toward Nithogar. "And do you know who Re-Magul is? Even I, cloistered away, know of this hero and his position as the eldest of the giants."

Nithogar spat something like a laugh. "Like that means anything to me, the eldest of the dragons—"

"You forget yourself, ancient one. I may not be as old as you, but I am old enough to remember great Erixalimar, who still lives."

Nithogar shook his head at the mention of the name, as if shooing away a buzzing insect.

"So an old giant and an old dragon meet . . ." Re-Magul said, rubbing his beard.

"Two old dragons," Cohalisaram added with a lilt to his voice that seemed strange coming from the massive creature.

Re-Magul smiled in spite of himself. "Either way," the giant said, "it sounds like the beginning of a joke a faen would tell."

Cohalisaram laughed loudly and long, showing teeth that looked like sharp stones.

"Very well," Nithogar said when the other dragon had finished. "Evening comes, and with it more rain, most likely. You have stopped our battle before it really started, which is fine with me. Why don't the two of you move along somewhere else now?"

"Oh no, Nithogar," Cohalisaram said. "We haven't even told the giant about the dramojh within the rock."

* * * * *

Re-Magul stared at the master dragonstone, then back at Nithogar. He once again gripped his weapon in both hands, as though readying an attack.

Nithogar wondered at the other dragon's motives for causing him this trouble. He had no problem slaying the giant if he must, but Nithogar did not have the stomach for fighting another dragon this night—particularly one that seemed to have honed his draconic nature in new and unknown ways.

As the sky darkened, Re-Magul finally broke the uneasy silence. "Dramojh? In the rock?" He prodded the stone with his sword. "Impossible."

"Once again," Nithogar replied, "we find your knowledge of the possible to be sorely lacking." The dragon tensed, raising his head high. "What my . . . brother, here, says is true."

"That cannot be," Re-Magul said softly, more to himself than to the dragons. "They are all dead or driven from the world. We saw to it. We were thorough."

"Indeed," Cohalisaram agreed, his manner betraying a respect for the giants that Nithogar did not share.

"Calm yourself," Nithogar said. "The dramojh are all gone. If there is a dramojh within the stone, it is dead."

Re-Magul's brow furrowed in confusion and perhaps distrust. Cohalisaram looked at Nithogar expectantly.

Nithogar sighed and glanced around distractedly before speaking. "I put a spell on a number of dragonstones and sent them to sites important to us. The spell was a contingency, so that if ever the dramojh were destroyed, some of their essence would remain preserved within them. Time has worn away the enchantment on the other stones. This is the last one, but it is the most powerful."

"And here," Cohalisaram said, "the spell remained and performed its function."

Before Nithogar could ask the other dragon how he knew this, Re-Magul shook his head, his eyes wide. "Why? By all that is holy, *why?*"

Lies filled Nithogar's head, but his anger wouldn't allow him to speak them. "Because I wasn't done with them, giant! There was still work to be done!"

"Work? Those . . . demonic things . . ." Re-Magul sputtered.

As the giant and dragon faced off in rage once again, Cohalisaram opened his mouth wide and, from deep within his throat, a thin stream of silver and green energy poured forth. It did not move in a straight line, nor was it necessarily quick. It danced and meandered through the air. Re-Magul cried out and lifted his sword defensively. Nithogar just stared.

The energy worked its way around the giant and instead struck the dragonstone. The rock glowed silently with the stream's silvery-green essence. The surrounding hills had grown as noiseless as the three of them standing there, looking at the stone.

A creature stepped forth from the glow. It was dark but glistening, like the web of a spider, and translucent. Nithogar had seen such a creature before. "A ghost . . ." It had a body like a scale-covered mockery of a spider, too many legs splayed out from a twisted form. It had a long, serpentine neck and a demonic face that seemed to be all teeth and eyes. Fluttering, nervous wings like those of a bat curled on its back. The thing did not move, it seeped, as if it were oil and the air a sieve.

It was a dramojh.

* * * * *

"No," Re-Magul said, "it can't be real." He looked to Cohalisaram for some kind of explanation, but somehow the dragon was gone. Just gone.

The dramojh was a liquid shadow. Each second that passed seemed to cause a ripple to move along its surface. It looked around, as if attempting to gain its bearings.

Every nightmare that had ever haunted Re-Magul's sleep or shook his waking thoughts had suddenly come true. Like so many of his brethren, the giant had sworn to never rest, never allow himself to exit the Wardance, never stop hating, until the demondragons were gone. Now, one stood in front of him, dripping darkness like a festering cancer. His soul cried in anguish at the sight of it, but his determination fought to keep his mind clear.

This thing was a dramojh, but it was different, too. Ephemeral. Ethereal. Like the dragon had said, a *dead* dramojh. This was not one of the creatures Re-Magul had struggled for so long to destroy. It was the shadow of one of them, preserved by perverse magic—a crime against the land, to say the least.

The shadow of the dramojh focused its gaze on Nithogar, ignoring the giant.

Father/Betrayer. Kin-Abandoner. Maker/Forsaker. Scion-Slayer. The shadow's thoughts were Re-Magul's thoughts—and Nithogar's as well, presumably. Re-Magul had experienced telepathy before,

but this was different. There was no other voice in his head.
The ghost spoke to him with his own mental voice.

Left us alone. Left us to die.

"We had to leave," Nithogar whispered.

Fearful. Distrustful. Incapable of dealing with the consequences.

"No," the dragon shook his head ever so slightly. "I was going to
come back. Sooner. Much sooner. But the West. It held . . . things
. . . unknown to the Conclave. Things became very complicated."

Nithogar seemed to shrink.

We are forsaken. We are gone.

"Damn right!" Re-Magul said, pointing the tip of his sword
at the creature.

The shadow turned toward the giant, looking him in the eye
for the first time. *Slaughterer. Murderer.*

"Of horrors like you? Yes!" Re-Magul launched himself at the
ghostly dramojh and swung *thu-terris* in a wide arc. This must
end. The shadow had already contaminated the world too long
with its unexpected presence.

The warmain's magical blade flamed through the shadow,
tearing at it like a hand splashing through greasy, thick oil.
And, like oil, the blade slicing through it did not seem to affect
it at all, except to cause its surface to ripple slightly.

Worse, *thu-terris* clouded over with a darkness that oozed
into its blade like blood into water. Without warning or threat,
thu-terris, the Blade of the East, died in Re-Magul's hands.

* * * * *

Nithogar saw the light fade from the giant's sword like a candle
snuffed. He watched as the shadow dramojh focused its dark
abhorrence toward the giant, and imagined that, hundreds of
years ago, such a scene would have been commonplace in the land
where they now stood. The dragon wondered at his creation.

Even as he watched, he could not help but remember his last
experience with his scions. His plans to wrest control of the

Conclave from those dragons who opposed him had reached its fruition. Dramojh by the tens of thousands swarmed over their mountain palace. Dragon fought against dragon, but the sudden appearance of the squirming horde of the dramojh made the outcome of this final battle a foregone conclusion. Scales were torn from dragon flesh, and flesh was rent from dragon bone. Dark, thick blood, rich with power, flowed down the mountainside in grisly torrents. But even as victory belonged to Nithogar, he saw his creations turn against him and his allies. Like an infection, the dramojh suddenly had no cause to discriminate—they swarmed over all dragons.

Nithogar surveyed this scene, even now calmly monitoring the unplanned contingency, wondering how to control the new situation, or at least turn it to his benefit. But then he saw her.

Jelissican.

The dramojh, born of a fusion of his own essence and the dark but potent magic of the tenebrian seeds, the result of his matchless intellect and dauntless pursuit of power, swarmed like hungry locusts over his lair-mate. In his mind's eye she fought valiantly—Jelissican's physical power matched or exceeded his own—but the dramojh were numberless. For every five that fell with a sweep of her rending claws, ten more took their place. For every dozen consumed in the fiery blasts of her breath, two dozen more swarmed over their remains to renew their sorcerous attacks.

Nithogar did not see Jelissican die. Her green and golden form was buried in black dramojh bodies, spreading over her like the darkness spreading into Re-Magul's sword.

There was no way to turn this situation to Nithogar's advantage. Somehow, just as all his plans had reached fruition, everything that mattered died.

He had heard much later that the day ended with Erixalimar's arrival on the scene with a host of celestial beings who, together, eradicated the dramojh horde and sent the last few survivors squirming into deep holes in the Bitter Peaks. But Nithogar was long gone, fled to the West.

He could not speak for the dragons who came with him, but he knew that with every beat of his wings he fled from himself. He fled from what he had wrought.

And now, after millennia, he stood before his progeny again.

* * * * *

Hate. Revulsion. Disgust. Contempt. Loathing.

With a taloned claw, the dramojh reached for Re-Magul. *Thuterris* was cold and dead in the giant's hands, and he could not move it to block the strike. The shadow's hand seeped through his armor as effortlessly as it seeped through the air, and the giant felt a coldness—felt a *darkness*—enter him. He cried out.

"After all these centuries," Nithogar whispered. "Guilt is an emotion for lesser beings." His voice grew louder, but he spoke as if reciting a mantra. "Truth is not a goal unto itself."

The dramojh shadow continued its attack upon Re-Magul. The giant quivered, helpless to act, engulfed by the cold and darkness only a dead demon could wield.

"I was wrong," Nithogar said.

The shadow ignored him.

"I should have known, then, as I watched her last moments. Passion served nothing, I thought. Revenge, guilt, anger—these could not serve me, I said. I only had to forget. I had thought I could exorcise these feelings through absence, but I was wrong. After so long, I know now that I must remember."

Nithogar rose to his full height. He seemed to draw power from the hill itself and fill himself with it.

"You were a *mistake!*" Nithogar's front claws came crashing down upon the specter, shimmering with a power all their own. Out of the corner of his eye, Re-Magul saw the shimmering fire, and recognized its color and texture. He had seen it before, in the pattern deep within the rune of every runechild and the heart of every spell. It was the power of the land itself, and it tore through the shadowy demon, spattering darkness and defilement across the hill and across Re-Magul.

The ghost wavered and drew away from the giant, whirling like a vortex of black water to face Nithogar rather than Re-Magul. It hissed within his mind incoherently.

Re-Magul lay in the grass, blackened and charred from the dramojh's eldritch power. His sword had been torn from his grasp. He fought to remain conscious, his heart and lungs so cold that he could not breathe; his blood had almost stilled within his veins.

Dragon and dramojh clashed in mid-air, like a moth crashing into a flame. But which was which? Re-Magul shielded his eyes from the brilliant blaze of power and darkness—a conflagration that both lit up and dimmed the twilight upon the hill.

And then he was alone.

Nithogar and the spirit had vanished. The dragonstone was sundered into two halves, although Re-Magul was unsure how it had happened.

But no, he was not alone.

Cohalisaram once again stood on the hill, also gazing at the stone. His massive form looked almost like part of the hill.

Re-Magul said nothing. He walked to where he had dropped *thu-terris*. A dark streak still cut across the silver of the blade, but it had stopped spreading. The sword still felt cold and heavy. Lifeless.

The giant felt likewise.

"I'd like to hear the ending of that faen joke," Cohalisaram said, lowering his body to the ground, resting his head on his folded forelimbs.

"I am a very old giant," he said quietly. "And still I have never taken the time to learn the art of jokes."

The giant continued to stare at his sword, and Cohalisaram did not reply. The hilltop was silent for a time.

"I have been sustained by anger and hatred," Re-Magul said finally. "A need for revenge. My hatred for dragons—for dramojh—seems to have sustained me as clearly as Nithogar's magic sustained him."

Cohalisaram snorted. "And I by my fear. My need to hide.

"But now," he continued, "I believe that need must pass. Perhaps I should no longer hide between the moments, but become a part of them. It is time I came forward, like today."

Re-Magul studied the dragon. "Are you saying we must change? Adapt to the present . . . or the future?" The giant sheathed his dead sword on his back. "I think I am too old to change."

Cohalisaram laughed. "My friend! Have you paid no attention at all? You may be the oldest of your kind, but did you not watch, as I just did, one of the oldest beings of all recognize his mistake and decide to change?"

"And it killed him." Re-Magul gestured at the empty air.

"Oh, I don't know about that," Cohalisaram said. "From the tales I've heard, it might take a lot more than that to kill a dragon like Nithogar. Whether he is gone or not, I am heartened by what I saw."

"And you think a giant can learn from a dragon?"

Cohalisaram raised a claw as if to mirror the giant's gesture. "Two dragons."

Now it was Re-Magul's turn to laugh, something he had not done for a long time.

"Perhaps you are right," Re-Magul said, still laughing. "Perhaps I have it in me to change."

"I have it," Cohalisaram said, his monstrous visage brightening. "A dragon and a giant meet on a hill. A dragon and a giant leave a hill. But it's not the same dragon—and it's not the same giant."

"I'm no faen, but that's not very funny."

"Perhaps it's more of a proverb then a joke, then. You giants like those, don't you?"

"Dragons teaching giants proverbs," Re-Magul said, laughing again. "What could possibly come next?"

"I, for one, will be interested to see," the dragon said.

WOLFGANG BAUR

Wolfgang Baur is a game designer and editor who has written more than one hundred game books and articles, including Beyond Countless Doorways *and* Frostburn. *This is his second short story for Malhavoc Press. He lives in Seattle.*

RICHARD LEE BYERS

Richard Lee Byers is the author of more than twenty novels, including The Shattered Mask, The Black Bouquet, *The Dead God Trilogy,* The Vampire's Apprentice, Dead Time, *and the bestseller* Dissolution. *His short fiction has appeared in numerous magazines and anthologies. A resident of the Tampa Bay area, he spends his leisure time fencing, playing poker, and shooting pool.*

MONTE COOK

Monte Cook has written more than one hundred roleplaying game products, including coauthoring the 3rd Edition of the Dungeons & Dragons® *game. A graduate of the Clarion West writer's workshop, he has also published various short stories and two novels:* The Glass Prison *and* Of Aged Angels.

BRUCE R. CORDELL

Bruce R. Cordell is known in the roleplaying game community for his many adventures and rulebooks, and lately his novels, including the Oath of Nerull, Lady of Poison, *and the upcoming* Darkvision, *as well as the short story "Hollows of the Heart" in* Children of the Rune.

ED GREENWOOD

Ed Greenwood lives in a farmhouse in rural Ontario, Canada, with about 80,000 books—but his mind dwells in the world he created, the Forgotten Realms®. *Not content with playing in one imaginary world, he's since created several others and is happy to visit the Lands of the Diamond Throne, too.*

JEFF GRUBB

Jeff has written fourteen novels, over twenty short stories, and more game products than you can shake a stick at. A founder of both Forgotten Realms *and* Dragonlance®, *he often vacations in other domains. Jeff lives in Seattle with his wife and coconspirator, Kate Novak, and his cat, Emily.*